"Ware has successfully blended elements of science fiction and epic fantasy to create a unique story in a landscape that has just enough of a modern, dark edge to elevate it from a traditional fantasy journey to something new and compelling. Ware writes with an eloquence that is not often encountered in genre fiction... With a language almost of his own, and a witty inner monologue to match, Ecko is a captivating hero... A successfully fresh 'something for everyone' approach to genre fiction."
THE BRITISH FANTASY SOCIETY

"*Ecko Rising* is an incredible read, with completely unexpected twists and turns... The worlds described within the book are complete and understandable, and you might want to live in at least one of them. The author's diverse knowledge of subcultures within our society is evident and well used. The cliff-hanger at the end has left this reader aching for more." GEEK SYNDICATE

"Ingenious... The story itself is engaging and totally unique, a plot that pushes the boundaries not for the sake of it but clearly to offer something different." SFBOOK

"Danie Ware effortlessly juggles a dystopian hard sci-fi environment with a fantasy world with its own very specific set of rules, and comes up with a story that keeps you gripped... This is a strong debut; I suspect Ware will be a name to watch out for in future." SCI-FI BULLETIN

"*Ecko Rising* mixes science fiction à la early years Michael Marshall with the comedic fantasy of Terry Pratchett and the sprawling authenticity of J. R. R. Tolkien's Middle-earth... staggeringly impressive in both its richness and detail... A hugely enjoyable genre mash-up that promises great things to come from first-time author Danie Ware."
ALTERNATIVE MAGAZINE ONLINE

ECKO BURNING

ECKO BURNING
DANIE WARE

TITAN BOOKS

Ecko Burning
Print edition ISBN: 9781781169087
E-book ISBN: 9781781169094

Published by Titan Books
A division of Titan Publishing Group Ltd
144 Southwark Street, London SE1 0UP

First US edition: June 2014
10 9 8 7 6 5 4 3 2 1

What did you think of this book?
We love to hear from our readers. Please email us at:
readerfeedback@titanmail.com, or write to us at the above address.

To receive advance information, news, competitions, and exclusive offers
online, please sign up for the Titan newsletter on our website.

www.titanbooks.com

FOR MY BROTHER ALAN,
TO WHOM SO MUCH OF THIS BELONGS

CONTENTS PROLOGUE 13

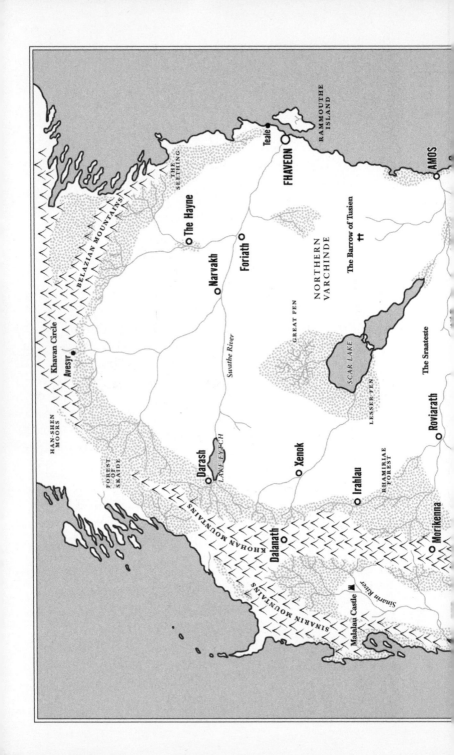

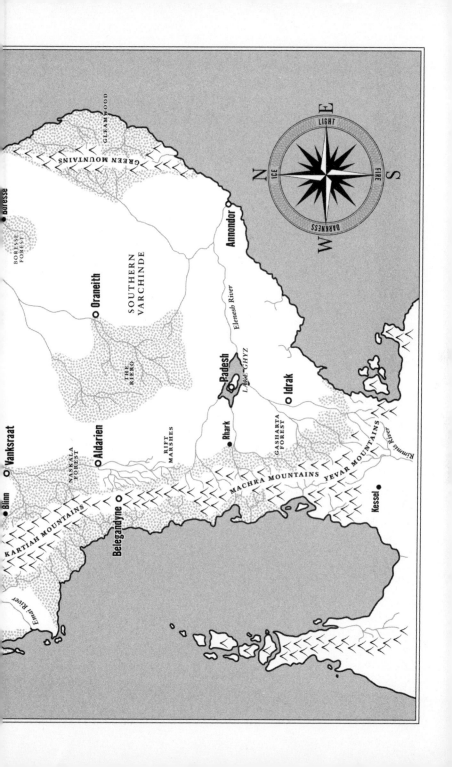

PROLOGUE AEONA

She'd walked their halls of decadence with wonder.

Now she leaned out over the parapet, breathing in the sunlight, the salt air, like amazement. They watched her through their shared eye, their curiosity whetted and mutual.

"But how do you *do* this stuff?" She turned to face them, bright with attitude. She was defiant, mischievous and confrontational. "Does anyone know? The Great Library, the Bard…"

Anticipation cut through them both, savage and immediate.

I want her, I want –!

No. Denial was absolute. *I'm not giving you one this young. She's mine. You know why.* The creature in his soul slavered at him.

Hungry.

I said "no". Ice-cold, he forced it down. *The Count of Time has brought her here for good reason.* It glowered at him for a moment, considering, then fell silent.

Patience, he told it.

He turned back to the girl, laughing with her. "I have all the company I need," he said, amused. "Aeona's my home – everything's here; my work, my art, my life. It's quiet here, I don't want it invaded." He joined her, age-spotted hands on worn, pastel stone. Beneath his skin, ink writhed – marks he could never lose slid across his fingers and circled his wrists like serpents.

When he turned to look at her – one eye seeing, the other, the dark one, covered – she caught her breath.

"Shar," he said her name with affection. "You've seen only the beginning." His gaze caught hers, held it. "Would you like to see more?"

"You can't have anything else!" Her laugh was casual, thrown away by clean sea wind. Blue water dashed into whiteness on rocks far below. "Why are you even out here?"

Ah, little one. So many questions.

Her lips were parted; her varicoloured eyes shone. He liked her eyes, one blue, one green – they were unusual, they'd caught his interest like a portent. He thought he might keep them.

"Come," he said.

Light flooded the high garden, the stone cloisters; a glitter of autumn leaves hung from the pergolas and danced in the breeze. This time, she stared more at the scatter of creatures, his menagerie, his creations and artworks. He walked with purpose and she occasionally ran to keep pace, feet swift on patterned mosaic. Dapples of sun slid over her skin.

"What're they for?" she asked.

"Themselves." He gave her an amused shrug. "Me. I like them, and they have a good home here."

They passed across the shadow of a statue, a creature of hooves and horns loomed above them.

"But why don't you let them go?"

"To what end?" He raised his one eyebrow. "Freedom isn't a gift to one who can't use it."

She frowned at him.

He pushed open a door. "Here."

Yes, draw her in. Make her –!
Be silent.

The room was dim, shelves heavy with books. He let her wander, her fingers trailing over their spines. Somewhere in his heart, the creature hissed with heat and helpless fury.

Let me taste her. Or I will rend your insides to bloody shreds. I will tear myself free of your flesh, rip down the skies and rain death on this accursed rock –

Peace. Your melodrama bores me. I'll bring you what you need – in time. You wait until I say.

I starve; you perish. Where is your learning then?

I won't let you starve.

He laughed again and the girl turned to look at him, soft in the grey air.

"Come here," he said gently.

She came, still cocky as she laid a hand on his shoulder. Her chin tilted sideways, assumption and invitation. For a moment, he allowed himself to be charmed by her brazenness.

The creature in him trembled.

And the blade opened her throat.

A single slash, a red line, a ripping, widening smile. A flood of rich darkness that covered his hands, concealed the ever-moving sigils. He caught her as she fell, bubbles on her lips and a final look of shock in those strange, two-coloured eyes. He was sorry to waste her this way, but he – they – sought answers. As if those eyes were a harbinger, a warning from the Count of Time itself, they sought answers now.

They laid her out on the stone floor, life running forgotten to the sea far below.

A single blow shattered her sternum. It took the strength of the creature within him to crack her ribcage and part the two sides like doors – tearing her open to reach the truth that lay within.

Her lungs fluttered; her heart beat desperately, struggled, and was still.

The creature in him pulsed with blood and eagerness; his skin bulged to contain it. Slowly, he raised a bloodied hand and lifted the covering on his darker eye.

Tell me, he said silently. *Tell me what you have seen.*

It repulsed his clinical nature – but his need for knowledge was absolute.

Foolish! It was laughing, the sound immortal and terrible. *The world is wounded, riven to her heart, and now a canker spreads through her flesh. Despite Maugrim's failure, Roviarath will fall to her knees. Fhaveon lies trembling, her pale thighs wide. Old forces muster at Rammouthe; they have waited so long. And the Bard is gone...*

The creature paused.

What?

Ineffectual, his presence or his absence matter not.

Its scorn was like a blade, it severed his consciousness, thought from thought. Under the full onslaught of its presence, he could barely remember who he was – even as it spoke, it pried into his mind with hot, curious fingers, baring his innermost weaknesses, laughing at his doubts and fears. One day, it would tear his soul to screaming shreds.

But not today.

Tell me what you have seen! he demanded.

I know that the world has found eyes, it said, sounding faintly amused. *But they're crazed and broken, and she struggles to focus – to mesh thought and memory once more.*

It paused. He found he had to stare at the girl, blood congealing on her skin.

And I have seen something new, something different. It was piqued – he had never heard it sound so... curious. *Something that had might enough to thwart Maugrim's growth. Something dark, cruel, tortured. Something insane. Something that walks as though in a maze of its own mind – and something that –*

The creature caught itself.

Something you'll want, my estavah. Something that may hold the key to the greatest knowledge of all.

The creature could not suppress its hunger: it flooded the man's mouth like warm red wine. He swallowed.

You can't fool me, my creature. The want is yours. What are you withholding from me? He pushed back, demanding. *How does the world find her vision? Seek her memory? What has happened to the Bard?*

It laughed at him then, displaying a cruelty and power so vast he found himself shuddering physically, backing away from the torn-open corpse of the girl.

Ah, my old friend, it said. *Do you not trust me, even now?*

The girl's head turned. He thought he saw her exposed lungs inflate, her bloodied lips make words. *Trust me*, she mouthed silently. *Trust* –

He dropped the covering over the eye.

The girl was still, ripped open like a bweao's uneaten kill. She had not moved.

You seek ultimate comprehension, the creature said, its tone enticing, a dark charisma that teased sweat from his shoulders. *This – man – believes he has it. You should bring him to us, my friend; my captor.*

Struggling, he said nothing, thought nothing. Mind empty, he stared down at the girl. Her eyes were open, that look of shock still on her face. She'd given them answers, but raised only more questions.

Sea birds cried as if in mourning; the breeze rattled the shutters. He shivered.

The creature was hiding something, something he couldn't touch. It was laughing at him. And yet he needed to know, *had* to know.

Aloud, he said, "'...that walks as though in a maze of its own mind.'"

The words echoed hollow in the silence between them. The girl cooled on the floor.

Bring him, it said. *Coax him; make him come to us. He cannot be broken, but he is in need of a mentor, a father, and you can make him trust you.*

Why do you care, creature? What do you want?

I? The creature was grinning – a white slash of savagery in the darkness. Somewhere, embers smouldered in yellow eyes. *Trust me, my estavah, my brother. The greatest knowledge requires the greatest risk. Bring Ecko to Aeona, tear him wide, and you will craft the greatest creations of your life.*

PART 1: NODES

1: AFTERMATH THE GREAT FAYRE, ROVIARATH

The Great Fayre, the trading heart of the grasslands, lay ruined.

In the long light of evening, the fading sun stretched red fingers between the ruined stalls, touching at the remnants of lives that had been. Though the surrounding grass burned a thousand glorious shades of autumn, here the ground was churned to muddy ruts, the pathways littered with wreckage.

Scavenger birds circled, their cries harsh.

Surrounding two-thirds of the walls of Roviarath, the plains' central city, the bright jumble of the bazaar had been shattered to fragments. Gone now were the traders and the tellers and the tricksters, the fakirs and the forgers, the bullies and the beggars. Gone were the creatures that had assailed the Fayre's vulnerability, that had been assaulted and thrown back by the city's rallied forces. And gone too were the opportunists, the looters and the pirates that had followed in the wake of the fighting.

About its edges, there remained a scatter of unbroken stalls – now home to the displaced and the desperate. Figures loitered silent, watching through eyes that were hard, or broken, or expectant. They watched the lines of workers that combed the devastation.

Ribald and vocal, the workers paid them no attention – instead, they called jests to each other across the debris. Steadily, they picked over the Fayre's wreckage – strewn trade-goods, pieces of blackened, superheated stone. Through-routes were cleared, neat stacks were piled, orders were barked and passed along. Bookkeepers noted trade-routes and craftmarks, and took careful tallies of what little remained.

Sometimes, there would be a flicker of fur and shadow, and a skulking creature would steal through the ruins. Then the workers would stamp their feet and throw things – but their archers did not shoot, though they were arrows nocked and heads turning, aware of the rising dark.

Watching them, Ecko had kinda guessed their targets had two feet, not four.

But that was fine – like they could see him anyhow.

Slipping through the debris, his chameleon skin shifting to the colours of sunset and shadow, he was a tattered ghost, unseen, unheard. He'd been out here before, helping himself to the good shit – hell, he had a whole stash to replace – and knew full well that he'd be a porcupine if they saw him. But face it, these guys had about as much chance of seeing him as they did of booking him a ticket back to London Heathrow.

Bring it on, guys; give it your best Robin Hood...

Stranger in a strange world, Ecko had come to realise one thing about this medieval mudbath – no one had seen anything like him before. Might even go as far as saying the culture shock was theirs, not his.

He watched the workers' progress, grinning.

Over them, the evening light faded, and died. The sunset glow deepened to darkness, and eventually the crews withdrew. The city's lighthouse tower swelled slowly to a white star of hope.

This is Roviarath, it said, *central and victorious. This is the heart of the Varchinde plain.*

Yeah, thought Ecko, *this is the city whose ass I just saved.*

*Call me "Child of Prophecy", tick the "Dungeon" box, an'
gimme my fuckin' gold coins, already.*

Yet when the final horn-call sounded and the gate swung
closed, he was still outside its walls.

The great wooden doors gave their final thudding, a
reverberation like a heart's last beat.

Orphaned now, the Fayre looked like some derelict carnival,
garish and spooky – a perfect playground for the rising, brain-
hungry shamble of the recently deceased.

But this was Ecko's third night out here, and he'd not yet
found a single zombie, shambling or otherwise. He hadn't quit
hoping though – and, hell, if he was gonna hope for zombies,
he might as well hope for shotguns and baseball bats while he
was at it. He prowled the ruin, his enhanced vision flicking
lowlite and heatseeker, his super-charged adrenaline poised,
eager, right on the edge. If he couldn't have zombies, then he'd
settle for the local alternatives: for beasties and bad guys, for
the Thing-style stone mcnasties that had assaulted the city from
the depths of Maugrim's tunnels…

His hovering adrenaline spiked as he glanced up at the
warriors on the walls.

Yeah, Maugrim whose bad-guy ass I kicked.

An' did I even get a thank-you card? Flowers?

Over the rocklit defences, the sky was starless-black.
One moon, full and gold and far too big, hung fat like some
Christmas bauble – it streaked the mud with piss-bright yellow
and made the garbage hunker like a nightmare. Higher up, its
smaller, silver brother shone cold and distant.

Together, they made the moonlight bizarre, cross-hatched
and entirely fucking impossible.

Chrissakes. Ecko aimed the thought at the silent city. *I did
your Noble Quest. I mushed your bad guy an' saved your world.*

I found your treasure and got your hot girl – well, kinda. I saw the truth, whatever the hell that was. An' I get what? A pat on the back? The ends of his stealth-cloak fluttered, laughing at him. *Where's my level-up, for chrissakes? My weapons upgrade? My skills package? My unlocked achievements?* He wanted to rail at the impossible moons. *An' why the hell didn't I score my ticket home?*

The cloak billowed harder, agitating. It was a soft mass of folds and layers; had covered him from allies and foes alike, from eyes unwanted. For a moment, the flap was intolerable and he was tempted to tear it off, throw it down amid the garbage... but it was part of him, a shielding layer, something quintessential. He could no more tear it free than he could lose his own skin...

Again.

Chrissakes, enough. Get a fucking grip.

London, the tech he called Mom, who'd undone and rebuilt him, they were a world away, unreachable. Whatever the hell he had to do to get outta this program, this reality, this whatever-it-was they'd plugged him into... apparently kicking bad-guy butt wasn't it.

Yeah, all right already, like it was ever *gonna be that simple...*

In his dark heart he knew it: This whole thing wasn't just about completing some scenario. It was Virtual Rorschach, too complex to be solved that easily. Around him, his reality was an expanding fractal, based on his thought patterns. With every decision he made, every reaction and movement, he shifted those patterns and changed his possible futures. And every one of those futures was projected by the algorithm of Collator's AI, watched by the therapist Eliza. Put simply, every new pattern was a multicoloured rebroadcast of his tiniest thought, no matter how subconscious or dark or humble. Eliza could see every single thing his mind was doing.

Every. Single. *Thing.*

Machine, mathematics and medic, in perfect harmony, twining through his brain like some inescapable hangman's knot.

The city stood silent, not offering an answer.

From somewhere, there was a rising *yip-yip-yip* of a critter, loose in the Fayre's ruins.

Ecko flicked out his cloak and began to move again, scanning the wreckage for loot. This fucking program wasn't just about beating up bad guys, he kinda knew that already. To get outta here, he was gonna hafta tick Eliza's boxes, prove he was *sane*.

And he couldn't even fake it.

Looking at the moonlit ruin of the grasslands' central market, Ecko wondered if that was even fucking possible.

Or if he was gonna be in here forever.

The moons slowly dissolved, tumbling under their own weight down towards the waiting mountains.

Cycling his oculars, Ecko was systematically ransacking the debris – with the loss of The Wanderer, down the hole into the Pit of Doom, he'd lost his hoarded stash. He was out of kit, weapons, and food.

The Fayre, though, was just about out of swag, place'd been picked cleaner than a nightclub drunk. He was finding almost nothing, now – fragments of broken pottery and ceramic, edges of fabric, rotting into the mud. The half-eaten corpse of some rodent-thing, its skull gleaming golden in the light. There were pieces of seashell, long since shattered; there was half of some tiki-type carving that seemed to have been made from bone.

As he picked up the tiki-thing, something shuddered in his skin, a subtle creeping, like fungus, a crawling sensation that spread across his shoulders...

And he knew *exactly* what the fuck that meant.

Shit.

He dropped the carving, pulled out of the thoroughfare and

found cover – the remains of the nearest stall. He pulled his cloak tighter, kicked his oculars into the brilliant grey-green of starlites and turned to look for the predator.

Come on then. Heeeeeere kitty, kitty, kitty...

The dawn light was failing. The grey clouds thickened, closing over the fading moons and the city's lighthouse tower.

The first spits of rain were cold, like gravel.

But Ecko didn't care. His adrenals had kicked, elation and eagerness; their tremble spread slowly through his system, lifting and charging him, making him shiver. He felt faintly sick – and he fucking *loved* it.

Trembling with anticipation, he waited.

Just as he was creating the wave, teetering on the very tip, beginning to tell himself there was nothing the fuck there, for chrissakes... there came the sudden crash of toppling garbage.

The sound made his heart hammer, nearly scream straight out through his ribcage. He held his breath for a moment, throttling the immediate need to lash out, that instinctive knee-jerk adrenal reaction...

But damn, it felt so good...

He stayed as still as he could.

A moment later, there was a sharp snarl, close. This wasn't Yippy, it was bigger – sounded more like a bear than a dog.

Did you get bears in artificial realities? Surely, they'd be in the woods? Or maybe this was gonna be His Greatest Fear Made Manifest.

Yeah, like I did that one already.

Ecko found his grin had spread wider, a slash of darkness.

He looked over the front of the stall.

Though the clouds were really massing now, a rising army of grey, his oculars could still see them clearly – two rangy, bone-thin critters, four-legged and taller than his hip, with heavy, protruding lower jaws. They fought for a discarded horse skull, shredding the last of the flesh from the bones of its nose. Its teeth clattered as they shook their heads, worrying at it.

As he watched, they pulled it to and fro, then dropped it. He could see them, noses lifting, heads turning, their eyes flat as mirrors and shining in the darkness. His breath froze cold in his throat – were they looking for *him*?

But there was no fucking way they could know he was here. He had no scent, no sweat, no fucking pores, for chrissakes. He made no noise; he cast no light, no shadow. Back in London, his tech had made him to be...

Yeah, right – this wasn't London. Like the impossible moonlight, these critters could probably do anything. They might have motion detectors. Or radar in their butts. Or –

One of them bared its teeth, and snarled.

Fuck.

Ecko pulled back, realising he'd make a rookie mistake – he hadn't left himself with a route *out* of his stealth position. If he needed to flee, he'd have to go over the front of the broken stall – and over the fucking critters.

The second one was slinking sideways, now, shoulders low – it knew exactly where he was, and was flanking him.

Teach me to be a fucking smart-ass. Shit!

He took a moment to scan the stall – weapons, ideas. Gifts of the gods, for chrissakes, a plus-five magical whosit of beastie-skinning...

There was a long, wicked-looking wooden splinter – too light to throw, but perfect for eyeballs – and that was about his lot.

Bloody efficient fucking patrols!

The thing in front of him had lifted its chin, was still turning its head this way and that. For a frantic moment, Ecko tried to remember – was the wind supposed to be going from the critter to him, not the other way around? Hell, he'd never had to pay attention to this shit before.

Yeah, love the learnin', Eliza, thanks for that. Gimme the download next time, willya?

But his blood was running high, his adrenaline was thundering in his ears as it hadn't done in days. Hell, this was relief, release – trapped in the city, he might've been burning shit down by now, just to have something to fucking *do*…

Come on, critter; let's see if you're smart, shall we?

The creature came forwards, flap-like ears up – what had he said about radar? His starlites could pick out the other one, now to the right, just about visible through a split in the side of the stall.

No sweat. With his adrenaline kicked, he could be over the stallfront and this thing would be a carpet –

It sprang.

And *fuck* it was fast!

He was taken absolutely by the speed of the thing; his targeters tracked it a beat behind, their crosshairs flashing as if struggling to keep up. It was almost as fast as he was. He went over backwards, one arm raised, smashed into the back of the stall, falling awkwardly, debris scattering over him, the jaws of the thing right in his face, filthy and stinking and layered with shreds of fuck knows what.

The other one was a split-second behind it, slamming into the side of the stall hard enough to come clean through, surging forwards to help hold him down. He felt its heavy jaws slam shut a second away from his other arm.

Spittle slicked him.

Shit!

In the back of his head, something yammered, the litany of suspicion that never left him. *Are you trying to teach me something, Eliza? That I can't do this alone? That I need my friends? That I'm s'posed to be part of a fucking pack? Are you?*

But the thought was a moment only; he had bigger shit to be worrying about.

In his raised hand, he still had the long wooden splinter. He flicked it through dextrous fingers and rammed it in the upper gums of the beastie in front of him, rolling sideways as he did so.

It screamed foxlike, burbling blood and drool; the sound seemed to shred the clouds, like the fabric of the stalls themselves. Through the rent, the dawn light was returning, and the back of the stall was splintering under his weight, splitting where he'd fallen into it. One critter off of him now, he flipped to his feet, tangled in cloak and wood bits, and turned back for the other.

It was there, still beside him, teeth bared, breath as toxic as its mate's had been.

Come an' have a go, if you think you're beast enough…

A flash of memory: Kale, the Bard's werecook, facing the doomed Maugrim – a flicker of over-image that made him think again about friends.

If Eliza was really trying to tell him something, she'd picked a helluva way to fucking ram it home.

Bitch.

But chrissakes, this whole reality was like that. It was like he couldn't trust anything, like everything was some sorta tutorial, or assessment, or message –

Not now!

The thing beside him leapt, but he was already moving – one kick brought the back of the stall down completely, flapping and awning and all. He leaned down to tear the broken upright free with a savage jerk. Spear, or javelin.

Eat this, you motherf–

It was then that he saw the rest of the pack.

He came back to the city as the climbing sun streaked pink the tessellated streets. He was hurting, shaking, injured, but he'd taken out five of the fuckers, sent the sixth whining home for Mommy with its tail between its legs. Damn thing had taken a chunk of him with it – he hoped it had fucking choked.

Yeah, I still got it. The fight's adrenaline had made him feel more like himself than he had in days. *Stick that in your bong and inhale.*

Around him, the tight streets of Roviarath were already wide awake. Maugrim may have been defeated, but he'd opened his darkness at the city's border, thrown his monsters at her walls. The city herself was untouched, but her people were unforgetting and restless – and without the Fayre, they'd gotten fuck all to do.

And nowhere to live – for chrissakes, the streets were *rammed.*

Traders crammed the corners, bodies packed the roadways, the homeless slumped against the walls, hands outstretched. Despite the early hour, a surfeit of bazaar stalls had already grown out of the buildings, like some haphazard and multi-coloured mould.

Jade's soldiers were prowling, watchful – but there was no violence.

Yet.

One hand wrapped over his chewed arm, Ecko slipped through the chaos, a muttering, wounded wraith. He needed treatment – hell, that wasn't s'posed to be funny – but had no wish to go to the hospice and answer a stack of nosey bastard questions. Besides, his improved antibodies should be enough, proof against tetanus and septicaemia and whatever else you got when a pack of beasties held you down and tried to fucking *eat* you...

When he got back up to his tiny room, though, he realised Eliza was still testing him – that he was never gonna get away from this shit.

Oh fucksake. Heeeere we go...

They were waiting for him – his erstwhile companions.

His *friends.*

Triqueta, rider and warrior, slight and warm and golden.

Her skin and eyes and hair all gleamed in the light from his tiny window, the stones in her cheeks glittered opal. She was sitting on his bed as if Eliza had put her there, poised and gleaming, just to push his buttons.

Looking out at the city below was the girl Amethea, the leech they'd freed from Maugrim's cathedral. She stood frowning slightly, her long blonde hair in a braid that reminded Ecko forcibly of fusewire.

Chrissakes.

Their presence made him feel trapped – like they were part of that hangman's knot. He was never gonna get away from all this, every whichway he turned, he had to face the same conclusion – he had to surrender himself, and learn to be what Eliza wanted.

Dance, Ecko.

Yeah, like on the end of that hangman's *rope...*

"Ecko!" Triqueta was grinning, up on her feet as she saw him. She went to clasp his wrist, smack him on the shoulder. "How you doing? Killed anything yet? Burned anything down?"

Her face was leaner; there were dark lines in her sunshine skin. He remembered the daemon Tarvi kissing her, the way the time had *bled* from her body...

He shuddered, pushed both her and the image away.

"Jeez, get off me, willya? How the hell'd you two get up here?" he demanded.

Amethea turned, a smile lighting her face. She, too, wanted to touch him, she gripped his shoulder as if he'd fade away or something. He flinched from under her grasp.

"It's good to see you," she said. Her eyes sparked mischievous. "You're looking a lot... better."

"Better than what?" Their warmth was freaking him out, they were too close. "What d'you want?"

"Us?" Triq said innocently, winking at Amethea. "We can't just come visit?"

Visit.

The word was affectionate – a joke, an embrace. It was camaraderie and friendliness, reunion and welcome. It was everything they'd been through, everything they'd shared, all right there in the tiny room.

Visit.

"Redlock sends apologies, but he's in the hospice." Amethea was saying. "He's still coughing. And dead grumpy." Her smile was like the sun coming up. "He asked after you."

Visit. Asked after you.

And *that* was the problem, right there, it was why he'd stayed away from these people: Redlock's wound *worried* him. He fucking *cared*.

About these people. These pixels.

These ink-blots.

These devices that'd been set here to lead and control his behaviour.

He shrank back from them, said in a voice harsh as fear, "Get the hell outta here. Bonding, bondage, whatever it is, I ain't playin'. Emotional reunions so not gonna happen."

"Good to see you too." Amethea chuckled, pointed at the mess the critter had made of his forearm. "Anyone looked at that?"

"Yeah, you just did." He was shrunk under his cowl, hiding. "Now you got five seconds before you take a flyin' lesson. Why'd the hell d'you come up here?"

"Oh put a cork in it, will you?" Triqueta stretched the kinks from her shoulders. She looked tired, weary figments crowded at the corners of her eyes. She'd clearly been drinking, regularly and a lot.

But he didn't *care*.

She said, "CityWarden sent us to find you. He wants you to stop upsetting his patrols."

He snorted. "CityWarden can kiss my ass."

"CityWarden's had better offers," Triqueta said. "You're

rattling around here like a dried grain in a skin drum, scaring the grunts and helping yourself to stuff you shouldn't be." She raised an eyebrow. "Larred Jade's a good man – but you're pushing his patience. He wants you to do something for him. A little trade for the stuff you've collected."

"Oh, lemme guess." Ecko crossed his arms and grinned. "He's got – what? – a sewer rat problem? Local bandit lord needs spanking? Evil necromancer? C'mon, there's gotta be –"

"Ecko, serious for a minute." Triqueta flicked a ball of lint at him. "Jade's working hard to fix this city. The Fayre can't run from scattered stalls, they've got no way of tracking their stuff, knowing what goods go where, or what comes in return. No one can tally or allocate anything. Given enough time, the plains' whole trade-cycle will come apart."

Ecko's targeters followed the lint, he caught it, flicked it back. "I've just saved his fucking city."

"*He's* just saved his city. Personally went out there to fight the monsters. His people think he's a hero and he might just save this place yet – but you're making it hard for him. And it's about to get harder."

"What the fuck is that supposed to mean?"

Amethea said softly, "The plains are diseased."

That one caught him broadside. "What?"

Amethea shrugged, said, "I don't know. I'm not sure I even understand it, but when the Monument fell, when the The Wanderer…" Her expression clouded, she changed tack. "Around the edges of the hole, around the pit where the Monument was, there's some sort of *rot*. I don't know how, but the grass is blighted."

Triqueta was scratching at her hands – her increase in age had given her eczema between her fingers and she agitated at them, flaking the skin. Tiny fragments of her life fell to the floor.

Amethea put a hand on her friend's wrist. "And it's not only here," she said. "Jade's sent flying bretir with messages, riders. To The Hayne, Fhaveon, Annondor, Idrak," she named the Varchinde's outermost cities, "to Rhark, Blinn, Aldarien at the foot of the Kartiah, Darash on the shores of Lake Fytch." Her face was clouded fully now, darkened with tension and uncertainty. "They think it's the same blight everywhere, creeping inwards from the edges of the grass."

The words fell heavy, lay stone-naked on the floor.

Ecko said, "So what the hell does that hafta do with me?" His voice cracked and he was silent. Then he spat, like a last line of defence, "Jesus, why should I even fucking care?"

"Because *we* did this." Triqueta said. "I don't know how, but we made this happen. Dammit, Ecko, I was only waiting here for Redlock – I just want to go home. To pull the blankets back over my head and forget everything that happened. But how can I? How can any of us just not care? After everything we've been through and everything we've *lost*." The lines in her face were as clear as if they'd been drawn. "I may be older, Ecko – but apparently I also have to grow *up*."

"Ouch." He glowered at her.

"The Bard trusted you," Triqueta shot back. "For all your horseshit, he believed in you. He *died* believing in you."

He died believing in you.

Ecko's adrenaline spiked, hard enough make him stagger, swallow bile. That hurt like hell, like she really had punched him, like his nose had crunched under her fist, like he couldn't fucking breathe. Somewhere in his head, he could see that hangman's noose, a silhouette against a clouded sky.

You bitch, Eliza. This whole fucking thing...

Somewhere, he could hear Eliza laughing like broken glass, surrounding him with a hundred sparking shards of mockery. *Ah, but there's the choice, Ecko! If you want to leave the program and come home, then you'll do as you're told. You'll play nice with your friends, eat all your greens and be in bed before 10 p.m. You'll go sane, Ecko, go safe – you'll learn to be* normal.

And Collator: *Chances of successful scenario currently rated at –*

"Oh, you are taking the fucking *piss*." His words were soft, but vicious. Both women looked at him, then at each other.

He died *believing in you.*

He found that he was holding Lugan's lighter, cold and square, like an anchor. He was trapped. Not by some pre-ordained path, some questing goal of necromancers and gold fucking coins – but by a new target, one that was as much anathema as it was unattainable.

You'll learn to be normal.

He could see himself now, his own pale skin and red hair, his scrawny wire frame in a suit, his little Pilgrim tablet every morning... *I am happy in my servitude.*

He wanted to scream, throw things, burn the fucking place down, but he held himself still.

Somewhere, in the darkest parts of his mind, somewhere deep enough that not even Collator could find it, an idea was beginning to take shape.

Something that would take that noose away.

Mildly, he said, "So – okay, we did this. Whadda we do now?"

"You're running messenger," Triqueta told him, "to Amos. Lord Nivrotar needs to know about this and it's too complex to send by bretir." She grinned. "Time to trade for your keep."

"Christ." His hand was cramping; the lighter was cold. He stood still for what seemed like an age, his chin up and his hood falling back, letting his face shift to the colours of the rising sun. "And – lemme guess – you're comin' with me." It was a statement – he already knew the answer. "Just to make sure I don't go AWOL."

"We are," Amethea said, grinning. "We're going on a little river trip – Jade had a bargemaster make space."

"A *boat*?" His flash of genuine horror made Triqueta chuckle.

"A boat." Amethea said. "The city'll give us what we need

– think she can spare that much. And Redlock'll catch us up –"

"No shit."

"And I need to see my family," Triqueta said. "Ress and Jayr went to the Amos Library, looking for stuff about centaurs. I've missed them. I want to know what they found."

2: HARVEST FESTIVAL FHAVEON

Harvest time had come to the great city of Fhaveon. Celebration danced drunken through her zig-zag streets.

Harvest was a time of thankfulness, of rejoicing in family and abundance, of celebrating the incredible wealth of autumnal colour that washed the open Varchinde. The crafters and the traders, the storytellers and the warriors of the city amassed their wares and moved to their tithehalls, waiting for the incoming wagons of meat and bone and clay and leather. The bookkeepers of the Terhnwood Harvesters' Cartel went through their notes and records for the previous return, and stole down to the city's sanctuary to assure themselves that the security stockpile, hoarded against crop failure or extreme winter weather, was enough to guarantee them safety.

Harvest was also a time of sorrow, for the colours in the grass meant it would die, that the vast emptiness of the Varchinde would be scoured back to barren soil and bared rock and scattered scrub, waiting, bereft, until the spring growth came again. Everything the people of the Varchinde needed for the winter had to be gathered when the double harvest moons rose from the eastern sea. If they failed to gather enough to survive, there was no contingency plan.

Like the ancient rule of Heal and Harm, the harvest was both life and death – and it told that there must be balance in all things. The people of the city's manors knew this in their blood and bone.

In the city herself, though, where the wild colours of the grasses were hung from garland-banners and woven into decorations, such traditions were sometimes easy to forget.

Surrounded by the noise of Fhaveon's bazaar, an ageing scribe sat beneath a pale awning, spectacles perched upon his nose. His parchment was pinned to its easel by ingenious fibre clips. He drew with a deft hand – not letters, but swift curves and features, charcoal lines of body and face. The parchment flapped occasionally as the wind chased through the tent, but the scribe continued with his work.

Above him, upon one of his upright support-poles, a long pennon fluttered like a live thing, snapping in the salt wind. It bore a symbol advertising his skill to the people of the topmost streets of Fhaveon, the people who had left kiln and needle and hall and workshop to enjoy the festival. The scribe's name was Mael, and he was a well-known character of the sunlit street-sides. Once, he had kept records for the hospice, but he was too restless for the methodical work. Now, he made his living raising a smile and a gift from those who watched him draw.

Around him, Fhaveon's decorous walls and shining, tumbling waterways shone with rare autumn warmth. Wreaths of grass, studded with berries like drops of blood, adorned the stonework proclaiming the city's double holiday with indulgent glory. More garlands, red and yellow and umber and ochre, wove through the wide streets, covering the city's topmost heights as if they'd grown from the very clifftop.

Beneath them was the wine and food bazaar: stalls that offered gifts and jewellery, most made from ubiquitous and gloriously decorated terhnwood, some few pieces of real ravak, red-metal worked by the craftsman of the distant Kartiah. Gamblers called to passers-by to roll their dice, try their fortune. Storytellers flourished and boasted. Animals were here, too: exotic beasts in embroidered collars, doomed and squeaking esphen, bright birds in cages. The smells and the noise were incredible.

Harvest time – the celebration of the Varchinde grass.

And a perfect time for the city's new powers to take advantage.

The crowds stirred and eddied. In among them were performers, troubadours and jongleurs, attracting gatherings when they paused for a song and a jest. The tales they performed were carefully selected: the lineage and beauty of the new Lord Foundersdaughter, the necessity of trade and terhnwood, the long wisdom of the Council of Nine. Some sang of lively rogues and troublesome maidens, older tales chosen for both fiction and familiarity, each accompanied by the pulse of the drum or the skirl of pipes.

The people gave them food and wine, sometimes trinkets.

Sometimes things rather less savoury.

At the heart of the revelry, a huge, abstract mosaic lay basking under the fat, autumn sun. Here, the wind was keen and the area was free from the bazaar; here, the people broke away from the crowds to eat and wander, to watch the sparkling fountains and look above them at the tip of the city, the ten shining windows of the High Cathedral, the valour of the Founder's Palace, both flawless against the azure sky. Up there, looking away from the plaza and out over the sea, stood the imperiously motherly statue of the GreatHeart Rakanne, keeping her eye upon the silent shores of Rammouthe Island.

The Lord's face was blunted and salt-rimed with age, though its decay could not be seen from below. Had she but turned, behind her and to her left, she could have looked down into one of her own creations, one of the joys of the city – her sunken, half-circle theatre. This morning, the tiers of seats housed a scattering of people, shaded by canvas roofings, like horizontal sails, that flapped tightly in the breeze. The theatre was behung with flying pennons of more woven grass – like all the others, they would be burned when the evening's dancing began. For now, though, they framed the single herald and the pair of sparring fighters that occupied the stage.

The harvest tourney, a long city tradition, had begun.

Ousted combatants wandered freely back into the stalls and the roadways, garments stuck to their bodies with sweat, garlands hung about their necks. Some sought wine in solace or celebration; others eyed the kaleidoscope of wonders on offer, and plotted how to win in the following return.

One of these paused by the awning of Scribe Mael.

Intent on his sketch, Mael did not look up as something large blotted out the sunlight. He was putting the finishing touches to a picture that was unmistakably the new Lord Foundersdaughter, her face petulant, her curves overstated, the grasslands behind her rippling under a dramatically stormy sky. It was accurate enough to show Mael's artistic talent, cutting enough to be funny, funny enough to ease the inherent disrespect.

Several people were tittering behind their hands, but as they saw the fighter approach, they stopped and sidled away.

Eventually Mael glanced around, saw that his audience had gone, and scowled.

"You damned great oaf, Saravin," he said.

"I'll have you hauled in. Look at that picture."

The two men had been friends for more than thirty returns, one settled in the hospice records room, the other roaming the city's tithed farmlands as one of Fhaveon's few warrior freemen, a sort of one-man Range Patrol.

Mael pulled the picture from the easel, and handed it over.

"Here, keep it if you want."

Saravin took it, grinned. "You trying to get me in trouble?"

The scribe stood up from his stool to stretch his back. He was a small, slim man, stooped from returns of peering at manuscripts, and lately framed with a faint atmosphere of nervousness. Beside him, Saravin was as big and as furry as a northern bweao. The contrast was marked, but there were similarities in body language, in inflexion, which marked their very long friendship – in many ways, they'd grown up together.

"Her Lordship going to show her face, later?" Mael asked. "Join her party?"

Saravin eyed the picture. "Doubt it. Reckon her days of freedom are over, poor love."

"Love?" Mael sniffed, began to tidy up the inside of the tent. "Love is for –"

"Poets and fools, I know." For a second, the big man's grin broadened. "I taught her everything I could – think my days are just as done as hers." The grin vanished below his beard. "Being... deniable has its downside." He eyed the picture thoughtfully. The young Lord's hair and skirts flowed free in the wind – the same wind that rippled the autumn grass, that was even now –

Mael grunted humorous assent with an edge of resentment that caused Saravin to frown and study his friend more closely, but the scribe shooed the warrior from the front of his stall, followed him out. He began to let down the flickering, shifting curtain.

"And how did your heat go?"

Saravin chuckled. "Was drawn against Lithian, first thing this morning." Saravin cast his eyes above, then his grin broadened and he winked. "I'm through again. Next bout this afternoon."

"Interesting," Mael said.

A collection of young, off-duty soldiers knocked into them, spilling wine from skins and goblets. They caught Saravin's eye and muttered an apology before moving off into the crowd once more, spluttering with laughter.

"You think you'll get it?" Mael said. Again, that hint of annoyance.

With a quick, impish chuckle completely at odds with his size, Saravin shrugged.

"Get what?" the warrior said, with a wink. "Foundersdaughter's Champion? Rhan's empty seat on the Council of Nine? Can't think what you mean."

Mael hissed, and Saravin chuckled again, a brief, sweet sound, oddly boyish. Then he lowered his voice, and said, "Someone has to do something, Mael. If not me, then..." He shrugged, let it tail away.

The curtain was stuck, and Mael tugged at it harder, speaking as he pulled.

"This is all madness. Haven't you heard? There's something wrong with the harvest." The old scribe glanced up at the garlands – a veneer of hope that concealed a leering, unspoken fear. How much grass had been wasted in their making – in the celebratory burning that would come? "The city's still in shock from Rhan's death, we should be in *mourning*." His eyes flicked to the palace above them, back. "So much is happening around us..." For a second, he glanced about them at the revelry. When he spoke again his voice contained a knife. "I can't find my feet, gather my thoughts."

Saravin chuckled again. "You? The young prodigy who's unlawful learning once cured a warrior doomed?"

Mael frowned at the memory, said nothing. He tugged harder and suddenly the curtain came free, closing off the tent with a sharp slide that nearly made the old scribe stumble. Saravin caught him easily, then indicated a long pennon that flew from one side of the plaza.

"You need an ale."

"You're fighting this afternoon – get drunk and you'll be a warrior doomed all over again."

"I'll stick to water. Save you saving me twice. You're a bit long in the tooth to be remembering those forbidden books now, old friend."

"Don't you 'old friend' me."

Saravin laughed.

They wandered slowly in the direction of the pennon, pausing to admire the stalls they passed on their way. The stallholders nodded at them, knowing both of them well enough by sight.

"Pure terhnwood resin, straight from the plantation itself. Craft with this, it's smoother than a maiden's…"

"First round's always a winner, seek your fortune…"

"Paints and colours, inks and powders! Dyes all the way from Southern Padesh…"

The scribe hesitated for a moment to look at the colours offered by the dyer's stall.

"This is all crazed," he said, his attention on the display before him. "You mark my words."

"Prophesying doom again?" The stallholder, it seemed, knew Mael's ways. "What ails you this time, Brother?"

The scribe shot a glance at Saravin, but the warrior had moved to the next stall along the row, where he was chatting with another of the morning's fighters. Saravin slapped the woman sympathetically on her tanned shoulder.

Mael turned back to the dyer, picking up a fragment of coloured cloth.

"I'm afraid," he said. "Afraid of the future. And afraid of –"
He caught himself, but his eyes must have flicked to the palace – or to the statue – because the stallholder leaned forwards.

"Hush!" He grabbed Mael by the shoulder of his tunic and leaned to speak into his ear. "Your thoughts are well known, Brother, to many of us here today. We stand on the brink of a new age, a new fear." Tension rode his words. "The harvest has not been rich enough. The Council can't help us – that poor girl…" The trader's voice was fast and low. "She's a child, she's not ready to rule! We have to help ourselves!"

Mael backed away, suddenly unsure of the trader's urgency.

"What are you –?"

"Quiet!" The stallholder peered about him, face etched with concern. He noted Saravin, still talking to the woman, and lowered his voice to an intense thrum. "The Angel on the beachfront, next Calasday, at highsun – ask for Fletcher Wyll. And don't bring *him* with you!" "Him" was obviously a reference to Saravin, noted with a quick jerk of the trader's chin.

Suddenly changing attitude, he picked up the fragment of cloth that Mael had let drop.

"The brown, Brother?" Now, his voice was loud enough to carry. "A perfect shade, don't you think?"

Catching on, Mael made a show of examining the colour in the sunlight, squinting at it, and wishing he hadn't left his spectacles in his tent.

"No, I don't think so, too sombre. I want something –"

"This cloth has crossed the Varchinde, Brother! From the farthest south, it has been marked by merchant after merchant, it has fought its way past brigands and pirates, past bweao and..." The shadow cast over the trader by Saravin was unmistakable; the trader's voice grew brittle. "Good morning, there."

For a moment, Saravin said nothing. When he spoke, his tone was so mild and affable that Mael was not sure if his question was a threat or a jest.

"Would you care to face a test, trader?" he asked.

Conscious of a sudden tension, the scribe held his breath.

"You may forget," Saravin went on, "how sharp a man's ears become when he spends thirty returns listening to the plains wind." The trader's eyes flicked to the peace-bonded weapon and back to Saravin's face. "You may also forget that 'that poor girl' learned much of her rural lore at my side, and that I grew very fond of her. You may forget, but it's probably wiser if you don't."

"On the contrary," the trader said, smiling with all innocence. "I have a very good memory. And I remember you, Saravin."

"Delighted to hear it," Saravin said, beaming. "Then you'll

remember that I've told you to leave the girl be. Let her do her job."

"Let Phylos do her job."

The dyer's mutter was barely more than a breath, but Saravin's hearing was as sharp as he'd claimed. Still affable, he grasped the man's shoulder in one huge, hairy paw. His voice was bare-edged. "Tread careful, trader."

The trader folded his arms deliberately, looking up into the fighter's face.

"Everyone treads careful round you, Saravin."

Tension locked them together for a brief, silent moment. Then Mael laid a sun-wizened hand on his friend's arm. "Go easy," he murmured, "you're seeing things."

For a second, Saravin didn't move, but the trader sat in bland-eyed innocence, and the warrior let him go, glowering.

"You're too long in the plains, old friend, too long alone," Mael said softly. Under his hand was the scar that had nearly reft Saravin of his life some thirty returns before – the bite of the gangrene from which Mael had saved him. "I've seen what that open space does to a man's mind. It changes you, 'Vin, remember?"

Saravin grunted, patted Mael's hand as if it were a child's, smiled. "Remind me how to think city?"

Mael laughed quietly. "At least you've got the city's respect. But if you win this afternoon, win anything, you'll have responsibilities."

Shaking his mass of hair, Saravin turned away. "Maybe I'm seeing shadows," he said. "*Arta ekanta*; figments that aren't there when I turn to look close. But these rumours of disease – we've got no –"

"This is a city, Saravin, you can't treat its people like pirates."

With his flash of his childlike grin, Saravin quoted a Fhaveon axiom. "'Guilty until proven guilty.'"

Mael moved him away, catching the trader's eye as he did so.

Almost imperceptibly, the trader nodded in acknowledgement, then turned to a couple of brightly clad ladies who were examining his colours. He did not look up again.

"It's all games." Saravin smiled and shook his head as a younger woman pressed herself against him, her eyes vivid with kohl and sincerity. "If the harvest really is threatened, then we must stand together, city and farmlands both, or we'll all die."

Mael wasn't so optimistic, but he let the matter rest.

At the edge of the plaza mosaic, a simple bar had been erected – no more than a waxed cloth roof and a makeshift wooden table. Behind it, warm in the unlikely sun, a small, walled garden gave a place for drinkers to loiter and chat. Even though it was early, the space was packed and people had scattered outwards into the sunshine, needing to make the most of both weather and break.

Scribe and warrior began to shoulder their way through to the bar.

Conversations paused as Saravin passed; gatherings of traders and workers and celebrants were silenced by his presence, then fell to muttering at his back. Mael's hearing was sharp enough to catch fragments of words, tantalising hints of public opinion, concern about the harvest, several comments about the city's new Lord. He could only imagine how much Saravin could overhear, but the warrior's face was stone hard under his heavy beard. They reached the bar without comment.

"A tankard of the tempest," Mael said, "and –"

Before he'd finished his order, the girl thumped two leather tankards down in front of him, spilling ale on the bar top. Her eyes did not meet his.

"Won't you..."

But she had gone to serve another, further away.

Saravin stared after her, checked a sigh. By the tension in his movements, he would far rather be in the garden than clustered in with all these people – Mael saw him watching the light dapple the green space with a certain well-disciplined wistfulness.

Mael picked up his drink, and turned to lean his elbows on the bar. Unlike his friend, he avoided the outdoors whenever possible – the inadequacy of the harvest was an almost academic problem to the scribe, one of numbers and weights and allocation rates. He understood that any shortage meant the farmlands would struggle with the winter. It meant their manors wouldn't hit their required autumn quotas, that the city would decline full recompense, refusing to exchange with them the goods and materials they needed. He understood how this could become both complex and disastrous. But he had not *seen* the failure, had not felt it in the soil as Saravin could.

Tensions stole through the crowd like figments, stole through the city entire.

The creeping blight was not the only problem.

Lord Foundersdaughter Selana Valiembor, only child of her dead father Demisarr, was painfully inadequate for the role to which she had so abruptly ascended. Her father murdered, her mother raped, her family's timeless guardian accused and condemned. Selana's grooming had been good – but she was too young, too traumatised, and she was an open opportunity for exploitation.

Her increasing reliance on the Merchant Master Phylos was both apparent and worrying – and it didn't take a scribe's wisdom to know where this story of a new and naïve ruler could end.

Mael listened to the fragments ebb and flow, took a thoughtful sip of his foaming ale.

Something about Rhan's absence was deeply, fundamentally unsettling. He had always been here; his presence like the stone the city was built upon, the wall that defended her cliffside face from the water. Yes, he had been irreverent, his behaviour was both legendary and humorous, but his loyalty was unquestioned and his defence absolute. Without his experience – his authority to balance Phylos's manipulation and ambition – the city was rocked to her foundations, trembling headless and vulnerable. Out there, right now, a heady mix of fear and drink was working upon the people's anxieties – one strong voice could lead them almost anywhere.

Had Rhan really been a champion? Or had he been as Phylos painted him, the stagnant deadweight that prevented the city – and the Varchinde – from developing? Had he murdered Demisarr? Forced his wife? Caused the harvest to fail? Who would take his critical seat upon the Council of Nine? With Phylos in ascendance, would this promise of a new age really come to save the city, the grasslands?

Saravin had drifted away, gone to find the open air. His head full of questions, Mael continued to idly observe the crowd.

And what of Fletcher Wyll's meeting? Priorities warred within the old scribe. Though young, Selana was the only child of her father, and Fhaveonic traditions were as deep as her wells. Enough people would support that principle to make insurrection scattered and unlikely.

People like Saravin. His heart was true, but his loyalty...

Mael found himself looking through a gap in the drinkers – following the direction that Saravin had taken. The big warrior stood in the garden with his bearded face turned up to the sunlight, feeling the cool wind of the autumn, brisk this high above the sea. The seethe of plant life around him was almost overgrown – an oddity for the upper reaches of the city where the soil was thin.

At the very rear of the garden, on a stone bench with a gargoyle grimacing at one end of it, sat a young woman, cloaked, hooded, and alone. She sat silent, her hands and most of her face concealed. Mael gazed at her blankly for a while, not really seeing what he was looking at, until something crossed his line of sight and he suddenly blinked, aware.

There was something wrong with the woman's *skin*.

It was hard to see – the sun was behind her, behind the low wall of the garden, and her face was in the shadow of her cowl. The stonework over her was hung with vine and creeper. There was something wrong with her hands –

Good Gods.

Mael's grip tightened on his leather tankard and he found himself staring, breathless and wordless, the blood draining from his face.

The girl's hands were in her lap, in a dapple of sunlight. They were soft and uncallused, yet her skin was blotched and suppurating. There were patches of rot, like lichens, growing through and in her flesh. As she raised her face and her hood fell back, he saw her hair was matted with it, that her mouth was full of... he swallowed in spite of himself, felt sick... her mouth was full of *moss*.

Saravin, closest, must have seen Mael's expression. He seemed to turn with almost comedic slowness, his hands going to the peace-bond that held his belt-blade. The woman parted her lips, tried to speak to him, but no voice came. She lifted those hands, tried to reach for him but the creeper held her back and she struggled like a trapped thing, and the people were looking up now and wondering who she was, why she was trapped with her hands reaching outwards...

Mael stared, stunned.

Then someone pointed and screamed, and suddenly all around him was disbelief and scrambling, scrabbling bodies. Someone tried to scramble over the bar, and was forcibly repelled.

Saravin was moving, but something in Mael could not. He was...

Fascinated.

He didn't think about why.

As the people backed and fled, some of them panicked,

hissing like water over stones. Mael moved forwards, out of the bar and into the garden, towards his friend.

"'Vin?" he called softly. "What's that?"

"Damned if I know…" Saravin's voice was hoarse. Mael had never heard him sound scared before. "You?"

A thrill of terror went through Mael's blood.

The woman tried to speak again, but whatever was growing in her mouth had coated her tongue and her teeth, the insides of her cheeks, and no air would come.

"I've never seen anything like it…" Saravin tailed off, his hand still on his belt. "What in the name of the Gods is the matter with her?"

The bar was empty now, people had fled shrieking across the plaza outside and the soldiery would arrive any moment.

The woman opened her mouth again. The overgrown plant life of the garden seemed to reach for and through her.

The scribe edged closer, ignoring Saravin's combatant bark of warning. Mael had no weapons, couldn't use one anyway, but he needed to see her close-up – needed to see what was happening. In long returns at the hospice, he had seen many illnesses and injuries, many types of grief and pain, but he'd never seen anything like this. And if Saravin, also, had no idea…

Something in him moved – like pity.

And then she came for them.

She was thin, savage and slavering; her eyes glowed like windows into the Rhez itself; and her gnarled hands slashed, desperate and claw-like. She came at them as though she'd been *waiting*. She thrashed and tore herself from her cloak, arms reaching and fingers outstretched as though frantic to tear the skin from their faces.

She was trying to speak.

Unreal in the gentle dapple of sunlight, patches of her skin shone cold round areas of roughened darkness. She wore garments overgrown with moss, fibres rotting and torn by the garden's plant life.

"Gods!" Mael breathed.

Both men had fallen back – the change was so sudden, so *wrong*.

For a moment, she paused in her struggles. She opened her mouth again and exhaled, a long stinking breath. She snarled.

A tremble went through Saravin's body, a pulse of absolute, focused fury.

Softly, Mael said, "Wait!"

Shivering with tension, he crept closer, until the overgrown garden had swallowed his boots to the ankle. He paused, transfixed, studying. Something about the fecund reek of this thing's breath, something...

...*familiar*...

The woman met his gaze. She half-heartedly swiped at him with one arm – as if she knew he was out of reach. Her eyes were pure madness now, burning cold.

"So," he said softly, watching her, "this your garden?"

Saravin muttered, "What are you *doing*?"

The woman cocked her head to one side, gave a second, open-mouthed hiss. In the still air, it stank like a farmer's compost pile.

"There are herbs for that," Mael said.

In response, she gave a plaintive whine and stretched one hand slowly towards his mouth. Yearning.

Now *that* was creepy.

"Mael," Saravin said. "Come away. Come away *now*."

The hiss became an inhalation, a sucking of air, a seeking. The woman coiled back, watched them through crazed, unblinking eyes. Then she hurled herself forwards, tugging frantically, struggling, shredding her own skin. Ripping the bramble clean from the dark, city soil.

Wearing it like a blood-garland.

Mael backed up sharply, tripped over his heels and went down on his arse. The woman threw herself at his face, clawing to reach his jaw and mouth, inhaling, her lips parted as though to drain his very breath. And Saravin was there to meet her, punching his blade's quillons straight into her eyes and grappling for Mael's collar with the other hand.

"I said, come away!" he gasped.

One eye popped in a splash of darkness but her hands caught Mael's shoulders. They clung, clawed – she was trying to pull him into her embrace. Her other eye was fixed, glaring-chill.

Viciously, Saravin slammed the blade into her ribs, undercutting. She keened, a horribly human noise.

But she opened her mouth anyway.

The sweet, lush stench was overpowering, a grass-harvest pile left too long on a hot day, a farmer's vegetables rotting by the roadside. The stench smothered Mael's breathing, breakfast and fear roiled in his belly – he was going to throw up.

And Saravin was there, blade discarded, hands closing on the woman's shoulders, bodily dragging her from Mael. With a vicious shudder, he threw her down to the overgrown path and slammed his boot into the side of her head.

A wet, cracking sound.

Again.

For a second, she seemed confused. The tension left her body, the crazed blue light faded from her eye. She blinked, tried to focus, her mouth worked as if to say something, but only a flood of dark fluid came from her ears and lips.

Kneeling, Saravin punched his oversized and hairy fist clean through the front of her skull. Almost unwittingly, Mael rolled to the side to throw up.

And he saw.

The young woman, now faceless and broken, was still in the regulation garments of a Fhaveon city servitor.

3: FAMILY AMOS

Amos, largest and oldest city of the Varchinde, a dark sprawl about the mouth of the Great Cemothen River.

Over the jumble of her tiled and tessellated roofs, the yellow moon had shrunk to half-full, liquid and gleaming; her smaller, higher brother now faced away from her as if sulking, glittering white in the starless sky. Melding with the moonlight, torchlight pooled across the cobbles, flickering, and bright rocklights glinted from shadowed doorways. Grass-garlands danced from window to window, fluttering, beckoning the milling crowd down toward the river and the heart of the city – then onwards to the broad, bustling spread of the Estuary Wharf.

Over the river's myriad mouths, music skirled like night wind. Carried by its promise, the people laughed and danced.

Somewhere among them, hemmed in by tight and gleeful bodies, the slim, bright figure of a woman caught a toe in the hem of her skirt and half-tripped, splashing wine down her embroidered bodice. The movement was almost clumsy, as though she was unused to fine dress.

About her, ale and humour ran freely – the accident was greeted with cheers.

She did not acknowledge them.

Triqueta blinked as the streets seemed to waver in her vision, then downed the last of her wine. Staggering, she found herself caught in the centre of a great crowd, laughter all round her, buoyed tidal through widening roadways. Pressed close, the people of Amos drank carefree, their hair woven with coloured grass.

From somewhere, a hand produced a pottery carafe, and refilled her goblet.

Rumour raced round her; boasts and dares. The Lord Nivrotar, CityWarden of Amos, had herself been seen dancing in the streets. She was unarmoured, they said, jesting with those who came close. Her prowling bodyguards were few and seemed unworried by the masses. As Triq was carried forward to the huge swath of the Estuary Wharf, the mood around her was expansive, and lavish.

Yet some part of her was withheld, and unable to let go.

She should be revelling in it, she knew that, she had every reason. She had success and fortune. She had notoriety. She had wealth to squander and no reason to withhold. She was a cursed hero, for the Gods' sakes, reunited with family she'd missed and now carried high on their shoulders...

Family.

The word was bitter.

Triqueta found she'd stopped. The crowd tutted and pushed to get round her, heady smells of scented flesh and spiced food, but she didn't move. She had a shadow in her heart, something that hurt like a bruise. She had seen things she could never unsee.

She had family hurt, and no idea how to help them.

With a gesture like need, she threw back the wine. It was sharp, almost made her splutter. She shook herself, shrugged the shock away, started to move – and tripped again on the hem of her ridiculous, whimsical finery.

What in the rhez had she been thinking, wearing this?

That she was some great lady, some cursed champion? Going to some carefree revel?

She was Banned, body and bone, born to the saddle and the free grass of the Varchinde.

But the tide still carried her forwards.

Below her, scattered through the awnings and lights of the Estuary Wharf, the taverns had overspilled, and drinkers crowded shouting. Songs grew in volume and then scattered into laughing fragments. Yet from up here, crushed in flesh and festivity, the party seemed oddly hollow, the laughter forced, the colours fake – like shadow-puppets.

Somewhere in her soul, doubts burrowed. They sent tremors through her slight figure. She needed more wine – needed the warmth and the blur.

So here I am: Amos. A city where I can indulge my every whim, gain anything wealth can buy...

...except ignorance, the world back the way it was.

Triqueta was desert-blooded, short-lived. She celebrated life and lived only for the moment... but now when she needed that celebration, that freedom, that innocence, needed to lose herself in it... she found it flaking through her fingers like soft ash.

Ash.

"My lady?"

She had stopped again. Her hands hurt where her fingernails were curled into her palms, cutting.

"Can't breathe. Need air," she murmured. Whoever they were, she pushed past them, shoving into the crowds and the smells and the noise, right through until she reached the outermost wharves, where the fisherboats were tied up and silent. There was room to think out here; the great coast-hugging triremes sat without judgement. The wind was soft and chill.

Triq leaned back against the wooden wall of a wharfside storehouse, still faintly warm from the autumn sun, and closed her eyes.

Damn that daemon bitch Tarvi – she took more than just my physical time.

In a flash of pique, she threw her goblet into the water, watched it shatter the sparking-bright moonlight. It almost collided with an oversized, muscular figure.

She challenged it, her blood rising.

"Hey, you! Watch where you're walking!"

Elaborate, carved scars glittered where they caught the moons. Her friend Jayr, the girl they'd once dubbed the "Infamous", grabbed her elbow and steadied her.

"Good thing about that frock," Jayr said, "makes you an easy person to find." Her grin was brief. "I didn't want to leave him, but I had to find you."

"Nice t'see you too," Triq said. She didn't want to see her friend – didn't want the truth she'd brought or the pain that went with it. But they were Banned, and they were family, and that was all there was to it. "Where we going?"

Jayr snorted. "Where d'you think?"

It was late, the moons dying on the rocky slopes of the distant Kartiah.

In the dingy interior of a backwater tavern, Triqueta picked up a small pottery cup. She knocked the contents back in one, wanting the burn, welcoming it – but even the harsh spirit wasn't enough.

Around her, layers of filth belied the bright moonlight outside – this was a place of hard eyes and hard liquor, a place she could come and drink herself, quite deliberately, under the table.

Wordless, Jayr filled her cup again.

"But how…" Triq was slurring. "You and Ress came here looking for answers, for help. How the rhez did he…?" Her elbow tumbled from the tabletop and she narrowly missed dropping her cup altogether. "How'd he end up like that?"

Her voice cracked and she didn't care.

The questions, she knew, had no answers. Triqueta had come downriver as an escort for Ecko, but she'd also come looking for her Banned family, her best friends – and she'd found Jayr changed, older somehow, calmer in spirit.

What had happened to Ress was beyond comprehension.

Madman, frothing and gibbering, a scrabbling figment of his former self. The horror that had crawled over Triqueta's skin as she'd seen him…

Gods!

She shuddered, downed another cup.

Jayr had told her the tale – how she and Ress had been in the Amos Great Library. She'd told of the paper he'd found, how she'd watched the life and hope and mind just drain from his flesh and gaze, told of her helpless fury at Amos's Lord. Even going over it again, in the thick, dark air of the tavern, it still made no cursed sense to either of them.

Triqueta emptied the carafe, called for another. While she drank the dismay and the hurt and the guilt to a dull sense of disbelief and a roiling core of anger, she struggled to make it all fit, somehow. To make it fit with the tales of the daemon Kas Vahl Zaxaar, with the blight, with the rumours of hostility to the north – but she was no damned scholar, by the rhez, and all she could think of was the empty look in his eyes, the disfocus of his pupils, the lax wet of his mouth…

The fact that she should've come sooner.

Ress had not even known her – he'd looked straight through her, barely noticed she was there. He'd scribbled on the wall, tried to cut himself, pissed his trews, screamed wordless and terrifying. She'd felt like nothing, a phantom; she'd felt like railing at the sky, like shaking Jayr until her teeth cursed-well rattled…

How could he be so broken?

"Dear Gods." In the thin light from the windows, Triq's hands were cracked and dry and pale. Her words caught in her throat.

She lowered the cup and blinked at it stupidly, her eyes almost as unseeing as Ress's. "But Jayr. How could you *let* him...?"

"I didn't *let* him." Jayr seemed oddly subdued, in helplessness or guilt. She leaned forward over the filthy tabletop, her own cup still untouched. "I've told you, it was only bits, I could barely read it. It made no sense, time and light and this and that, I don't even know what it said."

"Ress taught you to read." Triqueta blinked, confused.

Jayr glanced about them, lowered her voice. "Lord Nivvy's done everything she can, but her lot can't even touch him, they're worse than hopeless. Unless your clever apothecary friend – Amethea – can pull an esphen out her arse, I don't know what else to do. He's screaming crazed, and if I didn't force feed him, he'd be in the long ditch by now."

"Gods." Triqueta's mouth shook, she put her head in her hands. "Poor Ress. Oh my Gods. I should've come sooner, I should've –!"

"Something I can help you ladies with?" The male speaker was casual, grinning and masculine, handsome and fully aware of it. His eyes flicked over Triqueta and her unlikely frock, dismissed her, moved to scan the breadth of Jayr's heavy shoulders and the swell of her breasts under the leather vest she wore. "I'd be only too happy to... lend a hand."

Jayr eyed him briefly and snorted, not even bothering with a response.

But something in his stance, his arrogance, in the way he'd spoken – or in the way he'd dismissed her – sparked a flash from Triqueta's liquor-sodden temper.

"And how's... how's that your problem?" Drink-addled or not, she could still put a blade in her tone.

The man grinned. One of his back teeth was missing. Still addressing Jayr, he said, "You're an odd pair, aren't you? You together?" He met Triqueta's gaze with a smirk. "Or does this ol' lady just barter for you?"

Old lady.

The phrase caught, stuck. Around her, the noise of the tavern retreated to a dull buzz and she stared up at the confidently grinning, gap-toothed man. Her face was still streaked with tears, but her grief was rapidly congealing into something else entirely.

"*What* did you say?" she demanded.

Jayr hadn't reacted – Triq could only guess the scarred girl hadn't quite understood the implication. Moving through an odd, unreal fog, her motions unfolding before her eyes as if performed by someone else, Triqueta picked up the pottery carafe of spirit.

It was cold against her itching skin.

The man laughed outright at her. Her age. Her dress.

"Put that down, love." There was a long terhnwood blade at his belt. "Before you hurt yourself."

Jayr said, "Triq? What're you doing?"

Triqueta stood up, swaying. She didn't know quite what she was going to do, whether she was going to put the carafe down, or smash it into shards on the filthy floor, or slam it in the man's smug face...

Jayr said, warning, "Triq..."

But the man's hand had strayed to the blade at his belt. His voice tinged with mockery as he said, "C'mon love. Don't embarrass yourself, hey?"

The phrase stung like a whip-strike, like a slap across her face. Her grief igniting now, burning into furious, white-focus temper, a necessary outrage and outlet, Triqueta dropped the carafe to shatter on the tabletop and slammed the heel of her hand, hard, into the man's face.

"Fuck *you*!" Sometimes Ecko's colourful language had exactly the impact she needed. "I'm losing a friend. What's your excuse?"

The man rocked back, one hand to his nose, scarlet seeping

between his fingers. From around them came the familiar rhythm of shouting and benches scraping, the ripple of impending violence.

"You cursthed bith!" The man's other hand was drawing his belt-blade – there was no braided, peace-bonding string at this end of the Amos wharf. A moment later, it was in his hand, gleaming dully in the rocklight. The crowd closed round them, whether to watch or participate Triq had no idea.

Come on then. I can still do this... you just watch me...

Then, in a harsh scraping of bench, Jayr stood up.

The noise ground across the room, made people cringe. There was a moment of complete stillness.

Triqueta blinked. Swallowed.

When Syke, Banned commander, had named the girl "Infamous" it had been a jest – a tongue-in-cheek comment on her pit-fighter past. Many a wager had come in its wake – in two returns with the Banned, Jayr had fought just about every soldiery and Range Patrol champion from Amos to the Kartiah Mountains and back.

Now, she filled the room like a shadow, like a bared threat. Her Archipelagan features had an odd, haughty beauty, her scalplock was exotic, her shoulders carved with flat muscle, her Kartian slave-scars shining white – in this tavern, there would be no damned doubt as to what they meant. She was a crossbreed of cultures, exotic and impossible. She folded her arms, said nothing.

She didn't need to.

The man fell back, garbling an apology, resheathing the blade and pressing his other hand to his nose.

After a few rustles and mutters, the rest of the surrounding drinkers returned to their seats.

Apparently, the show was over.

* * *

Triqueta wiped her bloody knuckles with the silken fabric of her skirt.

Her head was pounding now – the booze-fuelled flare of anger had left her, and she felt empty and cold. She struggled to focus through vision and thought that blurred. Everything swayed, and she felt sick.

Jayr was sitting quietly, her face troubled. Something about her little display had bothered her, but Triq was too sozzled to quite get her head round it.

Jayr said, "We should get back. Don't like leaving him for long."

But Triq couldn't face the wreckage of her friend – not yet, not like this – the thought of it brought a rush of tension to her blood that woke her up faster than a well-placed bucket of water.

She said, managing to enunciate clearly, "Did you ever take him back to the Library?"

"Gods, no. Never want to set foot in the place again. I'd burn it down if I could."

"Maybe we should look? Maybe we'd find something to –?"

"To make him better?" Jayr gave a short, humourless laugh. "There isn't anything. We should just put him the rhez out of his misery."

Triq blinked. "You said you were fighting to keep him alive."

"I am. But what's the point?" The girl bit at her nails, spat out tiny, bitter fragments of white. "He can't tell us what he saw, he can't help us fight the bad guys; he can't wipe his own arse. We're *Banned* – we ride free, trade free, no one tells us what to do. If he was a horse –"

"He couldn't wipe his arse if he was a horse, Jayr." Triqueta said it with a straight face, but Jayr stared at her as though she was screaming loco.

Then Triq cracked a smile and they both chuckled, a shared warmth and relief that eased the tension. On an obscure impulse, Triqueta gave the younger woman an awkward hug.

"You'd never abandon him. You stupid mare."

Then someone by their table cleared his throat.

Suspecting another idiot, they parted, ready for trouble, but this man was older, thinner, his hair greying and his face weathered by long returns in the sun. He shot furtive glances to either side and bobbed an apology for interrupting.

"I'm sorry, I couldn't help overhear you. You're Banned? You've come from Syke, from Roviarath?"

The last whispering remnant of booze thrilled out of Triqueta's blood. She was trembling, and had no idea why.

"What's it to you?" she snapped.

The man glanced round again, then held something out to them.

"I need help. With something. I found this, I..." He swallowed. "I've come south, from Teale. I found this on the edges of the town, and I wondered if you knew... if you knew what it was."

Teale was a small, northern outpost of Fhaveon, the Varchinde's Lord city. It offered the capital a harbour, trade of fish and shell and salt and scrimshaw. It also supervised the growth of much of Fhaveon's terhnwood crop – the quintessential trade- and craft-material that provided the plains with everything from tools to weapons to jewellery.

The man held out a terhnwood belt-blade, the resin cracked and the fibrous centre somehow swelling, splitting its way free. The wooden grip was smoothed, the leather sheath rotted and moss-grown, the stitching tearing. As he put it on to the table, Jayr said, "What the rhez happened to that?"

Triqueta blinked at it, trying to focus.

"Please." The man was self-conscious, as though worried they'd think he was loco, send him packing with a bloody nose. "You said about trading, about Roviarath, and I thought... I thought you might know about terhnwood, about..." He let the request hang. Triqueta and Jayr exchanged a baffled glance.

"Please – can you just look at it?" He extended a hand, pushed the thing towards them like an appeal.

Jayr picked it up, turned it over looking for a craftsman's mark. Triqueta said, "Where did you – ?"

"I told you: Teale. There's disease there, the harvest's been poor, grass and terhnwood both. There were people who went out to the farmlands, to try and help…" The man was shaking. "I found a… a woman. She was asleep, I think. She was all – I don't know – overgrown, like the roots had pulled her down. She… was carrying that."

"What?" Triqueta stared at the shuddering man. "What do you mean?"

He shook his head, wrung his hands one over the other.

"I don't know. I wanted to find someone who'd help me, who'd understand."

"This is messed right up." Jayr had taken the little blade from its sheath and was holding it up to the dirty moonlight that filtered through the shutters, turning it this way and that. "You ever seen terhnwood do this?"

The man shrugged, helpless to explain. "I only found it, I don't know what it means."

"Nope," Triqueta said. There was an odd shiver in her skin. She eyed the blade for a moment, then said, with a crawl of nervousness, "It's craftmarked."

Jayr glanced at the mark and shook her head. The man looked from one face to the other and shrugged, wordlessly pleading.

"Not a clue," Jayr said. "But whatever it is, I'm betting Nivvy can tell us the full story."

Roderick the Bard had once described Amos to Ecko as the "City of Darkness".

Hell, every fantasyscape had to have one.

This one, though, wasn't populated by a load of Gothic

architecture and tentacled dominatrices in unlikely armour. Like Vanksraat, like Roviarath, the other cities he'd seen, Amos was a seethe of muck and noise and people and poverty, ludicrously tiny compared to the vast conurbations of home.

Now Ecko was here, though, walking the city's streets and looking up at her above him, he found that she'd grown and swallowed him whole, sucked him down into the warm and dirty closeness of her belly.

Amos was the closest thing he'd seen to proper urban sprawl: she was twisted and dissolute, rotted and ancient, archaic and ornate. She was tumbledown in some places, overgrown in others. The buildings were tall and cramped and irregular, they seemed to lean upon one another as though wearied by time. The streets were narrow and meandering, the alleyways seemed woven one through another as if they'd been born in a tangle – twisted and wrong – as if they'd never had builders, had never been new or full of hope.

Poetry? Ecko administered himself a mental slap. *Okay, now I've really lost the plot...*

It kinda piqued him that he was at home here. As he turned around to look up at the narrow buildings over him, at the endless statues and sculptures, at the random artworks that seemed to lurk at every corner, loom in every archway, he wondered what Eliza was playing at.

But hell, after five days on a fucking *boat* and a view of nothing but patchwork grass, Ecko would've been happy to get off the water at Westminster Bridge, security and all. Some huge part of his rotted soul wanted to just *go*, to say "fuck it all" and piss off through the streets, leave everything and climb up the side of the nearest building, run the rooftops, free...

Sod Eliza and her fucking cunning plan, he'd stay here, stay Ecko...

Like, who the hell'd miss him if he really ran away?

Yeah, an' I bet I don't have even that *choice...*

A crumpled harvest-banner caught for a moment on a stone, then whirled away in the rush-flood of rainwater.

People splashed, cursing, down the main thoroughfare behind him.

Damn you, Eliza, damn you an' your fucking program. I'm not gonna just give in to this.

He took Lugan's lighter – now refilled from Maugrim's stash – out of a pouch and began to spin it over the backs of his knuckles like a road-trickster's coin. Raindrops hit it and shattered. The lighter was too heavy to move with any skill, and when it fell, his targeters sparked and crossed and he grabbed it before it hit the cobbles.

He was caught between impossibilities – knowing he had to capitulate, but refusing to be led. Knowing he cared about his friends, but refusing to let them touch or weaken him. He was fucked, whichever way he chose.

I'm so not gonna do this. You're not gonna make me play splat-the-bad-guy again. Not demon-summoner 101, not dungeon-bash, not dragon-flight, not save-the-maiden, not fight-the-fucking-final-war. There's gonna be a way outta this.

"Angry, Ecko? There's a change." Triqueta was a leaning wall-shadow, stark in silhouette like some sort of film-noir poster.

"Shit!" Preoccupied, startled, he found himself boosted and shaking, combat-poised to take her head clean off with a squarely placed foot. "Where the hell did you come from?"

"Your dreams." Her expression was perfectly blank.

He said nothing. What the hell was he supposed to say to *that*, for chrissakes?

The rain was thinning to a gusty drizzle. The wind was cold, bundling wet garbage in whirlwinds down the empty street. Over tall buildings, the gold moon was so close he could've reached up and gutted it with a slash, watched molten metal flood down the buildingsides.

Triq stepped further into the light – she smelled of spirits, of tar and tallow smoke.

"Good to see you're awake." Her words blurred at the edges. "Got me now?"

"My early-warning system's kinda fucked. So what?"

His *friends*.

She grinned at him. "I thought you'd be out here – though you're a hard man to find." She glanced down the side street, the clawing tree-fingers, the high walls. "Going to tell me what you've been up to?"

"No." His cloak writhed, swelling and billowing like a live thing. "Whatever you want, I ain't got it. Now –"

"You're supposed to be seeing Nivvy, remember? Did you get distracted?"

"An' what're you now, city militia?" He snorted, only half in humour. "Sell-out."

His accusation set her expression like drying ferrocrete. The moonlight left deep gouges in her face – lines under her eyes, down the sides of her nose and mouth. There were shadows beneath the gems in her cheeks where the flesh was softer, beginning to drop.

The image was as sudden as a flash-projector, footage burning white-hot into his retinae...

Tarvi.

Hot lush flesh, gasping, hand reaching behind her to pull him closer, hair in his face, turning to look back at him, her profile in the moonlight soft through the –

Stop it!

His adrenaline had redoubled, screamed silent in his throat, choking him. For a moment, his insight, his defiance, his realisation – all of it – were swamped by a rush of very real physical need.

"Say that again." Triq was glowering at him, belligerent with booze. "I'll strip the skin off your body one limb at a time."

Inexplicably trembling, Ecko curled his lip.

"Been there, done that." The words came out like a challenge, daring her to touch him.

"Yeah?" She swayed slightly. "Then you'll know just how much fun it is when I start sharpening the *blades*."

"I don't have time for this." He shook himself, bared his teeth. "I delivered the message, already, dropped it at the gate. Tell Lord Whatsit you never found me, an' crawl back into your bottle. Carafe. Whatever the fuck." Then he forced himself to turn away. The memory of Tarvi kissing her, feeding from her, draining the very time from her skin, was pounding too hard in his blood. "I'm done here."

Startling him, she said, "You fucked her, didn't you?" It caught him, hooked into him like a grapple and held him fast. There was a twinge of bitterness to her tone, a need to understand something.

"'Fucked'?" The word sounded odd in her mouth.

"You use the word often enough. I know you fucked her."

"I think she fucked me."

"I think she fucked everybody."

"I think you're right." He snorted mirthlessly, understood what she was asking. "An' no, I dunno why she took your time and not mine." Glancing back past the edge of the cowl he could see that she was watching him, waiting.

Blood and adrenaline raced under his skin. He didn't move.

Then she dropped her gaze, looked at the cobbles, the pooled moonlight. His chest was tightening, just like she'd wrapped her thighs around him and squeezed.

"I'm done here," he said again. It was softer than he'd intended, he'd no idea if he was telling her, or himself. He searched for his defiance, made an effort to snipe. "No more games."

"I need you to see something." Undaunted, Triq stepped after him.

"Chris*sakes*!" Now, he paused to round on her, a harsh black grin slashed under the cowl, a focused effort of rejection. A loose piece of cloth blew into his arm and stuck there, flapping. "What the fuck –?"

"Something Jayr's taken to Nivvy, something… something we don't understand. I need your eyes, your fingers…" She waved a hand as though she'd run out of words. "Guess I thought you might be able to see –"

"See *what*?" He peeled the fabric from his skin, held it up and let it go, whirling over and over down the street.

"Ecko, please." Triq half-stepped forwards, blinked as though struggling to focus. "This is important. Critical." She grinned, briefly mischievous. "Come on, or I'll drag you by force."

"Like you could." He met her gaze. Gold in blazing moonlight, it shone like she was Queen fucking Midas, like everything she touched…

Fuck!

She was closer than he'd realised. Under the reek of cheap alcohol, she smelled like soft leather, like horsehide and sunshine and spring. She snorted, warm air on his skin, said again, "Please?"

He found himself backing away from her, like she was some sorta siren, luring him to a rocky doom. "I told you," he said it again, hammered it home, "I'm fucking done here. I played your errand boy, okay –"

"Ecko, we all went through the rhez together," she said. "What happened to friendship? Camaraderie? Loyalty?" The stones in her cheeks glittered. "You came here because you *had* to?" Her tone was disbelieving.

I don't care, I don't care!

"Yeah," he said, bitterly. "Now, I don't only hafta be a superhero, I hafta have a fucking *team*."

"Name of the Gods." Disgusted, she turned her back on him and went to walk away.

In the darkness, he could see the world around him shattering like glass, the halogen-lit green walls of Eliza's lab stark behind darkly broken, pointed shards. He could see the expression on her face as it melted under his flame.

He called after her, "I'm not gonna be controlled, Triq. I'm gonna find a way outta this. Gonna find the flaw and drop a grenade in it. A dragon-load of C4. A psychological fuckin' tac-nuke!"

He curled his palms tight, twisted them into hard, controlled fists, crushed his sensitive fingertips into his own grip, hurting.

Triqueta stopped, turned back. In the moonlight, the stones in her cheeks glittered as though she had four eyes, all of them looking at him.

She said only, "Keep sulking, Ecko. Bitch and whine until the grass-rot kills us all, kills the world under us. And then you'll be stuck here. Alone. In a dead world. Until the end of the Count of Time. But hey – at least you'll never've given in."

And then she turned, and walked away.

4: PLAYING THE GAME FHAVEON

Scribe Mael had decided that Fhaveon didn't offer the best ales – but that he'd better have another one, just to make sure.

The festival of the harvest had ended. It was late now, the traders and merchants were packing up and Mael had drifted away from the last shouts of the bazaar. Leather tankard in hand, he had found himself a place at the very back of a rising tier of stone seats, looking down at the half-circle of open sand that was the city's theatre.

It was still hot, breathless and unsettlingly so. His pince-nez, precious ground glass from the Archipelago itself, had kept sliding down his nose until, irritated, he'd taken them off. He could still see at distance, though, and he was half-watching Saravin pour a well-earned horn of water straight over his head. The big freeman had won his latest round clean, taking the elite guardsman Gharran by two points. The well-drilled posers of the soldiery had speed, but they couldn't match Saravin's experience – or his repertoire of dirty tricks.

The old scribe sat back, grimacing at the lukewarm froth in his tankard. The seats below him were mostly occupied by off-duty soldiery. They were relaxed, loud and boisterous. As their numbers grew, they cheered and jeered the various combatants and entertainments. Their ale was plentiful and free-flowing, much of it brought to them.

One of them nudged his companion and nodded down to where Saravin stood, dripping water into the sand. They both chuckled.

The sound had an edge.

With another sip of ale, Mael watched.

Around him, the wind was picking up; the garlands flapped against their moorings and fragments of autumn grass blew free, spiralling through the air. The scatterings of soldiers beneath threw their tankards at each other and roared with good humour.

Mael was uneasy, though he could not have explained why. He glanced this way and that, not sure what he sought.

The next round would be a given, so it was said. One of the city's older warrior freemen, a man named Mantine, had been blessed by the Gods even to get this far; he was no match for the soldiery's darling and champion, the veteran tan commander Cylearan. The winner would face Saravin in the final round, the climax of the contest and the height of the evening's revelry.

And then?

Mael sipped ale thoughtfully.

In the arena, it seemed as though a rag-coated jester had almost heard his question. The jester looked up at him and smiled, made grand gestures, announced a tumble of his fellows. Armed with vastly oversized, softly padded weapons, they raced across the sand and up into the stands, shrieking and having mock battles, imitating certain of the combatants with exaggerated gestures that had their audience roaring. Their performance was embellished and humorous – the sounds rose into the evening and the seats of the theatre slowly filled.

The combat-tourney was a regular sideshow at holidays such

as these, something rarely taken seriously. The winner usually received a ribbon and a pat on the back.

But not this time.

This time, Merchant Master Phylos had made a big noise about the tourney. He'd donated a little something from the Terhnwood Harvesters' Cartel – a craftmaster's blade, marked with his sigil, a weapon of such finely created beauty that it was worth almost more than metal.

And Saravin had already implied that there was more at stake here than simply the victory itself.

Was that why the event was so popular, this return? Why the seats were filling with soldiers, carrying ale and laughing, calling for their friends?

Mael leaned back, squinting at the closest seats, peering at the furthest ones. The theatre was fuller then he had ever seen it.

He made an effort to master his thoughts.

The Angel. Ask for Fletcher Wyll.

He still didn't know if he would go.

The sun sank lower, the light long and warm and fading. At any moment, it would meet its death upon the peaks of the far distant Kartiah, pouring its light down the sides of the mountains and into the plainland. It suited the mood of the holiday, the wordless unease that had tainted the crowd throughout the day. The odd restlessness had crept in here too. Somehow, in the dying of the light, Mael could see Rhan's fall from the clifftop, the darkness that had flooded to fill his absence…

…that shadow was under everything.

Mael watched the jesters, watched knots of young warriors slide between the seats, seeking an empty place.

The comedy seemed ludicrous, playful and painful, a game of touch and ego. A prank.

But the soldiers below him were roaring with laughter – the seating was almost solid with them now. Phylos's offer had been a good one, it had piqued their interest and they were calling aloud, a scatter of combatants' names, wanting one of their own to do well. Shouts of rivalry between the differing tan were few – the occasional scuffle was inevitable and good-humoured.

But how could they not understand… How did they not see…?

The people's fear was being managed, Mael realised – that was where the unease had come from, the feeling that the holiday was hollow. And that fear made them easier to lead.

Still watching the jesters, Mael understood that Rhan himself had not been forgotten – the new regime was too smart for that. No, Rhan had been *blamed*. The city's guardian had been uncaring, oblivious – he was a scapegoat.

But wasn't it also true?

Under the new rule, Selana's rule, the people would have to work harder. There were rumours of disease in the harvest, now being controlled with strategic crop-burning. If the people were willing to tighten their belts, do without luxuries, ration everyday items, then they would all win through together.

Mael sipped his ale.

All of that, though, still didn't explain why this tourney was so populous – why the entire soldiery had mustered to watch the outcome – or why Phylos had thrown his hefty weight, and the weight of the Cartel, behind it. Mael tilted the tankard again, and realised that he had found the bottom.

He blinked, rummaged for his pince-nez.

The herald was chasing out the jesters, returning to his place. Mael found his glasses, blinked again, and looked around him.

Double took.

At the back edge of the arena, the opposite corner to Saravin, stood Mostak himself, tan commander, a shorter, sharper, tighter version of his dead brother – and ruler of the city should anything happen to his niece. He was cloaked, his hood up against the sun, but Mael knew the way he moved, the lines of his body and his half-hidden features. He had drawn the man a hundred times.

Saravin, too, still loitered at the arena's edge. As Mael watched, he moved to wish both new contestants a good fight.

Now, the herald held his arms high, bellowed for silence. The soldiers gave short jeers and calls, but they sat back. When Cylearan appeared, the theatre erupted in cheers that bordered on frenzy.

Mael held his breath, empty tankard forgotten. He watched Mostak – but the commander stood stock-still.

A rustle of tension went through the seats. First out onto the sand, Mantine was the oldest of the fighters, a freeman of wagon and manor, who'd been wielding staff and spear for nearly forty returns. The crowd called his name almost derisively, there was a faint "boo" from someone Mael didn't see, though they were swiftly shushed.

The soldier Cylearan was younger, though not by much. She was a seasoned Range Patrol veteran, still a very handsome woman, tanned and slim and elegant. There was a languorousness to her that shouted like massive confidence, as if she had the entire soldiery behind her. Half of the youngsters in the audience must have trained under her at some point – the other half wished they had. She'd disdained her Fhaveon shield with its winged device, disdained any kind of parrying weapon; she carried only a long, single blade, which rested almost casually over her shoulder. In the sun it glinted like real metal. Her hair was tied back tight, military fashion, her garments were functional, but she wore them like the finest gowns. As she walked – sauntered – out onto the flat sands, she played her audience like a performer.

They loved her and she knew it.

Mostak shifted. Though he was a distance away, it was almost like Mael could feel the commander's unrest drifting upwards like smoke. Behind him, way down at the base of the hard-walled cliff, the sea shone with the dying of the sun.

What is really happening here?

Mael found himself on the edge of his seat, its stone biting into his flesh. Somehow, this event had become pivotal, and he had no idea why.

Mantine leaned on his quarterstaff. From somewhere behind him, a fruit rind struck his shoulder and rolled into the sand. He didn't flinch.

The herald raised his arms, called the rules – contact only, first to three touches. He indicated watchers, five of them, spaced about the semi-circular front of the arena. They bore pennons of various colours that they could lift for a touch.

"Samiel be your witness!" The herald's ritual call seemed barbed with irony. "Begin!"

From the opening, it was apparent that Mantine was outmatched; Cylearan was playing with him. Mael had not been watching the tourney up until now, and the Gods knew he was no warrior, but he found himself wondering how the rhez Mantine had got even this far. The man was a solid fighter, spinning the staff end over end with a double-handed efficiency that he must have learned defending land or caravan.

But Cylearan was a vet of twenty returns' experience. The pirates that Mantine had battered as a hobby, Cylearan had trained to batter professionally. He aimed one end of his heavy staff at her ankle, then spun it backhand to feint at her shoulder, then spun it back again to catch her hip as she ducked into it. The moves were good, they were almost too fast for Mael to follow...

But they were not too fast for the soldier.

She sidestepped, ducked as though she was dancing, caught the third blow with the edge of her blunted blade hard enough to split splinters from the wood. It was a fast cross-parry – forceful enough to slam the staff away from her, to leave her with an opening.

But she didn't take it. She backed up, indicated with her free hand for Mantine to come at her again.

Below Mael, the soldiers were absolutely silent, their breath caught.

Cylearan was grinning. Mael couldn't see from up here, but he could guess that the expression was similar to the one that Saravin wore sometimes – that tight, combat-grin of real, physical elation. Her hair was drifting free of its tail and wisps framed her face. Maybe she was laughing.

Mostak watched the performance from the arena's edge, his tension palpable. Saravin, too, stood watching.

Mantine came forwards again. The sand under his feet was dark and solid. Again, the staff did the left-right-left. This time, Cylearan's real metal blade met it three times out of three, each impact sending it bouncing back to pivot again. With each parry, her footing was flawless.

But this time, Mantine didn't stop; he drove her back, the staff hammering alternate upswings, his grip reversing faster than Mael could see. Cylearan met every one by pure instinct; her gaze didn't leave his. It became a rhythm, and, unable to bear the rising tension, the crowd broke into scattered cries and cheering.

Slam, slam, slam.

There were no rules about overstepping the edge of the arena, tripping people up, or hitting them when they were down. A touch was a touch. Your blow should be pulled, minor injuries were inevitable but cost points, a major one could cost you the contest. The staff moved in a blur of fire-hardened wood.

Then, suddenly, Mantine changed tactic.

Cylearan was on her back foot, at the very edge of the arena. The soldiers in the seats behind her had scrabbled out of the way. Half of her attention was turned behind so she didn't fall backwards over the rising stone. And Mantine changed the angle of his blow. Rather than left-right, he came back in again with the left-hand end of the staff, straight at her right ear.

A tight breath of shock came from the audience entire.

She caught it with a circular parry, pushing her blade outwards and downwards, turning the staff away from her. Then, swift as a thought, she cut clean back inwards, with a noise that could almost have been a laugh.

Mael didn't see the actual touch. He saw the flag though, a flash of blue fabric, saw Mantine step back and raise the staff to indicate that he'd lost the point.

One.

Below where the scribe sat, there was a rumble of low, rhythmic cheering, a rumble that spread and grew in volume. There were also scattered hisses – the soldiers expressing their displeasure at Mantine's tactics?

Cylearan's smile was like the sun. As they headed back to the arena's centre, her walk was buoyant, energetic. Mael glanced at Mostak – the commander was talking to an aide. After a moment, the young man nodded and slipped upwards through the seat tiers, hugging their very outer edge.

As the combatants circled again, Mael watched the aide go, wondering what his errand could be.

And he saw a flash of blood-scarlet.

Phylos.

Right at the back, in the corner, at the very top of the seating – almost directly opposite where Mael himself was sitting. With him was Selana, new Lord Foundersdaughter, young and blonde and completely overwhelmed by the force of his presence. The aide saw them, hesitated for a moment, then cut sideways across the crowd before vanishing over the top of the seating.

Mostak was intent on the arena and had not looked up.

Saravin however…

What was this game – move and counter-move?

In the damp sand, Cylearan was playing, her free hand spayed wide and her blade-tip darting forwards more like an arrow than a sword. Her slashing attacks had allowed the staff to spin sideways and parry; a thrust was a harder thing for Mantine to block, and now he was on his back foot, retreating before a jabbing onslaught of almost-sharp, sun-sheened metal.

Mael tore his eyes away, back to Saravin.

For a moment, his gaze crossed that of his old friend and they both paused, watching each other over the heads of the crowd. For a moment, Saravin seemed to be trying to tell him something – his fingers moved with subtle gestures – but Mael had no idea what he meant. Out in the Varchinde, the Range Patrols had some kind of sign language that they used to communicate silently or across distance – or both, he thought – but he'd never learned it. He had no idea what the old sod was trying to tell him. For that moment, they were caught on each other, on an edge of desperation – then another blue flash caught the attention of both of them and the moment was broken.

Two.

Mantine had a graze on his cheekbone. Even from here, Mael could see that it oozed darkness. There was a scuffle at the arena's edge, but Mantine shook his head at the apothecary and went back to stand at the centre.

Mantine seemed angry, controlling it. He was a fat old man and he was being made a fool of. Perhaps he'd realised that something was wrong.

The cheering was gathering, clapping and calling. Cylearan almost danced with it, the halo of hair around her face shone with the death of the sun.

Watching her, Phylos had folded his arms across his massive chest. He stood like a blood-statue, tightly controlled. He needed her to win, Mael could see it. But why?

What was this woman that her victory should be so critical? Was she supposed to also beat Saravin, win Phylos's blade and ribbon? Was *she* destined for Rhan's seat on the Council?

No, something about that wasn't right. Cylearan was a warrior; she'd have no place on the petty politicking of the

Council of Nine and she had too much experience to be a yes-woman. So, why…?

Down in the sand, the combatants circled each other again.

The crowd was shouting now, "*Cy-Lear-An! Cy-Lear-An!*"

The sunlight from the woman's hair was dazzling. As the sun itself dipped lower, down and down towards its death, Mael found the light was blinding him.

Something, some echo, something he was trying to remember…

Mantine had lost his confidence, his steps faltered and his blows were hesitant, unsure. He shook his head, once, twice, as though the cut on his cheekbone had dazed him. Cylearan had this now, even more than before; the fight was hers and she knew it.

And so did Phylos.

He stood immobile, huge in stature. Beside him, Selana seemed on her tiptoes, captivated by the fight below and trembling in anticipation of the outcome.

Mostak had not moved.

Saravin watched Cylearan as if he was trying to learn her flaws.

So many players – but what was the prize?

The Angel. Ask for Fletcher Wyll.

Mael knew now that he was going to be at that meeting.

Cylearan's blade was swift and merciless – somehow casual in its relentlessness. Mantine spun the staff as if he were in danger of his very life, retreating from the onslaught.

As if he was sure of his chosen warrior's victory, Phylos stepped back and was gone.

As he vanished, Mostak looked up – raised his chin, bristling like a silent promise.

In the arena, the blue flag rose.

Three.

Mantine was on his knees, but the crowd were on their feet.

* * *

It was almost dark when the herald returned.

In the corner of the arena, Saravin had slumped to his seat. The sky was darkening, vast and rich; Calarinde, the yellow moon was rising, brilliant in the pink-striped dusk – she swelled to gibbous, seeming closer than she'd ever been. Rocklights made the chilled stone glow with a warmth that the mercenary did not feel. His blade was as heavy and as cold as his belly, as his arse-cheeks on the stone.

He stood up, began to stretch his shoulders.

Around him, above him, the crowd was almost all soldiers, eager for the veteran Cylearan to cut him down as swiftly and smartly as she had cut down Mantine – as she had cut her way through to the very last bout. The woman was good – and she had the entire soldiery behind her. They'd gasped with every stroke of her blade.

Saravin had her age, her experience – Cylearan didn't frighten him, but she did make him wary. He had studied her closely and knew he couldn't afford a mistake.

He stretched his back.

He *had* to win this.

He wasn't even sure why.

As Cylearan walked out onto the sand, the herald could barely make himself heard over the noise. They bayed for her, they loved her and they wanted her.

Like an afterthought, Saravin heard his own name and he walked out to face his opponent, but the rising tiers around him offered little welcome – the audience was almost all soldiers. He could see a scattering of the city's people, no more, and Mael, tucked up there in the corner – Gods bless him for staying.

The herald held his arms for silence, then had to bellow several times.

And then there they were. Eyes on eyes and flesh prickling with tension.

I have to win this.

Close up, tan commander Cylearan was slightly younger than he'd thought, a scatter of lines in her tanned skin. She was sharp-eyed, eager and smirking, challenging him, wordless and secure. For a moment, Saravin had a huge and unprofessional urge to put her over his knee.

She flickered an eyebrow at him as though she could see his very thoughts.

Then the herald called upon Samiel.

Cylearan moved like a dream, swift and sure. The hair prickled down Saravin's back.

And the crowd began to roar.

Saravin's world shrank: he forgot Fhaveon; he forgot the sand under his feet, the sky over his head. Enclosed by sensation, by rocklight and stone and the eagerness of the layers of people, he was acutely aware of the hot rise of combat-tension, that sharp-edged, bright and terrible focus that marked a real warrior.

There were voices round him, shouts scattered and brutal, but he had no time for them. As Cylearan began to shift, sideways and watchful, her rocklit shadow swelled about her like an aura, shifting behind and around her wherever she moved. It was strong, some shadow-figment that replicated her motion as her eagerness rose.

It was palpable. He could *see* it.

What?

Saravin had been too long in the open Varchinde, too long alone – all that space did strange things to a man's mind. But *some*thing was raising the hair upon his arms and shoulders until his skin prickled with it; something was sharpening his mind until his awareness was poised, painfully acute. The cheers sliced through him, the air on his skin was tangible, the shadows almost too sharp. He could feel them.

And – there was something else.

It was almost lost under the mass of the crowd, but it was at the bottom of the steps – something that had come to watch the fight. For a moment, Saravin almost turned, but Cylearan was stalking the ground, her strange, dark energy-shadow giving her a halo of menace.

In his head, Saravin imagined he heard a voice, *"Senphana, Cylearan"*, like a breath of hot wind.

Cylearan advanced like an oncoming storm, close and overheated. Gone was the performer that had beaten Mantine, the cocksure woman who had walked out to meet him – she was suddenly blood and steam, her thought-cloak a daemon of fear. Her eyes had drained of light, humanity, recognition – her focus was only the play of muscle and weapon. As she struck, lightning-fast, then struck again, Saravin had time for a single realisation – that blade was sharp.

Reversing, parrying frantically, he kept it from slicing his skin – ridiculous that something so small should pose such a threat! With such short-range weapons, Cylearan was right in Saravin's face, forcing him into constant retreat, and making his longer blade suddenly clumsy in his hand. She was a flurry of hands, knife and shield both used offensively with fantastic speed. She rammed the shield rim into Saravin's teeth. Saravin twisted sideways away from under it, managed a swift attack that was met with contemptuous ease.

The shadow-cloak became an arc of after-images, following Cylearan's motions, each one burned into the rocklit air. Cylearan had bitten her lip, red trailed down from the corner of her mouth. Somehow, she had become an avatar; she was a flame-limned monster whetted for blood. Amid frantic defence, Saravin was dimly aware that only he could see this.

What was going on?

The not-voice breathed again, *"Senphana, Cylearan."*

Cylearan pressed forwards, her eyes flashing with the heat of the image that rode her. Saravin swung his sword two-handed, blocking every shot by instinct alone, his arms starting to ache with the strain. Tension and fear rose in his body; he was pressed backwards and backwards. He wanted to simply flee, but he could not gain enough of a distance between them to break away without risking injury.

And if one of those strikes hit, it would not be to win a ribbon. It would be to kill.

Cylearan slavered, her energy levels soaring, her image frenzied with bloodlust.

Somewhere above him, the GreatHeart Rakanne glowered with a motherly affection at the stage. The audience bayed like animals.

This is crazed!

Summoning his courage and resolve, Saravin tried to fight back. His sword was blunted, but he could inflict enough injury to slow this daemon-possessed fighter, enough to flee her. He had an advantage in blade-range, but he could not pass the thought-speed shield that defended Cylearan's body. A line of wet fire opened across his chest as the blade hit; still, he was being forced back.

He stumbled to the edge of the arena and fell backwards into the walkway between the stage and the first tier of seats. He landed, clumsily jarring his spine, and the avatar crouched upon the stage's edge, blood trailing across her chin.

The audience saw the blood that now stained Saravin's chest, and a new wave of feeling broke from them – disbelief, panic, anger, eagerness.

"Get away!" Saravin shouted, scrambling backwards on his feet and backside. "She's crazed, get back!"

The herald moved, surprisingly calm, to take charge of the shrieking crowd. Some surged forwards, eager to see, some tried to back up into the press of their fellows. Saravin tried to scramble to his feet, but in the chaos an unknown foot hooked his wrist, and he fell again. The voice rang in his head: *"Senphana, Cylearan!"*

Dropping her shield, Cylearan hurled herself forwards.

Saravin rolled sideways – too slow! There was a harsh slash of pain across his belly, another. The daemon was in his face, slavering at him, eager for blood.

But a third figure had shoved its way through the throng of people and now hurled itself bodily into the struggle. Saravin barely recognised the sharp, slight man as Mostak himself, before the commander wrapped his arms around the flame-avatar's body, and knocked her sprawling. Saravin tried to scrabble upright, but his belly was cut and his legs were shaking.

Lights were exploding behind his eyes.

As Mostak's tackle rolled the woman over, she laughed outright, a sound of fire and cold and darkness. She laughed like steam.

She said, "You're finished, all of you."

There was a terrible, cracking snap.

For one horrified moment, Saravin saw the woman's energy levels falling, then it was only Cylearan, her neck askew, her eyes rolled back.

The soldiery was screaming, livid.

Then: "Sara*vin*!" Mael's voice, as if from some huge distance. He tried to speak to his old friend, reassure him, but his hands were full of greasy greyness and that probably wasn't a good thing.

It was too much, and the darkness came anyway.

5: NIVROTAR _{AMOS}

In the vaulted stone hollow of a silent crypt stood a little man whose skin and garments were patterned in slants of coloured light.

Around him, the air was cold and still. If he so much as breathed out loud, he would set it in motion, echoes upon echoes – ripples of sound that would waver the walls with reaction.

But he had long since learned to breathe in silence.

This was Amos's underbelly, her true darkness – tucked and secure beneath the great beast of the palace. It was the personal office of the Lord CityWarden Nivrotar, the location of her deniable meetings, the chamber where her real decisions were made. He would've bet his fucking eyeteeth that this was the last room many in Amos had seen – that there was some Traitor's Gate out onto the river that was the flick of a James Bond switch from where he stood right now.

This was where the work got done – where the Lord Nivrotar kept her bollocks.

And hell, Ecko was kinda curious to see if Nivvy had bollocks or not – and where she was gonna hang them. The walls in here were all carved in friezes of one sort or another and they didn't leave much in the way of peg-space.

Nivrotar herself watched him carefully – every bit as silent as he was. The Lord of Amos had no use for adornment, ceremony, legions of goons or crowns and jewels – she was unarmed, unarmoured, sitting thoughtfully before him on the edge of a stone step, one long white hand stroking a flawless white chin.

Watching him, just as he was watching her.

Nivrotar felt like cold, and power. She felt like a bared blade, a chill caress down his cheek. She made the colours of his skin flicker as she shifted.

She was also absolutely drop-dead motherfucking gorgeous.

Hell, in an another underbelly, far from here, somewhere deep under Camden Market, there were still flesh parlours that would take four hours and six hundred eurobucks to make some goth wannabe look like the Lord CityWarden Nivrotar.

"So, you have come to see me after all," she said, her voice curious. She had been sitting with her back against some carven font-like thing; now, she leaned forward to hook him with a question like a monofilament barb. "Tell me, Ecko, what changed your mind?"

Keep sulking, Ecko.

"Nothing." In the dust and the cold, his response was harsh, hacking jagged through the air. Unrepentant, he grinned. "Maybe I was… curious." There were edges of echoes, mocking – they made his cynicism sound oddly empty as if the crypt itself was answering him back. He dared it, grinned wider. "So why the hell d'you care?"

She raised an eyebrow. "Why the hell do you care, *my Lord.*"

"Thanks, call me Ecko." His cloak rippled with a mock-elegant gesture, an almost-unconscious imitation of the Bard. "Silent 'G'."

For a moment her eyes tracked the flickers of colour as they crept across his garments. Then she stood up, tall and slim, her hair gleaming with an oil-black sheen.

She said softly, "What happened in Roviarath?"

Huh?

It wasn't the question he'd been expecting.

"We kicked the bad guy's hairy butt. I brought you your message. You know this already."

"Don't be clever." The cold seemed to coalesce on her skin, to glitter like frost, like the faint metallic veins that glimmered through the floor. He'd kicked his heatseeker, seeking the inevitable super-power, the ice-enchantments, the blade-up-the sleeve, the concealed goons behind the pillars – but found nothing. Her skin was cold but not impossibly so; she had no weapons, no support. She was unmagicked and apparently alone.

She spoke again, with a faint glitter of edge. "I asked you a question."

He bared black teeth. "What, your spies on vacation?"

"Maybe I'm recruiting."

"You can't afford me."

"*Look* around you." In her pale face, her eyes were dark as bruises, but a flash of passion led his gaze to frescoes glimpsed between pillars, champions battling monsters, each panel worn to a blur by years without number. She ran long fingers over the closest, the battle-scene that decorated the font-side behind her. "Do you know these legends?"

"How the hell would I –?"

"Nor does anyone else."

The finality in her tone floored him; she was playing battle-chess with his head and he'd no fucking *clue* where she was going with this. It was unbalancing, deliberate, and it was pissing him off.

She said, "This mounted and noble warrior that spears this great beast, sheds its blood to feed the trees... Whatever the saga, it is long since forgotten."

"Chrissakes, I came for weapons, not art. Willya quit playin' silly fuckers and just show me this... knife – whatever the hell it is?"

Her smile flickered. Somehow, his impatience meant he'd lost a round. He bridled, pissed, then reminded himself that he didn't fucking care anyway. He was only playing 'til he found the exit.

Made the exit.

Tore a big goddamn hole in the side of reality.

Oh yeah, he'd come for weapons all right...

Nivrotar pushed her long shimmer of hair behind one perfect white ear.

"Fhaveon is falling, Ecko; Rhan is gone. The Merchant Master Phylos, controller of the Varchinde's trade, now rules the city's Lord. He's taken the Council of Nine and his forces consolidate, even now. Do you know what this means?"

"You need an assassin?"

Her smile deepened for a moment, genuinely amused.

"A good theory – though sadly, something more insidious would just take his place. No, whatever else Phylos may be, he's obvious. His moves are brutal and easy to anticipate." She shrugged, twisted a strand of pure black hair round her finger in an oddly coquettish gesture, smiling still. "Ecko... as Phylos rises, so the Varchinde falters. We tumble towards the little death of winter, and the loss of the Great Fayre will critically damage our trade – will cause great harm, and widespread misery. The cycle cannot turn without its hub. My goods cannot travel inland without their redistribution point, their secure destination – and without my goods outgoing, their balance does not return here to me, and to my people. Do you understand our culture well enough to ken what this will do? There will be strife, and shortage, and I mislike that Phylos will turn these things to his advantage, and use them to spread his power beyond Fhaveon. Perchance, had he controlled Roviarath also, the outcome would have still been more fearsome – but the loss of the Fayre is terror enough for now." Somewhere above her, there were glass panes in the ceiling and the light flickered as feet ran over them. "All of this, and there are these... rumours... of rot in the grass." Distantly, there were shouts. "Tell me, do you believe CityWarden Larred Jade can rebuild the Great Fayre?"

Ecko shrugged.

"Why the hell you askin' me this shit? I'm a sociologist now? An advisor? Ask Triq, ask Thea – they know how your trade-whosit works. I came here for one reason, and if you don't have it, then I'm gone." He turned his back on her, took a step across the stone.

"Where, Ecko?" She made no move, her tone was amused. "Where is it that you're going?"

Where is it that you're going?

The question picked him up, spun him, threw him down, pinned him to the shining floor as neatly as a nailgun through each palm.

Keep sulking, Ecko.

Nivrotar was watching him, intent and quiet, one white finger idly caressing dark lips. She still had that faint smile, as if she could see his thoughts, see the wheels turning.

He quelled a sudden and powerful urge to lash out, to goad some other reaction from her – hell, if he'd wanted to know where that Traitor's Gate was, now looked like a re-aal fine time to ask...

He said, "D'you have this blade, or not?"

Studying him, she raised her voice and called. A small door opened in the crypt's far side; she barked brief orders at a servitor and the figure withdrew, closing the door. Then she focused back on Ecko as if she'd rip him to gobbets.

With a flicker almost too fast to follow, there was a resin gleam of terhnwood in her hand.

You fucking touch me with that, you'll be swimmin' through that gate yourself...

But she offered it to him hilt-first.

He glanced, didn't take it. He was still half-expecting her to manifest as some giant demon mcnasty, some squawking harpy, any fucking second... She stood tall and cold, her expression clouded with storm.

"This is what you wanted, isn't it?" The question was a slap. "Take the blade."

"Or you'll do what? Stick me with it?"

For a moment, he thought she'd move, she'd surge forwards and bury the thing in his throat. His adrenaline kicked, ready to hit back, to throw her down and deal with whatever grunts came through the side-door – but she held herself absolutely still as if her control was pure ice.

She said, "The grass tells me many things – I had heard, felt, a taint in its autumn but the message that you gave me..." She paused, then said again, "Take the blade."

This time, he looked, his targeters crossing instinctually. As he realised what he was looking at, his telos spun for more detail, and his hand was moving – he was raising the thing to the light like it was fucking Excalibur or something, studying the ruin of resin and fibre.

Confused, he blinked back to normal focus and looked at the Lord.

She said softly, "What do you see?"

"Look, I dunno shit about your terhnwo–"

"Tell me!" It was a bark, cold as a slap.

His telos spun back, studying the intricate micro-patterns of the crafted resin, the stilled writhe of the fibres that gave the weapon rigidity and shape. "It's gotta mark, like a maker's mark."

"All crafters have one – it's used to tally movements and trade –"

"Yeah whatever, whole thing's rotted as... holy shit."

"What do you see?" Nivrotar's question was a thrum, intense.

"It's growing." Ecko's answer was a fragment of honest surprise. "I can fucking *see*... Shit, it's fucking *growing*!"

He could actually watch it. The fibre was budding, tiny but unmistakable. The movement was minute, he could only see it with his oculars, but surely... "Look, green stuff not my thing, didn't even smoke it in college – but this shit's all the fuck wrong." He was fascinated, watching the tiniest of nano-movements, the minuscule thrust of new life – and yet something about it didn't feel healthy, it felt like it was rubbing against the palm of his hand, somehow, as if the fibres on the inside were struggling to get *out*...

He shuddered, and he wasn't even sure why.

He wanted to ask her what the hell it was – but the question was a hooks, a lure, a step down that path he was still refusing to take.

Keep sulking.

Instead, he spun the blade in his hand, the movements inhumanly fast, then stood the thing on its point on the tip of his index finger.

"So. You got zombie plant life – not the zombies I was lookin' for, but hey. What the hell does it prove?"

She reached out and took the blade from his finger.

"Ecko – blight in the grass will be fatal, to our life and our culture, our farmlands and our cities. Blight in the terhnwood will gut us like esphen, leave us gasping until we perish. If I cannot offer my crop, Amos will not only have no terhnwood, she will have no stone, no wood. And if I cannot trade with my farmlands, she will have no food – unless I choose to take it by force. And if the grass also perishes..."

Ecko's ears were humming, tinnitus and adrenaline and rising horror.

Scouting through garbage to find out where the hell he went from here.

Because we did this!

"No, you can't guilt-trip me like this, goddammit. There's no fucking *way*..."

But Nivrotar was still speaking. "My eyes and ears in Fhaveon tell me Phylos tightens the grip of the Cartel upon the people. I knew the city was stockpiling – now I know why. And if he can turn this blight, too, to work for him..."

"Chrissakes." From nowhere, memories of Tarvi squirmed, and Pareus burning and dying. *He* died *believing in you.* "You're not gonna yank my fuckin' chain with this..."

The Lord ignored him. "Without Rhan, without Roderick, without the Great Fayre, and now without the very grass, the very terhnwood, the basic things that sustain us... Ecko, Phylos is up to something – just as Fhaveon controls most of the Varchinde's terhnwood, so she also trains and distributes almost all of our military... She holds all the dice, Ecko, and she weights them in her favour."

The humming in his ears rose. He could hear the Bard in her voice, see his stance in her movements, in the colours of her hair and skin.

No, you can't make me care about this shit, you can't make me...!

She took a step forwards, lowered herself gracefully to one knee and placed a long white hand on his cheek.

"Ecko," she said. "You're the only one left. Without you, the Powerflux falters and the world will die."

He wanted to rage at her – so fucking what? – but he saw the plains seeping and rotting and raw, saw the wide grass dead and the soil barren, saw the cities stark and ruinous against the sky. He saw forces, marching and dying, heard voices lorn and lost.

The picture cut him like a hard blade, deep and into his heart.

He felt responsible. Guilty. Afraid.

He hurt.

Cared.

Then his savagery returned with a rush, reactionary and furious. *No, I don't care, I don't care! It's a fucking desktop wallpaper, no more – you can't make me care about a picture!*

Daaance, Ecko...

He was caught, cornered, just as neatly as if he'd been tied up while the bad guy outlined his plans to blow up the world.

He'd been cornered by the very sensations he'd had Mom peel from his body, tear from his mind. By emotions he'd denied, buried, surrendered, rejected, so many years before...

And the Lord Nivrotar didn't give two shits about his personal fucking drama.

He couldn't say yes, wouldn't say no, had no idea which way he would fall. Both sides yawned at him, a tumble into a decision he could never undo.

In an effort to cling to the edge, to buy time, space, rescue, he said, "Christ, all your speechifyin', you even *remind* me of the fuckin' Bard. What're you anyway, his mom?"

He was poised for her comeback – *wanting* her to spring for him, needing the outlet. His adrenals were kicked – ready for anger, violence, the call for palace guards to pike-spit him and stick his head on a bridge somewhere... and he was utterly thrown when she laughed aloud, her humour ringing from the stone vaults of the ceiling.

"His *mother*?"

Ecko stared, baffled. His adrenaline leaked out of him like piss down his leg.

Her glowering darkness gone, she bore a smile on her face that was almost girlish.

"I'm Tundran-born, Ecko, though not of his blood." Her laughter brought light and life to her pale skin, sunshine on snow. "Like Roderick, I seek lore and preserve what parts of my culture I may."

Damn the woman and her fucking mood-swings, she was like running on rubble – he'd no clue where she'd trip him. He was shaky now, he'd so been anticipating the confrontation, the revelation, the Epic Truth That Would Make Him Change His Mind... Hell, she'd make a great case-study supporting the use of Doctor Slater Grey's little magic tablets.

"What the hell is so funny?"

"You are – I should keep you here, my Dark Jester." Her eyes flashed with what might've been mischief. "Tundran culture made an error, Ecko, many returns ago. We're long-lived, but a slowly diminishing people – fewer children in every generation, and fewer of those surviving. We cling. Perchance that's why Roderick hoards his knowledge with such obsession."

"An' I thought he was jus' getting out of doin' the real work."

"Don't be naïve." The Lord's smile vanished, sunshine behind a cloud. "I *know* how long he waited for hope, clung to his faith alone – and I know how much your arrival meant to him." Her passion was rising, there were shades of deep colour in her cheeks. Her voice was layered with frost and terror and need. "If we've lost him, Ecko, really lost him..."

Lost him, really lost him.

"You're doomed, I get it already." His rasp hacked into her chill, shattered it. "But I don't do guilt trips. If he's that fuckin' critical, you find him yourself. Send your *spies*. Find Rhan. Find the Pevensie kids and crown them all king. You can't *make* me..."

For a moment her expression darkened, eyes like thunderclouds, like the threat of snow. Then her face set into an icy, humourless smile.

"You will walk away?"

Yes. No.

Fuck!

"Try an' stop me." The words were reflex. His targeters twitched, adrenals shivered: he was ready to dart for the stone stairs to the courtyard above – or to crush her white throat with a foot if she came for him.

But the cold held her where she was. She said only, "I am the Lord of Amos, and if I say so, you will obey me in word and deed and thought. Yet I would rather you made that choice for yourself. Listen to me, Ecko, and realise: by just standing with me, my enemies are yours. In the friendship of the Bard, you have secured your own death. In thwarting Maugrim and ensuring the survival of Roviarath you have angered foes far more dangerous than simply Phylos the Merchant Master. And those enemies will not forgive you – from them, you cannot choose to walk. They will follow you, hunt you and catch you – and your defiance will mean nothing. We are together – we have enemies wherever we look and we must face the unravelling of our culture as well as fight to preserve it. You stand with me Ecko, not because I choose it and not because you do – but because everything else that stands, stands against us." She rested her cold hand on his cheek, the colour of her skin seeping into his own. "I will not prevent you from walking. But if you do, I will not help you when they find you."

"If they kill me," Ecko said, his voice as soft as rust, "you, Phylos, the grass, all of this, ceases to exist."

"And what in the world," her smile was gentle, dangerous, "makes you think they'll just kill you? There are more unpleasant ways to teach people obedience."

That one had him thinking for a very long time.

6: MWENAR AMOS

Resisting the urge to blow on her chilled hands, Amethea watched the old crafthouse.

Down beside her in a tangle of overgrown garden, Triqueta was motionless, one blade drawn and the beginnings of a smile flickering at the corner of her mouth. It was cold, the sky was bright and clear, but Triq's desert skin looked warmed from the core of her soul. Her breath plumed in the crisp air.

Triq watched the sprawl of the house for a moment longer, then shook her head, the stones in her cheeks glittering.

The building was deserted.

Before them, mist and creeper clung to the cracked flagstones. It was barely the birth of the sun and the air was still cold, the night's chill lingering. They were a way from the city's heart, here; it was quiet, and an old wall separated them from the outer streets. Amethea watched every direction at once, starting with every stirring of a leaf.

The quiet was disconcerting, but Triqueta didn't seem to care.

Amethea suppressed a shiver.

The crafthouse was a long, low shadow, and it clearly

hadn't been used in returns. It was half tumbledown, its empty windows Kartian-dark, hiding nameless fears. Once, this place would have been a craftmaster's home and workplace – one of the single most important buildings in the city. There would have been a workshop here, and pure liquid terhnwood resin of the highest quality, brought straight from the plantation, braids of treated, dried fibres. The craftmaster would have had his moulds and ovens here, and from his skill would have come the finest weapons and ornamentation that the city could offer in trade – sigil-marked items that would travel from trader to merchant, merchant to bazaar, bazaar back to trader, all across the Varchinde.

And in return, he would have been one of the most privileged citizens of the city.

Now, there was nothing. Only his long cellars, empty and lined in stone.

Saint and Goddess, like I haven't had enough of stone rooms! Amethea thought, and the faint breeze sighed again; enough to stir the mist and scuttle the fallen leaves like insects about her boots. The cold was stiffening her knees.

Frankly, she'd rather be fighting to prevent poor demented Ress from clawing his own eyes out than here, flexing her stiff fingers and trying to stop herself from throwing up from sheer nervousness. She'd run scout for Vilsara in Xenok many times, but this?

This was not the same beast at all. They were following the craftmark on the blade they'd been given in the tavern – the whole thing was creeping her skin, and frankly, she wanted to be back behind the safety of the high palace wall.

Any wall. Any wall but this one.

But the old crafthouse was silent, its shutters closed and sagging, its heavy wooden door sealed.

Figments of white mist gibbered laughter in her head.

Stop that!

She swallowed, found her mouth was too dry and smothered a sudden cough, a plume of pale breath rising like steam. As she did so, Triq moved as though released, swift and almost soundless, easing quickly and carefully across the weed-edged flags.

Triq had drawn her second blade, held them both folded back along her wrists. Amethea drew her own little belt-blade and watched her friend's progress.

Any moment now, she thought, *the attack, the ambush, the monster...*

Nothing happened.

The weeds writhed silent and the white mist eddied into spectres, pale shadows of emptiness.

Triq threw a glance at her. Grinned.

This is crazed.

Amethea did not want to go into this place, did not want to know why half the roof had fallen in, why the creeper had grown through everything like a disease. She was no warrior; faced by the centaurs, then by Maugrim, she'd not been able to save Feren's life or her own sanity...

Stop that! Think about what you're doing!

Triq had taken cover beside a sculpted guard-creature, a rearing beast of stone and teeth, ever watchful and ever blind. She paused for a moment, then beckoned with a sharp movement of her shoulder. Amethea gathered her courage and crept forwards. As she moved across the courtyard, she mouthed a silent, pointless prayer.

Lot of good that'll do me.

But there was nothing, no motion, other than the mist; no sound, other than her heart in her throat, her blood in her ears.

Birds on the river, greeting the newborn sun.

As she caught up to where Triq was crouching, the Banned woman gave her a wink, then gestured for her to stay put. Triq checked the open flagstones again, then made a swift and quiet race for the huge, carven stone doorway.

Above Amethea, the guard-creature snarled at nothing, poised in his roar until the end of the Count of Time.

Amethea waited. Carefully, Triq extended a hand to the heavy door.

The crash as it fell into the hallway made them both jump. Triq dropped to a crouch, both blades ready.

But the seething mist settled, and the creature above Amethea didn't creak into motion and sink its stone claws into her shoulder.

Not that I'd expected it to. No. Not at all.

The stones in Triq's cheek flashed again as she took a moment to look up and round. Then she carefully, carefully, crept into the waiting maw.

But still, nothing. The crafthouse was peaceful, and the pale early morning light tumbled softly through the broken roof.

Amethea dismissed her fear, and went after her friend.

The building stood empty, bereft of life.

There should be a pirate nest under here or the scattered homeless of the city's outskirts lurking in the cellars. There should be the crumbled fragments of the craftmaster's works – tight containers split, and the resin slowly solidifying as it contacted the air. There should be the cut stalks of the plant, rotting now with the past returns. There should be old tally-books, no longer needed – and equally old bookkeepers to go with them.

There should be...

Stop it!

The monsters lived in her mind, her memory. They danced at the corners of her vision, tempted out of the darkness by her lack of sleep. They were *not* here, they couldn't be. This was Amos and her threats were solid and real and "normal". Getting her throat slit by a local pirate was a good deal more likely than encountering stone and darkness and fire and blight and her own blood spiralling across the floor –

Name of the Goddess. Stop that!

Shaking herself, Amethea struggled to focus, to banish the lurkers that skittered, jeering, through the soft shadows.

They are not in here! Look for yourself!

Ahead of her, the hallway was long and low and empty; the pretty, patterned mosaic on the floor was broken in many places. The walls were stone; ranks of pillars held up curves of vaulted roof, and shadows pooled about them, grey under the morning. There were more guard-creatures here, smaller versions of the beastie outside, but they showed no inclination to move.

An old, carved water fountain was long dry – even the lichens had perished.

The stone creatures in Maugrim's wall. They could be here...

Okay, she was annoying herself with this stuff now.

Vilsara, Amethea's childhood teacher, was a solidly practical woman – perhaps that was why Amethea hadn't returned to Xenok. Vilsara wouldn't have understood; would never have tolerated –

"Sst!" Triq snagged her attention back to the cold draughts of the hallway. Under the tumbledown end of the roof, the back of the hall led out to a pillared promenade, now shattered and almost inaccessible. On one of the sidewalls was a balcony that may once have been a place for archers.

There was nothing else. The place was absolutely empty. Triq looked round and shrugged. Then she sighed, straightened her shoulders and slipped along the left-hand wall.

Amethea stifled a groan.

They scouted the hall quickly as the light slowly swelled above them, one crouched and watching, while the other sought information, insight, anything. Outside, the city stirred to mundane morning life; inside, the corpses of vermin had long since rotted to stone-stain and pale bone.

Slowly, Amethea's terror waned into a faint sense of irritation.

There was nothing here. Not a dusty grain, not a stinking vagrant, not a gang of kids or a lost pirate. Not an empty sack, still bearing the mark of its farmland. Even the scavengers were desiccated remnants. Whatever had caused this one crafthouse to be abandoned, it was long gone.

Or at least she hoped.

They reached the hall's far end, where the open promenade was mostly buried beneath shattered stone, where the wall had crumbled and the shutters had failed in their last desperate cling to the stonework. The guard-creatures had fallen here, too. Derelict in their duty, they were no more than powder and final, determined fragments.

Broken bits of faces that still looked up at them, caught in their snarl.

Triq picked her way across the jumble like a dancer, light-footed and graceful. Amethea did her best to follow, but the occasional creak of the pile made her shudder. Several times, as she stepped from stone to stone to jutting timber strut, the mass moved under her like some giant and sleeping beast.

After a few moments, Triq hissed and again twitched her shoulder in the motion that meant "come here". Amethea's thumping heart nearly broke out through the front of her chest. Monsters, she'd known all alo–!

Stop that!

"Oh, good Goddess." The words were a breath of shock, and the teacher stared.

At the hall's far end, hung from the very last two pillars, were two beautiful silk hangings, torn now and their colours fading. They flanked the remnant of the doorway that led out to the promenade. In the functionality of the crafthouse, they seemed out of place, incongruous.

Amethea was trembling, but this time it was not with fear. Her face was hot and she pressed her cold hands to her cheeks.

The two women crept closer.

The silks had been painted, delicate and flawless. Every tone of flesh and facial expression was evocative, enchanting, the colours still rich. The images looked as though they would come to life, would pull themselves free from the silk to dance across the shattered hallway.

Amethea's heart was hammering, choking her.

One hanging bore the image of a lounging woman, indulgent and soft and full-fleshed, her blue-black hair spread out like nightfall. She was lusciously naked, one hand between her thighs; in the other, a goblet the size of her head.

The other hanging bore a man, scholarly and slender, his dark hair shorn short and his garments woven with pattern and wealth. One eye socket was empty, but his self-assurance was tangible and the remaining eye was alight with humour. In spite of his youth, Amethea could see a hunger in him – in his hands, in the straight line of his mouth – the hanging seemed almost to burn with it.

Something about him – his stance and attitude – reminded her of Maugrim.

Her temples pounding, her face burning, Amethea looked at her boots. For a moment, the image of the man's single eye was all she could see – it felt as though it was burning into her mind.

Little priestess.

Triq punched her. Hard enough to make her jump. She shook herself and looked back at the images.

The pictures were painted, not woven. They bore no craftmark, no evidence of their artist. The silk, too, was anonymous – there were no anomalies in its smoothness or stitching that would tell them anything about its origin. By the style, they'd been crafted within the last twenty or thirty returns, but the vibrancy of their colours suggested that they had not been hung for that long.

So had they been hung *after* the hall had been damaged?

For a long moment, both women stood and stared, half-distracted and half-baffled – then Triqueta suddenly nudged Amethea's shoulder and pointed, "It's moving."

Her voice was soft as sand.

"What's moving?"

"The wind's wrong," Triq said. "Can't you feel it? The inside of the building is warmer than the outside, but the wind's going *that* way." She nodded. "Our lady friend here seems to have a mind of her own."

"Not just a mind."

"Stop it, I'm serious." A poke in the ribs. "I reckon we might find the workshop – it's still open. Somewhere down there."

"If the next words out of your mouth are 'secret door'..."

"Secret, my arse. Keep an eye out, will you, this shouldn't be too hard..."

It wasn't.

The promenade was pillared like hospice cloisters. Between two pillars a stone arch framed a doorway, a mouth onto cold, worn stone steps, littered with leaves and debris.

From somewhere close by came air, a breath like alchemy, rank and thick with scents – herbal and medicinal, old sweat, the tang of rotted flesh.

Amethea's laughter was gone now.

They exchanged a look, then carefully, quietly, crept forwards to peer into the building's broken throat.

Silence.

Close to the hole, the smells were stronger and mingled with them now was the odd stench of scaled flesh – something Amethea didn't recognise. Triq wrinkled her nose and said softly, "Mwenar. Desert creature. Predator, six-limbed, 'bout so high." She held a hand to mid-thigh, then caught Amethea's eye. "And very lost."

Neither of them moved.

There was nothing down there, no motion. In the dim glow of a long-faded rocklight they could see a smooth, grey stone floor. Close to the doorway, it was still scattered with rubble; further in, it was as smooth as if it had been...

...as if it had been in use.

Amethea gripped her little belt-knife more tightly, and wished she was Redlock.

They listened.

Then Triq said, "Stay here, watch the door. If anything moves that isn't me, caw like an aperios or something and we'll get the rhez out of here."

"You're not going down there alone."

"Thea, I love you, but you're dead noisy." Triq grinned. "Watch the door and count to three thousand. If I'm not back, go tell Nivvy the monsters ate me."

Monsters...

"Triq..." Something in Amethea knew that the Banned woman's motives were all wrong; this was all about her age, her capabilities. "Triq, don't..."

But she'd already gone.

And the monsters crowded in from the corners of Amethea's mind.

The workshop was a series of small store rooms and records rooms, all of them empty. Between her fingers, Triq's skin itched enough to drive her loco, but the air was still, and the smell was strong. There were remnants scattered in dust on the floors – a scrap of cloth, an old sack, a bradawl with its fibre-tip broken.

The smell teased as if it coaxed Triqueta on. It was a desert smell; it didn't belong here, not in this cold stone, in all this emptiness. It smelled out of place, it smelled *wrong*.

Triq wondered how long this crafthouse had been abandoned. A master of this quality was the centre of his own small community, even his incoming trading was tightly supervised by the Cartel. The Cartel gave him his records-keepers, his workers and distributors, his traders and merchants that came straight to his home – he had his own tithes, his own neighbourhood and politics and rivalries and tales. Why this building should be hollowed out like this, that little community bereft –

The air changed.

It was larger, colder. It raised chillflesh down her arms. The smell grew suddenly, sharply stronger as if a doorway had opened, or a barrier had come down.

She paused, listened. She dropped back against the wall, blades in hand. Her blood now alight, alive with anticipation.

I can still do this!

Carefully, she eased forwards.

And then she understood why they were here.

A small sound made Amethea turn.

There was a man in the empty hall with her, standing suddenly close upon the haphazard rockpile of masonry. He was a slight, slim figure, pale haired and weaponless – yet he looked as if he could raise his arms and call lightning from the very sky.

His presence was close; it was tiny, and massive.

His presence was wrong.

Her stomach curled in on itself, knotting with fear. The monsters at the corners of her vision had withdrawn, but they seemed to be somehow *waiting...*

Morning sunlight slanted through the broken roof, pale stripes that lit the hallway in glow-perfect slants. One of them angled down to the rubble and touched the man like a benediction.

Amethea was backing away, her breath balled in her throat and choking her. Now, she could see that his clothing was worn, crusted, torn and stained; his skin was darkened somehow, as though something grew within it, within *him*. What flesh remained seemed to have caved in upon itself. His face was grown with creeper, in his mouth, in his eyes.

The lucid part of her mind told her to scream for Triqueta to help her, but she gagged, was almost sick.

The man was pale, blotched with lichen – moss grew from his ears and jaw. There was need in him, a ravening; a desperate hunger that made her quail from the passion of it. And there was such loss that she would have pitied him, despite her fear.

Once, Amethea would have trusted the World Goddess Cedetine to come to her aid, to give her strength to understand this madness, to help. But she had seen so much, too much...

The monsters crouched, grinning.

Stop that!

The man's head turned, his senses fixed on her, seemed to focus. The need sharpened, somehow became more wheedling, almost as if he sought to coax her. He started to move, stumbling as he came higher up the shattered pile.

The snarling beasts, broken under his feet, did not move.

Amethea's fear threatened to suffocate her, to shove her screaming heart right out through her chest. One hand tightened on her ridiculous little belt-knife. She half-crouched, looked for something to throw.

Somehow, he reminded her of the sick feel of the craftmaster's knife.

Triqueta had found the main workspace. It was very dry, very cold, and it *stank* of mwenar.

She had paused on its outermost edge, watching inwards and trying to follow the long stripes of dying rocklight. Pillars were wreathed in shadows and shelving marched away into the distance, their ranks interrupted by still-full sacks that lurked silent as if to trip them up.

But the sacks no longer contained terhnwood fibres.

Triq moved like a figment from pillar to pillar, touching nothing, glancing at the labels on jars and pots – long names she didn't understand.

In places the pillars stood guard over tables decorated with inexplicable contraptions, instruments that stood patient as if awaiting skilled hands. Wicker cages along one wall contained creatures, long mummified by the dryness of the air. A huge, cold fireplace lay in one wall, a blackened stone chimney piece leading to the hole above it. Something else might have been a crucible-oven, also cold.

It was absolutely deserted.

But if this place was abandoned, Triq asked herself, why did she feel as though she was being *watched*?

The hairs on the back of her neck prickled.

Responding to her instincts, she put her back to the chill, smooth stone of the nearest pillar, and looked around her, scanning for signs of movement. In front of her was one of the long tables, stretching between the pillars and towards the far wall. Underneath her boots, the flag floor was hard.

New weeds grew in the cracks, coiling colourless with the absence of the sun.

For some reason, their presence made her nervous.

She continued to scan.

Ahead of her somewhere there was rocklight, casting long streaks of shadow back from the pillars, layers of loco darkness that offered both cover and nightmare...

Then the light was gone.

The eyeless man was coming towards her.

His overgrown mouth was open, sucking in air as if he sought to find her by her very breath. His own breath steamed like plant life rotting on a hot day. Her first instinct was to stand still, silent, in the hope that he would lose her and drift away...

...but his need was too strong.

Still crouched, she got her hand on a decent sized chunk of roof, threw it, threw another. She was a good shot – one hit his shoulder and rocked him, the other caught him smack in the forehead and he lost his footing and toppled, skidded down the back of the heap.

Got you! Now just you stay –

Somehow, she couldn't even muster surprise when he got up again.

In the basement, Triq stayed stock-still. Ghosts of light kept the darkness limited to many shades of grey, but it was more distracting than helpful. Still there was no sound.

Trying not to think about the colourless weeds, she shut her eyes. Resisted the urge to stamp her feet.

Slowly, she became aware of a new smell – something under the saturating smell of mwenar. It was a smell of gangrene, of rotting herbs and death; a sweet, cloying smell that was oddly familiar.

Then the noise began.

Amethea was no warrior – but she did have a good, solid helping of sense. As the thing came again to the top of the pile, its eyes grown over, its feet skidding now, the wound in its forehead dark but unbleeding, she swallowed the inevitable mouthful of fear and tried to think.

Her mouth tasted like sand, like rock-dirt and horror.

How did she stop this thing?

It was closer now, skidding down the near side of the pile, corners of masonry tilting under its feet and making it lurch, awkward and angled. Its eyes were cold, its mouth still open and she could see the faint steam of hot, swift breath in the chill, bright air.

Was it trying to speak?

Help me.

Was it trying to say something?

Help me.

Frankly, Amethea decided, that was more than enough. Her hand closing around the biggest piece of stone she could find, she backed to the stairway and gave her best impression of a cawing aperios.

They were getting out of here. Whatever this was, Nivvy had a full quota of soldiers and Range Patrols and other armed and dangerous things – and this was absolutely *their* problem.

The voice that sounded almost in her ear made Triqueta slash a deadly response.

"Surprise." Ecko's scratchy tones ripped into the darkness and her blades were cutting from reflex alone. He cackled. "An' besides, you missed."

What the rhez…?

Triq had no time to recover from the shock, to even formulate the question. The darkness was shattered by another noise, a noise that made her shudder to the soles of her soft desert boots.

The noise was a hiss, a cold, wet, open-mouthed hiss of pure hate. It was a distance away, somewhere at the end of the long gap between table and wall.

And she had no idea what'd made it.

"Holy *shit*," Ecko said softly. He almost sounded awed.

The chilling hiss sounded again.

Triq's hands tightened on her blades. She turned her head, trying to orient on the sound.

Then, through the darkness, another noise reached her, the noise of something heavy dragging itself across the floor. The smell of mwenar was rising, but more than that – there was the herb smell, the smell of thick moss and wet lichen, and a rich, familiar scent that was unmistakably female.

"Triq? What the hell *is* that thing?" Ecko's awe had a note of real fright. "You gotta tell me what it is. Jesus Harry Christ, what is this, Clash of the fucking Titanics?"

Triqueta had never heard Ecko sound scared.

The slithering came forwards, slowly.

Something was coming.

In the deep grey layers of light, it was only an outline, feminine but wrong somehow. Below a tangled mass of dark hair, its shoulders were low to the ground, and after a moment, she realised that this was because it was dragging its lower body behind it. Its arms pulled it torturously across the floor.

Fear screamed at her to run, *run*!

But she couldn't move.

"Triq?" Ecko's voice was almost quavering. "What is it?"

"What's *what*?"

"Oh Jesus Hairy Christ on a fucking motor scooter." Ecko took a deep breath, let it out. "Let's just get this over with."

"Ecko? Get what…?"

"What I fuckin' do best," Ecko muttered. "Jus' remember, whatever happens now? It's not my fault." He took another breath and stepped in front of the beast, shadow within shadow. A tiny flame flickered for a moment, then there was a fizz and the flame became a little brighter. "Fire in the *hole*!" Ecko said, and the tiny flame arced up the room.

Knowing Ecko's foibles all to well, Triq crouched and put her hands over ears.

The resulting explosion created a whoosh of hot air that made tables rock, brought shelves off the wall, and shattered pots all over the room. Even with her eyes closed, Triqueta could see the erupting flower of light. She heard Ecko whoop beside her and then cackle, his fear forgotten; heard the furious, feminine scream that came from the creature. The smells of mwenar and herb were lost under the rich scent of burning meat.

But the thing was still coming.

It took a few moments for it to sink in that no one was coming to answer Amethea's call. It was a few moments too long, moments wasted, and the echoes of the harsh cry scorned like laughter.

Like it was already too late.

The man was even closer, now, stumbling down the near side of the pile. He didn't scramble sideways, or put out his hands like a normal man would, he staggered eyeless like the blind things in the rug, like he was already –

Oh that's it. Enough.

With a rise of irritation at her own desire to be a victim, Amethea took note of the weapons she had. The man paused, his head up and his breath still steaming as if his very insides were cooking in the cold. He seemed to realise that she was up to something.

Help me.

The strange half-words sounded again, mingling oddly with the dawn sounds of the city and the last echoes of Amethea's cry.

Help me.

But this time, she'd really had enough. Her little belt-blade was more tool than weapon; throwing rocks would only slow him down. As he began to move again, his foot rocked one of the timbers, sticking half-out of the pile.

She couldn't lift it... but maybe...

As he came close enough for her to smell the rotting-mulch stink of his breath, to see the lichens that had eaten his eyes, she planted one booted foot against the long wooden beam.

And the monsters in her head paused to watch, curious.

* * *

Still a fair distance from them, the creature hauled itself from the flames. It was alight, its hair and skin burning, but that was not what bothered her.

It was female, a grotesque and bloated parody of former beauty. Once, her blue-black hair would have been lustrous and long – the envy of her generation, now it was tangled and matted and afire. Her upper body was naked, revealing two sets of rotting breasts and four fat, white arms. Moss grew on her skin; parts of her flesh were missing altogether, eaten by the plant life that she housed. Her overhanging belly was sunless-white, and where the triangle of hair should have been, there were scales, peeling and dry. She had no legs. In their place was the body of the mwenar, stumpy forelimbs struggling to support the weight. It was as sick and bloated as the human half, and it was this that she dragged behind her, a slick trail of moisture following.

Two of her human arms were helping this rotten weight move. The other two were reaching forwards, even as the fire melted her flesh.

Now, she rose upright like a rearing snake, both sets of sizzling-fat arms spreading to meet her attackers. Her hair and skin were still burning, the flesh on her face was beginning to melt like tallow, but she seemed to feel no pain.

Fear began to grow in Triq's heart. Fear – and nausea.

Beside her, Ecko paused, the female thing in front of him burning, naked flesh dissolving in heat and fire.

With a second cry, a cry of defiance and denial and fury and outright rebellion – at the man, at the monsters, at her own Gods-damned fear. Amethea slammed the beam with her foot.

It rocked, but didn't move.

She kicked it again. And again. She kicked it harder, and harder; she kicked it even as the man was walking along its length, and reaching for her, his hands too blotched with green. She spat through gritted teeth and nearly cried.

Move, damn you. Move. *Move!*

Then it rocked. It jerked and slid. It moved. The end tipped from its perch and the beam fell sideways, twisting as it went.

It threw the man – the monster, whatever he was – sideways into the rubble... and a whole slide of stone came down on top of him.

Filthy, dusty, crying and exhilarated and relieved, she screamed defiance at the pile.

It didn't move again.

In the work room, the bands of fear that bound Ecko and Triqueta were released; they were able to move.

Ecko threw himself at the burning creature, his peculiar hand-and-foot fighting too fast to follow. At the same time, Triqueta sprang past the creature and landed behind her, blades slashing at her back and tail.

The creature screamed in fury. She twisted faster than Triq realised, her tallow arms reaching and agile and fearfully strong.

Ecko was moving, but he was not fast enough, not this time. One burning hand caught Triq by the throat, searing her skin and tearing her breath from her body; the other slapped her, setting off an inferno in her skull.

She felt the impact, the rush of air, the strike of the wall... then nothing.

By the time Amethea reached Ecko, screaming at him to stop, to *stop*, it was too late.

Triq was slumped in a heap at the base of one of the pillars, and the black-haired woman, the same woman whose image was on the hanging in the hall, had been torn to fragments and ash.

Whatever clue they were supposed to find here, it had been burned away.

7: CATALYST AMOS

Stuck in the hospice like an invalid, Triqueta was restless.

A day – only one! – and she already itched with impatience. She had too much to think about, too much to do. The world moved on around the walls of the hospice, and she wanted to be a part of it.

If she raised her fingers to her face, she could feel the dressing under her opal stone. The burn was slick and patchy, the skin tight and hurting. The dressing covered her face right down to her jawline.

It was taking all her concentration to not scratch the shit out of it.

Burn or no, however, the serene air of the hospice was driving her loco. She wanted to see how Ress was, talk to Jayr, to Amethea; she wanted to go to the Library, she wanted to rail at Nivrotar for sending them to that damned crafthouse in the first place. She wanted to know what the rhez Ecko had been doing there. She wanted to go back to Roviarath, for Gods' sakes, do *some*thing to help…!

Amethea counselled her, advised patience. For now, Triq had to sit tight and not talk too much. Triqueta had the robust physical health of most Banned, but her age scared her and she was not mending as fast as she used to. Thea was good, though, she'd managed to save the opal stone – thereby rescuing her friend from a lifetime of misfortune.

"How are those things even in there?" Amethea had asked her. "They're right in the bone."

"Had them since I was a babe," Triq had told her, carefully trying to talk out of one side of her mouth. "Gift of the desert, mark of your sire's family, his 'Banner', embedded at birth. And no, I don't know why they still fit."

Amethea had chuckled. "That's not possible. Stone can't –" The statement had come out as bitter, bitten off short. They both knew full well that stone and flesh could do all sorts of things they weren't supposed to. "Sorry. Still understanding, I suppose."

But Triq had snorted. "Nothing makes sense. Should've interrogated the mwenar."

The unspoken thought had hung loud: *If Ecko hadn't torn it to pieces.*

But Amethea had said, "We're all crazed, we'd have to be to be mixed up in all of this." Then she'd turned her attention back to the burn. "You're lucky, this could've been so much worse. Don't mess with it, and you'll heal pretty clean. When you feel ready, go down to the bathing room and have a look – but come back up here and let me re-cover it."

Have a look…

The phrase had been so simple.

But Triqueta had not looked at her own reflection. Not since…
…and *that* thought didn't need finishing.

Now, though, she was dirty and itchy and achy and restless, so she found her courage and an armful of cloths, and padded softly down the curve of stone stairs, down to the bathing pool, silent and shining under the stone of the city's ancient hospice.

The burn was a timely reminder – if she was going to face

whatever was coming, she better have the cursed nerve to face herself.

Even if descending the stairs did feel like she was walking to her own execution.

For a moment, as she came to their foot and saw the water ahead of her, the dance of its reflection on the vaulted stone of the ceiling, the memory of Tarvi's kiss coiled around her fear, laughing with a pretty girl's sweetness and guile. Gods know, it thrilled her blood still; Triqueta had known enough lovers in her life, but a kiss like that...

She still didn't know how many returns the bitch had really taken.

Holding the cloths like armour, Triqueta stopped short of the edge of the pool.

A look...

One more step.

She was going to be sick.

Swallowing hard, Triq glanced around her, assuring herself that the chamber was empty, that no one else had to see this. The circle of stone benches was cold and silent; between them, the incomprehensible dance of statues had their blind faces turned away. In the centre of the pool itself, a flat stone platform served some forgotten purpose.

She was alone. The air was cold.

Okay.

Slowly, she took off her belt, her old Banned leathers. She could see her own chillflesh, prickling over her body as if in dread.

I can put an arrow in the eye of a running esphen. I can hang from one foot in the stirrup of a racing horse. I can out-fight and out-drink a warrior twice my size – and take him to my tent afterwards.

She answered her own thought with a tang of bitterness.

But for how much longer?

The water was calm, absolutely still. She could see the old

mosaics in the walls of the pool. One more step.

And there she was, looking back up at herself.

The woman in the water was not the Triqueta she knew – she had more curve, her skin was less tight, her belly softer, her thighs dimpled with shadow. The dressing on her cheek was crisp and clean – smaller than she'd thought. She raised her hands to her small breasts, lifted them to where they should be.

Let them go.

How old? she asked her reflection. *How old am I?*

The statues about her stayed silent.

"Okay," she said aloud, needing to hear the words. "It could be worse. You look damned good for your age, sunshine. Whatever it is."

The last phrase twisted in the roof, echoed back at her.

One kiss. One second where her basic desert instincts – *Laugh! Live! Love!* – had got the better of her –

Oh, who the rhez was she kidding? Her desert instincts had got the damned better of her all her life – too many lovers, too many gamblers, too many fights. With a wry grin at her unfamiliar reflection, she turned sideways, trying to see her arse, then stepped forward to dip a bare foot into the water.

It was cursed cold. She bit back a yelp and grinned.

Then she waded into the chill, careful to keep her face clear. She merged with that other self and the ripples shone as they spread across the stillness.

"Triq!" The voice was as warm and familiar as the touch of a terhnwood blade – and cut her skin just as readily. "Thea said you were bathing. Looks like my timing's perfect."

She turned, heart hammering, face burning, wet hair sticking to her shoulders...

Redlock.

Redlock of Idrak, once Faral ton Gattana, manor lord and hub-controller of his local farmlands and tithes, now freeman and warrior without peer, was grinning like a bweao, just as dangerous and as boyish as she remembered. His broken nose gave him a rugged air, hard and scruffy like a tavern brawler; his greying red hair was roughly braided. His garments were still road-stained and there was mud on his cheek. She kicked out and struck for the shore. Inexplicably, her heart was thundering like running hooves.

At the memory of her own reflection or as though she hadn't really expected him to come back.

He called to her, "Stay there, silly girl!"

Then he dropped his axe-belt, unlaced his boots, kicked his way out of his battered garments. He was fit as a horse, grey scattered through the hair on his chest. His freckled skin was sunburned only to his throat and elbows, and littered with a storyboard of scars.

One side of his ribcage was badly dented where Maugrim's chain had thrashed him, the scar was still vividly angry.

He said, "What did you do to your face?"

"Long story," she replied. "Jayr and" – her voice caught on the name – "Ress are here. And Amethea." It sounded inane but she could think of nothing else. Her heart was in her throat and she struggled to form words past the ache in her cheek. "And Ecko..." She left the sentence hanging, changed tack. "How's Syke? And Jade? What's happening in Roviarath?" She got it out in a rush. "The blight in the grass...?"

"It's some damned scary shit, is what it is." In removing his shirt, he'd tangled the neck lacings in his hair. He tugged, and swore. "Poor bastards, they're doing their best. But even so, when I left, Roviarath's traders were starting to scatter, taking their tables outside the walls. By now, they'll be all over the place and Jade'll have no way to keep track of them." He stopped to untangle the string, his muscled body prickling with cold. "The whole system's broken, Triq. It's too complicated, too fragile. Stuff from all directions is piling up because the hub just isn't there any more." He freed himself, looked up. "It's all coming apart."

Triq said, "So – what about the disease? The hole where –?"

"He's got a watch on it," Redlock told her. "That damned thing's putting the wind up everybody, though it doesn't seem to be getting any worse. Dear Gods, why is it so cold in here?"

Three steps and he was wading manfully into the water, grimacing at the chill.

"I'll go tell Nivvy – but I wanted to be at least halfway presentable before I went in there. Brrrrrrrr." He shivered.

"Now who's a girl?"

"Ha!" Then there was a splash and there were hands on her calves, trying to pull her under.

"Don't – my face!" Suddenly giggling, she kicked away from him, took a breath, twisted out of his hands. The water was clear. The pool's mosaics hinted at battles glorious and forgotten. With a hand on the rough-edged artwork, she knifed swiftly round the central pillar.

But he was already waiting for her.

She tried to turn; her own momentum carried her into his arms.

He caught her, grinning, leaned in to kiss her.

One kiss. One moment of weakness…

No!

Startling herself, she shoved away from him hard, her face and chest hurting. A moment later, she was hanging on to the central platform by her elbows, panting, her hair plastered down her back.

The rocklit air was cold on her skin.

What the rhez just happened? What…?

"Triq?" He exploded up beside her, took a gasp of air and shook his braid like a courier's nartuk. His heavy shoulders bunched as he unconsciously copied her position. There was a tail of weed on his arm, reminding her suddenly and forcibly of the moss-grown mwenar. "You okay?"

No. Yes.

"Sure." The answer was reflexive, though her thoughts were tumbling, panicked. *He was too close. Why was he too close?*

"It's good to see you, Triq." He rested a hand on her back, smiled, eyes searching her face. "You look…"

"I know how I look." With a rush of movement, water sheeting from her skin, she pulled herself onto the stone. Suddenly, acutely conscious of the changes in her face, in her body, she stood tall, turned to face him, arms crossed under her breasts. "Well?" she said.

She was shivering. Damn that water was cold!

"Triqueta." He pulled himself onto the platform. Water ran down his face, dripped from his hair. "You're Banned. You're fierce, you're proud – you're as terrifying with a set of dice as you are with that damned lop-ended bow of yours." A smile creased the suntan lines round his eyes. "Your beauty's unchanged."

She watched as the water ran down the sides of his throat, over his shoulders and scars.

Get back on the horse.

In the house of the burning beastie, Ecko had found a miracle.

A key. A fucking *sign*.

He'd found it in the alchemy lab, guarded by the monster in proper traditional style, and now he was all bundled up with it, turning over what it was, and what it meant, and what it could do, and where it was gonna take him.

He knew one thing for sure – whatever Roderick believed, Nivrotar pleaded and Triqueta slapped him round the head with… he was going to find a way out of his trap.

His fucking Catch-22.

Around him, the city's hospice was quiet. The open-sided corridors that surrounded the central quadrangle were empty, shaded with dusk. The sky was darkening and layers of cloud were sinking over the dark roofs of Amos, rain scattered. The first glimmers of rocklight lit the quad's central sculpture into something ghoulish and ugly.

Whatever the hell the statue was. Ecko didn't really look, he was too busy roiling in the dark glee of his own thoughts. He'd disdained any kind of treatment, pulled his hood over his face and now skulked right into the wall, less than a shadow, less than a nightmare, less than a fragment of forgotten horror. He was himself again, he was *arta ekanta*, demon figment, that single image, forgotten upon awaking, that yet still haunts you throughout the day.

And he wasn't really looking where he was going.

"Ecko..."

His name like a breath, too soft for alarm. For a moment, he thought it was in his head, that Eliza, Collator, Lugan, *some*one, was trying to reach him through the screen or the gap-between-the-worlds or whatever the fuck he was supposed to call it...

...and then he woke up and it was all a dream...

...but the voice was here, with him in the corridor.

He stopped dead, his heart pounding, shrank back. His oculars shifted options, searching.

Found a man crouched in the corner, filthy and stinking like some elderly London hobo. He had some sort of rotted hemp bag gripped in one hand.

The man was staring back at Ecko as if he was some dark and manifest archangel.

What the hell?

The guy looked in his sixties, weathered and lined but pallid under the rocklight. His beard was grey, his hair awry. There was a scarlet line from one corner of his mouth that crusted down toward his ear. Scans showed the massive, erratic flickerings of the man's body temperature and Ecko had to make an effort not to back up even further.

They continued to stare, mutually compelled and horrified, and the world shrank round them, spiralled in on that meeting, that moment, that single laser-intense gaze. Then the man's expression fluttered and twitched. He flinched, blinked, mouthed words of nothing. His temperature fluctuations redoubled, flashing through the front of his face and skull like flame on water. His empty hand batted querulously.

Ecko had no idea what he was supposed to do. Every instinct told him to get the fuck outta there before it all went to hell in a handcart, but some part of him was completely, utterly compelled. He dropped into a full crouch, studying the guy like some kind of specimen.

Or was *he* the fucking specimen?

The guy smelled like incense and old sheets, like wrong flesh and ill-health.

It was a scent that suddenly and forcibly reminded him of Slater Grey. Of home. Of Pilgrim. Of –

Don't go there.

"Man, you fuckin' *reek*."

At Ecko's rasp, the man's temperature peaked, his gaze sharpened, and one wasted arm lashed out. His eyes were intense, demented, one pupil larger than the other in a way that screamed *lunatic*. His hand was fast as a whip – and even with his adrenals kicked, his oculars tracking, Ecko was too slow.

The man's hand clamped round his upper arm like a manacle.

"Shit!" Really freaked now, Ecko jerked his shoulder, tried to back away, but the man's fingertips were digging into his woven flesh like he'd sprung some fucking bear trap. Instead, his efforts nearly pulled the guy to his feet. "What d'you want? Small change? Meths? Get off of me, for chrissakes."

"Change." That made the madman smile. "Yes, change. I

came… to tell you… something." His words were spittle and desperation; he fought to focus.

Ecko had no idea who this fucker was – or why he'd been ambushed. His oculars scanned, but there was no one else in the cloister. *No cameras, no security, no Pilgrim…*

Yeah, all right already. Joke's on you, asshole…

Ecko smirked, kicking his adrenaline after all – the welcoming thrill that unrolled along his muscles like relief, like a cheap backstreet high. Swiftly, he glanced back and forth down the corridor again, turned his oculars on the quad.

Nothing.

Now I gotcha…

His hand clenched tighter round his prize.

"Tell me *what*?" Now, he crouched down, his oculars targeting – eyes, jaw, throat. "What the fuck –"

But the man was speaking, low and severe. He leaned forwards, words falling from his mouth like gobbets of blood, like spat lumps of tobacco. In the front of his face, heat ran like liquid through his forebrain. "You have no eyes… eyes like pits, like the pure element of dark. Smile like a blade of death. You've come… for me?"

What the hell…? Ecko bared his teeth, trembled with the surge of blood through muscle. "What is this? What the fuck're you doing?"

The scent of Grey's experimentations was tangling his brain in horrific knots of nostalgia and resentment. Images tumbled and he pushed them away.

The steel hand ground into his bicep. "I can see myself in your black eyes." The man was looking straight through him, his pupils were blood-dark, haunted; his forebrain was on fucking *fire*. "Myself and myself and myself, like mirrors, going back into the Count of Time. Pattern endless and repeated." He cocked his head to one side, a motion almost mechanical. "What does that mean?"

"You totally snatch today's prize for the cryptic mystic visionary mad dude." The grip on his arm was hurting. "Now get the hell offa me."

"Time. You're outside the Count of Time, he can't *touch* you!" The sentence ended in almost a laugh, a flood of realisation. "He has no power over you!" The bear trap released and the hand rose between them, reaching forwards as if it expected to pass through him, to find that he was some kind of phantom. In the guy's skull, the colours calmed, muted. *"'Time the Flux begins to crack'! You!"* The word was cry, a paean of elation. "You're the cat... the cat..." The word fragmented into physical shaking. Ecko's skin was shuddering with adrenaline.

Catapault? Catamite? Catatonic? Catalytic fucking converter? He pressed his lips together to keep quiet.

"...catalyst!"

The madman was grinning with absolute wonder, like the sun coming up, like Ecko's baby sisters, long ago, with a favourite toy. "You... it was written for *you*!" He was nearly crying. "Are you even here at all?"

Are you even here at all?

Here at all?

You think this world is real?

You think that it's not?

Incense and old sheets. The stink of unwashed flesh. Grey's base. The people eaten from the inside out by the tablets, by Nothing, by... What did they call it here? The word came from Ecko though he wasn't even sure what it meant. "Kaz... *Kazyen*."

"Yes!" The madman was in tears, now. "You understand, you *understand*!" He was like some abandoned creature meeting a friend for the first time, overcome with more than he could express. "You don't *need* to remember – you *know*!"

"I know shit." Ecko was fascinated and appalled.

"I can see now! Time doesn't touch you – and I can see

myself, over and over and over and over and over and over…"
He tailed into muttering, tears streaming down his face. "I
know… I know what I must do. I can fix this… I can… I can
help you fix this…" He cried, tears glittering in the rocklight
like shattered glass. "Roderick was right all along…" The last
words were a whisper. The madman lifted his face to the pattern
of light and let it bless him; lift him. Whatever his revelation, it
was profound enough to leave him sobbing like a child. "It all
fits. And it's going to be all right!"

Then he started to laugh.

His laughter was demented, high-pitched and half-scream
– it was elated, it was grieving, it was celebratory, it was
downright fucking terrifying. Ecko's targeters flashed again;
his muscles were absolutely *bunching* to play soccer with this
fucker's head…

But.

"Shut the hell up! Shut up! What the fuck is so funny?" he
demanded.

The laughter faded, the madman collapsed into gulps as like
crying. One hand ferretted beneath his blanket and emerged in
a tight clench.

When he opened it, it was empty.

"Figments!" he said. "Maybe that's how we win!" His
cackle began again, demented. "Win, lose, sane, insane. Inside
and outside. You understand, you *understand*!"

"Understand this, mofo." Ecko shook him, hard, held the
treasure right in his face. "This is a building block; it's a first
step. You want figments? This is the One Thing that I'm gonna
drop in the Ass-Crack of Doom and ker-*blooey*!" Right in his
face. "Bitch can't force me to change."

The old man's face crumpled. He cocked his head to one
side, looked quizzical, almost fatherly. He said, quite clearly,
"So you'll just break it, if you can't have your own way?" This
seemed to make him think for a minute. Then he laid a calming

hand on the side of Ecko's face. "When you go home, what happens to us?"

What happens to us?

You think this shit is real?

For just a moment, the impossibly gentle needle of the question slid under Ecko's skin and injected him with sharp, cold horror. His stomach lurched with nebulous terror; his knees went. He was on the floor, nauseous and shaking, crouched at the old man's feet like some sort of acolyte, his cloak mottled the colour of rocklight and dread. *You're not real. You're not fucking real.*

He wanted, he wanted...

Then he remembered who the fuck he was and what he was doing. He'd found the fucking *answer*, dammit. He found his snarl, his anger. Right under the madman's nose, he opened his hand.

Showed the old man his prize, the thing he'd found in the crafthouse.

The solution, the key, the "One Goddamn Thing".

Sulphur.

Frankly, Triqueta thought, they could've chosen a more comfortable location.

Resting along the line of the axeman's body, head on his shoulder, hand on his dented chest, she was realising that the stone under her was cold and slippery, that her hip hurt and that her back was twisted at a painfully funny angle.

The dressing on her wound had come loose – but the healing skin was cool, it no longer itched like dust and fire.

Her grin was wicked, tight at one side. *Romance, love of the Gods. These are the bits they never tell you!*

Suppressing a chuckle, she reluctantly sat up to stretch the kinks from her spine.

"You okay?" Redlock was grinning too, amused at himself, her, or the loco circumstances, she didn't know.

She peeled the dressing completely off, wincing, and threw it at him.

"Not as young as I was," she told him, her tone half humorous, half dare. For the first time, the phrase didn't hurt quite so much.

"Me either." Ruefully, he rubbed at the dent in his ribs, then shot her an evil smirk. "Race you."

As she stood up, his foot lashed out and snagged her ankle, tipping her with a shriek into the water.

Shit!

She came up blowing swearwords, just in time to watch him arc over her head and dive clean into the pool.

"Show off," she muttered.

The ripples reflected on the stone roof, dancing rocklight across the arches. She watched as Redlock pulled himself once more out of the water, dried himself with his shirt, then caught a wet foot in the leg of his trews and hopped suddenly sideways, swearing.

Master Warrior, for the Gods' sakes! Her laughter was clear and real.

It felt good.

"I should see Nivvy," he said, when he'd found his balance and secured his drawstring. "When I left Roviarath, Jade was still holding it together, but I've been five days on the river and I've got no idea what's happened since." He sat down to reach for his boots. "The restlessness isn't organised – it's quiet, got no leader, and no real teeth. If we're lucky –"

"The people *like* Jade," Triq said, her teeth chattering. "He's smart."

"True enough." Redlock tipped a stone out of a boot. "But think about it – all those smugglers' hubs and illegal bazaars. The Cartel in Fhaveon won't be able to track anything once it's reached the city – they'll have no way of knowing where anything goes, they won't get their expected returns. And then –"

"They'll blame Jade." It was a statement, not a question. She stared at him. "Oh dear Gods. *That'll* be his excuse!"

"Whose excuse? For what?" Redlock raised an eyebrow. "What did I miss?"

"It's too complicated to explain. But if Phylos gains power, he won't stop with Fhaveon –"

"Then Jade's screwed," Redlock said. "He's fighting on two fronts already – not only the loss of the Fayre, but the city's manors now scared that the harvest'll fail. If they've got nothing to tithe for the stuff that they need…" He tailed off to a shrug, glanced at her. "And if they hoard, then what does the city do? Whole thing's a cursed disaster."

"Can't he help them?"

"You know how the cycle works – it's all wheels. And if Jade doesn't have the trade coming in from outside, or the tithes coming in from the manors, Roviarath will be gutted like a clean kill. If Jade's lucky, the people will just *leave*."

"You said the traders were already –"

"It was happening when I left, Triq. Roviarath will be as a big a damned hole as her next-door neighbour."

"And Syke? Taure?"

"Worried about the grass." Redlock gave a rueful grin. "They miss you."

" I miss them. I miss… I miss all of it. Simpler times."

"Aye," Redlock said softly. "Sometimes, I wonder if this warrior business isn't just getting too much." His grin was faintly rueful and he covered a cough. "Even for me."

She had no idea how to answer him – but turned as she heard her name, a scatter of hasty boots on the steps.

"Triq!" Amethea was wide-eyed, out of breath. Her blonde hair caught the rocklight. "You're needed…" She took in the half-naked Redlock at a glance. "Both of you."

"What? Why?" Triqueta's heart stopped cold in her chest.

Ice spread across her skin, frosting the sparkling drops of water. "What's happened?"

"Nivrotar wants us. All of us. Now."

In the corridor, the air was tight as stretched paper.

Waiting.

The old man was hunched and mumbling, one dirty hand smothering his nose and mouth. He was curled in on himself, shaking like an old hippie on a happy-pill crash-down. His shoulders were sunk into his blanket, and his breath was catching wet in his palm.

Whatever mind the poor fucktard had left was leaking out his ears like so much brain fluid.

His other hand was gripped round Ecko's tiny, yellow sulphur crystal – so white-knuckled hard that Ecko expected to see claret seeping from the clench. He was desperately trying to keep it, hold it, to huddle it to his chest.

But Ecko was right over him, black eyes burning, mottle-skin seeping with the dappled rocklight of the corridor. One burn-scarred, hyper-sensitive hand was locked over the old man's own, the other was round the madman's skinny wrist, fingertips digging into the bones. He was fighting the madman's strength, was twisting his arm, this way and that, trying to make him let go. The old man was rocking with the force of the motion, but his fingers were absurdly powerful and his hand was locked tight.

As though that tiny piece of sulphur was the future of the world itself, he fought to keep it out of Ecko's grasp.

Ecko bared his teeth, stupidly, angrily, feeling like some picked-on street kid trying to get his music pod back.

"Gimme that... chrissakes, *give* me..." His voice was a husk in the quiet. "Leave *go*, you asshole!"

Looking up through the splayed fingers of his other hand, the madman began to snigger, a high, horribly nasal sound. His grip was like a steel fucking pincer and he was not letting go.

Yeah, you fight me for it. I got you on your ass now, bitch, and you know it. How you gonna get back at me this time, huh?

He had to fucking ask.

Absolutely on cue, the door at the corridor's end slammed open to the sound of feet. Not releasing his grip, Ecko shot a glance.

Double-took.

The woman was like bad temper made manifest – she was almost Lugan's size, powerfully muscled, with a shaven head and an awkward, aggressive attitude. As she came into the cloisters' rocklights, Ecko saw that she was young – incongruously so – and that she was carven with elaborate, deliberate, heavy white scars. Kartian scars. She was a shout of contradiction, a full-on bona fide freak.

She was also stampeding towards him at a fairly terrifying rate.

"Get off him!" she bawled. "Get off him, you little shit, or I'll break you like a *stick*!"

Yeah, whatever.

Ecko turned his back on her and twisted the struggling lunatic into a knot.

"Come on, you fucker, come *on*."

But the old man was looking back at him through his filthy, splayed fingers, his pupils maniacal – all wrong, the wrong sizes, the wrong directions. He was twisted all sideways now, and still sniggering like a horror-story clown. He raked his other hand down his face, leaving four nail-weals of hurt, dragging the skin of his eyes and mouth into some batshit comedy mask.

"Jesus shit. You are shot *away*." With a wrench, Ecko finally secured his prize, turned back to check on the incoming woman.

"Jayr," the madman said, quite distinctly. "The world is going to change now. Fast. We have to *go*."

Ecko would have asked him what the hell he was talking about, but cowardice being the better part of discretion, he'd already fled.

8: BROTHER

THE TRADE-ROADS OF THE NORTHERN VARCHINDE

The camp looked like a gale had torn through it, shredding its contents to grief and destruction.

No matter that it was not a Range Patrol campsite – that it had been set up a way back from the road by smugglers who'd had no interest in Phylos tracking their cargo or whereabouts. No matter that it was now silent, seeming abandoned by the pirates that had built it.

Those that had survived.

The walker was long past concern for Phylos's power, or for the irony of coincidental minutiae.

His world had shrunk to the grey cloud that wrapped him.

No matter that the site was devastated, or that it was scattered with bodies. No matter that the predator, human or animal, that had ripped through here may still be nearby.

Whatever it was, it could not harm him – not for long.

He was cursed, more than any creature living.

He was immortal, was not permitted to die – there could never be so simple an end, not for him. He had failed, his people, his city, the Varchinde entire – he had failed utterly and in everything, and there was no way out. No release, no conclusion. No "enough".

Several times, he had tried to take his own life and failed – his injuries healed, his consciousness gasped anew and then limped slowly onwards through the grey.

The metal fetter that Phylos had put upon him still cramped his wrist, and he was bereft.

The fetter was a prison, a barrier.

With it upon his skin, he was bereft of the Powerflux, the world's shifting, cycling, elemental field. It was like being blinded, deafened, having his fingers burned away and his tongue cut out – with its cold touch upon him, he was without senses, trapped within his own skin. Without the ebb and flow of the world's elements, surrounding and carrying him, his defeat and misery and weariness had multiplied, self-perpetuating and closing off his awareness of the world that surrounded him. His depressive inertia had sealed him within himself, hopeless.

And so he'd walked, directionless and endless, because it was the only thing that kept the hollow at bay; a repetitive, unthinking action that brought him something resembling peace.

It was the last barrier between himself and that dreadful lethargy, that depressive listlessness that sucks the will and the spirit and leaves just the grey, the empty soul, the "Nothing", the very essence of Kazyen.

He walked on.

He did not notice the passing of the Count of Time, did not notice that the traffic on the trade-roads was lessening with every day and halfcycle; that widening swathes of rot marred the spectacular burning of the Varchinde's autumnal colours. He did not notice or care in which direction he was heading; he did not respond as other travellers hailed him, or eyed him warily and moved to keep out of his way.

He did not notice the rain or the wind, the wondrous skies

of the dusk and dawn, the night movements of the moons over his head.

The skies were forever denied him. He had been created to be a creature free, yet Samiel had held him out over the edge of paradise...

And had let him go.

From this time forth, you are "rhan", homeless. You are charged with the care of the mortal world. If you fail me again, you will be nothing.

Yet now, even that no longer mattered.

Nothing.

He walked like a blind man, oblivious.

Rhan Elensiel, once Seneschal of Fhaveon, First Voice of the Council of Nine, Foundersson's Champion, was a broken thing. Four hundred returns he had stood beside the family Valiembor, mother and son, father and daughter, guarded and guided them and upheld the strength of the Lord city. Four hundred returns he had secured the grasslands against foes and strife and warfare, had watched the terhnwood grow, and the trade become the Varchinde's lifeblood, buoying the comfort of all.

Four hundred returns – until the plains were so secure that he had grown bored.

Taken that comfort – and his own – for granted.

Four hundred returns, and he had failed in his Gods-given duty – grown too lazy, too complacent, too downright *smug* to even notice the danger until it was upon him. Until the enemy was manifest – and by then it was too late.

Phylos had taken control of Fhaveon. He had cast Rhan down, thrown him from the very walls. Rhan had murdered the Lord Foundersson, had forced his wife, Phylos claimed. Rhan had lost city, legacy and purpose to a man who would destroy the Varchinde entire.

But what could he do? Why fight when he had already lost? There was no point.

Grey. Kazyen.

He walked not because he was looking for anything. He walked because there was nothing else to do.

What stopped him, he did not know – but he stumbled to an unsteady halt as if becoming aware of the world for the first time in cycles.

He ached, in knees and in belly. There was no hurt, exactly, he wasn't hungry – like the peculiar, nebulous pain of his self-inflicted injuries, such things were mortal danger signs that he understood only academically. But the endless walking had taken its toll on this bland and slender body. He was… he was *tired*.

He also had no idea where he was.

The air was bright and crisp and chill. The newborn sun was behind him, throwing his long shadow forwards over misted ground. His own gloom loomed ahead of him to touch this small abandoned camp, this mess of rubbish and fear and discarded mortality.

In the east, the sky was dawn-pale, streaked with a blush of pink. Ahead of him, the glowering dark loomed low, making the mist seethe on the cold ground. A small cart lay shattered, one wheel struck from its axle; a livestock pen had fencing damaged and strewn wide. The scatters of bodies were overgrown with moss and rotting with rain; some were gnawed to the bone in places, or missing eyes where the inevitable aperios had spiralled down upon them.

Somewhere, something in him envied them.

But they were dead, beyond his pity, and their presence was not what had stopped him.

He moved to look more closely.

The camp had been set up round a single building – a slightly tumbledown, half-stone cot. Its turfed roof had fallen in on one side and it had no door.

Where was he? The thought crystallised at last and it made him blink, bewildered. *North, inland. Was this Foriath? Narvakh?*

In spite of the dawn, there was no birdsong.

Staring dazedly at the building as though it could offer him an answer, he became aware that it contained movement – there was something in there, something still alive. As the thing came into the light at the doorway, it took a moment for him to realise what he saw.

A girl.

Pale, slender, filthy, almost grown enough to be a woman. Her underdress was ragged and her face and hair were streaked with grime. Her arms were covered with scratches and dirt.

When she saw him, she stared for a moment, then stumbled out of the building and started to cross the campsite, falling almost immediately.

She shouted at him, tears streaks of clean through the grot.

"No," she cried. "No, you must go, you must go *away...*"

But it was far too late, and he was right in the middle of them.

The camp was already occupied.

Three of them, tall and laughing and moving with a grace that baffled him, an impossible gait. Their shadows stretched long and wild over the grass.

They knew he was there.

As they turned, he saw their faces were masculine, striking; they were more than human, more than animal; crueller than both. Their hair was long and braided with fragments of bone and thread and colour; from their temples came horns, wide-spaced and curving like those of a mountain tsaka. Their skin was whorled with blue stains, decorous and elegant. They had a beauty to them, and a barbarism, that stirred something in the darkest corners of his heart.

He knew them. Didn't he?

Somewhere, memory stirred, old ash and broken edges.

The figures were moving swiftly now. Their eyes were a chaos of colour, no iris or pupil – windows of madness.

Quickly one of the creatures was on the girl, towering over her on legs that bent at the knee, and then bent back again, all the wrong way. It was hugely tall, reaching for her with strong hands outstretched as if to pick her up, embrace her against his bare and painted chest.

Her angry shriek tore across the morning and hard into Rhan's awareness.

It was a strike across his cheek, a sharp slap awake.

Now, he shook himself, took in the scene at a glance – he was a way back from the trade-road, the northern route that led inland from Fhaveon and later branched to both Darash and Avesyr – that would account for the trees. The building was an old hospice-refuge, long abandoned. Its more recent inhabitants showed little concern for its disrepair.

Instead, they closed about him and the girl.

Rhan had lost his elemental attunement – the true life of the world was unknown to him, he could neither feel nor touch it.

The girl pounded her fists on the bare chest of her attacker, trying to push him away. For a sliver of a moment, his own memory jarred him...

Valicia, Demisarr's wife. Fighting.

...and the recollection took him too long. The girl fell, shrieking, the weight of the creature on top of her.

Rhan moved, but the other two had flanked him.

Something about them stank of wrongness, of twisted, gnarled life. One of them had a symbol on his flawless chest, a sigil, something... They paused for a moment, eager, their sharp teeth bared with anticipation.

Rhan had murdered the Lord Foundersson, raped his wife, lost his city – if these things tore him to pieces, perhaps Samiel would take pity on him and take him home...

Love of the Gods, if these things tore him to pieces, perhaps he'd be fully damned after all. He could join the waiting ranks of his damned brother Kas Vahl Zaxaar, and awaken at the end of the Count of Time to wreak his vengeance upon the unready world...

Even that had to be an improvement.

The thought was a crux-point; a timeless second that was somewhere between defiance and despair, ascendance and damnation. *Let them take me. I don't –*

But the girl screamed again, furious, a sound that rent the brightening dawn sky.

And he could not abandon her.

One of the creatures went over backwards – a fist in its perfect face sent it sprawling, its furred legs kicking. With a back-slam of the same elbow, the second was down in the grass. It made a high, thin keening noise that shredded the air into painful strips.

And Gods, the violence felt *good*.

For the first time in cycles – *How long has it been, how long?* – he felt like himself. His skin was shivering with tension and vitality and he could feel fury stirring in his heart.

Oh yes. I remember this.

The girl was fighting hard, swearing like a wharfside trader – she'd gained her feet and a belt-blade and she was swift and vicious. The thing was right over her, grinning – it reeked of predator.

Yet there was something about it...

Something...

As one of them recovered, reached its long hand for him, he realised that the *wrong* sensation was familiar, that it tied in with that ghost-memory, that figment at the back of his mind. Like the creatures themselves, he *remembered* it, knew it well. For a moment he almost had it – like the echo of a tune, a half-remembered dream – then it was gone again, evaporating in the morning light, and the creatures were rising from where he'd struck them down.

As they came up from the misted ground, he stared at where the thought had been.

What?

The creatures were standing now, taller than he, and they had got between himself and the girl. One of them stood directly ahead, a broad shape against the lightening sky – its blue designs seemed to writhe in its skin, caress like strands of silk. Its gaze was pure insanity, yet its movement was precise as it reached to take Rhan's face in one steam-warm, long-nailed hand. It bared sharp teeth in a grin; it was demented, and absurdly gentle.

It stroked his skin like a lover.

Rhan shuddered, raised an arm to throw it off him. Touching it held that same evasive, pervasive sense of *wrong*.

But it was like...

Like family...

What?

The Count of Time left him. The creature's gaze, its odd caress, transfixed him. As it leaned forward, that grin close now, it was his brother, his lover, his father, his friend, his life's loss. He could not pull away from it.

Then something hit it from behind, something small and angry and very, very fast. The thing turned, and the compulsion was gone.

She shrieked at him, "What are you *doing*? Don't meet their gaze, they'll suck you in!" And the girl was rounding on the creature with her little knife.

She put out the thing's mad eye.

And Rhan realised the other two were still standing.

He called to her, "What are they? Where did they come from?"

"My family were taken by the grass, infected by something. I was hiding. Then these things came. They were... I don't know... different..."

Rhan eyed the moss-grown dead, but they made no movement.

The things reached forwards, their eyes alive with chaos and steam, with lust and joy, as hot as the rhez. Rhan needed the Powerflux, needed the pulse of the world's heartbeat, her blood flow, needed and wanted and craved the light, but they were everywhere and they were tall and ink and hair and bright eyes and bared teeth –

The girl spun and slashed. He guessed that she was a smuggler herself, raised on the trade-road. Her blade cut at a creature's face.

And it keened, bled just like a man.

Rhan grabbed one of them by a heavy shoulder, picked it up and threw it bodily into his fellow, sending them both tumbling. They were quick, though, picking themselves up and circling in with their faces eager and their great hands outstretched as if to claw chunks from him and the girl.

He wondered what the rhez would happen if lunch just happened to be immortal – and decided he didn't want to know.

Or did he?

Could he die here? Really?

Rhan was rallying – but he was still a mess. He was confusion and hesitation and doubt. The creature that had been the champion of the Foundersson, the greatest warrior in the Varchinde, could not focus, could barely fight a load of randomly wandering beasties.

He was awash with fear.

Not of them, of himself.

And this time, his doubt was fatal.

He heard her scream, again, one last time. He saw her go down under another of the creatures, its mouth kissing, biting, tearing her flesh. He saw the ink on the creature's body thicken and grow stronger, saw the girl kick and scream.

Again, that sense of familiarity. He knew what he was seeing, on some level, he *knew*...

But her shriek, pain and fear and horror, overwhelmed both the lingering figment and his own self-pity. Whatever these things were, they were not mortal and human – they were merciless – and if they pulled in his life and they grew stronger, Gods alone knew where it would end.

No, whatever they were, they had to go.

Now.

He may not have his attunement – but he still had his fists.

Rhan Elensiel stood alone, surrounded by debris and moss and the shredded remnants of the dead.

Even fettered as he was, he could still fight like a...

...like a daemon. Like Kas Vahl damned Zaxaar himself.

You hear me, my brother, my estavah? It had a hint of his more usual sardonic humour. *Perhaps I'm not done yet.*

His elation was brief. He had his victory, he was here, and now, and living – but the girl who had fought so hard for him was dead, and now lay by the lichen-fleshed remains of her family.

Her family. Something about the growth of the moss in their flesh was wrong, but he had no idea what it could be. His senses were truncated, blinding him, infuriating. What in Samiel's holy name...

He knelt by her, so small and broken, and stroked a filthy hand down her thin cheek.

"What happened to you?" he asked her. "What happened to them?"

An apology seemed facile – he had no words for her bravery. How long had she been hidden here, her family dead around her, waiting for what?

Rescue?

Poor child. His skin spasmed in pain.

He looked around, at the ground, at the scattered tools – wondered if he should return her, return all of them, to the world. The trees were tall here, and the roots spread wide, perhaps there was no need even to dig.

The world would care for her own, take them home.

And me? Rhan wondered. *Where do I go now?*

The girl was smiling, oddly peaceful – he was glad for her, but she had no answer to give him.

Where do I go now?

Rhan stayed kneeling, almost as if waiting for direction to come to him.

He should return to Fhaveon and face Phylos. He should trace the unnatural steam-heat in the Merchant Master's aspect all the way back to his fallen brother. He should rise up, raise a war-banner, muster the force to regain his city...

But the girl lay there, answerless and unmoving, her family around her. And the creatures lay there too, their dead flesh steaming like a shimmer in the clear air...

Steam...

Oh dear Goddess.

With a hot, sick rush that almost made him tumble sideways, he made the connection.

He was on his feet in an instant, staring down at them, feeling elation and terror and *kicking* himself...

How could he have missed the link? How could he have missed it!

That *was why he knew them!*

He'd seen such creations before, of course he had. Hundreds of returns before, these were creatures created to assault the white walls of Fhaveon, creatures designed for warfare. They had been crafted long ago, crafted by the hands of Kas Vahl Zaxaar himself. Crafted from...

Crafted from *flesh*.

Vahl was Rhan's brother, closer than any mortal creature could ever be; anything he'd touched carried the richness and glory and taint of his presence.

And Rhan could *feel* it, metal fetter or no.

Vahl's presence had ridden Phylos like a cloak, a shadow. But if he was really *awake*...?

Samiel's *teeth*!

Rhan was trembling, pacing. The understanding was like a drop-key in a lock, a perfect and flawless fit – he had no doubt that his conclusion was true. But it led to only more questions.

These were vialer, he remembered them now. He'd thrown enough of them down. They were foot troops, fought in knots or from chariots, dispensable, and they'd once raged in their hundreds. But why were they here, now? Why had they come out after the girl, her moss-rotted family?

Vahl, you old bastard. What are you doing?

The girl stared still; her eyes open to the sky. There were aperios over the trees, attracted to the reek of death – it would take them a moment to spiral down. Their appetites were ghoulish, but he did not fear them – they, too, had a task to perform.

Rhan turned to pace again, the grass under his boots now soaked in gore.

He remembered Roderick, remembered the old stone guardian that had fallen from the walls of Fhaveon – a fragment of lost Tusienic alchemy, seeking absolution and answer.

Have you not felt it, Master of Elemental Light?

He had scorned it then, concerned only with Fhaveon and her petty politics, concerned only with returning to his hedonistic life. But now this had all raged out of control. He had seen Vahl's shadow, but had thought that he had time to rally, to reconsider and to counterattack before –

Had Fhaveon fallen that far already?

That thought brought him to a halt; his skin crackled with ice-cold horror.

Fhaveon *had* fallen already – and without even a battle. Vahl had charmed Phylos, his vialer were loose in the plains. Rhan had lost the war before he'd raised a weapon...

He had no weapons to raise.

Rhan lifted his wrist so that the metal band caught the sun. His sudden terror flashed hot and cold, disbelief and dismay.

By his feet there were crawlies creeping, seeking the girl's flesh. Around her, the three vialer lay shattered, taunting him with the knowledge that he could still fight if he had to.

But how many more were there? Where were they coming from? Did they already walk the streets of Fhaveon – the very streets he had thrown them from, four hundred returns before?

Rhan needed the Bard, needed his vision and insight, his direction.

Rhan needed an *army*.

His despair loomed grey, a cloud over the morning – *This is too big, you have already lost, why bother now?* But he would not, could not, leave Vahl to victory.

A glint of morning sunlight caught his notice, and he bent down, unclipped a small red-metal brooch from the girl's shoulder. It was poorly crafted and held little value, but he lifted it anyway and held it to his own shabby cloak, the disguise he'd taken when he'd left the city.

And, as the rising sun touched down through the canopy, and the autumn mist began to evaporate from the grass – as the aperios descended with their ominous cackle – Rhan stood with the brooch glinting at his shoulder.

Have you not felt it, Master of Elemental Light?

He closed his eyes, raised his face to the dawn.

And he tried, one last time, tried to fight past the barrier that numbed him. He willed it to happen, opened his mind, his heart, his soul, to the Powerflux – to the great web of life that enwrapped the world, to the cycling rhythm of day and night and season and element. To the souls of the elements themselves – to the thrill of the pulse and thrum that connected them, to the light of the drowned OrSil.

He was Dæl Rhan Elensiel, the last of his kind undamned.

He had not failed in his duty – not yet.

The great cycling of the Flux would be his succour and knowledge. Light could be savage, an element used for battle, but it could also bring understanding – illumination.

He would stretch his awareness throughout the Flux itself and feel – feel the presence and absence of those whom the world knew, feel his friends and his foes, the health of the Flux entire.

He would know what to do.

But there was nothing. A grey hollow of despair where the Light should have been.

Once – how many cycles ago? – he and Roderick had discussed their next move. Where they would go from here.

He remembered, he had said to the Bard...

"You hold the thoughts of the world in your mortal mind and your beating heart – and they overwhelm you. I know the fear that lives in your soul, that it eats you by the day and haunts you in the darkness... Trust me, trust yourself. If this fails – and it might – then we go to the one place that can answer every question. Probably the one place that you should have damned-well gone to start with.

"We ask Mother."

Rhan could not relocate, but he could walk.

And he could walk north. To the birthplace of Roderick the Bard, Guardian of the Ryll, to the border city of Avesyr.

And then onwards, through into the Khavan Circle and the waters that it protected.

To the one place where the thoughts of the world were made manifest. To the one help that may yet remove the metal fetter from his wrist. To the heart and mind of his mother.

To the Ryll.

9: FIRE WITH FIRE AMOS

The Lord of Amos stood silent, a shroud of deep bruise-grey swathing her from feet to chin. Her hair was darker than black; her flawless face corpse-pale, all shadow and cheekbone.

She was in her study, her private space. This was not a room of the court, not even a room of business – this was her personal retreat, hidden at the very height of the palace's north-eastern tower. The arched windows were unshuttered, their ancient glass thrown open to starless cold and white moonlight. And scattered throughout the square room were the last remnants of her personal hobbies – books and papers, and things that might once have been an orrery, an astrolabe, and a fantastical, elemental compass.

Now, they were abandoned, useless. Each one was old red-metal, ornate, covered in verdegris and dust tails. Nothing up here had been touched in returns.

She could barely remember what she had used them for.

Like the ancient stone about her, the Lord's memory was crumbling – the Count of Time too much to bear.

Why had they come here, those first settlers – where had they come from? The Bard had gleaned much, but the world's memory, the Ilfe, was as lost as the might and knowledge of the city's Great Library. Soon, there would be nothing left.

Nothing.

The word made her shiver.

She leaned her hands on the cold stone of the sill, watched the almost slender curve of the white moon, Alboren, rise slowly over the black water, the dense firefly-sparkle of the city's Estuary Wharf. His golden sister, her crescent curving the other way, would not rise for a time yet – the son of Samiel was alone and Amos glittered beneath his light.

The city's noises carried clear over the river.

Breaking the long quiet, Amethea said, "My Lord?"

"So, news comes from Roviarath and Fhaveon alike." There was no tension in the Lord's voice; rather, she sounded weary. "The Count of Time moves more swiftly than I would wish – Phylos's consolidation is startlingly efficient. We must make some hard decisions." She flicked an eyebrow at them. "Thank you for your competence, Faral, and for your return. Your experience is a solid thing in a world made of doubt."

"Thank you, my Lord," Redlock said.

"Now, answer me a question." Nivrotar turned fully from the moonlight, and her expression was lost in shadow. "Do you believe that Roviarath is holding – can hold – against the troubles of the trade-cycle, and against this rise of blight?"

"Not indefinitely." The axeman raised both eyebrows and let out his breath in a long and dubious sigh.

As the Lord turned to look at them, Amethea saw the wall beside her housed a dark stone plaque – ancient wording now blurred into silence by returns without number. It held a solitary handprint, like a signature, long-ago pressed into the stone. She wondered to whom it had belonged.

But Redlock was still speaking. "Jade's a smart man, my Lord, canny. And many of his people see him as a hero. He's got time."

But not much.

He didn't need to say it aloud.

"I have ears in Fhaveon," she said. "Messages reach me that the Council of Nine has become a jest, that the soldiery itself has been – shall we say 'acquired'? – through Phylos's charm and manipulation. He is the young Lord Selana's only advisor, and holds control of her word and ruling. He'll use her name to uproot and destroy any attempt at resistance. Tell me – what do you smell?"

"Horseshit, my Lord," Redlock snorted. "We're up to our ears in it. I'm more tactician than strategist, but Fhaveon trains, despatches and rotates the soldiery for the entire Varchinde – and if Phylos holds command of that soldiery, he doesn't need to pick fights. He can mutter something about the threat of the blight, occupy any city he chooses, stuff it to the brim with his grunts, and – "

"It's 'bow down or else'," Triqueta cut across him, shrugging. "It's just so damned *slick*."

"He's got us over a barrel, all of us," Redlock agreed. "Oiled and ready for whatever he wants. He holds the very city that was built to be the plains' defence – he won't need to start a war, he'll just *occupy*. Every soldier in the Varchinde is already answerable to the bad guys. My warrior's opinion? We're stuffed."

"Then he will grind us into the diseased soil and that will be the end. This end is not acceptable." Nivrotar turned away, dismissed the idea with such force that it made Amethea shudder with unease.

Below the tower's windows, the palace held a roof garden rich with herbs, its design ornate and its significance long forgotten – in the rise of daylight, they might have seen that it edged a fantastical maze, flower-hung walls as old as the Varchinde itself. The Lord was staring out over the top of the puzzle, her pale face as cold as the white moon. Amethea wondered – did she look north to Fhaveon, too far away to see?

She ventured a thread of hope. "Vilsara used to say the Gods have a pattern, though they'll never tell us what it is…"

Nivrotar turned back over her shoulder. "A pattern?" she said. "You suggest that the blight and the might of Fhaveon and the rise of Kas Vahl Zaxaar are intertwined? Why would even the Kas blight the very land they aim to possess? Undermine their own city's strength? Ah, little priestess. Perhaps they have a pattern of their own?"

Little priestess… Maugrim's name for her. The words robbed Amethea of a response and she fell back, biting her lip.

"I gotta question." Ecko had been skulking, scuffing his feet in the dirt, paying them little attention. Now, though, he was grinning like a black-toothed bweao, a grin at something only he could see. He said, "Who's your boss, Red?"

Redlock frowned. "Only these." He patted the axes, then a huge grin began to spread across his face. "Oh, you clever little shit…"

Ecko was almost cackling. Triqueta looked from one man to the other. "What? What?"

Redlock laughed, then paused to cough. "Triq, it's a thing of beauty, think about it. How big is the Banned? Combatants, I mean. How big?"

She blinked at him, her opal stones glimmering. "I don't know. Fifty, sixty, could be a few more. It's rare we're all together in the same place."

Redlock watched her expression, waiting for her to catch up. "And how many warrior freeman worked out of the Great Fayre? If you had to guess?"

Triqueta said, "Oh come on, you know that more than I do. They're scattered, I don't think anyone tallies their numbers. They're just that, freemen, not soldiers, they're an integral part of the trade-cycle. They're not answerable to… Oh for Gods' sakes."

Redlock was laughing. "With me?"

Nivrotar watched them both intently. Ecko eyed the ceiling with mock innocence, as though he'd just solved all of the Varchinde's problems with his own sharp wit.

Amethea said, "What are you on about?" Her humour was arch. "Some of us don't actually kill people for a living."

"It's so simple, it's perfect." Redlock gripped her shoulder, still grinning. "There are warriors across the grasslands that aren't a part of the Fhaveonic military – we're freemen, usually operating out of a single city or location. Some trade purely on reputation – I do. Others work as units, sort of crafthouses in their own right, I suppose, though their trading's with the craftsmen and tithehalls directly, rather than with either the military, or with the Cartel." He shook his head. "You with me? Ecko's a cursed genius."

"And then there's Syke and the Banned," Triqueta said, "currently holding Roviarath – if they muster, that's a small damned army right there. Ready and waiting. Jade understands the trade-cycle, he must know what'll happen…"

"Of course he does." The axeman turned to meet the Lord of Amos's gaze. "Would you face Phylos? Challenge this?"

"Directly?" Nivrotar smiled. "Probably not. But if – when – Fhaveon overextends her borders, could we muster enough strength to defend ourselves?"

"Whoah, you hold your fuckin' horses, there," Ecko said. "You lot couldn't fight your way outta wet paper bag – you haven't gotta fucking clue, no discipline, no army, no tictacs. You're gonna need more wellie than idealism an' a buncha loose grunts."

Triq snorted at him. "Why are you even up here? Your conscience got the better of you?"

He didn't quite look at her. "I had that shit removed."

Amethea said nothing. Ecko's slight, slim figure was cloak-shrouded, cowl-shadowed, almost impossible to see in the black-and-white moonlight of the tower, the angled shadows of the Lord's devices. His thin face was exotic, wrong; his black-pit eyes expressionless – she'd no idea in which direction he looked, if he was watching her, his companions, the Lord or the city. Redlock and Triqueta were a known quantity – more or less – but Ecko? He was still unknown, an outsider, a stranger in a tavern tale. He seemed on edge, more so than usual, and she wasn't sure why.

He felt almost... eager. Like he knew something they didn't. She wondered what it was.

"I need numbers," Nivrotar said. "Information. If we're to rally a force here, and one in Roviarath, to resist the expansion of Fhaveon, then the Count of Time is against us. We must do this quickly. And quietly." She shook her head for a moment, looked out over the garden. "For this, I need the Bard. More now than ever."

The comment was followed by silence. After a moment, she went on. "I will send bretir to Larred Jade. And we must hold this information in reserve. The time may well come when we'll need to strike back, so let us seem quiet, and keep our fists concealed."

"So now we recon?" Redlock said. "If you need info, we can be in Fhaveon in –"

"Not you," Nivrotar said. "Your red hair is a flag, Faral ton Gattana, your reputation a spark that will light Phylos's eyes to suspicion, and have them roving to where they are not wanted. Triqueta, Amethea, you will be known to Phylos's forces, your lives will be forfeit. And Ecko – you and I have spoken of this already. You are marked, all of you, and will make very poor spies." The second moon was rising, a yellow smudge behind low cloud. In the high room, the air glittered with a faint and gilded highlight. "For you, I have perhaps a different task."

Ecko snorted, "Chrissakes, here we go..."

But Nivrotar cut straight over him. "I need you to tell me of the alchemist you visited. Of the House of Sarkhyn."

There was an odd weight in her voice, an edge to her question that brought quiet to the tower room. Amethea and Triqueta exchanged a glance.

Redlock crossed his arms and raised an eyebrow at them. "Been having adventures?" he asked.

Ecko shrugged, said, "The House of Sarky's toast."

The Lord of Amos leaned back on the deep sill of the window, the moonlight making her hair shine.

"Sarkhyn was my friend, Ecko. Once. She was a woman of true vision, a creator."

"That's one vision we'll all be havin' for years." Ecko didn't sound particularly contrite. "But hey, it's not like she didn't leave a legacy." He was fidgeting now, restless and tense, bouncing on the balls of his feet. Amethea watched him, intrigued.

Nivrotar was still speaking. "Her legacy was her lore. She believed that alchemy, like elementalism, is divisible into light and darkness, fire and cold. Fire alchemy we understand." Her eyes held Ecko's. "But the others? Can dark alchemy animate the dead, can cold preserve life? I had hoped you would find me information, maybe weapons. Something with which I can equip our new army."

"Weapons." With a certain air of triumph, Ecko opened his hand. "Like this one?"

"Saint and Goddess!" Amethea gawked and pointed. "You've got brimstone!"

Something in Amethea's tone caught Ecko's attention, arrested it like a high-street cop.

Brimstone.

She stared at his treasure, glittering in the moonlight like crystallised piss.

"Where did you...? You didn't find that in the crafthall?"

Ecko snorted. "Now, that's just dumb."

Amethea said, "I used… Vilsara used it for treating the skin, but we almost never saw the stuff. It comes from the Yevar, somewhere. It's incredibly rare."

There was a puzzled pause, broken only by the sound of Nivrotar's fingers, rapping a restless tattoo on the wall behind her. The noise was tense, as if she were waiting, or thinking, or scheming.

"So," Ecko said, his voice soft with anticipation, "I gotta ask a question. I've looked, an' there's none of this stuff in your markets. Where do I get more?"

"Ecko." Redlock's alarm was tangible. "What're you doing?"

The Lord watched them intently, her sleek body tight with anticipation. But Ecko no longer cared. He was almost cackling; almost letting his sudden rush of eager, dark glee spill out through his voice, saturate the tower room like oil. He turned back to the apothecary, almost not wanting to hope. "Sing it, sister, where do I get more?"

"Just wait," Triq said. "What is that? What do you want it for?"

"Let her answer." Nivrotar held up a white hand.

His blood alight with elation, with incredulity, with coiling tails of lust, and anticipation, Ecko stood poised and breathless. This tiny piece of crystal was his catalyst – and he'd found it right *there* in the crafthall, right *there* under his goddamned nose. A tiny scrap of potential, a miracle, a rarity…

His victory. His route out.

Oh, you just fucking wait!

Unable to control his exhilaration, he began to laugh.

It wasn't his usual twisted cackle, his cynical snort. This time he was really laughing, a grotesque writhing cold sound that wound out through the open window and up into the moonlit sky.

They turned to stare like he was fucking demented.

Yeah? Well maybe you gotta reason.

Amethea said, "Ecko?"

Nivrotar said softly, "Answer him, little priestess."

Answer him.

"See this?" He held the crystal up between thumb and forefinger, a citrine gleam, an eye of yellow. Moonlight refracted on his skin and the mottle of colours shifted in response. They gaped, unnerved, as if wondering what the hell he was gonna do next.

Yeah, he'd got them like he'd got Maugrim's fucking pocket watch.

The comparison made him grin like the broken edge of his sanity.

"This," he said, his rasp soft and absolutely evil, "is a key. It's a magic goddamned stone. And if you've got a decent alchemist, an' enough of this shit, it's the only fucking weapon you'll need." He turned the tiny stone to tiny yellow glints along its surface. "Now. Where. The hell. Does it come from? The name of the trader, the source, the market, the roadway it came down; the volcano, the salt deposit, the damned science museum *gift* store. *Where* do I get more sulphur?"

Amethea stuttered, said, "It's brimstone, you powder it. It comes from the Yevar, I think, from the Taes – the open-mouth mountains to the south. I don't know who brings it north, but I know... I think I know... where Vilsara found it. Sometimes." She was hesitant, awkward, as though she was hiding something. Ecko had to control the urge to pounce on her and shake her until she spat it out. "She kind of... didn't ask too many questions."

His laughter ghosted down the corridor. "Why? What is this shit? Contraband?"

"I don't know – like I said. It's just incredibly rare."

"Rare," Nivrotar commented slyly, "or controlled." Her smile was like the edge of an axe.

Oh, now I've fuckin' gotcha...

He was grinning like he'd split at the ears.

"Spill it, sister – what's the deal here? You dabblin' in illegal pharms now?" He cackled. "Starting to see you in a whole new – guess it's a whole new darkness."

Triqueta said, "How is this stuff supposed to help us against Phylos?"

"This is sulphur, so-called because it *burns*. You wanna beat your bad guys? Spank the daemon? Win the fucking final war?" It was pure fucking genius. "I say you *are* the bad guys. And you fight fire with *fire*."

Now, the Lord of Amos was chuckling, a sound deep and rich and dirty.

Oh yeah – we're gettin' somewhere!

The pieces were falling into place. The yellow moonlight spread across the roof garden, lighting the maze to cross-hatched angles of madness. He was getting the hang of how this shit worked, and how he could break out of it.

Fight fire with fire.

Triq lowered her gaze.

Amethea said, "Fire? I had no idea. All this time..."

"It's black market meds, Doc. You track it down; I'll blow it up."

Redlock said, "You do know what you're doing with this stuff?"

Ecko grinned like a nightmare. "Trust me."

Much later that night, movement outside caught the Lord's eye.

From the tower opposite her own, there came a sudden clattering, a rise of voices, outraged and angry. The rocklight was uncovered – illumination spilled from the unshuttered window – and she heard Jayr, heard the abrupt, stark crash of violence.

She moved to the window, intrigued – and with a glimmer of tension.

It was too far to perceive clearly. Jayr's heavy shoulders filled most of the light – though it was apparent that something had happened to Ress. To *Ress*.

Without looking away, the Lord rang swiftly for a servitor.

The voices continued – the strident anger was Jayr, the softer tone Jemara. As Nivrotar was trying to see, to listen, a flurry of waterbirds took to the air, cackling.

She stifled frustration. When they'd passed, the whir of wings taking them inland, she discerned a third voice, neither male nor female. It brought a flush to her face and a chill to her very bones – it was a voice she was sure she knew.

It *was* Ress.

And yet.

Her white hands tensed on the deep stone of the sill. She'd never heard him speak like that. His voice was massive, multi-layered, as though something else were using his throat for utterance, some vast power that had dwelled within him and was now manifest.

And it was *angry.*

She could hear Jayr, striving to calm him down. Jemara, the palace leech, sounded afraid.

Then there was a scuffling. Jayr's shoulders were gone from the light. The shape that replaced them was Jemara, round and shrinking back – terrified of something in the room.

Of Ress?

Nivrotar heard his voice again, heard a grief so huge that it made the entire night ring. It echoed out over the still city as if the very world herself were sobbing with failure.

The Lord stood frozen, uncomprehending, barely daring to breathe.

Jayr shouted again, an edge of desperation in her voice. Nivrotar saw Jemara shrink back, saw what she thought was her hands go to the sides of her head.

And she *keened*. A high sound of pure and absolute agony.

A sound that sliced clean through the fabric of the night like a thought-sharp metal blade.

The gentle knock on the door behind her nearly made the Lord leap from the window. She paused, trying to still the pounding of her heart – but couldn't tear her attention from the light in the opposite tower.

Ress had fallen silent, but the huge presence had not faded – if anything, it was stronger. It was larger than the city below, larger than the night above, larger than the white moon that cast his light across the world.

The knock came again. She ignored it.

Jayr's voice was now almost a shout. It seemed to echo like ripples under the weight of that presence, under the *something* that was happening across the night's gap.

Jemara's keening shattered into broken fragments. "No," she seemed to be saying, "No, please don't, no…"

The knock came a third time. The Lord tore herself from the windowsill and, with short shrift, flung open the door.

"Come with me," she said.

Her grey shroud billowing about her as though she were the Count of Time himself, she was out past the lad and heading for the sharp angles of the descending stairs. Behind her, the last of the broken keen was fading into a gasp, a plea, into the sound of Jayr's voice, angry and horrified.

Then even that was gone and the Lord was at the bottom of the steps, throwing open the door to run across the front of the building like a hurrying girl.

As she did so, the huge presence, whatever it was, whatever it had been, was fading like Jemara's final cries.

Lifting her grey cloak into an undignified bundle, the Lord of Amos ran up the opposite staircase.

But she knew full well that she was far too late.

INTERLUDE: UNINVITED GUEST LONDON

For just a moment, Roderick of Avesyr had felt that empty, stomach-lifting sensation of falling.

And then –

The sickening jolt. His belly in his throat and his blood in his ears. Sparks shooting through his thoughts, blinding and baffling him –

The room folded in on itself. His legs crumpled. He clung to the table, felt it slide. Long used to The Wanderer's movements, he wasn't ready for the soul-ripping wrench that tore them from the heart of the Varchinde, from everything they understood...

There was screaming, shrill and high – Karine? Silfe? There was an odd, hollow howling, a scrabble like the last denial of the end of the world. There was the stern bellow of Sera, roll-calling names. There was a snap, like a breaking bone. The Bard lost the table, found himself on the floor, sprawling where it had come up and kicked him. He could hear voices, the harsh pound of feet, the blare of some kind of alarum.

As he scrambled up, fighting to hold his belly in place, his shaking knees still, a harsh, cold light sliced through the windows of the taproom. It cut squares into the floor and made glitter of the tumbling dust.

Roderick raised his forearm to shield his eyes.

What?

The room stilled. He turned, looking for the rest of his team.

Silfe was there, sitting on the floor with her hands in her hair, her face drawn and pale. Karine was over her, picking her up, telling her that it was okay, it was okay.

The words were reflex. Like the light, they made no sense.

"Are you all right?" Sera was close, like a wall, his hands cool and strong. His strength was enough, and the Bard was able to stand straight, to find his voice.

"I'll manage, help the others." He shook his head, realised that the odd, hollow howling was fading, changing note...

Even as he tried to locate it, it was gone.

Kale? Where –?

He turned, looking for answers, something. The quiet was swollen with possibilities, with threat.

And then a heavy boot smashed in his front doors.

It all happened in a heartbeat, in the space between one world and another.

His blood was pounding, choking – he realised he was already moving, instinctual and compelled, straight for the doorway. Sera was with him. Karine was on her feet, her fists clenched. Silfe was gasping, pushing herself back, her horror sucking all the air from the room...

The white light was a square of jagged unreality on the floor.

And there was a shadow in it.

"On the ground, hands on your heads! Now!" The owner of shadow and boot was a heavy-set warrior, his unfamiliar garments pure white. He was crouched behind a two-handed weapon, holding it to his eye and moving cautiously into the room. "I said now!"

A tiny red dot like a blood-drinking insect flitted from face to face.

Sera stood like a rock, implacable. "Put the weapon down."

The red dot stopped on the doorman's chest.

Behind the warrior came a woman, her garments similar and her hair shining like white-metal. Her eyes were covered by a strip of reflection and she, too, bore an odd hand-weapon and an attitude of naked aggression. She grinned at their shock – casual in stance, unhinged in expression.

Sera said, "Both of you. Put the weapons down. Now."

The warrior gave a faint shrug, a slight ducking of his head...

...and the world exploded.

Deafening noise and splintering furniture; detonations of alchemical burning that assaulted nostrils, that billowed dust and sudden thumping terror. The metal-reek of blood, the crash of a shattered table, a body hitting the floor.

A high, single shriek, like crystallised horror.

Sera!

Roderick was moving, but not fast enough, not *fast* enough. Karine was already running to where Sera had half-spun to the floor, one shoulder punched clean through as if by some giant bradawl. Flesh and gore had burst from the back of the wound. Silfe had her hands over her face, buried in her hair; she was screaming, screaming, rocking back and forth. The shrill sound shredded the air and nerves.

Over and over, like eternally shattering glass.

"Christ, shut *up*, you bitch." The man turned, the weapon detonated again and Silfe was falling, the screaming torn down, the back of her head completely gone.

Gone.

Roderick stared. The Count of Time slowed to a tumble of absolute impossibility.

Gone.

Silfe's expression was one of shock, her eyes were open and her lips still parted on that final scream. She fell, with exquisite slowness, through the Bard's disbelief, her head falling back and her hair flying wide, a pale glow about her face. She fell backwards as if through a fog, through a thickening of the air, through a rising, heart-pounding cry of denial.

That last scream echoed from the walls.

Gone.

The Count of Time had left him. The Bard wanted, needed, to move, but the thick air held him like mud, like dismay, like incredulity. He'd no understanding of what he'd just seen.

Gone.

It was too much.

All of this. Too much.

As he watched the girl fall, his mind, stupidly, spun old memories. Down through the returns, the tavern had manifested in many places, in cities outside the Varchinde, in poverty and desolation and desperation, in the halls of the Kartian CraftMasters, in the semi-mythical ruins of the Kuanne. Many times, they'd been met with superstition and confusion, with outright violence.

But this? This broken brightness, this stinking air. They were lost to lore and a world from where they should be... How could they face this assault? Face death at the flinch of a finger, face traumatised people even more damned scared than they were?

Gone.

Karine's voice slammed into him; her words hit him like fists. She was shielding Sera, shouting incomprehensible words one after another, a raw torrent of fury and hurt. Roderick staggered, found he could move, breathe. He'd grabbed the end of the blaster and tried to take it before realising the heat of it had blistered his hand.

He heard his own voice. "Get out. Or I'll tear you to *pieces.*" It was lethal, as sharp as a fibre across an exposed throat.

Then he felt the kiss of cold metal as the mouth of the woman's weapon caressed his cheek. Her other hand cupped his buttock.

She smiled at him. "Not before I spread your pretty face up the wall."

"Awright, enough! Strafe, 'Eels, what the 'ell is goin' on?"

The bellow brought quiet. The two warriors stepped back, but they exchanged a look that chilled the Bard to the core. It reminded him of Ecko, somehow, of something that was no longer human – something that didn't care…

Another figure cast a shadow in the doorway.

Tall as the Bard, Archipelagan in build, Banned in attitude. This man wore leather, battered and black, and his eyes flickered with a faint, fire-spark blue. With the harsh white light behind him, his face was hard to make out – but the shaven head, the blonde beard, the ink that decorated the skin of his forearms…

Suddenly, everything snapped into place.

It was real, it was all real.

Grief and shock and tension surged in the Bard's blood, making him stare, stare again.

Dear Gods.

"I'm Ade Eastermann," the man said. "Me mates call me Lugan." He looked the Bard up and down for a moment, then punched a huge, inked fist into the doorframe as if to assure himself of its solidity. "And you can't park this 'ere."

Jesus Hairy *Christ* on a fucking motor scooter.

Lugan stood in the front garden of a quasi-medieval *pub* that had just beamed-the-fuck-down-Scotty in the middle of his chop shop.

Its landlord was some mock-goth long-hair with a taste for high boots and loose sleeves, all now blood-slicked from a fucked-up first contact. The only other still-moving person was a woman, crouched on the floor over her injured mate – fuck's sake, one dead and one terminally wounded was not how this shit was supposed to go down.

Lugan had access to some kickarse meditech. But not yet.

Right now, this was just too batshit.

Strafe and Heels, the unhinged twins, had been banished back to the office. In the bar-room, Lugan's ocular scanners were showing him body heat but not much else. His brain tried to rationalise an explanation out of 3D printing or holographic projection, but he kept getting distracted by the pub sign.

It depicted the legend, "The Wanderer".

Well no fucking shit.

Fuller rattled in his ear: *Density scan confirms: timber-framed, stone foundations. It's not showing on the National Grid, hasn't accessed our data, power, plumbing or sewage. Whatever it is, it's a self-contained entity. Furball's prepping the scan.*

Lugan said, *But it's solid? Close Encounters of the Beer Kind?*

'Fraid so. Two storeys, total height at roof apex just under six metres – means it hasn't breached the railway bridge. No internal security I can ascertain. Does have a sizeable cellar system – we've lost access to rooms three through seven.

Collator?

Analysing for nanotech bio-polymer and showing weather systems in Guatemala. I think he's got a headache. Not much help, doing this old school.

Lugan snorted, watched the strange building. *What 'appened to Miz Gabriel?*

Floored her Beamer and fled. You want her traced?

Keep an eye on 'er willya? And get a full chemical scan of every-fucking-thing she touched. Check the air recyclers. If we're trippin' our nuts off, I wanna know.

Will do.

The sub-vocal exchange had taken barely a moment. The goth-type was crouched, looking down at the dead girl, at her last, shocked expression.

Lugan shifted faintly awkwardly, his boots making scars in the grass.

The man didn't look up. When he spoke, his voice was rust and steel.

"She was a child. She did nothing to you."

The commander glowered. "Is this some sorta joke?" The body with half a head was just another impossibility; this whole thing was a movie, a brainrig, a trip. "'Cause it ain't funny."

The goth-type shot him a glance. Somehow, his face was too young for the lines that carved through it, though his expression was hard as setting ferrocrete.

"I require an apothecary," he said. "And an explanation."

"Not sure that one needs a doc." Lugan was brutal and didn't bloody well care. "I dunno 'ow the fuck you got this in 'ere, but you get it the fuck back out. Before I bring in the JCB."

The goth raised an eyebrow. He stayed down by the girl as if he were guarding her, and said, "My name is Roderick of Avesyr." He threw the words like weapons, daring. "And I'm a friend of the man who calls himself 'Ecko'. You know him. He has a silent G."

The commander skidded up short, lunacy screaming like jammed-on brakes. "What?"

Now, the goth stood up, as tall as Lugan, lighter on his feet. Lugan's scans showed no enhancements, no wacky trip-colours, only body-heat – body-heat and anger.

"You heard me," the man said. "Now, I require an *apothecary*."

The commander snorted. "Or you'll do *what* exactly? Conjure dragons?"

The woman had her hands on the injured man's shoulder in an attempt to staunch the bleeding. It took a minute for Lugan to realise that she was pressing the front of the wound, not the back.

As if she felt Lugan looking, her chin lifted and her expression was hard as a promise.

Christ on a *bike*.

Lugan was catching himself up – and wondering what the

bloody hell was going on. He felt like he'd walked onto a set, like he'd dropped some big fat pill and was tripping his nuts off, like that little bitch Tarquinne, Ecko's sister, had come in here and spiked his tea. He punched the wall again as if expecting it to move, to splinter and waver and fade under his fist – but the goth was still speaking, anger thrumming like a bassline.

He said, "I know you, Lugan. I know the mission you sent Ecko upon. I know about Pilgrim, about Grey. Now, if you want an explanation, you get me a damned *leech*." The last word was a snarl.

The mission you sent Ecko upon.

About Pilgrim, about Grey.

Fuming now, helpless, confused, guilty, Lugan surged into the doorway that Strafe had kicked in – but he wouldn't go through it, not yet.

He said, "Whatever this is, it ain't fucking funny. Ecko failed 'is mission, 'e *died*. An' if you don't shut your mouth, you'll be –"

"Joining him?" The goth came forwards, facing him, fearless. "How many of my friends with me? Is this usually how you treat –"

"This ain't fuckin' 'alloween, mate." His anger was focusing now. Lugan pressed the goth for a reaction. "You ain't 'ere an' that's the end of it."

"How do I prove it to you?" The goth was opposite him now, staring out at the workshop, the oil stains, the bits of bike and old posters. "Ecko believes you abandoned him, threw him away." He was fast, merciless. "Use of your name angers him. He misses you, though he would never admit it. Do you need me to tell you how tall he is? What of your cybernetics he offers? What he likes for his noontide meal?" His face set. "Do you?"

Lugan lifted a fist, but the woman shouted up at them, "Oh for Gods' sakes, stop it! Silfe is *dead*. Sera too if you don't do something! Put your cocks away and *help*!"

"Jesus fucking *Christ*!" Lugan's head was spinning. If Tarquinne had been here to put something in his bloodstream, then it might explain why he felt like was going to chuck up.

Fuller? You there? What the 'ell –?

Chemical scan negative, Luge; the air-recyclers are pure. Furball's on stand-by – you can save that guy's life if you get the gurney in there now.

"Bollocks!" Again, the commander slammed a fist into the wall. This time, he split his knuckles and a spatter of blood baptised the brickwork.

He had no clue what the fuck he was supposed to do. There were too many connections, too many coincidences, too many impossibilities – it all roared round his head like the Wall of Death at a rally, and the engine noise was deafening him. He reached for explanations, tried to make sense of it, gave up.

This is bullshit!

Fuller's calm tones still spoke in his ear. *Bio-polymer scan negative. And last I heard 3D printers weren't that good at granite. Luge – either we're all tripping... or that thing's really here.*

We're all fucking tripping, mate.

Roderick said, his voice soft, "Ecko was here, Lugan. His kit is in my cellars, his memory burned across the minds of my" – his voice cracked – "of my *staff*."

The word was an accusation, helpless and bereft. The man dropped his gaze, exhaled, rubbed thumb and forefinger over his eyes.

Shit. Lugan reached for a dog-end, lit it, blew a stream of greasy smoke in the goth's face. "You bring 'is kit out 'ere, and I'll send in the doc."

"Come in and see it for yourself." Upset or not, the goth didn't even cough.

Lugan hissed tobacco between his teeth.

Any further response was drowned out by a rising, thunderous rumble, a heavy-weight of noise that gathered force and fury – the 16:03, right on time and right over their heads. Tools jumped on their wall-nails, pottery wine containers clattered in their racks.

A roof-tile slammed edge-first into soft garden soil.

The train deafened them, then faded.

The goth took a step forward, coming right to the inside of the shattered door.

"Lugan," he said softly. "Upon my life and upon my word as once Ryll Guardian, this is The Wanderer – and we are really here. Ecko is my friend – though that friendship can be hard to manage." He paused, looking for the connection, the point of shared empathy. "Please. These people mean the world to me. Help Sera."

Canny fucker. Lugan labelled him. *Talker, fixer, dealer.* Over the link, he said, *Fuller?*

Voice stress analysis right off the scale – has a level of sincerity I've never heard. He believes what he's saying – completely. Heart rate's failing on the injured guy.

Lugan leaned down and picked up the roof-tile, fragments of soil and moss clinging to its edges, pieces of another world. One sharp blow to the head, a couple of strategic detonations and a night trip down to the river... This whole mess would just go the fuck away.

Fuller said, *I'm getting no electrical signature whatsoever, no data-feed, no security systems. No external comms. No plastics, no man-made fibres. And this is weird – I'm getting almost no metals, pure or alloy.*

Cam?

We've got audio, can't get the angles for visual. Furball's good to go, Luge.

Awright! Quit the guilt trip!

Dog-end stuck to his bottom lip, Lugan squinted through the rising smoke.

"If Ecko *was* 'ere," he said, "then where's 'e *now*." He dropped the tile, edge first, into the soft soil and put his boot on it, driving it down.

Roderick took a step out of the doorway, breaking the barrier, looking up at the workshop that surrounded him. In the light, his hair was blacker than any goth's, his oddly young face drawn in suntan and white lines.

"I will tell you everything I can." His voice was lambent, and contained a tension that went somehow beyond the situation. "If you will help Sera."

Stepping past him in some bizarre act of symmetry, Lugan's boots hit the floor of "The Wanderer" with a one-two thump. Oculars spinning, targeting, analysing, he surveyed its warm, wooden interior, took a deep, smokeless breath.

As his eyes adjusted, he saw properly the girl on the floor, the back of her skull shattered, her eyes and mouth still open in shock. He'd seen such things before, but this one... She was a slender little thing, maybe sixteen, and there was a tiny piece of pale-pink ribbon tied round one wrist. He wondered where she'd come from...

How he would ever fucking apologise.

Shit.

Swallowing hard now, he ran a callused hand through his beard.

"Awright," he said. Then to Fuller, *Go Furball*. He dropped his dog-end and stood on it, leaving an ash stain on the floor. "Look, mate. I don't know who you are, where the fuck you came from, or whether I'm just havin' the biggest motherfuckin' trip of my life. But that shit?" He nodded at the girl. "Ain't funny. An' I'll fix what I can."

The goth turned, nodded. "Karine," he said to the woman, "leave Sera with me – please find Kale."

* * *

Walking the building cellars to roof was not a short task, but its conclusion was gradually clear – the cook was missing.

Karine had found his last moments – deep gouge marks in the kitchen doorframe, repeated and desperate as if he'd been scrabbling, trying to hold on. The door itself was open, but it showed only the small garden at the rear of the building, now flooded with more of the harsh white light.

The kitchen floor was covered in splinters.

Looking at the marks of the struggle, remembering the awful, fading howl, the Bard felt his heart shrinking. He'd no idea if Kale was loose in Ecko's great grey London, or if he'd simply fallen and was lost somewhere outside the Count of Time.

He had lost one member of his team today and almost lost a second.

And enough was enough.

When the Bard returned to the taproom, he found Lugan behind the bar, eyeing some of the barrels with curiosity. Sera had gone; a sheet covered Silfe.

Without looking round, Lugan said, "Your bloke's in prep for surgery. There ain't no one else in 'ere – I could've told you that much."

"How do you know?" Roderick said.

Something in his voice made Lugan turn to look at him with an odd expression in his eyes.

"Info, mate. Communication. It's everywhere, all the time." He flashed a grin, teeth stained and yellow. "You just 'ave to know how to get it."

For a moment, the weight of the comment missed him. Roderick said, "Then Kale –"

"'E's not 'ere. You should've asked."

And then the Bard realised the sheer enormity of what Lugan had just said. His system shot through with adrenaline, as powerful as anything of Ecko's. His stomach roiled.

He touched the thought like an injury, tentative: *It's*

everywhere. All the time. You just have to know...

He found he was shaking. He couldn't speak. He was staring down at the stained sheet that covered Silfe, at the shape of her body under the fabric, at the hard shadows cast by the light.

Ecko had told him and he'd not understood the might of it, the sheer scope of the power they wielded...

Communication. Everywhere. All the time.

By the Ryll! This... He had spent his *life* looking for this. For lore. For answers. For a way to *understand*.

Everywhere. All the time.

For –

Cutting his tumble of wonder dead, Karine said, "Then do you know where he is? We've got to find him. Kale's" – her voice turned plaintive – "Kale's dangerous."

"Dangerous 'ow?" Lugan chuckled. "'E gonna jab someone with a big sword?"

"Don't jest," Karine told him. "Kale'd tear you to bits."

Lugan's chuckle gained a hint of guffaw.

Roderick shook himself; his mind was still reeling but the thought of Kale loose in the city was critical, immediate.

He said, "We need to find him. Before any harm comes to him – or anyone else. Karine, you should stay with The Wanderer, with Sera, with Silfe..." His voice held the name, just for a moment. "I need to find Kale. Lugan, I think that you and your lore should come with me."

Lugan blinked, shrugged huge shoulders. "Any second now," he said conversationally, "everything's going to slide the fuck sideways. There's gonna be a seething multi-colour of Mathmos-lamp background and I'll be rollin' one more before bed..."

"We must find Kale," Roderick said. "And you – your communication, your information – you need to help. You need to find him before he causes trouble that cannot be undone, before I lose anyone else. Before your Pilgrim finds something it will not understand." His expression said, *Please*.

Something hit home. Lugan looked at him sharply, chewed his lip for a moment, then seemed to reconsider.

"Awright," he said at last. "You wanna do this? Let me take you by the 'and an' lead you through the streets of London. Someone's mind is gonna get a fuckin' change."

"Bollocks."

Lugan spat the dog-end from the corner of his mouth and said, very softly, "Walk with me, quick and quiet. Keep your eyes off the sky. And don't say a fuckin' word."

I don't understand...

His hand on Roderick's elbow was cold stone, as uncompromising as his attitude, as the jut of his bearded jaw. Already spinning from the sight, the sounds, the smells, the strangeness, the great city's assault on his senses, the Bard did as he was told. What choice did he have?

This was London. Ecko's home. It clamoured and it stank and it overpowered his senses. It grew around him – upwards and inwards, it grew into the sky like some vast glass-and-metal canker. It was too big, too much. It bewildered him and he could only cling to his confusion and hope to survive.

"We gotta lose this bitch," Lugan said. "Stay close."

On the other side of the roadway, there was some sort of disturbance, flashing lights and guards with arms outstretched; strips of fluttering fabric sealing off a part of the road. Over it, flying things hovered. People drifted past, showing little curiosity – between their movements, the Bard thought he saw a man slumped, dark blood spreading from his fallen body.

Fear flooded his mouth. He only the saw the man briefly, but he knew who it was...

Kale?

"Move!" He only realised he'd stopped when he felt a tug

on his sleeve. He stumbled in Lugan's wake like a blind man.

Kale?

It was too much to take in, unreal. Silfe had gone, and now Kale. Out here, impossible, in the road, stone and winding streets. Claustrophobia. Coughing. Pulling on his sleeve. Something following them. And then, suddenly, they came out from between the crowded, crazed buildings and there was a river. Wide and slow and filthy, but a river nonetheless.

His thoughts reeling, the Bard tried to stop.

Please do not run on the Millennium Bridge.

But the faceless, pointless monotone seemed to speak at him alone; it surrounded him, closed him in, preyed upon his ears. He couldn't think through the noise. It shut his throat and filled his mind with –

"Dammit, move!"

Spray can make the surface slippery. Please do not run...

Propelled by the man's huge, stained hand, Roderick blundered, still in shock. He was crazed, tensed, choking, a tumbling mote at the centre of colossal impossibility. How...?

Even if he asked the questions, the answers would make no sense. And why could he not breathe?

Spray can make the surface slippery...

Lugan didn't let him slow down. Their boots rang in rhythm on the slender metal span. The people before them jostled them blankly, uncaring, unspeaking. They bore themselves like the weight of the sky pressed them down. They muttered emptily, lost to Kazyen, as Lugan elbowed them out of the way.

"It's following us from the accident we passed. We stay in the crowd, it can't touch us. We need to lose this fucker. Like now."

The accident we passed... His thoughts reeled. *How does it know who we are?*

He couldn't grasp it, it was as strange as the sky, the water, the air, the colourless, blank-eyed populace. As strange as the bridge beneath their feet.

Metal. In the midst of his reeling bafflement, a question. How can there be this much metal?

He tripped. Lugan pushed him urgently on. The blonde man glanced back repeatedly, blue lights flickering like fire-sparks at the corner of his eyes.

So familiar!

But the Bard stumbled blindly, hanging tightly to his self-control while the world spun round him, questions unanswered. The water was brown, strewn with garbage, and it stank. The city's air was dense, choking-close, the cloud so low he could almost have touched it. Even here, it was smothering, too hot, thick and grey, somehow unhealthy; it tasted wrong. It ached in his lungs and he struggled to keep up, to draw breath. To comprehend.

Lugan muttered tightly, "Quit daydreamin' and shift your arse." He gave a wicked, half-threatening aside. "Unless you wanna swim?"

The water below them seemed devoid of life – only the boats that ripped up its surface, the desperate that combed its grey-pebbled beaches. For a fleeting moment, he wondered what they sought.

But Lugan was still pushing, tension in every line and movement.

And the grip on his arm did not slacken.

At the bridge's end, they passed a bright stall selling roasting foodstuffs, the smell rich, almost too sweet. His stomach turned, throat still full of nausea and tension.

Lugan shot at him, "If you're gonna puke, make it fast – an' make sure it's in the water."

Behind them, coming across the bridge, there was a flash of blue. Brilliant, azure blue. A cloak hem, the billow of a long skirt…?

The Bard lurched into motion once more. The colour faded into the grey and was gone.

"Keep your 'ead down and as many people between you an'

it as you can. Fucks up the pheromone trace. "Shit!"

As they left the metal bridge behind them, a barrier lay across their path – a thoroughfare of some sort, noisy, acrid and black. At its edge, the people had packed into an obedient block, controlled to docility by an incomprehensible system of lights and markings.

One of the blue-lit air vehicles – "drones" – buzzed them like an outsized insect and was gone.

Such chaos; such rigid order! It was all he could do not to claw at his own throat, tear open his windpipe in an effort to find clean air, space. *I have to breathe!*

But Lugan didn't stop. He jostled his way to the front, agitated, eyes on the light that commanded thought and movement.

"It's a 'sniffer' – hi-tech tracker. Can pick up your pheromones at ten metres, body-'eat signature at five and the spit from your breath at two. Short version? That thing gets up close and personal, it's gonna know all my secrets. Everything I got on record." He gave a brief grin, but it faded just as quickly. "But why the fuck is it followin' us?"

Communication. Everywhere. All the time.

The Bard's thoughts rolled like stones, sending ripples through his tension – his need for information was so strong it hurt. Sera's life, Kale's death, the life of the tavern itself –

The flicker of azure was closer.

"Don't stand gawping!" Lugan thumped his shoulder. "Drone gets a zap of your eyeballs, you're bagged." Insanely, the big blonde man was grinning, tight and whetted through his beard. "C'mon, you fucker, change."

On a small tower by the roadside, lights flicked colour. Obediently, the crowd surged into the road.

Lugan and the Bard were carried at the front of the wave.

The azure flash was at the back.

They had more room now, and they moved more quickly, dodging the incoming people and staying ahead of the swell.

Buildings rose ahead of him, carven stone, impossible glass. Unseen in the bustle, sudden steps tripped him to a stumble. The crowd shifted and muttered, but they parted for Lugan like the tall grass of the Varchinde.

The grass Roderick had left dying behind him.

"St Paul's," Lugan said. "Take a left – an' let's move it."

With still no idea where they were going, Roderick tumbled helplessly in his wake.

"She's still with us," Lugan said. "Bitch is right up my fuckin' arse."

Then, ahead of them, a high cathedral, a stern rise of scrubbed-clean stone that stood domed and pale against the grim and overheated sky. Upon it, weathered statues stared blindly outwards, uncaring of the sea of people below.

It was old, and beautiful – and it was soul-empty.

Kazyen.

As they pushed around its huge stone flank, he saw that the massive double doors were sealed closed against the tide of the lost. Instead, bright banners hung from tall stone pillars, vulgar and out of place. They bore the emblem of a man crouched under a heavy pack and were emblazoned, "Be Valiant. Be a Pilgrim".

Pilgrim.

Lugan was using his height and mass to carve through the crowd like an axe. The splash of azure was still behind them; here, there, somewhere, and closing.

"Fuck, fuck, fuck, *fuck*!" Lugan muttered. "What does it take?"

The monotone spoke over him, unctuous and smooth. *Welcome to St Paul's Cathedral. Please do not touch or deface Cathedral property. Cathedral attendants are on hand to ensure your visit is pleasant and trouble free. Welcome to St Paul's Cathedral...*

"Fuller, I need Collator!" A moment later, Lugan said, again, "*Fuck!*"

Just as Roderick wondered who he was talking to, he half turned and spilled swift words as if trying to explain.

"Collator's down, Fuller can't get drone coverage – 'e's in the system, but 'e can't do it alone. City security's like a coked-up pro, it's all over 'im." Another glance, another surge of speed. "No net, we're on our own."

The words were baffling, but the name – "Collator". It was the world-builder, the thing that Ecko had said was controlling how his reality unfolded.

Pilgrim. Kazyen.

Somehow, all this hung together. For a moment, he turned the concepts over, looking at them as if they were broken pieces of pottery, trying to work out what they made.

Communication. Everywhere. All the time.

No net, we're on our own.

Was it – was there some sort of elemental powerflux? A powerflux of information?

The thought brought a thrill, wordless and unexpressable, an excitement that made him tremble.

Around them, the press of people had become almost immobile, tight, crushing. Noise was constant, an endless, hovering hum; enough to chase him out of his mind, an enclosure of incessant sound.

The flash of reflected sunlight came again. He shivered.

"Fuck this," Lugan said softly. He paused to glance around, then, sharply changed direction.

He shoved people forcibly out of their path. Passers-by stumbled, retorts dying unspoken as they looked up at the leathers that had barged them. Rapidly Lugan and Roderick came to the edge of the plaza, to a row of garishly lit market stores, and a wash of scents too cloying sweet to think through.

She was almost upon them – almost close enough to feel them, to breathe their lies, their truth. Paused in the chill-draught doorway of the merchant store, they crossed gazes –

worlds apart yet pulled together by impossibility.

Roderick said, "Wait... wait. If I understand this, she is a scout? And she can feel us, know who we are?" He was grappling with the concept, not entirely sure what he was suggesting. "The man in the road, the accident. Was Kale. She must've realised..."

Lugan stopped, grinned and then slapped the Bard on the back hard enough to make him stagger.

"You're a fuckin' genius. Follow me, I've 'ad an idea..."

And they ran through the overstuffed streets.

Measureless, endless, a flood of noise and sensation; an almighty collage-sprawl of a city that unrolled in every direction, as far as he could dream. Narrow alleyways and huge thoroughfares, endless signs, garish boards, brilliant lights...

Lugan ducked and turned frequently – though not quite frequently enough. At every corner, there she was, her mouth open as if to inhale their very scent.

They ran on.

Great skeletal creatures, angles that lifted mighty weights, monuments to heroes forgotten, parks abandoned and trees filth-streaked and dying. And everywhere, everywhere, the soulless press of the people, *Kazyen*-lost. Their wealth was incomprehensible – and yet they had nothing.

It was coming closer. He could hear it now, a sharp tapping of metal on stone, a laugh like a girl's, caught and teased by a wind he couldn't feel.

Must... breathe... must... breathe!

He remembered, his thoughts running words to the rhythm it gave him, his boots thudding counterpoint on the hard flags.

"*Move!*" Lugan roared.

I was hailed as the hope of my people. The first guardian born in Avesyr in over a thousand returns. And I took a liberty – a blasphemy – that no mortal man may take.

I craved knowledge, needed to see. I touched my fingertips to the waters of the Ryll. And I alone bore witness to the world's nightmare, to the terror she has forgotten. In seeking truth, I found only a question I can never answer, a desire I can never fulfil.

He shivered with the possibility: *Until now. Here.*

The lore they possess, their communication, their information. Their powerflux. This is my answer. Somehow, I must understand...

Somewhere in his crowded heart, old images were awakening, thrumming like the strings of an instrument. He was skirting the very edge of his lifelong dream, of everything he'd ever needed to be.

Everywhere. All the time.

They ran.

His surroundings were becoming familiar – a huge, red-bricked bridge with rails of metal that stank like the breath of Vahl Zaxaar himself... Metal fences and discarded rubbish, coloured, angular artworks scrawled on walls.

The blue creature was very close now, an eager lover, seeking to uncover everything he had.

The monotone was fainter here, faded like a nightmare. He found he could fill his lungs – and then cough with the metallic taint that seemed to coat his throat from the inside.

And she had them.

They were cornered in a courtyard, the great bridge behind them, the blue stalker in front. Her eyes glittered scarlet as though full of blood.

"Eastermann," she said sweetly. "Alexander David. Alias: Lugan. Alias: Ade. Personal Identification Number, on record and correct. Geolocation –"

"Fuller?" Lugan took a pace sideways and said softly, "Now!"

The metal door behind him opened.

It rolled upwards like paper, a clanking and a clattering that drowned out everything the creature was trying to say.

But he heard Lugan's mutter, "If it's big enough to fuck Collator, love, it's big enough for you."

The creature stopped, stared.

At The Wanderer, flood-lit with every brilliant white lamp that Lugan's team could muster, dazzling and incomprehensible in the space that had been the Bike Lodge.

The creature twitched, swayed slightly, and tumbled sideways.

As the door started to rumble back down, Lugan loosed a triumphant snort, punched the Bard's shoulder hard enough to rock him sideways.

"Welcome to London," he said.

PART 2: PATTERNS

10: DANCING

TRADE-ROADS, SOMEWHERE OUTSIDE AMOS

Ecko sat calm, his guts in turmoil.

Evening wrapped him; the air was as cool and soft as a laundry ad. Amos was a dwindling shadow and the trade-road that'd cut through her manors and farms was now fading to a stretch of dilapidated sunbleach, tumbledown and quiet. They had moved out to one side of it, and its last buildings stretched reaching shadows over the fantastical flame-colours of the grass.

Behind them, a faint mist was gathering, loitering at their heels; somewhere ahead, the ground shrugged upwards into stubby, green-swathed mountains. Trees stood angled, stooped by the long wind.

Ecko's guts didn't care.

He sat hunched, almost daring the beauty to touch him. The whole thing was like a fucking postcard – not real. Something you'd find on the noticeboard in Lugan's office sent by a smug client – "Wish you were here".

Ecko had a lot of wishes. Postcards and smug clients weren't any of them.

In front of his cowled face, a small fire burned, warm and compelling. If he held up a hand, the colours of the grass were the shifting flame-shades of his skin. He'd sat before a fire like this one with Pareus and Tarvi, and the members of their tan who'd died defending him.

Yeah, an' if Eliza'd wanted to whack me round the back of the head with a bit of psyche-job-two-by-four...

Bitch.

The word had become a reflex, aimed at nothing more than his own resentment.

On the fire's far side, gold skin shimmering, sat Triqueta, her expression thoughtful and her eyes on the embers' glow. In the warm light, her increase in age was less obvious, and her face was gentle, its lean lines lost in the flickers of warmth and shadow.

Leaping sparks reflected in the stones in her cheeks, lighting them to flashes of flame.

He wasn't looking at her, anyway. Didn't want to look at her. Not in firelight. Too many figments danced in the heat. Memories of the Sical, the temptation it had offered him...

Worthy, you. Grant everything you wish.

He curled his fingernails into the palms of his hands, hurting.

And it wasn't like she was looking at him, for chrissakes. She glanced down from the firelight to the blades across her knees, the nicks in the edges, the splits in the resin. Terhnwood was perishable stuff, and it needed maintenance.

After a moment, he turned away.

A short distance from the fire, at the back of the peeling buildings, their lone pack-chearl was hobbled, its head down as it nosed the grass. Close to it, Redlock stood solid, both axes neatly parrying a series of cut and slash manoeuvres by a determined Amethea, her long belt-blade in her hand. The girl was sweating, teeth gritted, and concentrating hard. Each blow was carefully placed – a rhythmic sequence of slashing attacks to shoulder and hip that spanked neatly from the axe hafts. The impacts echoed in ripples from the wooden walls.

Then Redlock began to retreat. He crossed a long band of sunshine that tumbled through a dirty alleyway, and coaxed his opponent to move forward with each attack.

"Good, good! Watch your footing, place the blow carefully. Keep your distance constant. Now – defend!" As he advanced, one axe striking after the other in a careful, rhythmic pattern, she backed one pace at a time, circle-blocking each blow as it came in. After a moment, he sped the attacks up, pushing. She matched his speed, her face hardening with concentration.

"She's getting better," Triq commented. "More confident."

Redlock was grinning as the teacher blocked each blow. "Good, yes, well done! Now – back at me. Mix them up this time!"

With a breath like resolve, Amethea did just that, her strikes now coming randomly, slow at first, then gaining more speed.

Triqueta watched them, mischief in her face. As Ecko glanced at her – not that he was looking – she picked up a small stone from beside the fire, rested it in her hand. Redlock matched parry after parry, his haft blocks aggressive, strong. Aiming, Triqueta flicked the stone at him, the movement a flickering dance through the heat of the fire.

The axeman didn't even look. One weapon flashed in the light of the setting sun. There was a faint *tink* as it took the tiny stone clean out of the air.

No oculars. No reflexes.

Holy fucking shit.

Redlock grinned, but he didn't look round.

Triqueta chuckled, shook her head with what might have been admiration.

"He's too good for his own good, that one." The comment was conspiratorial, aimed at Ecko's huddle of silence. "Can you do that?"

Oh please. Mom made me. I can do things you've never even fucking dreamed –

With an effort, he swallowed a throat full of tangled, wordless envy, an undefined sense of inadequacy – as if his very enhancements were somehow about failure, about cheating. He picked up a loose strand of grass and held its end to the fire, watching it burn.

But Triqueta was still watching him, her eyes flashing gold.

"What?" He looked over the flame. Dared her, fucking *dared* her.

"I'm trying to work it out, Ecko. What this is all about. I'm trying to work out if you're not just here looking for the – sulph-whatever-it-is – and if you're not just going to grab it and jump wagon at the last minute."

"Jump *ship*, you jump off a *ship*, what is it with you people?" He held the tiny flame up, let it glitter from his black-on-black eyes. He had no fucking idea what he was supposed to answer.

C'mon Eliza. What'm I s'posed to do here? Pick her flowers? Sing?

From beside them, there was a sudden, masculine curse. Redlock had fallen back, slung one axe and dabbed a hand to his face – a hand that came away bloody. As Amethea gasped and started to apologise, he laughed at her.

"No, it's good – and that's enough for this evening. You've wounded me, Thea, wounded me sore."

"Gods, I'm so sorry, I wasn't –"

"Enough!" He grinned. "You got one through – that's good. Let's take a break and persuade Triq to go hunt dinner."

Triqueta called back to him, "Hunt it yourself!"

"You hunt it, I'll cook it."

She snorted. "There are quicker ways to kill people."

Chuckling, Redlock came to sit beside her and grinned at Ecko across the heat's waver.

"Axes are okay for firewood – but they're shit for downing passing esphen. Which reminds me..." He inspected their edges ruefully and rummaged in a belt pouch.

Ecko said nothing, watched the camaraderie with a hurt that might have been resentment, or anger. The smoke from the fire was getting in his eyes; the must/must not of his friendships tore at his mind and heart and skin. Christ, some part of him just wanted to put his fucking hand right in the fire until he could focus, control himself, another part wanted to get up and run and never ever come back. But he was as trapped out here as he had been in Amos, as he had been ever since The Wanderer had fallen into the depths. Trapped walking Eliza's path because these people were his friends and they fucking *trusted* him.

And he had to go along, no matter what the hell it was gonna cost him.

Dance, Ecko. Daaaaance...

Yeah, you just wait. I'll fucking show you how to dance...

Then, from the long shadows of the nearby buildings, there came a single, sharp cry.

Cut suddenly short.

His thoughts shattered, spun out into the sunset in a thousand sparkling shards. He was on his feet without thinking, adrenaline humming, muscles alight, targeters crossing on the threat...

There!

Amethea stood rock-solid, the resin glitter of a knife across her throat. Behind her was a tall, cloaked figure with a classic assassin's hood covering most of its face.

Bandits? Adrenalised or no, Ecko spent a second staring in genuine disbelief. *Seriously?*

But their presence made him cackle like a fiend, his mood suddenly lifting – *Bandits, for chrissakes.* These guys were about to have the worst night of their fucking lives. It hadda be more fun than warm milk and storytime and a nice early night...

There's a good Ecko. You just behave and everything will be fine.

His lip curled. *Yeah, you just wait...*

Redlock and Triqueta were both on their feet, hands splayed and visible but weapons within reach. As Ecko faded back into the patchwork colours of the long grass, two cronies joined the hooded figure, and the three of them stood there like they owned the road. At a gesture from the bossman, one of them reached to unhobble the chearl.

Ecko grinned. *An' whaddaya know, it's amateur night.*

The phrase reminded him of Lugan – and the grin spread across his face. Lugan'd proved that friendship was not a weakness, it was something solid as ferrocrete –

Lugan'd been a lying fuckwit who'd sold him down the river. Jeez, if this program was about teaching trust an' closeness an' teamwork, oh my, then maybe Lugan should've been plugged the hell into it instead.

Ecko's grin congealed.

Asshole.

And his humour caught light.

Y'know what? Fuck this. Fuck you and the bike you rode in on… If this is some teamwork 101 thing, then you can shove it. I'll do this my way.

The only way.

Collator: *Chances of successful scenario at…*

Whatever.

Angry now, he welcomed the burning, the singing in his nerves, the rush, the elation. It came with a sudden need to really refuse – to say fuck it all to death and just *go…*

But Redlock was coming forwards, the fire no longer blocking his vision.

He said, "We've got little you can take – the animal carries trail food, not much else. What d'you want?"

The cowled figure snorted. "Where's your sneaky friend? Get him back where I can see him."

"What friend?" Redlock's hands were on his axeheads; his tone was shameless.

"Don't mess me about, axeman. Bring him out, or the girl's gagging on her own gore. She your lover? Your daughter?" There was a grin under that cowl. "Both?"

"You're funny." Redlock didn't flinch.

The figures were up to their knees in the long grass. They wore cloaks and shirts and trews, dusty and patched, but there was something about the way they moved...

Something...

Oh for fucksake.

As the penny dropped, Ecko almost slapped himself round the head for being that bastard dumb – these guys had the perfect metre-stride of plainclothes' cops. Caught between his surging anger and a sudden rise of avid, eager curiosity, he paused to stare, quivering with glee and tension – and they were, they fucking *were*, they were walking in squad form even though the grass was past their shins.

These guys were goons.

His cackle returned, silent under his cowl.

Maybe they were renegades, AWOL, maybe they were on a super-secret stealth mission...

...or maybe they weren't Bond James Bond and they just were on some sorta road-patrol?

His adrenaline shuddered, but sustained. He felt sick. He stayed where he was, his oculars scanning, heat and light and motion. Whatever was about to go down, he *really* wanted to play.

"Come on, axeman, I'm gonna count to three."

It comes after two, y'know, in case you've forgotten...

...and after this.

Grinning now, he took a breath, focused on one of the wind-stunted trees. He gave them the hint of the Bogeyman's breathing that he'd once loosed in the base of Doctor Grey, a world and a lifetime away. Hollow, wet, dank breathing – a chill down the back of your neck, an unseen daemon lurking, oozing, in the grass...

The two goons, shuddered, exchanged glances, looked round. One led the chearl, the other had a spear, and their hands were white with tension. The tall figure with the blade didn't so much as flinch.

Smartass.

Ecko slipped onwards, circling to their backs as they advanced on the fire...

Nothing like giving this shit the personal touch.

Amethea was angry.

In fact, she could only remember being this angry once before – and that was with Maugrim, may he damned well burn. The fact that this figure had come out of nowhere and decided not only to remind her that she could be a victim, but to use her as leverage against her friends, was a bit much. All the praying in the world hadn't saved her last time – she'd had to do that herself.

Her thoughts were broken by the breathing.

It came from behind them, from the grass at their feet – dark, dank, wet breathing, breathing like a mouthful of blood. She shuddered, right to the core of her soul. But the man behind her laughed – a sound she felt rather than heard.

He said softly, "It's nothing, keep walking," and the blade pressed harder, a warm line of pain across her throat.

He called past her ear. "Call it back, or this one –"

"We can't." The answer came from Triqueta, gamer, playing for the Count of Time. "We can't call it back, it's... it's not human. We don't control it."

The man behind Amethea laughed again – she could feel the depth and timbre of it in her back, in her skin. The blade pressed into her throat and she pulled back from it almost without meaning to, pressing her head into the man's broad chest. She thought for one mad moment that he would stroke her hair with the other hand.

"Call it back, or you know what I'll do to your pretty little girlie here. You want to watch?"

Pretty little girlie?

Saint and Goddess.

And something in Amethea's soul remembered the pure stone, remembered that vast strength she had once touched, had felt within her skin...

Pretty little girlie.

She'd had about enough of this.

Ecko had gotten close now, right up to where they loitered, right *there*, at the edges of the trade-road. He was close enough to see the whites of their eyes – hell, the whites of their fucking kacks if they had any – and certainly close enough to see the fine red line that spread across Amethea's throat, the tickle of dark fluid that was easing down her skin.

But she didn't look remotely afraid. If anything, she looked downright pissed off.

Playtime was over. If his Bogeyman trickery was useless, then he had a whole fucking arsenal of other shit he could pull. Like a bluff against a bluff – see what these guys were really made of.

Like this.

The full-on high that he welcomed like the best class As on the market – *Oh now we're talkin'!* Redlock was moving forwards; Triq was using him to block their line of sight, pick up her bow.

The cloaked figure shouted, "Put the axes down or the girl – *shit*!"

His threat was cut short as one of his cronies cried out and fell, one kick to the back of the knee bringing him down in the grass with an explosion of dust and colour. The second strike with the same foot stretched the goon in the dirt, jaw shattered, eyes staring and mouth lax. Red leaked from his ear.

And Ecko said, "You lookin' for me?"

* * *

As Ecko appeared, both Redlock and Triqueta were moving –
the axeman forward in a roll, Triqueta stringing her lop-ended
bow. She had an arrow notched and to her ear when the lead
goon shouted, "Hold!"

Still held against his chest, Amethea felt the word throb
on her back like an ache. She'd no idea what game Ecko was
playing – why he'd downed the sidekick rather than coming for
the boss, but she wasn't in a position to be asking questions.

As Redlock stopped dead, his face etched with tension and
more dangerous than she'd ever seen him look, the goon started
to laugh.

"Don't be stupid. You know how this works. One move and
the girl dies."

Ecko said, "So?"

The word was a slap. Amethea gaped, held down the panic.
What? What are you…?

But Ecko shrugged, grinned. "You think I give a shit? You
slit her throat for all I care."

No, he was bluffing, he wouldn't…

Held still, the teacher felt a rush of absolute white-cold
fear – even in the stone tunnels of Maugrim's heat, her own
blood spiralling across the floor, she'd never felt such absolute
certainty…

I'm going to die here.

Really. Here. Now.

Her "Saint and Goddess" was suddenly hollow – words she'd
used too often for them to have meaning. She wondered if Vilsara
would miss her; wondered, stupidly, if Feren would be waiting.

The blade was tight against her skin now, cutting, hurting.
Hot and cold and pain in a tense line across her throat. Tickles
crept down her skin. Flashes of 'prentice classes came to her
– she knew exactly how deep it needed to cut before it hit her

windpipe, and exactly what would happen when it did.

Little priestess.

Feren had had courage. He'd fought his way across the plains because he couldn't abandon her. She owed his courage her life.

She owed these people her life.

This life.

Right now.

This life she wasn't going to give up.

The blade cut deeper, making her bite her lip to avoid crying out. The grunt jerked her body, as if making her dance.

"You move – any of you! – and the girl –!"

"I moved!" Ecko was closer now, and grinning, capering like some crazed market jester. "Hey, look, I moved again!"

"I'm not playing!" The goon was getting angry – she could feel it in the skin of her back, in the way she was held. His anger was good – it meant he was unstable, not in control. He was being made to look like a fool and he knew it. Amethea almost laughed – this whole thing was crazed, some sort of comedy mummery. The man's voice scaled upwards as he cried, "I mean it –!"

Ecko folded his arms. "Go on then. But when that one's dead, I'm gonna rip your fuckin' head off and play soccer with it."

The man was panicking now, trying to drag her backwards and away. Angry, she dug her feet into the wet soil, refused to move.

Then the solid thunk of an arrow took the second goon clean in the chest, dropping him like a rock, ripples in the grass. His groan as he fell was the sound of Redlock coming to his feet, his expression bleak as winter.

The chearl, freed from its captor, shook its spiked mane and went back to the grass.

But Amethea was damned to the rhez itself if she was going to be rescued again.

Instead, she lifted one foot and kicked backwards, hard as

she could manage, at where she thought her captor's kneecap would be.

Her aim was true. She drove her boot-heel hard, felt the contact, felt him flinch and groan and fold. As Triqueta was stringing a second shaft, her hands a blur, as Redlock was coming forwards in a lunge that would tear the life and breath and flesh of anything in its way, so she was out – the man's grip had slackened enough and she was ripping her way free...

She was turning and slamming that same boot squarely into his groin.

He toppled, clutching himself and keening.

And Ecko laughed outright, a sound that split cracks through the sunset sky, that shook the battered buildings of the trade-road.

Still curled from the impact, the grunt took a metal axe in his neck and fell sideways, the front of his throat tearing free as the blade cut through him. He toppled slowly, his garments and skin flooding red like the last of the sun.

When he hit the ground, he twitched for a moment, opened his mouth to speak – but it was too late.

Her heart like stone, Amethea stood over him and watched him die.

She stared at the fire.

In her mind's eye, the soldiers she'd crafted with metal and watched die; in her heart, Maugrim's passion and caress.

Little priestess.

It was a stupid phrase, archaic and clumsy. She was no more some damned priestess than she was...

...than she was a healer.

Lately, she seemed to be better at hurting things.

Heal and Harm; calls to saints and Gods. Denials of responsibility. Maugrim had told her this. She'd sat in his chambers and waited to be rescued, lost herself, crafted horrors because she'd not had the courage to refuse. In those memories now, "should have done" blazed in the fire, flames like regret.

Like *anger*.

Amethea's fingers touched the fine line that was scabbed across her throat, and then her hand moved to rest on the belt-blade that she'd been learning to use.

Strangely, it felt comforting – for the first time in her life she felt as if she was at ease with its presence.

"Got it!" Triqueta's cry startled her, made her look up.

The Banned woman had been going over the corpses, their pouches and packs. The sky over her was almost dark now, the moons crossing the ground with wonder and light. In the gleam, Triq had sat back on her heels and she held something that caught the light – a glimmer of moon through resin.

"Ecko was right," she said. "These guys're soldiers."

Soldiers.

Amethea felt her heart shrink in her chest and she wasn't even sure why.

Ecko had gone on patrol, hunting more bad guys, fading into the darkness as though he'd never return. Redlock was prowling uneasy, axes in hands. The trade-road itself was quiet – they were off the main thoroughfare here, and far enough out of the city that no one would know or care what had happened to them.

But if they were this far out, then why were there...

Soldiers.

"They're out of Fhaveon," Triqueta said. She shoved the corpse over on its face, and held up the resin tag. "Twenty-fourth tan, south city Range Patrol."

"Why the rhez're they out here?" Redlock stopped, turned. "They don't come anything like this far. That tag his, or has he stolen it?"

"They've all got them, same tan," Triq said. "And you saw

the way they moved, their stance, everything about them." She stood up, holding the craftmarker up to the bright moonlight. "Either these guys are renegade…"

"Or Fhaveon's patrolling the trade-roads." Redlock let out a low, awed whistle.

"Maybe they're looking for us?" Amethea said softly.

"How would they know we're out here?" Triqueta had acquired assorted other objects from the downed soldiers that she was now carefully sliding into various pouches. "Everything Nivrotar said – I think Redlock's right. I think Fhaveon's soldiers are spreading. Like some damned disease. I think the occupation's started."

Amethea shivered. Pulled her cloak tighter.

"Phylos's putting out his feelers," Redlock said. "Consolidating. If he controls Fhaveon, the Cartel, the military… If he wants to control the other cities, he's got to control the roads –"

"Does he have that kind of force?" Amethea asked, the fire warm on her skin. "If his goons are out here, then who's watching the home fires?"

The question was purely sense, but it made both the others turn to stare, then look at each other as if some light were dawning.

Triqueta said, "This place is the ass-end of nowhere, probably belongs to Amos to boot. Maybe Fhaveon *is* just after us –?"

"We haven't done anything." Redlock flashed a grin that said, *Yet*. He came back to the circle of firelight, then turned his back to watch the moon-shadowed buildings, the empty stretch of road. "I'm with Thea – if they're all the way out here, then they're spreading everywhere. And if they're spreading everywhere, then either Fhaveon herself is helpless – which I doubt – or she's building one rhez of an army."

Triqueta eyed the downed soldier, the marker still in her hand.

"We should go back to Amos, tell Nivrotar –"

"She already knows," Amethea said. "That's why she wants weapons. And I'm beginning to think" – the fire popped, startling her – "that all in all, the Lord Nivrotar knows a lot more than she's letting on."

11: RESISTANCE AMOS; FHAVEON

He was light as a child, bird-fragile, his body wasting even as they'd fled from the palace. She'd carried him in her arms like a child and he'd clung to her shoulder, silent in the gathering evening and more tightly focused than she'd ever seen. His thin frame was trembling, wound to the hilt with tension.

He'd frightened her. She'd had no idea that he was capable of –

Dear Gods.

The memory made her shudder and she shoved it away – as she had so many. It was how she moved forwards.

Don't think about it.

In her urgency, Jayr had taken almost nothing with her – a belt-blade and a waterskin, a bag on her shoulder. Benefits of her Kartian upbringing – she'd little need for *stuff*.

Poor crazed Ress. She'd striven to understand – what he was saying, where it'd come from. The thing he'd found in the Library that'd cost him his mind, seeing Triqueta, the terhnwood, the strange little man in the cloisters with the light seeping across his skin like disease. Ress had repeated his name like a mantra: "Ecko, Ecko, Ecko..."

Enough. He's had enough.

His hitting out hadn't surprised her. But what he'd *done*...

Jemara, hands pleading, knees folding, face draining of her flush and her puff and her cheery humour – toppling to the floor, eyes empty... lightless and soulless, her hands curling into claws and her mind just...

...gone...

Jayr didn't scare easy – but Ress had just sucked the life and the light out of her.

Impossible, and terrifying.

They fled – they had to. Once, Jayr had fled the great crafthalls of the Kartiah, fought her way free by sheer, brutal determination. Something deep in her heart still really wanted – hungered, lusted – to return. She wanted to make them beg, to make them *pay*, to hear them scream. She wanted to avenge herself for what they'd done to her, right at the last...

Jayr smouldered with constant fury. She'd no idea how she'd come to be raised in the pit-fighting slavery of the Kartians – it was just how it was, her life for as long as she could remember. She'd no recollection of anything previous – of parents, of siblings – no half-remembered dream, no understanding of why they'd not wanted her.

From as young as she could remember, she'd disdained emotional contact. She'd been raised to fight, fist and fury, her anger channelled and built, moulded and crafted. It had kept her alive when so many around her had died, many of those by her own hands, a scar for every one. And as her skills had increased, so she'd become noticed by her Kartian masters – and so they'd forged her like they forged their metals, into something that couldn't be broken.

Until the day they'd traded her body for something other than combat.

She'd killed four of them, and fled into the darkness. Raised without light, she'd been skilled enough – just – to reach Vanksraat, where Ress had found her.

And refused to leave her.

The Banned adopted misfits, or misfits joined the Banned. It'd taken Ress a very long time to help Jayr adjust, but he'd never given up on her, never left her side, and his gentleness and insight had been more than she could understand, at times. He'd reduced her to rage, to tears, to many times fleeing the love he'd showed her.

But she'd always come back.

And now, she would neither judge nor leave him.

He shifted in her arms, mouthing empty syllables. After a moment, he managed, "Jayr," forcing her name past his teeth, striving to focus on her face. "Look."

He was trying to tell her that they'd come to the edge of the palace's island.

Ahead of them was an open mosaic; on its far side, one of the myriad bridges that spanned the "moat" formed by the bifurcating Great Cemothen River. There were eight or ten of them, joining the little island to the main streets.

They were all guarded, though more from tradition than necessity.

To flee the palace, she would have to cross the open ground.

"We need to wait," she told him. "Watch."

"No time. No time no *time* no *time* no time like now." Ress had pulled himself up to her ear. He was struggling to speak, to cling to his sanity for long enough to form words. "Trust... me. We have to *go*."

"Trust you to what? Not pull my brain out through my eyeballs? I can't cross there without being seen."

"I can... do this..." He was tense with white-hot urgency, with single-minded compulsion. His skin was scorching; his blood afire in his veins. He was shaking with effort, his concentration was pure and absolute. "Just... walk..."

"Just walk?" she hissed back at him. "I'm Jayr the cursed Infamous, remember? People *notice* me."

"*Walk*." Ress's frame burned with intensity. "Now!"

Barely daring to believe, she walked out into the open.

The bridge guard didn't look up. He was young, bored, but too well disciplined to yawn. He rubbed his hands against the gathering evening.

As Jayr walked, her heart in her mouth, a faint sense of light-headedness crept through her, almost as though she were advancing through twilight, a fog, a dream. Her feet weren't quite touching the tiles, her flesh felt oddly...

Just walk!

What?

Disbelief and wonder held her breath in her throat. She came to the end of the carven stone bridge, passed a handspan in front of the guard's nose, close enough for him to feel the air they disturbed.

But he was watching the wheeling birds.

Ress... She looked down at the madman she held in her arms. *What the rhez has happened to you...?*

Ress curled motionless into her shoulder, Jayr of the Banned walked unseen from the palace – and from Jemara's empty mind.

Free.

From everything.

For a moment, she turned back, looked up at the dark, narrow-windowed wall above her – at Nivrotar, Triqueta, Amethea, the lost and blank-eyed thing that had been Jemara, the strange little man whose name compelled like a talisman.

Ecko.

Ress coughed, a tiny sound, like a warning.

She turned away.

Below her, the huge, broad stretch of the river rolled slowly beneath the stone – it would reunite briefly on the palace's far side before spreading out into the sprawling, bustling mass of the Estuary Wharf. There was movement down on the river, a gaggle of young man calling lewd jests at one another.

They didn't look up.

As they reached the bridge's far side, Ress suddenly went slack, the tension leaving his body. She clung to him, almost stumbling to her knees as her feet were suddenly solid on the roadway.

Swiftly, she ducked into a side-alley.

"Ress, by the Gods. What did you...? *How* did you...?"

"Fo-cus... un-der-stand." Held in her arms, he was smiling up at her, vacant and child-like, his mis-sized pupils staring loco. Drool sparkled. Watching him fight to speak was cursed creepy. "Believe," he said. "Just. *Believe.*"

"You're a real –"

"Just" – he was almost laughing, breathing and jaw both loose – "*lead*. People follow, always follow." Then he seemed to remember something. He said, "Leave the city, we must *go.*"

"We need to get the rhez clear before they start looking for us – once they find Jemara, they'll tear this cursed city apart to get us." She watched his crazed expression. "You need to go somewhere?"

He nodded, blinking as if he fought to focus his vision.

"North... coast-road. But quiet. We must go... *must go...*"

"Okay, north," she repeated. "I picked up barter-stuff, but not much. Where we going?"

"Fhaveon," he said. Then he pulled himself upwards and whispered in her ear.

She stopped dead, sudden chills chasing over her flesh.

"You're jesting? Even if we manage to get as far as the Lord city, we'll not find someone to –"

"We'll find... someone," said Ress. "We must. No time no time no *time*. Found my mind – my courage – Ecko showed me. We must *remember*!"

Remember.

For a long moment, Jayr said nothing, her mind turning over the implications of the intended destination – wondering at the sheer crazed impossibility of the idea. *Ecko showed me.*

She would be walking to her own death and carrying him with her.

But her resentment crystallised, shattered.

Why the rhez not? It's not like there's anything for us here. I trust you, Ress. I swear, you're the only sane one left.

She said softly, "It's a damned good thing you've got *me* looking after you, old man, 'cause I got nothing left to lose." A frown flickered across his features, his mouth started to move, but she spoke over him. "Fhaveon it is. If I have to carry you all the cursed way."

Assured that the injured Saravin was in the best hands, Scribe Mael had gone to Fletcher Wyll's secret meeting.

He needed to understand.

After the first one, though, it had been woefully apparent that Wyll, for all his ideals, had no idea which feet to put his boots on. He'd made a pretty speech, but when the time had come for planning, for decisions, he'd had no idea how to proceed. Political rhetoric was fine – but it was a great deal easier to descry the current situation than it was to build a new one.

Mael had noticed, at the second meeting, that many had not come back.

Already, he doubted the security of this neophyte movement. With the tan commander Mostak disgraced and remanded for Cylearan's murder, Phylos was now in absolute control of both the Cartel and the soldiery. His reach was wide; his might vast. The very future of the Varchinde now lay entirely in the Merchant Master's hands – his sheer power gave Mael the shivers.

Fletcher Wyll's second meeting had been held in the same place – the ironically named Angel, a small tavern cellar at one side of the city's lazy and decorous midriff. They'd had no rocklights, only tallow candles that danced ominous figments across the whitewashed walls. Stamping and raucous noises had come from above, causing trickles of wood-dust from the beams to tumble through the smoky air and onto the tables. The Angel's proprietor was a supporter of Wyll's sincere but haphazard cause – though, Mael thought, his ale might have been better.

However poor the ale, though, and however vague the group's intentions, Fletcher Wyll's concerns were genuine and his passion powerful. He was more idealist than organiser – a craftsman with a sudden and unexpected new vocation – and his call was strong.

"A core of strength," he'd said, his voice ringing. "A bold few who have seen the truth and understand what is happening to our city. The harvest falters – we know this. But Phylos hoards our terhnwood, arms the city's soldiers against her own manors and traders, and against the grasslands entire. How can I get wood for my arrows, when I have nothing to trade? How will I get twine, and glue, and feathers for my fletchings? And without my arrows, how useless is my bow? And is this not true for every one of you sitting here? Andrin – without tehrnwood, how will you have the fibres for the tools that shape your clay? Will you craft with your hands alone? Farrhon, without terhnwood, how will you craft your adornments so loved by the ladies? How will you trade for your family's food? And you, Mael, without terhnwood, how will you even have paper?" The use of his name had made him start. "And that is just where it begins – no weapons, no tools, no trade, no books or records. Our very structure will come undone!"

Mael had listened to him patiently, trying to sort out how he felt. In the city above – out there, over their heads – the Terhnwood Harvester's Cartel had brought in new measures. Terhnwood distribution was being rationed, now, it was no longer to be used for non-essential items, such as jewellery or personal decoration. The soldiery patrolled markets and bazaars; many had been sent out to the farmlands. There were rumours Fhaveon was withholding her terhnwood supplies to other cities; rumours that they, in response, would withhold stocks of wood and stone. Fletcher Wyll had a gift for seeing the truth of these things.

And yet, Mael mused, as he slipped up the stone steps and out into the early evening streets, word had come from the Council of Nine that there was no cause to be concerned. Terhnwood was hardy, it was a fast-growing crop – the Cartel was controlling the spread of the blight by burning. The people had only to be patient, and all would be well. They were clearing the fields, planting again...

The old scribe was so intent on his thoughts that he nearly fell over the beggar.

The roadway was a small one, an ascending curve that wound its way carefully up the side of the city. The death of the sun streaked a warm glow between the buildings. The shrouded figure was crouched at the side of the road, shadowed by a balcony; no one else seemed to have seen it.

Mael stopped, startled.

When the thin hand lifted a bowl, the scribe patted his pouches regretfully, wondering what he had to offer.

Around him, the people were heads down, all of them wrapped in their own thoughts and business. Tensions flickered between them like the wind-dancing dust – they paid the old scribe no attention. A glance told Mael that the area's soldiery were approaching, though still a distance away.

He looked back down at the dirty, road-stained figure. As the man moved, the dying sun caught his shabby cloak and gave him an odd glimmer of authority.

"I've nothing for you," Mael said, apologising. He leaned down. "You don't want to stay there, my friend, not for too much longer."

The man's extended hand was thin, and it shook. It had old calluses – but not from weapons. They were very similar to Mael's own, the distinctive bump on the middle finger that denoted a fellow scribe, a bookkeeper, a man with his letters. Something in Mael's blood shivered, like uneasy recognition. He glanced again at the incoming soldiers.

He leaned down closer, the plains wind picking at his thin hair. Discreetly, he tried for a look under the man's hood.

"I mean it," he said. "The grunts aren't very sympathetic up here. You'd best... Dear Gods."

It was involuntary, he drew back, his hands to his mouth, not quite sure what he'd seen.

The soldiers had paused to stop a woman, well-dressed and imperious. Her strident tones carried across the wind.

In odd counterpoint, the man was muttering, "No time, no time, no time, no *time*..."

Mael shook himself. Without quite knowing why, he extended a hand and pushed the man's hood slightly back.

No time.

As he did, he became aware that the beggar was not alone – that there was a heavy-shouldered shadow loitering further back under the balcony. His first thought was that the shadow was some sort of attacker, and he was torn with the risk of calling the soldiers for help and chancing their reaction. Then he realised that the shape was protective, not hostile.

The beggar had a *bodyguard*?

Another part of his attention, though, was taken by the old man's face, his crazed eyes, the sheer blazing determination of his expression. The sun was behind him and his face was in shadow; his hair and beard were greying, though haloed with light. His skin was weathered, and there was drool on his chin. But he had the single most compelling gaze that the scribe had ever seen.

No time.

Mael had a powerful urge to draw him, to exaggerate those features – to try and understand how any man's face could come to look like that...

...but he had no time.

The soldiers were moving again, coming closer. Mael crouched right down, allowing the people in the roadway to break their line of sight.

He said, "What do you want?"

The man's intense gaze did not leave Mael's own. His mouth worked for a moment, as if he sought the shape of the words to answer the question. His lips were cracked. Mael cursed himself for not bringing his waterskin – or a mug of the tavern's ale, no matter how poorly brewed.

Then the man said, articulating very carefully. "A... boat." He licked his lips, his expression tight with effort. "Need... trade... for passage."

"You'll have to go north, to Ikira, Teale, to one of the outposts." Mael was utterly baffled, simultaneously intrigued. "Do you even know where you are?"

The soldiers were close behind him now, it sounded like they'd stopped someone else. The scribe spared a thought to wonder why they were being so aggressive, but the man was still speaking.

"Fhaveon. Need.... a boat." Spittle flew. "Have... to trade. Please."

His gaze was brilliant with insanity. Mael had seen madmen during his days in the hospice, but nothing like this. The feeling of *focus* that came from this man was absolutely mesmerising. Again, he heard himself speak, as though the very words had been pulled from his mouth, "How can I help you?"

Then the bodyguard said, "They've turned this way, get back now." The voice was female – startling Mael slightly, though he wasn't really sure why.

The heavy-shouldered figure leaned down to yank the

beggar back against the side of the building. She, too, was heavily cloaked.

But Mael was sure he'd seen Kartian scarring, the deliberate, elaborate carven cruelty inflicted by the CraftMasters of the Western Mountains.

Who in the name of the world herself were these people?

He stood up, turning around just as the soldiers reached him. They were young, casually arrogant; they eyed him up and down with a certain sharp scorn.

He met their gazes, smiled politely, moved as if to go on his way.

They watched him for a moment, then continued downwards, around the bend in the roadway. Mael kept his bland smile until they had passed the Angel, Wyll's tavern on the bend's outermost corner, then he turned back to the shadow of the balcony.

"It's okay," he said. "They've gone."

He felt an odd sense of relief when both figures moved in response to his words. The crazed old man was huddled by the wall, shuddering, muttering. The bodyguard came forward and put back her hood.

Mael stared.

His heart was pounding.

She was young and very beautiful, classically Archipelagan in feature, high-cheekboned, tanned and oddly haughty. Her beauty was offset – or maybe enhanced – by the incredible scar-work that had been carved into her skin. Her head was shaven down both sides, also carefully scarred, and her remaining scalplock was long and heavy and braided down one shoulder.

For one moment, she reminded him forcibly of Phylos.

Then she spoke. "We need a boat."

"It depends on where you're going," Mael said. The setting sun was in his eyes now and he raised an arm to block out the light. "You'll need to get to Teale, or –"

"I'll need stuff to trade," the woman told him. Her attitude was defensive and abrasive, the bristle of someone who expected a fight with every breath. Whoever she was, she was as strange and intriguing as the madman she protected. "And I'll need a pilot – I can't sail the damned thing. Where's this 'Teale' – in the city?"

"It's north, though only a day or so," Mael said. "The passage should be clear. If you like, there are still caravans…"

As he spoke, he realised the caravans were no longer a certainty. Teale was a fishing outpost, though he assumed that fish and salt were still considered worth their terhnwood.

What there was left.

The woman blinked. Her eyes were dark, almost as dark as a Kartian's, though her skin and hair had the shades of the Varchinde. She was an oddity, fascinating. She glared at him for a moment, then nodded curtly.

"Okay," she said. "We'll go that way." She bent to help the muttering madman to his feet.

As she did so, a burst of sound came from the roadway. The madman crouched back against the wall, cowering with his hands over his head. The woman shifted, came to her toes as if ready and wanting to fight.

Mael had a horrible feeling that he knew what that noise was.

That noise was the door of the Angel being beaten down.

Hoping he was wrong, he turned.

In the roadway below him, there was a tan of soldiers, he recognised the emblem of their tan commander, Ythalla – one of the more vocal of Phylos's sympathisers. Six of them were carrying a heavy log of wood, chipped to a rough point. Three to each side, they swung it against the tavern door.

Mael said, "Oh good Gods."

The scarred woman stood, her fists tight against her sides. She was trembling. The madman had crept forward and was peering around the edge of the wall. His hand against the whitewash was clawed with tension.

Silently and together, they watched.

The door splintered but did not give. Mael could see over the tavern's roof, to figures spilling out into the small garden, glancing back, and then shimmying over the wall. There was Andrin, Farrhon, and others he recognised. As the door split, snagging the point of the ram for a moment, he saw there was another tan, a little further down the sloping gardens, waiting for them.

He said, again, more softly, "Oh good Gods."

Under Ythalla's stern discipline, the ram-team yanked the heavy trunk back out of the door and went at it with feet, splintering the wood around the drop-bar on the far side. In a moment, the doorway was clear and the soldiers were inside. Sounds of shouting and chaos rang back to where they crouched.

The people in the street had scattered.

The scarred woman's trembling grew tighter. She said, "What're they doing?"

The madman laughed, a soft noise that was somehow laden with grief. He said quietly, "They're dancing. A dance unchanged. See? No one has time. Not any more."

Mael said, "They can't do this. They can't just –!"

The woman's snort cut him dead. They could and they would and they were – and he knew there would be more of the same.

This wasn't just about hoarding terhnwood any more.

Something in him whispered, *It's started*.

Shortly after, two of the tan emerged from the shattered doorway, Fletcher Wyll dangling between them like a broken toy. He was bloodied and bruised, and they were laughing at their triumph. The scarred woman inhaled sharply, her anger tangible.

The man said, "No, Jayr. No."

Jayr. The name was familiar, but Mael couldn't think about it now. He watched as they dragged out the tavern's owner, equally battered. He felt his own rise of rage, of sorrow and helplessness, and he turned away.

Frustration pricked at the backs of his eyes.

"It was planned," he said. "Cylearan was popular with the soldiery. He made a martyr of her – just so he could buy their allegiance. Rid himself of Mostak. Consolidate. The whole damn thing was *planned*."

Saravin, his intestines spilling through his fingers. Cylearan, her neck broken – a sacrifice to ensure the soldiers' loyalty to Phylos. Mostak, seized; Valicia, damaged; Demisarr, dead. House Valiembor was gone, but for Selana – and Phylos forged her every move. The Council of Nine was a jest; it no longer existed.

Phylos had secured complete power in the city.

But *why*?

What did he actually want? Why was he hoarding terhnwood, consolidating his authority? He had control, but what did he intend to do with it? It seemed crazed.

Mael found that his eyes were wet and he snuffled, wiping a hand under his nose like a child. He was no warrior, no speaker, no politician. He was an old man, and he drew pictures.

The scarred woman – Jayr – thumped his shoulder and nearly put him on his arse.

She said, "You came out of that building."

"Yes." He could hear hammering, now, the sounds of workers placing a military seal over the tavern door. The street was absolutely empty and he knew that they'd have to move – and soon.

The madman was laughing, thin and high and crazed. His humour was severe and it scraped harsh on Mael's ears. Jayr bent to quieten him, but he grabbed her arm and stood himself up, shaking still.

His eyes were focused all wrong, his pupils different sizes. He lurched forwards like a drunkard and grabbed Mael's arm.

The intensity that Mael had seen in him before had gone, now he just looked insane. He said, "I can stop this. All of this. I know. I know the answers." He laughed again. "I know *everything*!"

It was a cackle, loud enough to make the heads of the remaining soldiery turn.

Jayr swore.

"Shh!" Mael placed his hands over the madman's cracked lips. "You're not going to get any boat if you make a racket like that. Come on. If you're going to get to Teale, then you need to move."

Somehow, helping them made him feel less helpless.

12: CRAFTMARK

THE GREEN MOUNTAINS, THE SOUTHERN VARCHINDE

Long days, sweating and itching and weary, walking and aching.

Long nights. Cold air and hard ground, looming trees and rising foothills; shadows that roamed flickering-free in the moonlight. In more than twenty returns as a fighting warrior freeman, Redlock had never been this far off the trade-roads.

And it was making him cursed twitchy.

More than once, in the small times of the night, when watching the sleeping hummocks of his companions, he'd started at a figment, a sound. He'd prowled the darkness, bristling with combat tension, then sat watching the fire, his back tense with the unknown.

Amos, Fhaveon, the Varchinde – they all seemed very far away now, lost behind the crumbled stone shoulders of the Green Mountains, shrugging their way free from the forest's heavy canopy. This was a place untrodden, of woven waterways and nighttime nacre. Triqueta had called it the "Gleam Wood", Ecko had called it firewood, Amethea had said something about ancient legends, now forgotten... the axeman had missed the details.

This was probably one of those places where you weren't supposed to leave the path.

If it'd ever had a damned path in the first place.

By every cursed god and his ale, Redlock didn't want to be out here. New weapons or no, this seemed all wrong – as if they were heading for something they had no way to understand. The bustle and strife of the trade-roads, the politics of the cities, he knew, but this? This was outside his experience and he didn't cursed well like it much.

Many times, there in the chill of the pre-dawn, he'd wondered what the rhez Nivrotar was playing at – why she'd sent them out here.

What she *really* wanted.

And whether she was expecting them back.

Sometimes, with his hips aching from the cold ground, his knee-joints clicking with the weariness of climbing and slipping and jumping, he wondered if they had simply been forgotten – and if the Varchinde had even noticed.

And then the coughing would double him over, hurting his ribs and flecking his hands with red. He'd done everything he could to hide it from the others – they trusted him and followed him, and he was damned to all the rhez if he'd let them see him falter.

He was Redlock, for the Gods' sakes. Whatever this endless cursed woodland hid within its glimmering tree roots, he'd face it, and he'd beat it.

Always.

Yet despite his solidity and determination, the woodland's eventual ending brought with it a huge sense of relief. When they climbed down at last from the forested foothills, and the dense trees began to thin and the scent of sea air filtered through the leaves, he felt his heart lift with light. As the dank and the moss receded, his doubts faded. He surged ahead of the others, and began to believe that the nightmare trek was over. It might, just might, be all right...

They weren't about to fall off the damned edge of the world, or anything stupid.

Silently, the axeman cursed himself for superstitious horseshit.

Over the crumbling mountains, the sun was lowering to the red glow of the day's end and Redlock stopped with an unnamed weight falling from his hurting shoulders. His undertunic was stuck to his back, his legs were aching with the long day, but he leaned on a bent knee with something like relief.

His lungs heaved; he spasmed hard with the need to cough. Smothered it.

Ahead of him, the ground became flatter and less harsh, the woodland parted to give glittering hints of open water. Beside him was a small river, frothing close to the coastline as if it really was the edge of the world. It ran swift, leaves like boats upon its surface.

On its far side, the ground had been thrown hard upwards as if the mountains had shuddered with some final spasm. A sharply rising twist of cliff tore free from grass and soil. It rose in grey rock striations to an odd lookout point, a Gods-crafted tower.

Redlock eyed it warily, allowed himself a moment to catch his breath. He shoved loose hair out of his eyes and glanced over his shoulder, wondering how far back the others had lingered.

He allowed himself the luxury of a cough, his breath barking harsh in the air.

And then something caught his eye.

On the opposite bank of the river and almost hidden by an overgrowth of the Gleam Wood's mossed trees, there was just about the last thing he'd been expecting.

A window.

Still leaning on his knee, sheltered by the edge of the woods, he stifled his coughing and stared.

Its arch was broken, tumbledown and ruined, but gradually Redlock realised that it was not alone.

Slowly, as the light stretched away from him, he began to see the angles of stone that showed amidst the overgrowth, the flat planes of mossed walls that had not been touched by human hand in…

He shivered.

…how long?

The shiver crept out across his shoulders, wonder and wariness. This was no more a place of merchants than the gutted wreckage of the Great Fayre. How long since anyone had lived out here, since anyone had come this far off the roadway?

Carefully, the axeman crept forwards to the muddied bank of the small river, and crouched by the bole of a tree.

Could there have been a village here once – here at the very outermost point of the Varchinde – charcoal burners, foresters? Could there have been some town reachable only by water, a place with no trade-road to tell of its presence? Scattered through the woods, there had been odd fragments of crafted stone, but at no point had they seen any sign that a road had carved this way – that any feet but their own had ever come around the edge of the Green Mountains and down into the wood.

By the damned Gods…

How had Nivrotar known this was here?

He began to see the ruins were not haphazard – there were pathways, cracked and splintered with time and growth, old stone buildings grown over by weaving roots, pulled down by their sheer strength. There were dead stone windows, empty and staring, old doorways gaping wide, steps that led from nowhere to nowhere.

And all of it overgrown by the seethe of beautiful, strangling creeper.

He stood upright, somehow trembling, oddly breathless.

He had no idea what the rhez he'd just found.

And in just that moment, there was no movement. Not a creature, not a bird. Not a human life, other than his own. If anything had ever lived out here, it had died a thousand returns before, rotted into the grass and been forgotten. Not knowing how far back the others were, Redlock was awed and utterly, utterly alone.

Then, behind him, something rustled.

The axeman wheezed, tried to swallow the urge to cough. It made his ribs burn, his vision blur – he struggled to draw an even breath, control his wracking body.

On the river's far side, the creeper danced at him, laughing silent.

He turned, shattering the moment.

Some distance back from the water's edge, Triqueta emerged from the wood, leading the chearl. She was lined and weary, her bright skin dusty, her hair straggled and stuck to her face. The laden chearl was restless, its eyes showed white and its hide was grimy, darkened with sweat. Placid though the beasts usually were, the Banned woman had her hands full, and her blades hung loose at her belt.

Behind her, Amethea was pale and swaying – her eyes darting from shadow to shadow, from dappled sunset to woodland sound. She caught sight of the broken stone walls, the last of the sunlight cresting the mountains and making them glow like fire, and her jaw dropped.

Even Ecko, barely visible in the seething colours of cloak and skin, seemed oddly subdued.

All of them were exhausted, weary from the endless woods. Redlock had no idea what they had found but he had the distinct and creeping feeling that their presence out here had little to do with chance.

And frankly, he didn't like it.

Ecko had been stuck with firewood duty.

All this fucking way, right out here in the ass-end of beyond, and he'd been lumbered – no pun intended – with collecting fucking *sticks*.

Dry sticks.

In the rain.

No one ever told you this shit – you only ever heard about the glamorous bits. It was all monsters and fighting and flirting and beer and sunlight and heaps of fucking treasure. No one ever told you that you had to crap in a hole, wipe your ass with wet leaves and then go hunting for dry sticks in the pissing fucking rain. Hell, finishing up this program could come after he'd skipped through the woods and sung a few songs and probably had a vision in a pond or something...

Chrissakes.

The only vision Ecko wanted was for this Noble Quest to be over, the sulphur in the bag.

He quit hunting sticks and crouched in the lee of a crumbling stone wall, his cloak hunched about him and the rain seeping cold down the back of his neck.

Sulphur, chrissakes. Never mind the Greek fire, right now he'd be better off inventing microfibre or something.

Fidgeting with irritation, he picked up a loose twig – a wet one – snapped it and wished he had a way to make it burn.

All the way from the trade-road, he'd been getting angrier by the minute: made claustrophobic by necessity, caught like a fucking trace-animal, forced to move in one direction. He felt like he was following footprints, some handy scenario pack. All he wanted to do was to kick this shit into *life. Make* it fucking happen.

Like now.

Like you jus' fuckin' watch me.

In answer, the rain grew colder.

Yeah, I know your game. But I'm gonna play this out, bitch, an' then I'm gonna bring this shit down round your ears. I'm gonna tear a hole right through the fucking sky...

Water ran down the inside of his neckline, daring him. It felt like he was being laughed at.

Of course you are. When you're finished collecting sticks.

Against Redlock's specific instruction, he'd crossed the small river, skirted the bottom edge of the rock they'd named the "lookout tower". He'd been hoping for more monsters, goblins and skeletons, prancing elves and luring dryads – hell, they weren't gonna be very dry in all of this – but the busted fragments of the ruin seemed deader than Eliza's sense of humour. Ancient legends, his mottled ass – right now, if he couldn't have his char-hole in the sky, he'd give his right bollock for geo-tracking, a silenced nine-mil and a thermos of fucking *tea*.

Tea. Chrissakes. He really was turning normal – this place was messing with his *head*.

He was cold.

He missed the Bard.

What?

The thought came out of nowhere. It was a twinge of conscience, a sudden wrinkle of doubt and hesitation. He somehow almost wished that Roderick *was* there, could help him, could tell him if he was doing the right thing...

Then he caught himself, threw the thought down and stepped on it. Felt it squash into the mud.

No. Lugan sold me out; Rodders fucking died. Fuck that. I don't need either of them; I don't need help. I don't need any other fucker to hold my hand an' tell me what to do. He was almost railing at the glowering sky. *I jus' wanna get to the end of this!*

Fuming, he fought the adrenaline down. Another stick detonated into fragments in his fingers, the snapping loud in the wet. He dropped the bits, shook them off like insects, like they'd bite him. Then he huddled up further as it began to rain more heavily, spattering down through the leaves.

Slowly, the sunlight died. The darkness rose to meet the cloud, and rivulets of dirt ran between his feet.

Then, as the nacre of the trees began to glimmer ghostlike, something caught his gaze.

Creeping silent, also this side of the water and close enough for his heatseeker, Triqueta was hunting. Her blur of warmth moved slowly between crumbling pillars. Curled against the rain to keep her bowstring dry, she was quiet as death, placing her feet with care.

Ecko stayed still. Breathless. Fascinated.

He wondered if she was on the trail of something – she was elegant and precise, somehow delicate; even in the rain she made no sound. As she passed across in front of him, he resisted the urge to scare the shit out of her, just for the hell of it.

Instead, he let her go, then slipped out behind her, into the full force of the rain. Keeping her just within range of his oculars, he began to follow her route.

Who knew, if he was lucky she might just be waking all the beasties up.

It was wet.

No, it wasn't just wet, it was absolutely *pissing* it down. Not even London got rain like this. It was a deluge, for chrissakes, a silver-grey sheet in front of his nose.

The soil under his feet was running with muck, slick with leaf mould. Roots wound under and through it, just waiting to make him stumble. His cloak had become a bastard nuisance – snagging on low branches and dragging down with water. He was almost tempted to dump it, but something in him couldn't part with his identity, with the things that remained of his London self, his real self, with the image of Ecko that he still needed to present...

Whether that was to himself or the world outside.

Inside.

Whatever.

His feet skidded again.

Then, through a fuzz of rain, he picked up the faintest blur of heat-trace, somewhere between the trees – not Triqueta, this was a new something, a breathing something, four-footed and prowling wary.

It was close. And it was too damn fucking quiet.

Now that's what I meant! Anticipation skittered, thrilling. *See? This is a helluva lot more fun than sticks.*

He skidded a third time. Impatiently, he picked up the cloak-hem and bundled it under one arm. In the faint gleam of tree-light, another corner of crumbled building loomed suddenly into view. He dropped low behind its cover.

Ecko was grinning properly now. Swap the canopy for the grey sky, the stone ruins for the tessellated buildings of London, and hell, he could almost be at home – this was more the fuck like it!

The blur that was Triqueta had paused. She seemed to be crouched behind or in something; a sharp, black line cut off her warm colour. A distance from her, the Something Else had crouched belly-down, like some giant street cat. A long tail curved over its back.

Triqueta hadn't seen it. Any second now, she was gonna be dinner – unless...

Oh for fuck's sake.

...unless he jumped in and rescued her.

Nice touch Eliza, just push my buttons whydontcha... Daaaaance...

Chances of successful scenario running at...

Then, out of nowhere, the thought hit him like a fucking jackhammer: *Fuck you, you bitch: what if I don't rescue her?*

What if I say, not any more? What if I walk away? What if I cut to the chase and go find the sulphur without playing Random Encounter Bad Guy?

Then whatcha gonna do? You'll lose your lever. Your strings.

How you gonna make me dance then?

It was like some dark epiphany, for chrissakes. The eagerness of it pinned him right to the spot, to the weathered wall he rested against...

See? I don't care. *You can't make me* care.

The beastie was close now, silent as nightmare. Ecko had forgotten the relentless sheeting of the rain, the cold light of the trees, his numb fingers. He was intent only on the critter as it stole forwards, low to the filthy ground.

Temptation beckoned him like the long middle finger of the dryad.

But Redlock was close, and he was a kick-ass fighter – pushing fifty or not, he'd chopped the centaur stallion to gobbets, and Maugrim had been a bloody, hacked-up mess. The axeman might just carve the beastie into beastie steak, already, and then there'd be a fuckton of awkward questions...

Shit.

Ecko's point of indecision teetered, swung one way and then the other; its breathlessness seemed to last an age. Triqueta shifted. The noise was minute, but the beast raised its head. In the patchy moonlight, its face was oddly flat.

What?

He didn't get time to register. Suddenly, the thing was moving. Fast.

And Ecko found he was moving after it, the moment gone, the test passed, the opportunity – if that's what it had been – lost.

The critter was fast, low to the ground with its odd arc of tail lashing upwards over its back. It had heavy, curved claws, which scraped on roots and stones, the noises sending shudders down Ecko's spine. He ran parallel, staying with it. Old walls loomed suddenly out of the darkness, but he was fast enough to miss them.

His adrenaline was pumping now: that familiar, glorious warmth, that flood-rush like a fix. The rain was slackening, the slippery ground was making him skid, but it no longer mattered. His telescopics spun, his oculars flickered to find targets – stonework, root-fork, monster's head and claws. His dark grin spread until it almost took in his ears.

Hell, Triqueta was still out there ahead of him. Maybe he should let the beastie get its claws on her, and then leap in at the last minute...

Ta-dah!

Like, if he *had* to keep doin' this hero shit...

The beast slowed, paused. It watched for a moment, then crouched, cat-like, tail quivering. As he closed on it, he could hear it breathing, a heavy, sensual sound, like a stalker's phone call. It was damned smart for a predator – intellect as well as instinct.

Was this one of those "bweao" things that everyone talked about?

He eased closer still, nervousness flickering but his grin gleeful and unholy. And even closer, until the beast was right there in front of him, its rear claws splaying and flexing, digging into the mulch. It was bigger than he'd thought, its fur was clumped and matted with water.

The rain gusted, patchy and thinning to drizzle. Triqueta was low to the ground, bow in hand, doing her best to keep the string dry – but the thing was downwind and hunting the hunter.

For a moment, the fantasy played out – the rescue, the gratitude – then he got a fucking grip, for chrissakes, and closed in as tight as he could go.

It was only as the beast threw itself forwards and its rear claws spat dirt that Ecko realised what he'd found.

It had a name – he knew it had a name – but for the fucking life of him, he couldn't remember what it was. As it left the ground, springing cat-like, the warning was out of his mouth before he could stop it, and Triqueta was turning, bringing up the bow.

But the thing was too close.

It was on her in a moment, slamming her to the muddy floor, its claws raking as it brought her down. Its tail was to Ecko, but he could see Triq's expression as she fell – a look on her face that wasn't fear, wasn't her warriors' focus, but something like pure horror – a look like she was trying not to chuck up.

It didn't stop her though. Nauseous or not, she went for the weapons at her belt.

The beast was massive, oozing muscle. Ecko didn't care – as Triq came back with both blades, he slammed a foot into the thing's rear end, knocking its ass sideways and making it roll –

Its tail struck at him.

Like a snake, like a whip – it lashed across the side of his face with an impact that made him falter, pain shooting through his skull. He fell back, his right ocular seeming to spark – or was it just his vision? – and Triqueta was on her feet, a claw-slash in her shoulder but both blades out.

She snarled at it, "Come on then. Come on then!"

She crouched low, moved one way. Ecko, nerves singing, face throbbing, cloak tangled with rain, moved the other.

The beastie, shoulders low, swung round to track him.

And then he saw what was wrong with it.

It had a face. It had a fucking *face*, a human face. It had a face that had been stitched or stuck onto a head like a lion; a face contorted with hate or with some terrifying need to speak. Its teeth were bared like a cat's, long and sharp, somehow too big for its mouth; they were yellow and bits of fuck-knows-what were caught in them.

For a moment, Ecko had a flash of the same piss-leaking terror that he'd felt in the House of Sarkhyn – that sickening sense of something wrong, something twisted, not only in body, but in brain.

Creature created.

Where the hell had that phrase come from?

He didn't get time to think about it.

The tail lashed at Triq but she was too fast. A single cut of her blade severed it. It fell, thrashing like half a snake, knotting about itself just like Ecko's guts were doing.

The human face contorted, tried to speak – mouth shaping word or cry...

Ecko shuddered.

Jesus Hairy Christ. Fuck this for a game of fucking soldiers!

He snap-kicked it in the teeth, kicked it again. Triq's blades bit into its hind end, slashed at tendons. It lashed its half a tail at her, bared its teeth at Ecko, reached for him with dinner-plate paws, with hooked claws that shone in the glow of the trees.

As he kicked it again, kicked it and kicked it and *kicked* it as if he couldn't shove the fucking thing too far away from him, as if he needed it to die at his feet, as if the fear that it generated could only be faced by the surge of adrenaline and blood and violence...

He could see that its mouth was moving – it was trying to cry out, to say something.

It was trying to speak to him.

He stopped, panting. Still shuddering with horror, he dropped to one knee in front of the thing's now-broken face, the blood that oozed from its too-human shattered nose, eyes swelling and blackening...

He said, "What the fuck are you? What the fuck...?"

Its mouth tried to form words with swollen lips, with broken, jagged teeth. It lashed its half a tail over its back, dropping gore into its patched fur. It said, carefully enunciating the symbols, "Eck... Oh... Eck... Oh..."

What the hell?

Shuddering, he kicked it as hard as he could, shattering its jaw and making it flop loose from its broken face. Even as

Triqueta slammed both blades to the hilt between its ribs, even as its face pulped under the force of the blow, it was laughing.

Human, mocking, cold.

It was laughing at *him*.

13: FOUNDERSDAUGHTER FHAVEON

Saravin finally died in the early hours of the morning, his last words lost. The wound in his belly had become infected, and his consciousness had been wandering. Whatever that final breath that passed his lips, if it uttered his greatest dreams or life's regrets, there was no one to care.

Almost no one.

A runner from the hospice brought the news to Mael, his tent closed now and his drawings increasingly rare and sombre. He nodded at the messenger, the news strangely unreal, not really sinking home.

For a while afterwards, the old scribe sat at his unshuttered window, staring out at the street. Mael did not have a magnificent view of the vast Varchinde, the descending slope of the city's wonder did not drop away beneath him like the decorous chasubles of the priests; instead, he could see a small and narrow roadway, these days almost empty of people.

A new power had taken Fhaveon. And it was fear.

The raid on the Angel had been one of many on that day – the city's military, now purely an extension of Phylos's might, had had little trouble locating the somewhat haphazard pockets of resistance and destroying them. Some were calling it "The Day of Reckoning". Others were calling it progress. Mael had few words for anything.

How did that old Range Patrol axiom go? "All that is necessary for evil to triumph…"?

But he didn't really believe in evil, nothing so prosaic. Many returns of studying people's faces had made him understand that things were more complex than that – in order to draw a caricature, you needed to understand how all the features fitted together.

People were complex things, made up of many different parts.

For a moment, he regretted not being at the bedside of his old friend, not reminding him of the crazed antics of their younger days, not holding his hand to the end – but his listlessness had sunk home now, and he simply stared out of the window, grey in the sky, grey in his heart.

Saravin was *dead*. His friend had been a game piece, used and cast aside. And he had not been the only one.

Was there even any point to resistance? Mael was not a man for a wager, but he could have bet that he would end the same way.

Long ago, in his hospice days, he'd had a word for this mood – this dejection, this pointlessness. It was not a black mood, not the savagery of depression or fear; it was a grey mood, an emptiness, an uncaring. The city could have crumbled around him and he would not have mustered the energy or decisiveness to actually get up and flee.

Once, he had found an old text that listed it as a malady. The faded inks had named it "Kasien", an old word, almost akin to the more modern Kazyen, the sort-of manifest nothingness that was somehow a part of the most ancient sagas.

For a moment, his mind turned to the madman and to Jayr, the strange Kartian-scarred Archipelagan woman that had come with him. He wondered where they had gone, if they had ever found their way to Teale or Ikira, then onwards to their destination.

What they needed to do.

But his eyes were still on the road, the birds wheeling under a sullen sky, and he couldn't find it in his heart to care. His beautiful city was rotting at the core. In Fhaveon, "nothing" seemed not only possible, but preferable.

Slowly, he became aware of a woman walking along the road. She was alone, discreetly furtive, peering at the doors and then scurrying on. As his eyes focused on her, the unlikeliness of her presence gradually crystallised through his grey. He wondered who she was looking for.

On another day, he might have gone out to help her, but his Kazyen, his nothing, had soaked into his skin and blood and bone and he could not find a reason to move.

She came closer.

In the roadway, the birds took flight as she walked.

She stopped outside Mael's small home, his own chamber a small part of the communal building that rose around him. The beams were low, but his scattering of drawings and herbal lore allowed him to live here securely. No one ever came to see him.

But the woman approached his door and raised a hand. She paused, tentative, took a breath, and knocked.

Stunned, though he had seen her coming, Mael was stuck to the spot, his heart thumping as if he had been caught in a crime. Like a child scared of the dark, he was absolutely unable to move. He stared out past the shutter, as if expecting her to fade away like a figment in the daylight.

But the woman took a step back, and looked in through the window.

She met his gaze, and his heart nearly came out through his chest.

Upon his front yardway stood Selana Valiembor, only child of the murdered Demisarr, last descendant of Saluvarith, and Lord Foundersdaughter of Fhaveon. And she was alone.

When he rallied his wits, Mael threw open the door and almost yanked the girl in off the road. Not even thinking to apologise, he slammed the door behind her and turned back to the window, slamming the shutters and then peering through them as though he harboured a fugitive.

Putting back her hood and dusting her – somewhat oversized – trader's garments, the Lord of the City watched him carefully.

She said, "Why did he die?"

The question caught Mael off-guard, but he knew whom she meant.

Saravin.

Turning back from the street, he bit down on a faint desire to be acerbic about the consequences of a blade in the belly. Instead, he said, "My Lord." The words were ludicrous and awkward. "Saravin... was very fond of you." He studied her, her pale and drawn features. "He was concerned for the future of the city."

"Why did he enter that contest?" She didn't meet his gaze. She was looking around her, and Mael realised that he should probably offer her a seat, a drink, his knee.

Instead, he managed a cautious shrug. "I don't know, my Lord."

"I think you do."

Now, she fixed him with a look. Something in her face reminded him, not of her dead father, but of her uncle, Mostak, the now-disgraced commander of the soldiery. She was young and out of her depth, but she was Valiembor to her fingertips.

He answered, not entirely honestly, "Rhan."

The name made her colour, high spots of violence in her cheeks. She bit her lip as if trying not to weep, but Mael took a risk and hammered the point home. "With the loss of the Seneschal, Saravin felt you needed a friend on the Council."

A frown touched her face. "I have Phylos."

Mael's silence was more eloquent than any response he could

have made. They stood in that tiny room, the young Lord and the old scribe, staring each other while an entire conversation floated between them, unspoken. When the girl turned away, Mael knew that every silent word had struck her, and that she was not as naïve as she appeared.

He was faintly surprised to hear himself say softly, "He died for you, my Lord. He died for Fhaveon."

He had meant Saravin, but Rhan's inclusion was both tacit and obvious.

The words made her falter. Her hands went to the tie-fastening on the front of her cloak and she dropped it in a puddle of fabric, threw herself onto one of the scribe's hard wooden seats. They had belonged to the hospice, long ago, and he'd become used to them.

Selana winced. "How do you sit on these things?"

Her flash of petulance made her suddenly girlish, out of her depth and struggling.

"Selana," he said. "My Lord." And this time, he bent his knee as he should, looked up into her face. "Saravin is... was my friend –"

His words choked off as she met his gaze. There was something in her look, some moment of the Count of Time, some taste to the air that made him stare with realisation. This girl, this woman, this daughter of Lord and niece of warrior – she was the city's future. Young as she was, she was the lynchpin of all of this – she was Phylos's ultimate gamepiece, the cover he still operated behind, at least in name – and she was sitting in his *home*.

She was an opportunity.

And whatever he said next could be absolutely critical.

He quelled a moment of panic – he was a scribe, not a politician, he was no one of any consequence. He was not a man for changing futures. And if Phylos's eyes should find her here, then the Merchant Master would be throwing Mael in the long ditch beside his old friend.

All that is necessary...

But she was *here*, delivered by the very Gods themselves perhaps, and he had to do something.

Being very, very careful about his words now, he said, "Did anyone see you come here?"

She shook her head. "Have I put you in danger? I'm the Lord of the City, I can go where I..." Somehow, she knew this wasn't true and she tailed into silence.

"Honestly, my Lord? I don't know," Mael told her. "But after the Angel, and the other raids..." He tailed off with a furtive glance through the shutters, realised that he was prevaricating and tried, again, to focus on the critical opportunity that was sitting in his front room with her hands in her lap.

"My Lord," he said. "I don't believe Rhan murdered your father."

"What?" She was caught unawares. Her jaw dropped and she stared at him. "My mother *saw* him, she –!" She bit off the sentence, though they both knew how it ended.

Mael realised he'd come in too hard, given her an abrupt chunk of information that was far too big for her to process. Frustrated, he tried to explain.

"Think about it, it makes no sense. Four hundred returns, and his loyalty was Gods-given, or so they say. Why would he throw it away? It was too much, too sudden, too... unusual." As he spoke, he found that he was gaining momentum. In explaining it to her, he was seeing it more clearly himself. "And he'd got absolutely nothing to gain. The city was secure, at peace; we had everything we needed. Nothing has threatened the Grasslands for hundreds of returns. It makes –"

"Rhan caused the blight."

"Why?"

"Because he was bored. He caused the illness so he'd have something to cure."

There was enough plausibility in *that* response to make Mael pause. Faint echoes of his grey mood lingered, tainting the air. *Bored.* Then he shook his head.

"No. I don't believe that. If he'd caused the blight, Phylos would have thrown him down for it publicly." A sudden thought occurred. "And why was it Phylos that carried out Rhan's sentence? Why not the Justicar, Halydd? Or Mostak himself?"

Selana twitched a shrug. "My uncle's dying, he's in the hospice. I can't even get in to see him."

"My Lord, you're the Foundersdaughter of Fhaveon." Mael took hold of the information like he was taking hold of her shoulders. "You can go where you choose."

She looked up, blinked at him.

"Mostak's your *family.*" Mael was thinking faster now, he was onto something here. He followed the thought through. "Or would Phylos have reason for stopping you?"

"My uncle's in isolation."

It was apologetic, and Mael knew he'd made the point.

"My Lord, we all heard the Seneschal's words, '*I love and guard this city with everything I am. And when my damned brother returns… My Lord, heed me. Without me, you and everything you love will perish in flames and screaming.*'" He could recite it flawlessly.

Selana was on her feet, pacing, her face pale.

"No. Rhan's a traitor. He hurt my family. I can't believe…!"

Mael was merciless, though his voice was gentle. "Try."

"My mother saw him!" The Lord's voice cracked as she rounded on him. "She was raped, she was thrown down and beaten. Are you telling me she made that up?"

"No, of course not." His mind was working now: he was sketching it in as he spoke, every last detail. "But there are substances that can make people suggestible, and Rhan… well, he had most of them in his house. If Phylos used them…" In a flash, he realised something else. "Oh dear Gods. Why do you think the Council charged Rhan in the first place?"

It was all fitting together now. It was like a rush, like those last few charcoal strokes when you realised that a drawing was going to be one of the best you'd done, when you had captured that moment absolutely flawlessly. Without quite knowing how, Mael found his hands on the Lord's shoulders, and he drew back, startled by his own intensity.

By the strength of his comprehension.

His grey mood had burned away completely. He felt *useful*, as though he mattered, and he could do something to help.

But as he let her go, Selana turned away and her face crumpled. He saw that her hands were tight, her teeth in her lower lip.

Belatedly remembering his manners, he said, "Can I get you something? A drink? A cloth?"

"No. Thank you." She drew herself up and her eyes gave the kind of flash that told him to hold his peace and his distance. He wondered what he'd overdone – the information or the contact. Or both. But he was an old man and he was onto something here, though he hadn't quite figured out how it fitted together. Lord or not, he was damned if he was going to apologise.

Selana dropped her gaze, turned back into a girl.

It was like a picture, lines around the outside sketching in towards the centre.

Mael was feeling better than he had done in days, since Saravin had been hurt, in fact. He could hear the old sod now, teasing him and demanding they go for an ale. *Shut up*, he told the memory. *I'm not done yet.*

The memory said to him, *Oh yes you are.*

Out of the corner of his eye, Mael caught movement on the quiet street. Selana saw his glance and turned.

She said, "Oh Gods. Do they come down here a lot?"

"You need to leave." He had forgotten her title, but neither of them cared. The tan commander Ythalla, she who had kicked down the door of the Angel only a few days before, would make short work of Mael's little home. "Back way, there's a communal cookhouse there, and a midden. It'll stink a bit, but –"

"I'll manage." She gathered her cloak and threw it about her shoulders. Her hands paused as she put up the cowl. She said, "Thank you. Saravin spoke of you sometimes, he said your eyes are the sharpest he'd ever known. He trusted you completely, in his own strange way." She grinned briefly. "I wish…" But she had no words to complete the thought.

He understood her anyway. "I'm sorry for your loss, my Lord," he said. "For our loss. He spoke often of you too." Again, that sense of fleeting but powerful opportunity, a need to say something that would open her eyes and her mind and make her think. "He said that you could be trusted to be fearless, and to do the right thing."

She mouthed the word "fearless", then pulled the cowl up over her face.

"You be fearless too," she said. "Ythalla's like some damned bweao, she's nasty." She laid her hand on his arm for a moment. "But she's also stupid. Be strong," she said, and she was gone.

Be strong.

When Mael turned to answer the door, he kept those words, that final touch, in his head.

They didn't arrest him.

Mael had found his glasses and he'd peered at the soldiers, carping and grumbling like some herb-addled elder. Disgusted, they'd searched the place and then gone on to bully the rest of the building.

By the time they'd moved further down the road, he realised that he was fighting the urge to pace. Selana, it seemed, had been bright enough to flee safely, and he could shove his pince-nez higher up his nose and retrieve a piece of his precious parchment.

He sat back down at his window, watching the moving tan through the slats of the shutters. His fingers retrieved his charcoal and started to draw.

In his head, though, there was another picture – a picture that was coming swiftly together, but that he had to take apart into its individual lines.

Phylos – hauling Rhan before the Council on drugs charges. The citizens of Fhaveon could be very pious about some things, and Rhan's unsuitable behaviour had offended certain circles for many returns. All Phylos had done was make that knowledge much more public. He'd also gained a large amount of the drug for himself.

The Merchant Master was as sharp and as merciless as a white-metal axe. He had held his peace, and held his peace, until all of this could happen at once – too fast for the city to gather its history and think, too fast for anyone to react. One moment, there was the Council, there was Rhan and Demisarr, and the next...

Mael was becoming increasingly convinced that Rhan's murder of his sworn protectorate, the rape of his wife, were a carefully crafted fiction – though he was not sure how. But what more flawless a set-up could there be? Valicia had watched her husband die, had been unable to save him, had been unable to save herself. And who would doubt her as an eye-witness?

And with the Foundersson and his wife gone, it left only Mostak – Valiembor-blooded, commander of the military, one of the most powerful men in the Varchinde. The harvest tournament, the event that had killed both Cylearan and Saravin, had been the Merchant Master removing his last real obstacle.

But *why*?

The one question that Mael still couldn't answer. "I hunger for power because I was bullied as a child" just wasn't holding any water, here. Phylos was Archipelagan, he'd been born elite. Or thinking he was.

For a moment, Mael's thoughts turned again to the scarred woman, Jayr, and to the madman she'd guarded. He wondered if they were a part of this picture, and if so, where they fitted.

But the picture in Fhaveon was too big, and he could not slot them into the image. Not yet.

He looked back out at the road.

The birds had come back, and they were pecking at something on the stones. He watched them absently for a moment, his mind and hands still sketching.

Phylos's manipulations were utterly flawless, equal parts calculated and savagely opportunistic. By controlling both the harvest and the soldiery…

Mael paused. The birds continued to peck.

The blight was the one thing that didn't fit the pattern, didn't fit with Phylos's rise to power. The harvest was faltering, yet tithes and trades were still being demanded, and the incoming goods were hoarded and held under guard. Messages from the surrounding CityWardens ranged from apologetic to hostile. Rumour on the road said that Larred Jade in Roviarath had ceased trading almost completely, and that his last bretir had carried a very curt message indeed.

The birds once again took wing, climbing up into the grey air with cold caws of displeasure.

Mael craned to see what had startled them.

There was a figure in the roadway, two.

He blinked, then took his glasses off so that he could see them clearly.

And then he stared.

The figures were not human. They stood on two legs, had two hands and two eyes, but they were not human.

They were almost seven-foot tall, long-legged and bare-chested and walked with a peculiar, distinctive gait. Their skin was tanned, decorated with ink and leather. Their hair was long and black and elaborately braided, decorated with small fragments of bone, stone and fabric.

Mael gawped, incredulous. The creatures were talking, laughing even. They had teeth like knives, eyes like roil and smoke. He had absolutely no idea what they could possibly be.

Then he realised they were wearing the belts and blades of the Fhaveon soldiery.

And they were coming down the road towards Mael's little home.

In his head, he heard Saravin, "Get out, you old fool!" He scrambled for a bag, for his charcoal and a handful of essential bits and pieces. There was food in the other room, he'd take what he could as he fled through the midden.

Almost as an afterthought, he grabbed the sketch that he had been doing, leaving faint prints of charcoal on the parchment. He looked at it for a moment, before shoving it into his pack.

He had drawn Jayr, scars and all.

14: CREATURES CREATED GLEAM WOOD

As they returned to their small and fireless camp, Amethea was on her feet. "By the Gods – what happened to you? You look like you found a war!"

Ecko had no words. The thing with the human face that had known his name – he was scared, he was fucking *scared* already, and his own fear was making him angrier than he'd ever been. His adrenaline was still firing, more anxiety than elation, and he needed it to pack its bags and fuck off.

Like now.

Eck... Oh...

Apparently, some Random Encounter Bad Guys weren't so random after all.

Well whaddaya know.

"Tell me," Triqueta said, "what's got the face of a man, the tail of a serpent and the body of some sort of damned bweao?" Her bow was across her back, her blades still in her hands, and she was as wide-eyed as he was. "Because whatever it is, it better not have any *friends*." The thing's half-tail was in her belt – she slung a blade and threw the tail down, twitching, at Amethea's feet.

The teacher, her pale hair glimmering in the tree-light, caught it before it hit the mud.

Lifting it, she said, "I can already tell you – I got given one of these last return."

"Jesus Hairy fucking Christ and little fucking *fish*!" Ecko was pacing like he'd never come down. His skin was crawling, and he couldn't make it stop. Medusa, fucksake, chimera – whatever the hell that thing was – how come it knew his name when he couldn't remember what he was supposed to call *it*?

Funny, much?

His mouth a tangle of black teeth and bitterness, he said, "What were you sayin' about ancient legends? I think we just woke 'em all up."

"The Gleam Wood's laden with superstition," Amethea replied, looking at the still-twitching half-tail in her hand, her expression a twist of fascination and disgust. "The main trade-route to Annondor goes over land – the coast's too rocky for triremes. Supposedly, this place hasn't seen human feet in hundreds of returns." She raised an eyebrow at them, held up the convulsing tail between thumb and forefinger. "Makes it the perfect place for pirates and smugglers... Are you even listening?"

Ecko snarled at her. "Fuck the geography lesson. What the *hell* did we just find?"

"And where's Redlock?" Triqueta asked.

"Scouting." Amethea shook the tail, turned it round to look at its other side. "He went up the lookout tower to see as far as the coast."

Triq snorted. "He can see in the dark now?"

Amethea shrugged. "He'd never admit it, but I think this place gives him the creeps." The tail twitched again, shuddered. "Can't imagine why."

Something in her voice brought the darkness to all of them – brought the awareness of the void of untrodden woodland, the ruins forgotten even to legend. Whatever really was out here, they were intruders, unknown and tiny against its time and history. Unconsciously, the three of them pulled together, peering outwards at the odd white light of the wood.

Ecko was starting to shiver – anger and adrenaline and come-down. The injury on his face was beginning to hurt. He wondered, stupidly, if he needed antivenin, if the bite – lash? – was gonna mess with his bloodstream, if his face was gonna swell up like the fucking Elephant Man...

Then his oculars caught it.

Not the end, not the hentai-flick nightmare this tail-thing had for a head, but the mark on its skin, like a miniature brand – a mark that was familiar.

Eck... Oh...

For a moment he stared at it, his adrenaline still shuddering, making his belly knot with tension. Then he said, "Gimme that." His targeters flashed and he grabbed it from Amethea, lifting it to see.

It writhed like a live thing. He had to look twice to be sure he'd gotten it right.

Eck... Oh...

But there was no fucking mistake about it – the thing bore the same craftmark as the terhnwood blade that had taken them to Sarkhyn's lab.

Redlock lay flat on the rock at the top of the lookout tower.

The rain had soaked into his garments, chilled his skin, plastered his hair to his face, but none of it mattered – not even the precious etched metal of his axeheads, now resting still against cold stone.

He lay in a silent jumble of disbelief, staring at the edge of the woodland and at the glitter of the eastern sea.

And at what lay between.

Over him, the clouds were thinning and the moons reached fingers of light through the gaps – prying apart the grey to look down at the rocky shoreline below. Their light glimmered on the seethe and rush of the water, on the spray that flew from the rocks.

And on the citadel that was standing there.

At the very edge of the world.

He hadn't seen it at first, but now he could look almost nowhere else – it was compelling, impossible, a wide, low shadow upon the glitter of the water. It was angled walls and shaped stone creatures, the last forgotten sentinel of the Varchinde plain.

And, even in the moonlight, he could see it was not a ruin.

He had no idea what it could be – some dream, some figment – some echo of his manor lord past come back to haunt him. Even as the axeman was telling himself not to be so cursed stupid, he was staring at it in disbelief, almost expecting it to thin and fade, to spread out upon the dark water and be gone.

But he was awake, and cold, and sober. And the cursed thing was still right there – the plains' last outpost, the forgotten city.

Forgotten, his right buttock. If it wasn't a ruin, then someone – some*thing* – was damned well living in it.

Swarming backwards on his belly, covering himself in muck, he found that his hands were on his axes, sliding with unexplained sweat. His knuckles were white and he wanted to cough.

To cough and cough and *cough* until the dust in his chest all cleared.

Until that cursed shadow-citadel was no longer there.

Or until its Lord damned well showed itself.

He paused where he was, body wracking with silent spasm. One hand went over his mouth, smothering any chance of noise. When the spasm receded, he glanced back at the water, at the building that loomed there, walls black against the shine.

It was hard to see in only the moonlight, but there seemed to be some sort of gatehouse, crenellations elaborate, at the mouth of the river – a building like nothing else he'd ever seen. And behind it a walkway? Or steps? They were almost impossible to make out.

For a moment, he was tempted to slide down the seaward side of the upthrust rock – to go out into the open, closer, and to see what in the name of every cursed God they'd found out here... But then something else caught his attention.

Movement.

They were below him, right below him, skirting the edge of the lookout tower – they'd closed almost about his feet without him realising. The moonlight was fading now, the clouds closing back over their prey, but he could see them, creeping between the ruins and heading for his camp.

Shit.

As silent as he could, he pushed himself back to his feet and slipped down the far side of the rock, boots scraping on the slippery stone, looking for a foothold. He tore his overtunic on the stone, but made it down without mishap. He eased around the edge of the rock to see what awaited him, here in the cold nacre of the Gleam Wood.

And then the white moon surged through the cloud cover, just for a moment, and he realised what he was looking at.

These were not villagers, not brimstone-hoarding pirates.

These were something else.

Redlock swallowed bile, smothered another cough.

Name of the Gods!

Here, in among the ruins of the buildings, there were the ruins of *flesh*.

These people were emaciated, thin to the point of starvation. Their garments were torn and their skin sun-darkened and cracking with dryness and salt. He could see now that their bodies were wrong – they had eyes in the wrong places, mouths in cheeks or shoulders, arms that ended in raw and bleeding wounds. Some were streaked with fluid; others had wound lengths of the flowering grasses about their heads or throats. A few bore weapons, clumsy and worn.

The axeman shuddered. The dark was pressing down upon him. He wanted to cough, but didn't dare move, or make a sound.

"Lost, are we?"

Starting, he spun.

Standing beside him, half-hidden by moon-shadow, was a cloaked figure, a cowl covering its hair. It was tall, impossibly so, and what Redlock could see of its face was strong and tanned and smiling.

But that was not what made him stare.

The thing's eyes had no pupil, no iris, they were a chaos of writhing colour. And its stance was odd, wrong: beneath the cloak hem it had hooves, wide and cracked like those of a road-running chearl.

The sight made the axeman's gorge rise; his flesh crawl. His cough rose again, and he controlled the urge to put a hand over his mouth.

The creature watched him, smiling, almost as though it could trace his reactions – as though it enjoyed them.

"I'm Varriera," it said, "once of Amos, now denizen of Aeona. The Lord Nivrotar would be proud, don't you think?"

Redlock controlled an urge to grab this thing by the neck of its cloak.

Instead, he replied, "What do you mean?"

Varriera – whatever the rhez it was – came closer, and that faint, ironic smile deepened into a chuckle.

"You're familiar with the market tales that tell you, you shouldn't leave the path? Aeona is the place you shouldn't find." Its face was still smiling. Its hands were decorated in old ink, leather wristbands. "We're a quiet community here, axeman. Few reach us, fewer still manage to leave. Certainly, no one leaves" – its smile spread, showing teeth – "unchanged."

Unchanged.

The word seemed to echo the twisted people, the overgrown ruins. As if the creature felt Redlock's shiver, it came closer still, laid a muscled hand on the axeman's shoulder – a gesture that seemed half-assessment, half-caress.

It said softly, "We should offer you our hospitality."

Redlock fought down the urge to punch this thing in the face, again and again and again, until those crazed eyes were not looking at him any more, were not watching his mouth, the pulse beat in his throat.

He said, "Take your hand off me, or lose it."

But Varriera met his gaze.

"Aeona is old, axeman, a place crafted to be forgotten." The creature's voice was rich and deep, almost Kartian. "Do you not know the darker edges of history? A scatter of these were built when Tusien fell, built to hold those who'd raised arms against the good of the Varchinde. Few now survive – and all have passed out of mortal ken." Its smile curved. "Including this one."

The word was a hard caress, like a hand about the throat. Redlock was pinned, unable to move.

"To the north," Varriera continued, "Fhaveon simply imprisons her unwanted – most of them." Its smile flickered. "To the west, there are those CityWardens who load them into caravans and send them to the fighting pits of the Kartiah. Here, we stand within the reach of Amos, of Annondor and Oraneith, of Padesh and Idrak. We have our manor and our Warden, axeman, and we, too, have our trade-cycle."

Redlock said, words like crushed horror, "You tithe flesh."

"Flesh is the tithe I take." Varriera smiled. "My return trade is one of learning."

Redlock tried to shake his head, clear his thoughts; tried to reach through the dark and the glitter and the clever words to piece all of this together.

"What is this place? What are *you*?"

"Ah, axeman. I'm as human as you are." The creature held up its hands, the ink upon its fingers. "I came here to find healing, new life..."

"And them? What did they find?" The axeman lunged a hand for the front of Varriera's cloak, said, "I don't know what this game is, but I've had enough."

In response, Varriera's curving smile was as soft as a pillow over the face.

They came out of the darkness, the ruins of the people that had lived here.

Ecko was moving, his hands and feet a blur.

Amethea fell back, her hands to her mouth. The wreckage that came for them was beyond anything she could ever have dreamed.

Triqueta, too, moved back, towards their poor chearl. She was feeling that familiar rise of panic in her gut; feeling her throat surge with that distinctive, welcome mix of elation and alarm.

She swallowed the deeper, darker flicker of fear.

Come on then. I can still do this.

I can still –

She was on the back of the chearl in a moment, holding it fast between her knees.

I'll take the lot of you, you see if I can't!

All about them, the throng were silent. They closed in softly, like ash, like blankets, reaching with hands and wounds and creeper and a desperate, choking yearning. A need that seemed pleading, almost childlike. They made her flesh crawl, the stones in her cheeks itch. For just a moment, she was a tight ball of absolute novice-terror – she missed her youth and her confidence, she missed her little mare. The chearl under her was big, too placid, too unfamiliar, too stupid – *I can't do this any more, I can't!* And then she shook herself, held the panic at bay, the animal with her thighs. She flicked her blades in dazzling wheels through her fingers, terhnwood gleaming, though the show was as much for her as it was for them.

"Come on then!" Triqueta was upright in the stirrups. "Let's see what you can do!"

They closed in tighter, a blur of horrors, one upon another in a way that made her stomach churn. Something about them *steamed* in the grey air.

Ecko had finally realised what had been frightening him.

As the misshapen throng closed in, a gentle pressure, the hand of a loved one over nose and mouth, stopping you breathing, watching you die – as the mangled things came inwards, he understood.

They were *family*.

Like the human-faced snake-tailed monster that had spoken his name – these things were like *him*: they were changed flesh, experimental, warp and twist and reach and gouge and open wound and mangled face. They were like Mom's creations.

Like her failures.

Had Mom ever had failures? Chrissakes, he'd never thought about it like that.

But the realisation was enough – with a snarl and a surge that raged denial of his own choices, his own life, he took the first one down with a circling foot, stepped over it, kicked the second – an older woman with a face like his mom, his real mom – and dropped her into the filth. The third was barely more than a kid, he fell back with his arm and shoulder broken, wounds gushing yellow fluid that shone unholy in the moonlight.

Ecko's targeters flashed – here and here! – showed him the weak points and the easy targets, and they were all moving so fucking slow it was like taking candy from...

In the midst of his own screaming horror, there were children, half his height, bowed under the weight of broken backs and extra limbs. There were half-creatures, things that were half-man; things that he recognised from his childhood, from the stories he'd heard as a kid.

And they closed like a noose, uncaring of how many of their number they lost, wanting only to reach out their hands and touch him as if he were some kind of saviour, some kind of hope.

He could hear them saying to him...

Eck... Oh...

And then there was something like the snapping of the Count of Time – everything was suddenly in motion.

Varriera, still smiling, cuffed the axeman across the face. The gesture was slow, elegant, yet absurdly painful; the strike detonated in his jaw. With a curse, Redlock fell back, his vision sparking stars.

What the rhez? He was Redlock, love of the Gods, he wasn't having this...!

His axes were out and in his hands, hard and familiar, metal glittering in the white light, but the creature's arm came out and sideways in a blow that seemed slow, an arc of fluid motion across the glittering dark. Redlock tried to move, but there was an inevitability to the strike that made him feel like he was drifting, somehow, or moving through mud.

Varriera's hand connected with the side of the axeman's neck. The hit was soft, but it sent him reeling, red pain exploding through his head and shoulders.

"Please," Varriera said. "Aeona has much to show you. If you will only let us."

But Redlock spat blood and got up, the red rage rising in his heart.

* * *

Astride the pack chearl right in the centre of the madness, Triqueta was surrounded by creatures – the huge throng of them now layering with nightmare, climbing one upon another. She had no idea how many there were. Her fear cried from her throat like defiance. *Come on then! Damn you! Come on!*

They closed about her, warm and helpless, pleading.

Triq shuddered.

Then one of them, sudden and swift, broke from the rest of the throng and came towards her. Its motion was hideous, wrong. Its head was cocked to one side and its expression eager, its body *cracked* as it moved. For a moment, she tried to see who – *what* – it had been, but the thought that it might have been human once made her swallow bile, and her fear was still yammering at her.

I can still...

It reached up to assail her on chearl-back. It had no hands: its arms ended in running sores, in weeping wounds that were open to the night sky. She hesitated – she couldn't help it – and then, furious at herself, she was turning the chearl's head to meet it, cursing the fact that the damned lumpish thing under her wouldn't move, wouldn't dance and fight like her little mare, cursing her own body for not moving as fast as she needed...

...but, by the rhez, she was fast enough.

She sat down hard on the pack-animal's back. With her heels tight at the chearl's sides, she found her grin. Pinned it to her face.

You bet I can.

The thing was within blade-reach, arms coming up for her, still oddly blurred in the sweating air. For the oddest moment, she had the feeling that the thing was something else entirely, that it wasn't really there, that the whole thing was only in her head, some figment, some nightmare...

Then it spat pieces of curse between its teeth, as if it were trying to speak.

And it was the release she needed. With the high, ululating war cry of the Banned, Triqueta sent the heavy chearl to slam it to the ground.

Apparently, this twisted creature was about to hand Redlock his arse.

And that really wasn't funny.

In another instant, he heard the movement of the chearl, heard Triq's high, insolent howl.

He heard his own blood-soaked cough.

Then another softly dancing blow connected with the side of his head, sent a slam of heat through his skull, and set him spinning, mind and body, as if he'd been struck by a cursed hammer. Sparks danced in his vision, his ears rang and his thoughts clanged back and forth.

Varriera was wavering now, its form unsteady.

It said, "Redlock. Please. Don't do this."

How did he know...?

But the axeman's head clamoured too much for him to fully formulate the thought. He was seeing double, the ruins, the steps, the sky, everything was swimming in his vision.

As Redlock struggled to focus, Varriera moved like steam, flowed forwards. The creature was compelling; the light seemed to focus in its eyes. It had no weapon, made no attempt at bravado. As he shook his head to clear the clangour, another absurdly gentle blow connected the heel of Varriera's palm to the centre of the axeman's chest and he just caved beneath the force of it, reeling and coughing and burning and hurting.

The axeman caught his heel on a root and sprawled on his back, wondering what the rhez was going on.

* * *

Eck... Oh...

Ecko was ablaze with fury and fear, an adrenaline like he'd never known. As the morass closed in about him, stretching hands to stroke his skin, he broke them in ones and twos and fives, his muscles screaming with the speed that was blazing through them. He wasn't even looking where the blows were going; the flash of target and the movement of limb were like the greatest fucking dance he'd ever done.

Daaaaaance...

Was this the dance you meant, huh, was it?

In that blaze, his anger at Eliza was finally venting, smashing into the faces and the mouths and mangled bodies of the things that were all about him, rising in a fury like he'd never known – like his very skin would catch fire as he would blaze like the Sical, blaze like Pareus, blaze like the dream of Tarvi...

Oh no you fucking don't..!

But there were too many. For every one he put down, there were another two, another three. There were no gaps, no exits. They were all around him, pulling him down to the mud, pulling at his cloak and his skin and his arms and his shoulders. Hard as he tried they were all upon him, layers of them, and their pressure was increasing until it was suffocating – until his vision was blackening and his targets were firing more slowly, until the blaze of adrenaline in his system was running down.

Until he had no more remaining and he was falling, falling under the weight of their need for him.

Triqueta's chearl was having none of it.

Ignoring the commands of thighs and heels, the beast planted its bulk solidly and refused to move.

What?

The twisted thing's arm reached closer. Triq slashed at it, shuddered, leaned back. She was swearing, horrified, terrified.

They were all around her now, their eyes gleaming, their faces an odd blur of darkness and heat and shimmering steam. Closer, closer. The smell of the wounds on the arms of the one closest to her was making her gag; she wanted nothing more than to punch her way out through the side, through the top, and tear screaming down towards the water.

But she couldn't leave Amethea. She could hear the teacher behind her, the horror in her voice an echo of Triqueta's own. Triq fought the obstinate chearl, thighs tight, trying to make it into the horse it... into the horse it had once been? Behind her, she could hear the thrub of hooves, a cry. Amethea was shouting something.

"Creature created. Creature created! Triq, it won't fight! You won't make it fight!"

Oh, by the rhez...

At the Monument, Amethea's chearl had recognised the centaur – Triq knew the story. The chearl had known the stallion for what he was, and they'd refused to face him. And now her mount recognised these – whatever the rhez they were.

Creature created.

The horse it had once been.

Understanding hit her like a cursed terhnwood shaft – her chearl and this accursed twisted thing, they were brothers, estavah, created by the same craft... Somewhere along the line, the chearl too were alchemically made and they wouldn't fight their own.

Horseshit! Now's not a time to find this out!

The things closed down upon her and her two little knives; they were freaks and horrors, flesh tithed to nightmare. Amethea was no warrior and Triqueta had no idea what had happened to Redlock.

I can still...

She saw Ecko fall, heard herself howl.

And the dark tide closed in upon her.

* * *

Redlock's head was spinning, his vision was blurred and his chest tight. The air around him was close, suffocating, and he found himself reeling, straining to breathe and trying to make sense of what he saw.

Before him, Varriera was height and hunger and flawless combat – as the creature moved, so repeated afterimages seemed to burn in the air. Its strikes were slow, impossibly slow, but they were still too fast for Redlock to react, and yet another blow caught his face and sent him sideways, pain exploding in sparks and lightning.

Somewhere in his head, the practical part of him said, *This can't be happening.*

The sky was bright and the ground was ruined and nothing here made any cursed sense.

Why had they come? How had they…?

But there was only that smile. Only the graceful movement of Varriera's impossible hands as another strike sent the grass and sky tumbling one over another.

Amethea pulled her belt-knife free, waved it in the face of the nearest thing that came at her. It stuck – or she thought it did – but it seemed to go straight through the flesh of the creature and emerge unscathed, seemed to strike only smoke and air. In front of her Triqueta sat astride the chearl, kicking and spitting and slashing, but the things were too many, and as fast as she repelled them, they came back at her, a silent wave.

Maugrim had shown Amethea the darkest corners of her soul and she was determined that she was going to learn from that vision.

Then there was a scream, furious and outraged, and Triqueta was pulled from the saddle, fighting savagely all the way down. The blur of creatures seemed to close over her, even as she spat fury.

By the Goddess...

Something in Amethea didn't quite believe this; didn't believe that they could come so far only to fail, only to fall here at the edge of the world in a fight that made no sense. She didn't even know what these things were...

Creature created.

As the things closed in about Triqueta, Amethea was remembering. Remembering the Monument, the stallion, the death of her friend. She wouldn't let this happen – not again.

Then the boil of heat and motion around Triqueta ceased abruptly and the things turned their thin, skeletal faces, their outstretched arms, the open mouths, towards her.

The tide was poised, about to close over them all, and there was nothing they could do about it.

Redlock's world was askew, a blur of confusion and pain.

Everything was sluing sideways, sliding like liquid and light, nothing made sense any more, and he could not even see the sea. Had there been a building here, had there been a town that he had been fighting in and for?

Varriera's last touch was as soft as a kiss, a hand across his eyes that closed them completely.

They did not open again.

Amethea heard a shriek – it took her a moment to realise that the noise had come from her own throat. She threw herself at the things around her, slashing and screaming as Triqueta had done – but it did her no more good.

They were all around her, hands upon her, soft and warm as a lover's embrace, pulling her down with a wave of twisted flesh, a wave that she struggled to reach the crest of... And then she failed, falling beneath them as if they could somehow fold round her and made her secure.

The last thing she heard was a voice.

"They've come. Take them down to the CityWarden."

15: TRIANGLE CITY FORIATH

Rhan arrived at the city of Foriath to streets that were seething with frustration.

Without quite knowing how, he found himself in the middle of it, carried forwards by a tide of outrage. The city's people were loose on her streets, pushing and shouting and all around him. They'd left homes and halls and were bunched and loud; the roads eddied with their fury. Their outrage rose like steam, and their voices carried across the morning, strident and righteous.

The slender, grey-haired man that had once been Rhan of Fhaveon caught himself, and stopped short at the end of a roadway. He leaned on a wall to catch his thoughts, and wondered what the rhez he had stumbled into.

This was not the Foriath he knew.

It was barely mid-morning, an overcast day and with a chill wind cutting across the dying Varchinde grass. There was no fiveday market due, no festivity or celebration. Rhan had been intent only on resting in the city, gathering his energy and then seeking a route north to Avesyr.

This, though, this was angry, and its implications frightened him, made him pull back tight against the wall to let the crowd pass, his thoughts all tumbling questions.

How had the unrest come here? How had it reached here ahead of him?

Foriath was a peaceful place, well fed and content. She stood with her sisters, Narvakh and The Hayne, the Triangle Cities that grew, reared and traded much of the Varchinde's ale and luxury food. These cities were populous, their manors and farms spread widely and lush with life and good soil. Their tithehalls and bazaars were numerous and busy, yet piracy was much less common here than in the cities of the coast.

Unrest was for the political hotbed of Fhaveon – not this place of round bellies and hearth fires.

But, in this time of monsters and looming threats, who could say how far such things would reach?

Rhan's grey mood had not left him completely, shreds of it clouded the edges of his mind, ready to close in if he lost his sense of purpose, even for a moment. *Why bother?* It taunted him, cold and mocking as the fetter on his wrist. *You'll only fail. Why even try?*

Many times on his way here it had made him stumble, hesitate. Rhan had lost his city, his attunement and his confidence, and now...

Samiel's *teeth*.

Foriath should have welcomed, her halls should blaze with rocklight and flame, her streets of stone and wood should be full of comfort. The Swathe River ran through her heart like a lifeline, crossed by several bridges. In many places the buildings ran right up to the water's edge, mooring points and small harbours lying at their feet.

In the wake of the crying crowd, though, the streets were empty. Rhan saw with shock that the once-mighty river was now home to corpses, white and swollen under the heavy grey sky.

The blight in the grass was closing, even here – and its harbingers were out.

As he moved forwards again, following the noise, horror teased his shoulders, jabbed at him and laughed.

He did not need to walk far.

He came to a stop at the head of a short flight of grey steps, an old, carven creature standing guard at his shoulder, one claw raised as if to beg silence. Down in front of him was an open square, a cross-section of roadways, now teeming with people, and jammed with indignation. They were packed hard, shouting, shoving, faces flushed and mouths open and red. In places, there was chanting that caught for a moment and then fragmented, drifting away to be picked up by others, a new set of voices, demands punching hard into the air.

Fhaveon was hoarding – the whisper of it had followed him northwards along the trade-road – but Rhan would've bet his no-longer-white arse it had nothing to do with fear or caution.

Phylos was an opportunistic bastard – and Vahl stirred, the vialer were aboard in the plainland.

Fhaveon was using the blight to stockpile.

She was arming herself.

And Rhan was afraid.

Watching the heave of the angry crowd, that fear was knotted cold in his belly, threatening despair and the rise of his grey mood, and tightening with every surge of anger below him. He felt helpless, the frustration in the crowd was a reflection of his own – vast and insurmountable.

His grey mood mocked him. *Why bother? You can't make this better. Give up now…*

He looked at his hands. Workman's hands, scarred – hands that suited the grey-haired, older and more serious appearance that he now presented.

He had only his hands.

Fhaveon had fallen – Vahl was rising within her white walls, rising like a cloud of steam and Rhan had raised neither blow nor objection. He had lost his city without even knowing how he'd failed.

And he'd hit the water, outcast and bereft. Again. Only this time, it was less like some streaking, glorious cursed comet and more like a bloody *rock*.

Oh, how are the mighty fallen, Rhan Elensiel.

Rain had begun to scatter from the heavy cloud above, the crowd pushed and heaved. As he reached the base of the steps and stood tight against the wall, he could see that there was a fountain at the intersection, a second great and clawed creature, and that it had become a rallying point. A single voice called out over the heads of the mass – the speaker was standing upon its stone edge as if it were guarding him.

Samiel's *teeth*.

That was all this needed.

Responsibilities pulled at him. He should stop this – but he had no might here, no power or strength. *Why bother?* And if things were already this bad, then he had to reach Avesyr, reach Mother and learn where in the name of the Gods he went from here…

Damn you, Vahl. How can I fight you when I don't even know where you are?

In the crowd, almost in front of him, there was a flash.

It was white-metal, an edge of sharpness in a glint of violence. With a shriek that was half-gurgle, an older man not two paces in front of where Rhan stood stumbled and fell. Behind him, a slim figure reached for his belt pouches and was gone.

Rhan held himself still with an effort, watching.

Around the motion, a pool of shock widened. A voice cried, "'Oo did that? 'Oo did that?" Hands reached to pull the injured man to his feet. A sharp ripple of jostling broke out from the angry cry; others took it up. Hands grabbed a second cloaked figure, innocent and surprised, and dragged him backwards into the crowd.

With a frightened shout, he vanished.

He didn't resurface.

The ripple spread, growing rougher. Several people tried to back away, but the anger was rolling now, spreading back into the people, and the seethe and press became more vicious, harder. The accusing voice grew louder, strident. It was echoed by others, all of them apparently righteous, seeking the thief, but their anger was self-serving and gathering both followers and momentum.

Retreating fearfully from the point of ignition, a slender young man almost barged bodily into the silent Rhan. With a start, Rhan saw the youth was desert-blooded: there was sunshine in his skin tone and a line of opal stones along his jaw. He muttered fearfully, not expecting to be heard or acknowledged, "Excuse me, excuse me..." and Rhan, on an obscure whim, grabbed his elbow and all but dragged him right up to the wall.

"Please," he said, soft and intent, "what's going on here? What happened?"

The young man looked at him, wild-eyed and wary. He was barely more than a lad, his garments were dirty and stained with the dust of the trade-roads.

He said, "I don't know, I don't know. Who are you, anyway? Get off me!"

Behind him, the crowd grew rougher, pushing. There were hints of screams. They were eager, they had the taste for it now and they wanted to find something else to blame.

Rhan released the boy's shoulder, spread his hands peaceably. "Please."

The lad relaxed, but still glanced back.

He said, "Fhaveon... we've always had a garrison here, a small one. But they're doubling it, demanding curfew. To ensure the trade-routes, they said, to make sure the tithehalls are unthreatened. There are soldiers every– By the rhez!"

He nodded at the square.

As if he'd called them, the new soldiery were surrounding the intersection.

They were human, but their faces were like stone.

And their weapons were sharp.

As the press came in, Rhan grabbed the lad by the neck of his tunic and pulled him from the wall and the crowd, back towards the steps. Where the horde had been unruly, angered and shouting, now they were furious, a united and defiant mob, calling and shoving with violence. Some had weapons – belt-blades, mostly, but they gripped them in hands turned white with resolve.

This was going to turn ugly. And soon.

At the head of the wide, stone stairs, there was a wall of shields, the colours Fhaveonic, but with the winged device – his own device that once adorned the city's soldiery – now gone. More of them blocked the three sides of the intersection. The figure on the fountain had vanished.

The boy said, "There's nowhere to go. Last time, they just pushed the people into the river. Hundreds drowned, it was horrible. They made those they'd detained pull out the dead from the harbours."

Samiel's...

Never mind.

Rhan turned from the intersection to the stairway and back, looking for a solution, a route out, but they had blocked every which way. He could see others in the crowd, heads turning this way and that, starting to panic.

Then a figure came to the top of the steps, raised her hands.

"People of Foriath! My friends!"

Rhan had never met CityWarden Jasenna, but knew her reputation well enough – she was small and round and happy, a peaceable woman with little liking for conflict. Jas was ideal for her city, but up there now she looked like a lost redfruit carried on an errant tide. Mutters and calls came from below.

Rhan could not possibly believe that Jas herself was responsible for the mess that Foriath had become.

Unless...

The memory of Penya was a painful one. Damn Phylos, he'd lever anything against anyone, and shamelessly.

As the CityWarden tried to shout, objects were thrown towards her with little regard for where they landed. Rhan saw a young woman take a heavy stone to her forehead and stumble, bleeding, but the press of the crowd was too close to even let her fall. The lad winced at the impact. Rhan's scarred hands almost reached for her, reaching for help, for air, for answers, for anything that would help him fix this...

Jas tried again, "People of Foriath!"

But Rhan had to fight the illness, not the symptoms. He had to take Phylos, take his city back, raise his arms against Vahl as he was always meant to have done.

But how? How can I fight an enemy that hides, that tricks and taunts, that plays games? How can I fight something that's rendered me powerless in my own city?

"People of Foriath, hear me!"

"Yeah, we hear you all right!"

"You come down here with your promises!"

"Tell us again how it's for our 'safety'!"

"I can't leave my house!"

"Your thugs killed my son!"

"I know times are hard!" Jas held up her hands and tried again. "I know that you fear, but there is no need! We must stand together! We must...!"

"Horseshit!"

There was laughter, but it had a cruel edge, an edge of threat. Voices threw back utter scorn. The surge and rush of the crowd grew yet rougher. Further back, the people were pushing to go forwards, goading those in front of them.

Jas sounded almost as though she wanted to weep.

"Please, people of Foriath!"

Behind the CityWarden, the tan of the shieldwall raised a hand, gave a sharp gesture that Rhan knew all too well. Horrified, he heard the three tan commanders at the edges of the square give a simultaneous barked command.

From somewhere behind the shieldwalls, the drums started, the sharp order to march. The sound rolled from the walls, threat and echo. Now, the shields were pushing forwards with a steady, heavy tramping, shoving roughly at anything, *anyone*, that got in their way. Slowly, slowly, they began to push the people tighter together, in to a seething, frightened knot. Shrieks sounded, scared, defiant.

On the fourth side, at the foot of the steps, the people did not move – they were watching the shieldwall above them. The crushing pressure behind them began to build. From somewhere, a stone missile flew, and another. Mouths threw spit and mockery.

"I plead with you, my people, my city, my *friends*…!"

But the CityWarden did not have the presence or the voice to bring control – she was a merchant, a brewer, a lover of ale and company and conversation.

There were screams, now, in among the throb of the drumming and the stamp of feet, there were cries for help somewhere further back in the crowd. And then, with Rhan caught there upon the great stone stair, the lad pushed still behind him, the pulsing broke, and the people surged forwards, roaring. It was like a dam had broken.

The boy whimpered, a tiny noise of absolute horror.

The mob ran for the stairs, all weapons and rage, they ran past him and up to where Jas stood, her flushed face etched in shock. He thought he saw her mouth, "No…"

Behind her, he saw the tan commander open his mouth, shout something, give a single hard gesture. The shieldwall raised, locked, braced; weapons came out and over, slamming down on the upper shield rims with a loud and unified, "*Ha!*"

The sound echoed from the walls, and the heart-throb of the drumming grew louder.

Rhan had no doubt the tan would use their weapons on the people of Foriath.

But the crowd did not care. They had no hope and no fear. They were drunk, not on ale, but on fury – and they were running up the stairs towards an armed, shielded force that simply stood and waited for them.

Pushed them into the river.

They would be cut down where they stood.

Standing there at the edge of the madness, watching the people run past him, watching their individual faces and expressions, Rhan was surprised to find that he was crying, that there was water in his eyes that was nothing to do with the rise of smoke, with the –

"Come on!" The desert-born lad tugged at his sleeve. "Come on, we can get away from this!"

"I can't leave them!" The answer was reflex. But much good was he doing, standing here like a –

"You can't help them. The soldiers are running everything. Narvakh and The Hayne are the same. We have to get away from here!"

The lad tugged at his sleeve again, and they ducked back against the wall, and then they were away through a cobbled alleyway that led down to the river.

And the bloated, rotting corpses of those who had been left to die.

There was an alehouse basement, right at the edge of the water.

There was a gathering of six scared people, faces pale in the rocklight.

There was a tiny, wooden wharf outside with a boat tied by its painter to the mooring – the river, they said, could still be travelled safely, corpses or no. If one walked the roads, there were questions and demands and the production of craftsman's symbols and maker's marks. No one bore belt-knives in public any more – unless they wanted trouble.

Outside, the rain speckled the slow brown roll of the water.

Inside, there was a long wooden table and a leather jug foaming almost to the brim. The desert-blooded lad was saying, "We should get a message to Fhaveon –"

"To whom?" An older man with grey whiskers and a wine-red face cut in with a scowl and shook his head until his jowls flapped. He picked up the jug and glanced around at the others, one eyebrow raised in a question.

"The resistance in Fhaveon fell before it could rise," said a dark-haired woman, her hand resting gently on the lad's shoulder. "Phylos cut it out like a canker. They took Fletcher Wyll, there's no one else to even try. Demisarr is dead, Mostak is gone. There's no Council. No, thank you, not for me." She shook her head at the offered ale jug.

There's no Council.

Other voices spoke, offering possibilities or denying them, hands held out tankards to be filled – but Rhan barely heard or saw them. The metal on his wrist was as cold as hopelessness. There was a hollow sound of horror in his ears, an echo of rising water and empty grey wings.

There's no Council.

"What happened to Mostak?" The voice was rough with alarm, unfamiliar. "To the Council of Nine?" It was a moment before he realised the questions were his own.

And he saw that the six faces in the room were staring at him, eyes dark under the rocklight. The stones in the boy's jaw gleamed.

"Who is this?" The man with the red face waved his tankard

at the desert-born lad, ale slopping. "Tesail?"

The boy, Tesail, opened his mouth, but Rhan was already answering for him, his wit catching up with his shock.

"I'm Sarastiah, of Fhaveon. I'm a... ah... craftsman, terhnwood, nothing special, goblets and such." The name and craft were a cover he'd used before. "Left the city when there was no work for me – arrived here this morning and was greeted by... well, you saw." He shrugged. "The roads are running with rumour," that much was true, "but I'd no idea –"

"He helped me," Tesail said, his yellow eyes wide. "In the riot out there, he helped me get away."

"You helped me, I think." Rhan gave him a brief smile.

The red-faced man took a long pull from his mug and then spoke through the froth on his lip, "Foriath is in uproar. This morning, they torched the stalls of the eastern bazaar, burned the stock where it stood. An 'example', they said."

"Who?" Rhan said, carefully. "Who torched the stalls?"

The question was weighted – he wouldn't put it past Phylos to sow the city with dissenters, voices to goad and gouge, sparks to kindle a flame – literally, in this case. The Merchant Master's eyes and ears were everywhere.

A crested black bird landed on the mooring-post. It croaked as if it were warning them, but no one turned.

Rhan trusted no one. Not any more.

His eyes, the only part of him unchanged in his now thin, lined face scanned the expressions round the table.

"We don't know." The red-faced man wiped his lip and met Rhan's gaze. "I'm Eorig, Jas is my sister's daughter. Some halfcycle back, the heralds told us Fhaveon was limiting her terhnwood cargo, something about preserving the city against the blight. The news spread like the pox, our own halls refused to trade and it has spread along road and river, west and north. Fhaveon's doubled her garrison – now she threatens to take our harvest by force if need be, to give us nothing in return." He took another long pull of ale. "We're not warriors, Sarastiah, but if we have to fight..."

Of course.

It was falling into place now – the vialer, the whole Gods-damned plot. Phylos had taken Fhaveon without a fight, using the blight as his leverage. As his soldiers spread through the Northern Varchinde, he could take the rest of the cities likewise – "securing" each one against the blight, against the unrest that it would bring. There was nothing the City Wardens could do, he could simply walk his soldiers in and start throwing orders.

He could take anything he wanted.

And the vialer he'd seen – had they been scouts? Were these forgotten creatures even now occupying Fhaveon herself, freeing up the city troops for their wide-ranging detail?

And the blight was *here*, like Phylos's damned ambassador, working for him, Rhan had seen it as he'd come through the farmlands. He'd felt the fear, the tension. The manors were scared. On a local level, their individual tithes to their cities were being cut back so they themselves could survive the winter, and the delicate balance of life in the tithehalls was faltering. The city populace of Foriath could face a war on two fronts – local and plainswide – or they could accept Phylos's soldiers and use them to take on their own farmlands...

The whole thing was diabolical genius.

Damn you. You're not going to do this.

He sat back, watching out of the window and over the river. The bird was cleaning its feathers, head tucked into its chest. He could scent the trace of smoke in the air and it rose with the grey in his mind... He closed his eyes against both of them. From somewhere, he could hear shouting.

Then he opened his eyes, and, almost dreading the answer, said, "What of Rhan?"

"Rhan!" The woman's scornful snort was like a slap.

"Rhan?" Eorig's tone was amused. "By the Gods, we're here

to find a solution, not make jokes." He poured himself another ale and the scent mingled with that of the smoke and brought with them images of the Bard.

Find a solution.

Not make jokes.

That was it, then. Four hundred returns of service and it was a joke.

But Eorig was still speaking, settling the jug back on the table. "There is one line of hope in Fhaveon – only one."

Rhan's gaze turned to pin him.

The red-faced man met his gaze, said, "Maybe you know this? In her youth, the Foundersdaughter had a tutor – a warrior of some note. He…"

The scent of smoke was growing stronger. Outside, the bird flew away.

Caught now, Rhan leaned forwards, watching Eorig's face as he spoke, the shake of his jowl and the way his grey whiskers gleamed in the rocklight. He had a feeling he knew exactly where this was going.

Saravin.

Warrior, Range Patrol, something of a loner. A man of courage and humour, nasty in a fight; liked his ale a little too much.

Saravin.

"But Saravin's dead," said the dark-haired woman. "Phylos's pet, the new tan commander Cylearan, carved out his tripes on harvest day. He died in the hospice."

"But we know there's someone helping her," said Eorig. "The Foundersdaughter still has a voice of sanity in her ear, a stabilising influence that's holding her strong against Phylos's propaganda. If we can find that voice, if we can make contact…"

Gusts of faint grey smog were billowing past the window, fragments of black ash whirling in the wind.

If we can find that voice…

Rhan would have bet Garland House and everything still in

it that he knew to whom that voice belonged. He and Saravin had enjoyed a cold ale together occasionally, down through the returns, and the big warrior had sometimes had a slender shadow, a quiet and unremarkable man who'd had eyes as sharp as quillpoints, and forgot nothing.

A scribe, an artist. For the moment Rhan had lost his name, but he could picture the old man in his head, stoop-shouldered and quiet. A thoughtful man who let others do the talking.

Something in his heart sang, *I am not alone!*

Then there was a sudden, harsh banging on the door.

They were on their feet in a moment, all seven of them, hearts pounding in unison as they stared at the doorway. The smell of smoke was very strong now. There were voices outside, demanding. The hammer on the door came again, and the wood juddered.

Eorig turned to the rest of them. "Go. Take the boat. Jas is my blood, they can't touch me."

I wouldn't be too sure of that.

The desert lad said, "I'll stay with you, I can help!"

"No, you go. All of you. Now!"

The hammering came again and the door rattled. The dark-haired woman ushered the rest of them out towards the little boat.

"Come on," she said. "Quickly!"

All except Tesail scrambled past her, but Rhan went only as far as the narrow wharf and stopped, looking back into the room.

As the door slammed open, there were the expected goons, shields and weapons, there was the expected tan commander, his face etched with grim certainty. Eorig drew himself up to explain who he was.

Without waiting, the tan commander punched him in the face and dropped him, spluttering, to the floor.

The commander turned to the boy. Met his gaze. Nodded.

You little shit.

Rhan turned back to the wharf, unhooked the painter, gave the boat a shove.

And then he jumped. Not into the boat itself.

Into the water.

Again.

INTERLUDE: KHAMSIN LONDON

Fog lay deep on the great slow roll of the river – a shroud of stillness.

Along Embankment, the glare of security lighting diffused the night to a white haze. The city's monotone had, at long bloody last, been shut off.

Somewhere to the north, muted laser-light gave evidence of London's continuing life. A short distance above them, the blue blur of hoverdrones patrolled the security-zone barriers at the Hungerford footbridge.

Audible through the city's rebroadcasters, Big Ben tolled a single, sullen note.

Half one in the morning.

If we're seen out 'ere…

Uncomfortable in an army surplus longcoat, collar up to hide his beard, Lugan stood tucked into the wall. He was phoneless, all enhancements on shutdown. He felt stark-bollock naked and prospect-nervous. Beside him, a similar coat covering his ludicrous garments and hair, Roderick was voiceless and wide-eyed, silenced by the great city, by her looming shapes in the fog.

Behind them, Lugan heard a single, approaching engine –

four-litre, beautifully tuned. Patrol-car headlights gleamed. Both men crouched closer to the wall, turned their faces away.

The car passed them and was gone, tail-lights receding into red haze.

"Chill." Tinkering with the lock on the expanding metal cage-door, the woman who accompanied them chuckled. "You're unseen, long as you're with me." Dusky-skinned, hair in dreads and body in layers of cast-offs, she had multiple piercings, blacklight-tats and way too many fingers. Her name was Thera, she ran "distraction", and she was another creation of the tech Ecko called Mom. The city cameras slipped from her as though she were a phantom.

She was also hot as fuck.

Mind on the job, mate, Lugan reminded himself.

"They don't see me," she'd told them, voice like velvet over gravel. When she'd held up an arm, the light tats ran like liquid round her skeletal, many-jointed fingers. "Magick."

"Gotta love a girl with good tats," Lugan remarked, straight-faced.

She grinned at him, white teeth bared in threat and humour. "You be watching your mouth."

She turned away, snicked open the cage-door and slipped it a foot or so sideways – it moved easily, well-oiled. With a final check, she shifted the graffiti-tagged board that covered the entrance to Embankment Station.

And the gutted, lurker-infested corpse of the London Underground.

Heart inexplicably jumping, Lugan squeezed his shoulders through the gap.

Stopped.

Too fuckin' surreal.

The ticket hall was so familiar, the smell, the taste of the air – the memory punched him in the face, almost made him reel with the force of it. And yet it was wrong – it was desolate, empty and grey, utterly cold. Silent, lit only by the faint rectangle of outside light, the station was layered with ghosts – a flickering mass of non-existent humanity, a city's population who'd once had the freedom to be thronging this hallway, trudging and pushing, hating the crush, swearing about the commute... now all gone. Safe in their bolt-holes, with their twenty-minute walk to work.

Old rubbish lay scattered across the black-and-white tiles. There were great gouges in the wall where the dispenser machines had been forklifted away. It was chilled in here, bigger than Lugan remembered. Gooseflesh crawled up his arms.

A city's bustling life, blown away like an old sheet of newspaper in a cold and empty wind.

"You be wanting the forgotten, the unseen, the unknown?" Thera said to them. "They all living down here."

Once the city's circulatory system, now the Underground was the place where she conveniently dumped her waste.

As the silent Roderick ducked in after Lugan, the thought came with a sharp realisation: what if the patrol car had seen them clearly? Was it only making sure they stayed within their boundaries?

Thera ran the cage-door closed, replaced the board. The hallway was suddenly in utter darkness.

"Don't you be thinking of nightmares, now." Her deep voice chuckled, wicked and throaty.

And, as Lugan turned, her tattoos came to life, dragons coiling in the darkness, fire that flickered over her skin. They were breathtaking, impossible – a circus light-show that limned her spider-hands, the shape of her face. A single thought and she'd transformed from invisible to prophetess, a manifestation of the city's continuing underlife.

Like hope.

He reached for a dog-end, cursed when he realised he'd left his cut-down in his office.

There was a hand on his shoulder.

"Lugan?" Roderick sounded surprisingly calm – on some level, he understood why, though he couldn't focus on it immediately. "Can you see?"

"Only the skin-job, mate. You?"

"The darkness does not bother me." He sounded faintly amused. "And the lights are very beautiful."

"Thanks, man," Thera said. "We going down."

Helplessly, they followed her spectrous writhe of light.

They passed what was left of the ticket barriers, descended the unmoving escalators, boots clanking on corpse-metal as they headed down, down under the city. A thousand noisy memories scudded through the emptiness – the tourists, the drunken party-goers, the laden shoppers and the frustrated families, the corporate security of the tube's last days...

...now just broken lights; ads forgotten, faded and peeling, lit only by the ghost-light that was Thera's skin.

All gone.

He lost sight of Thera's lights as she jumped from the platform's edge into cold, breezy darkness.

Lugan hesitated briefly, instinctively, then jumped down after her, followed her glimmer into the stinking black throat of the tunnel. Rails rusted in the puddles that splashed beneath his boots – somewhere down here there were flood-barriers, closed against the rising of the river.

The Bard said, mouthing horror for the first time, "People made these tunnels to live in?"

Beside them, frayed cables shed sudden sparks.

"No mate, they jus' live in 'em now."

He had no way of knowing where they were, no sat-access, no info upload, no fucking starlites. He missed Fuller, missed the aural link. Fuller'd *know* how deep they were, which line they'd crossed to, this time, and this one... Where the nearest fucking exit was...

Spark!

Yeah, awright, this place was spooking the shit out of him. His Manhunter ten-mil was a comforting weight.

After a while, Roderick said softly, "There have been times when The Wanderer has manifest within the great Kartian Crafthalls, guest of the Church of Sires." In the darkness, his voice was pure, rich melody. "They have always welcomed me, plied me with metal and bade me... entertain them." Boots splashed – they must've dropped down to the deeper tunnels, now, they were up to their ankles in water. The air was freezing. "Their darkness is vibrant, alive; this, I do not comprehend. Your lore and history is this close, it seethes in the air about you – and yet you have left this place by choice? It is as though you have abandoned your world's lore by... by apathy. By Kazyen."

Spark!

"The lore is still there," Thera said. She laughed again, soft and echoing. "But most don't care. They only live as they're told. Apathy has become a way of life, for most." She paused by a crumble of brick wall, a mouth of darkness even deeper than that of the tunnel. "You be stopping now. We here."

They turned sideways, stepped over a – broken? – hole in the brickwork and Thera's light-tats were gone, flatlined. Lugan could see absolutely fuck all.

Thera?

Behind them, there was the solid *boom!* of a slamming door, the clunk of a metal bar. He turned instinctively, but his orientation had gone – like some fucker had bunged a bag over his head.

Instinctively, his grip tightened on the Manhunter. He stretched out the other hand.

"Thera?" The sound was swallowed – wherever he was, it was fucking huge.

Somewhere to his left, Roderick said, "Lugan?"

The wall was warm and soft. "Sorry, luv." He drew his hand back sharply. "Rick? You awright?"

Movement, closer. "Here." The Bard's hand on his shoulder. "Rest easy, you can see with your hearing, your skin. There is no reason to fear."

The irony of their role-reversal was not lost on Lugan.

"Fuck that noise." He fumbled in his pocket. A moment later he chinked open his lighter and struck a tiny, bright flame. It flickered from the metal rings in Thera's nostril.

"Don't..!" She reached for it, but was drowned out by a hideous cry and the noise of something moving far above... something the size of a small truck.

Lugan shut the lighter with a snap and the darkness swallowed them all.

In his chest, his heart began to tremble. *What the fuck was...?*

"Don't you be using the lighter in here," Thera said. "Auntie keeping an eye on you boys – maybe she keeping more than one." A hand pushed, propelling him forwards. "Now, you move."

Roderick said softly, "'Auntie'?"

Lugan said, "I *don't* wanna know."

Blind as newborn rats, they moved.

As they stumbled forwards, the sense of space grew bigger, the air colder. Far above them, the creature called Auntie shifted unseen, a recurring nightmare.

Whatever it was, it was keeping pace with them.

And it was *big*.

Then a woman's voice, young, musical, soft, said...

"Stop."

They stopped.

Waited, straining to hear.

After a moment's tantalising pause, it spoke again, like a crystal bell, feminine, amused. "So, the mighty Ade Eastermann himself, here in my very lair. And you've brought your – friend." Her tinkling laugh brought a cold sweat to Lugan's shoulders. "Gentlemen, how is my Ecko?"

There was only one way to do *this* deal. "We need to ask you a favour."

"Oh?" The query was deceptively mild.

"We're lookin' for info. We busted a sniffer, brought down 'er 'arddrive."

"Why do you not ask your Collator? Does this drive carry some risk?" Her softness was lethal.

"Collator's off sick," Lugan said.

"Really." The voice was a sparkle, amused. "And what of my Ecko? I hear" – and she was moving in the darkness – "rumours."

"He is well," Roderick told her, "if you believe in the gaps between worlds."

Lugan smacked his forehead with an open palm.

"Worlds, you say?" The tech's laughter was like icicles, like crystal knives. "You're an alien, are you? Arrived in a spaceship, perhaps?"

"I arrived in a pub." Roderick's aplomb was impressive. "A pub in which your Ecko has been resident until quite recently."

Her laughter stopped dead. "Interesting."

Lugan flicked the Manhunter's safety.

And the silence swelled to bursting.

When she spoke again, all traces of humour had been stripped from her voice, like flesh from bone. "Well, what a fascinating creature you must be."

The Bard gasped – shocking, unexpected pain. "*Ah!*"

What the –?

Lugan was crouched in a second, ten-mil out of the holster, still concealed. Sudden anticipation – dread, certainly – tightened his muscles to a wary coil. Like that moment when you knew you'd fucked it and you were going over the handlebars... that endless, freefalling second before actual tarmac...

What had she done?

Now, her voice was tight with tension, sharply alive – need, fear, lust. "You're not human." The words were taut as a choke-hold, half-disbelieving. She wasn't playing any more, the darkness rippled with her urgency. "What are you?" Louder. Now harsh, clashing metallic. "*What. Are. You?*"

"Lost," Roderick said calmly.

Lugan pulled the Manhunter, coughed to cover the hammer, held it low.

And it was whisked from him, caught with a length of fishing line.

Slightly sticky fishing line.

Jesus.

The crash came. He slammed into the tarmac, skidded into the realisation: they were trapped in here, no exits, no comms. Only when they missed the 2:33 failsafe check-in...

Panic!

Suddenly scared to the soles of his boots, he bit down on the violence that screamed beneath his skin, begging for release in a demand for freedom, a detonation of righteous anger.

You're not human.

Then he sensed something directly before him, something significantly bigger than his own six foot four. Something metal-cold.

The tech said, "Give him to me, Lugan. Please." Her voice was an irresistible girlish flirt. It shivered round in his head with the knowledge of her sadism, the atrocities she'd committed. She'd flayed Ecko alive, for fuck's sake, eaten his eyes right out of their sockets.

Mom.

"'E's not mine to give, luv." He was still crouched, ready to go for the heavy, carbon-fibre boot-knife. "An' that ain't why we're 'ere. We're lookin' –"

"Give him to me, Lugan," the tech said, "and I'll answer your questions. All of them." Her breath was sweet, eager, like spring. "You want to ID your friend? That's easy. You want to know Tarquinne Gabriel's agenda? That's a little harder. You want to know what assails Collator? That's almost a challenge." She laughed, high and sparkling, like water. "Ask me anything, Lugan. I'm the soul and the memory; I'm the creator and the crafter. I'm mother and lover. The world seethes round and through me. I'm the *fountain* of all knowledge."

Oh, you're kidding...

His heart crystallised and shattered. He was a rat in a maze, helpless, manipulated. He knew what was coming – he was turning, trying to speak, trying to deny the absolutely *fucking* inevitable...

"I need that knowledge, more than I have words to frame." Roderick's voice was an impassioned thrum, his boots scraped as he moved. "I fear not your darkness, be it in your mind or in your heart. Perhaps I too, can strike a trade with you – my Tundran blood for your comprehension. My knowledge for yours."

It was like a meeting of worlds – like fucking *destiny* had just smacked him one, straight up the side of the head.

Are you fuckin'... Lugan found his voice, tried again. "Are you fuckin' barkin'?" *Destiny*, for fucksake, this was getting out of hand. "D'you know what she did to Ecko? D'you have any fucking *clue*...?"

"Yes." The word hovered in the darkness like a moth waiting for the light. "Lugan, I have done nothing for far too long. Your knowledge is vast, critical, its speed impossible – it defies everything I have ever believed." A hand gripped his shoulder, a brother, a plea. "Your powerflux – your 'net' – is everything I have ever wanted to be. This is my responsibility, the charge and dream I have carried since I was a child. I am a Guardian of the Ryll. I *must* understand – I must have your lore. And I must take that learning home."

"Fuller can give you a web-link anytime." Why did the sentence sound so trite? "Rick, look, mate –"

"Lugan, please." The hand gripped harder. "It is as if the Count of Time himself brought me here. All these pieces have fitted into place like steps of stone – eternal. We have come for a *reason*. I must understand your powerflux." Harder still, then let him go. "If I can take this home, if I can *remember*," the word was pure passion, "I can save my world. Would you not do the same?"

Would you not do the same?

Pilgrim. Corporate control, pharmaceutical control. London, great city now soulless, rotting from the inside.

The bloke was a fucking loony – but he had more guts than Mr Creosote.

"I wish I could, mate." The naïveté of it made him chuckle, wry and almost saddened. "But it ain't ever that fuckin' simple."

"Ecko believes it is," Roderick said. His faith was blind, resolute, untouchable. "It seems suitable that I visit his mother in order to help my own."

Something dropped in Lugan's thoughts – an old penny, tumbling finally down through an arcade maze.

Not human. Your DNA really isn't fucking human.

You – the tavern – it's all fucking real.

Mental brakes squealed as he stopped to look at the thought. *Real. Fucking* destiny.

You're 'aving a laugh.

Then he snorted. *Jesus Harry Christ, I reckon Tarquinne drugged that fucking needle after all. I'm gonna wake up in a minute with one bitch of an' 'angover.*

"Such idealism." The tech sighed like a shimmer, enticing. "My hatchlings have dreams – dreams I build." In the darkness, Roderick shuddered. "Tell me what you want – and let me make it happen. If you survive, nothing will *ever* frighten you again."

"I want…" For a moment, the Bard's voice broke, whether in fear, Lugan couldn't tell. "I went to the Council of Nine and they did not heed me. I need to wake the world. I need to make her people *listen*."

"The throat you have isn't enough?" Her sparkling laugh, chill as ice-water. "I'll give you a new voice, hatchling, a cry to bring down the very sky. Thera," the last words rang with dismal finality, "secure him."

"Voice?" The Bard's question was a breath, a tremor. "How will I –?"

"Don't worry, child. By the time it's yours to wield, you'll know it... intimately." She gave a final, shimmering laugh. "Stand down, my sister. As promised, I'll answer Lugan's questions. And let him go safely.

"Before I install *Khamsin*."

"You did *what*?" In the odd light of the tavern taproom, Karine stood in a too-brief night garment, hands on hips, outrage shouting from her skin.

Lugan dropped onto a bench with a solid thump.

"'E volunteered. Offered 'is blood to Save the World." He fully expected to be whacked with a frying pan any second. "'Ow's your bouncer?"

Fuller? You awake? Get your arse down 'ere!

"Sera's mending fine and *don't* you change the subject." Karine jabbed a furious fingertip. "You prove to me, mush, you didn't sell him out to buy information and I won't kick your sorry arse up one side of this room and down the other."

Lugan eyed her state of dress, thought better of the obvious response. Instead, he stood up, shed jacket and cut-down, pulled his tee over his head and turned round.

"There's a picture in your skin." Karine didn't sound impressed.

He turned back, massive bodybuilder frame earning him a sceptical, half-raised eyebrow.

"I don't betray me mates." His voice was stone.

What? Fuller sounded sleepy. *What's up?*

In the pub. You know which one. Get down 'ere.

"Put your clothes back on," Karine said. "You're not impressing anybody."

On my way, Fuller said. *Ten minutes. Put the kettle on, will you? This'd better be good to get me out of bed at four in the morning. Why can't you do this over the link?*

Quit whingin' and get down 'ere!

All right, all right. Coming.

Lugan picked up his tee, pulled it back on, realised it was inside out, swore.

"I'm fucking knackered," he commented. "But I got us some light – I know 'ow we find Ecko."

"And how we get home?" Karine's question was almost a plea. He looked at her for a moment – in the half-light she was suddenly vulnerable, very young.

"I dunno, luv," he grinned at her, wryly amused. "I still dunno if you're even 'ere at all."

They sat in the taproom, patches of fluorescent light spilling through tiny mica panes. Steam curled gently from the mouth of the herbal jug, smoke from the dog-end between Lugan's lips.

A grey-and-white cat prowled uneasily, sniffing at corners.

"Collator's still skewed," Fuller said. "It's responsive but the probabilities are way off. I've bypassed the building security feeds, they're straight to my flatscreen. We're good."

"You know this is all fuckin' 'atstand," Lugan said. "Maybe I am just trippin' me nuts off."

"I feel fine," Fuller told him.

"Yeah, but I could be 'allucinating you too." He blew a smoke-filled shrug, took another drag. "Still, best get the fuck on with it. Trip or no, it ain't gonna fix itself."

Karine grinned. "You're the soul of practicality. Herbal?"

"Awright." He shoved a leather mug across the table.

Fuller said, *Recording... now.*

"Friday 12th April, 'bout 2 a.m., Ecko buggered off the roof of Grey's base on the South Bank. 'E never 'it the floor. 'E fell through an 'ole in reality, and wound up in 'ere – where 'e went on some *mission* to save your world." His sarcasm was unavoidable. "Seems to be an 'abit with you people. Anyway, that's the easy bit."

"It's not impossible, Luge," Fuller said. "Over a million people a year vanish without trace. Crater, Earhart, Rockefeller. In 2017, Mark Domesday left his own gig and never arrived backsta–"

"Shut *up*!" Annoyed, Lugan stubbed out his dog-end, smearing soot on the tabletop. "In Ecko's skin, there're tracers – semi-passive, short streams of numbers at pre-set intervals. Their frequency rotates, but we can follow 'em. They geo-plot 'is location an' predict 'is next move. Simple." He threw a small, smart-nerved receiver into Fuller's startled hands. "The numbers'll give us 'is bio-rhythms – 'ow 'e's doin', when 'e's asleep..." He shrugged away the end of the sentence, reached for another dog-end. "I'm bettin' my fuckin' Shovel 'ead those numbers are still comin' from Grey's base. I wanna know what the 'ell went down in there."

Fuller inspected the device; a tiny LED winked back at him, teasing.

"The Philadelphia experiment, apparently."

Lugan glowered. "Fuller, I want Strafe and 'Eels after Gabriel. Get 'er scrawny corporate arse back in 'ere – let's find out if she's a part of this. Tell 'em to behave – she's a Big Fucking Noise and it ain't gonna be an easy job."

"Sure."

"Get Eliza on Collator. It's caught the clap – some kinda super-Trojan, still no clue what the fucker's carryin'. Nutshell: virused to 'ell. Quarantine it 'til Eliza can get 'er 'ead round what the fuck's the matter."

"Was semi-quarantined anyway, it's too vulnerable."

"And?" Karine's voice was blade-sharp. "What about the Bard?"

"God fuckin' save me from starry-eyed idealists." Lugan shook his head, stuck the dog-end between his lips, lit it.

Shut the recordin' down a minute, will ya?

Done.

Squinting through smoke-tails, he said, "If 'e survives, 'e'll come back. And you'd best be 'ere to meet 'im."

Silence fell heavy like a metal coin, rolled across the table.

Smoke curled in the air.

"Survives?" Karine's expression had congealed. "You didn't say..." Suddenly businesslike, she stood up with a scrape of bench, started collecting mugs. "You murder Silfe, you injure Sera, you abandon Kale, you hand Roderick over like some cursed fruit basket. You fill my air with that stink, you burn holes in my *table*." Her voice cracked. Furious, she flicked the extinguished dog-end at his chest. "I don't even know why we're *here*..."

Lugan pinched out the butt he was smoking, dropped it back in his pocket.

"Me either, luv. 'E's stronger than 'e looks, your bossman. 'E might talk like a big girl's blouse but –"

Luge... Fuller audio-nudged him, and he fell silent.

The hard line of Karine's mouth shook. For a moment, she fought it, inhaling a determined hiss of air through gritted teeth. Then that air emerged as a sob. Mugs scattered across the floor as her shoulders slumped, rounded and shook. She buried her face in her hands.

Lugan shuffled his boots.

"He has to come back." The words were muffled, hopeless. "He has to come *back*. And we have to go *home*. Please... can't you go and get him... *please*... We're all so *lost*..!"

Luge, say something...

"I'm sorry, luv." Uncomfortably helpless, Lugan patted her arm, but she shook him off, temper flashing from tear-lined eyes.

"*Don't* patronise me."

"We're all in the same bo–"

"No, we're *not*! You haven't lost your *world*! You don't choke on the air you breathe – you're not a prisoner, a *purposeless* prisoner, in something you used to love. The tavern's *broken*, it— it's not meant to be here. If we can't get home, The Wanderer will die."

"Fan-fuckin'-tastic." Frustrated, Lugan slammed a boot into the table and sent it skidding over, jug splashing into a dark stain on the floor. He came to his feet, shadow looming. "*Look*, I didn't send you people a fucking *invite*. Anytime you wanna try sortin' this out yourselves – and gettin' the *fuck* out my chop shop – is good with me."

Karine rounded on him, snarling through tears, "It's not my fault, don't –!"

"*I don't fucking care whose fault it is!*" Lugan was thundering now, his temper barely in check. He was fighting to control a lunatic situation he'd no way to understand and he'd passed "enough" three stops back. How the fucking *hell* had this insanity all become *his* responsibility?

His roar brought him wide-eyed quiet. The cat, unperturbed, was washing.

Ah, Luge? You okay?

With an effort, he grabbed his temper by the throat and choked the shit out of it.

"What d'you mean, The Wanderer will die?" His words were measured, tightly controlled. "If this is some kinda threat…"

"Two things can't occupy the same space. It's why The Wanderer's cursed to jump – place unto place, rootless, 'til the end of the Count of Time." Karine sniffed, wiped her nose on the back of her hand. "Here, it's caught. Snagged. And it'll disintegrate. Or you will."

Or you will.

"You're pullin' my fuckin' chain." Lugan leaned down to pick up the herbal jug, scuffed his boot in the stain on the floor. "Seems like we got ourselves a deadline," he said. He looked around him for a moment, almost as if he expected to see the walls of the taproom warp or fade. "Fuller, best time to case Grey's base – the sooner the better. We need to 'ave a little *word* with the good doc."

PART 3: DESIGN

16: FEAR AEONA

Ecko drifted through layers of consciousness.

"...interesting case." The voice was male, faintly familiar, though he couldn't place it. His head seemed clouded with a hangover of smoke and doubt. His body was heavy enough to sink into softness beneath him. "He was very deep, it's taken some effort to bring him back."

"Sure." The answer was clipped, female. Something about it sparked sudden alarm, deep but potent, a bright thread of awareness. Ecko held himself still, trying to wake up properly without giving himself away.

The air smelled faintly of old food, of...

Shit.

I know that smell.

The memory hit him hard, a slap that brought him awake with a hollow rush of horror, a rise of tension that made the awareness in him flare to sudden life. He kept still with some effort, but the voice above him chuckled.

"Seems our Mister Gabriel is waking – his 'mom' certainly crafted him some tricks. Sal, would you mind?"

Ecko felt the grasp of a hand, a pinprick in his wrist, felt the warmth begin to spread through his skin, up his arm, to lull him into that wonderful, easy feeling of contentment –

Oh no you fuckin' don't!

His adrenaline coughed, stumbled into life like it was exhausted, but it was enough, and the warmth began to recede. He struggled to sit, swaying but upright, eyes blinking at the man who stood before him, at the woman, at the tiny, familiar, room...

Oh no. Nonononono...

Denial clamoured, pointless.

It was a bolt-hole, a shit-hole. A corporate fucking special. It was familiar as childhood, as recurring nightmare. It was bed and wardrobe and console, the waiting world of anywhere-but-here. It was a mug of coffee; it was furred mould. Every part of this room was the same as the last time he'd seen it.

When he'd burned its occupant alive.

The memory brought its own adrenaline, a real rush this time, and he was down from the bed, on his feet and starting to rally, to fight back. Shapeless fury battered the lassitude that swelled through his body. The man – by every fucking God the *man*! – was tall, black hair in a ponytail, the sleeves of his white coat rolled up to reveal the needle marks that tracked the insides of his elbows. The woman was small, blonde, hatchet-faced. She had a small, folded-stock rifle against her shoulder.

Doctor Slater Grey.

Salva.

"Easy." Grey was smiling, holding out a nicotine-stained hand. "It's all right, Tam. I understand – but it's all over, now, it's all over. You're back, we've taken the 'trodes away. I understand you're confused, but nothing can hurt you, not while you're in here. Take a minute, and relax."

I understand you're confused...

He'd heard those words before, felt this massive sense of disorientation, seen the light glimmer from a long, black ponytail. All of this had a familiarity that felt like déjà-vu, like he'd already fucking been here...

Confused? You got five seconds to tell me what's what or I start breakin' shit!

"What the hell did you put in my vein, you fucker? What was that? What've you done to me?" Ecko made a clumsy grab for the man's white coat. He had a headful of uproar, endless questions tumbling one over another, but the swell of softness in his body was rising again, making him fall back. It rid him of words, of concepts, of understanding; it made him want to give up, to drift into apathy, into the grey and emotionless emptiness that brought relief from all things.

Why bother?

I am happy...

The doctor's hand rested on his shoulder, soothing.

Ecko gritted his teeth, fought back.

No, I'm not going under, I'm not...

"It's just something to make all this easier," Grey said. "You were very deep, but it's all right now – all that's gone. No more anxiety, no more adrenaline, no more pain. Not ever." He smiled like a snake. "No more transition. You're home now. Isn't that what you wanted?"

Transition.

You're home now.

Ecko could feel the lure, the gentleness of it, feel that wonderful nothing reaching to embrace him, to pull him down to contentment as it had pulled so, so many before...

But he was Ecko, and he wasn't fucking having any of it. He had been doing something, been fighting, been passionate and determined and reckless and confrontational and offensive and fucking mad and he wanted that shit *back*. He'd been in this room before – and he'd been *going* somewhere...

"Where was I? You had me plugged into that shit? Why? What the fuck did you do?"

"Not me, Tam. I'm your friend and you can trust me. If you let me, I can bring you peace –"

"Peace this."

He lashed out, but his targets slewed and Salva was moving and he found the rifle up his nose, perfectly positioned to spatter the back of his head up the wall. Her face was stone-hard. Something about her presence bothered him, but amid the struggle between motivation and apathy, the tangle of memories he was trying to unravel, he couldn't place what was wrong with –

"Get your fucking cock out my face."

In answer, she shoved the muzzle harder.

He slammed it sideways with a forearm. The violent motion helped him focus – and it seemed Grey had realised it. The doc laid a hand on Salva's shoulder and she drew the weapon back.

"We're friends here, Sal. No need for confrontation. We have to help Tam understand. Maybe we should use another needle?"

"You *touch* me with that shit...!" Ecko backed up as far as he could, right into the edge of the bed. He could see better now, see the outside edge of the bolt-hole, the halogen lights that illuminated the stacks of these fucking things that Grey had in here, all of them occupied.

Have I been here all this time?

Had there never been an Eliza, a Collator, a Virtual fucking Rorschach?

Images came at him, a tumble of sensation. The warmth of a tavern, a woman with opal stones in her cheeks, a young man burning, the rise of some creature of flame, stone ruins, endless vistas of grass.

Chrissakes, he *had* been somewhere. Somewhere *else*. A sense of crisis shuddered up his spine and forced the lethargy back further. He'd been fighting, creatures misshapen, white light and nightmare...

What the hell?

But that wasn't fucking possible. They'd pulled 'trodes off

of him and he was disoriented, confused...

Grey said, "Let me help you, Tam. I don't know how much you remember, but you made a mistake. In coming here, you've made yourself a danger to society, a renegade. You've blown your cover – finally and for good. If I let you go, you'll face trial and probably worse. The government of this country doesn't take kindly to terrorism. But if you stay here, I can help you."

Grey's voice sounded like the spread of lassitude in Ecko's veins.

He spat back, "You can fuck yourself."

"I've done so," Grey said, "and gloriously, many times in the past. You think I don't understand, that I'm just some callous scientist? I know where you are, Tamarlaine, understand where you've been. I know the forces that drive you and I know how terrible they can be, how they eat at your mind, at your soul." He turned one arm up, showing the needle marks like tiny, open mouths. "I lived in passion, and desire, and hopelessness. I lived a fucked-up life and it taught me many things. Now, I help, I bring calm. I've brought a society in agony to a place of peace, of productivity. No more poverty, no more want, no more need, no more struggle. No more rebellion. All you have to do is trust that I can bring you happiness. You'll never want for anything again."

For a moment, for just a moment, Ecko saw the warmth – saw the soft grey oblivion that would claim him. There would be no more urgency, no more need, no more drive. He could be content with what he had, always.

Trust me.

And then there was something else in his head, some flash of vision. This time, it was an old man, crouched in a corridor, his eyes all wrong, his pupils the wrong sizes. He was staring at Ecko, staring hard out of the memory, staring as if he were trying to say something.

As if he was trying to say, *Kazyen.*

* * *

Amethea could not see.

Her eyes were open. If she closed them and pressed the lids gently with her fingers, she could see colours in her vision – she was not blind, there was just no light. The air was warm and still. It smelled faintly of...

What *was* that smell? A taint of smoke? Scented woods, incense? Something –?

"Little priestess."

The voice was amused, familiar – it sent a hot shock through her skin.

A door closed, a heavy bootstep came towards her in the dark... and then there were hands on her shoulders. Warm hands, hands rough with calluses. Gently, they spun her about, but she could see nothing of him in the pitch-black.

She said, her voice a whisper, "You're not here."

"But you are." There was humour in his tone, and the power and confidence that she remembered, oh, all too well. The smell seemed to be coming from his skin. She raised her hands to push him away and they lay on his chest as if she had deliberately left them there.

His touch cupped her cheek, gentle. He said, "Amethea."

The lucid part of her mind watched her, howling, as she melted in his warmth. He touched her, held her; his attention was everything. All she wanted was his acceptance, that sense of belonging, that family, that need to be needed. She wanted him to look at her, to notice her, and she said his name in return, even as a part of her mind shrieked in fury at her own submission...

"*Maugrim...*"

* * *

Triqueta of the Banned was in absolute blackness.

She stood motionless, breathless, hands on weapons with her desert skin alive and trembling. Without her sight, she concentrated on her hearing, on feeling the air about her like some damned Kartian – the place she was in was large and warm, and the darkness seemed full of –

Threats.

A rough grip on her shoulder made her duck, grab the wrist and spin – but there were more hands, more than she could count. There was a press of bodies around her, and she was stumbling, suddenly, hard against a wall, wondering what the rhez was going on.

She heard Syke's voice say, like a whip, "Ress."

And there was light.

It was right in her face, too bright, an accusation. It made her blink and flinch backwards. She tried to raise her arm to cover her eyes but there were hands everywhere now, they were holding her back and down, pressing her into the wall and forbidding her to move.

She struggled, cursing. "What are you doing? What are you...?"

In the light, there was a blade, hard and fibrous, a worker's tool.

"You've earned this." Syke's voice came again. "You know why."

"Earned what?" She struggled harder, furious. "What are you –?"

Then the blade moved, buried its tip in her cheekbone.

Under the opal stone.

What?

Triq had seen Banned justice a couple of times in her life and the sight was an ugly one, swift and brutal.

This wasn't happening. There was no way...

Syke! What did I do?

Now, in the light in front of her, was Ress's face, calm and clear, his expression grim. Panicked at his closeness, his severity, she began to really struggle, dread closing her chest.

"No, *no*! I didn't do anything! What the rhez d'you think you're playing at? Get off me!"

It was Ress's hand on the blade, his eyes that tracked the tip as he worked it carefully into her cheekbone, under the edge of the stone. Triq had no idea whether he could take the thing out, what would happen if he did.

A new voice said, "You caused the blight, Triq. And you abandoned your family."

Dear Gods.

There, in the light was another face. A face like her own, masculine, older, a face with the same stones in his cheeks, the same lines, the same yellow eyes. Triqueta had not seen her errant desert sire since she was a small girl, raised among the dust and thievery of the trade-roads and ribbon-towns –

"No." The word was horror, disbelief. "No. We had to stop him, we *had* to –"

The blade twisted and her voice ended in a shriek – a cry as much of outrage as pain.

"No! Damn you all to the rhez, you bastard sons of mares!" She fought against the hands that held her. "You can't do this!"

From behind the light, Syke's voice was flat, unimpressed with her denial.

"You're no longer Banned, Triqueta, and you can no longer bear the stones of your sire's banner. You have no family. If any of us see you again, it won't be just a warning."

"But I didn't do anything! I was there, in Roviarath, I was trying to *help* –!" Again, the blade twisted, again, her voice scaled upwards. This time, there was a popping sensation, like an eyeball coming free of its socket, like a bursting boil, and then a welling of pain and loss, dizziness and fluid flooding in her cheekbone. She could feel the blood-warmth overflowing, streaming down the side of her face.

She felt sick. Her knees were starting to fold.

Ress's expression didn't change. Brutal and clear-eyed, he moved the blade to the other side of her face.

He said, "It's not just the Banned, Triq. It's Larred Jade. It's the Varchinde entire. You've damned us all."

"I didn't *do* anything!"

Her sire said, "You left your family to die."

"No! I came here to fight, I – *Ah!*" The blade went in again.

She was folding now, the taste of her own blood in her mouth, the warmth on her cheek a flood that was matting her hair, sticking in her ear, streaming down her jaw and into the collar of her shirt.

"I lost my mind," Ress said, "because of you. Jayr and I will both die, struggling to reach something that doesn't exist."

"What? Ow!"

She struggled furiously, righteous and outraged. The blade twisted, vicious, digging into the bone, digging into her face and into her love of her family, breaking the ties and pulling her away.

The second stone popped from its socket and that warm rush of stickiness came again, thick dark blood streaking both cheeks as if she'd lost her eyes.

She howled fury, but her head spun. Her legs would no longer hold her and she slid down the wall to the floor.

And then the figures around her started kicking.

Redlock couldn't breathe.

He was in darkness, lost. He was suffocating, stumbling, gagging, desperate to haul air past the knot in his chest. He slumped against the wall. One hand grappled for a hold, kept him upright, the other wrapped about his throat as if he would tear open his flesh.

And he coughed.
And he coughed.
And he *coughed*.

He knew he'd been foolish, knew he should have let the hospice heal him. He should have had the patience, allowed the time for his ribs to mend. But he was Redlock, for the Gods' sakes, he was Master Warrior, unassailable. Neither injury nor illness had slowed him for more than twenty returns.

Now, it seemed, the Count of Time was standing over him, one long grey hand reaching into his chest – and slowly crushing the life right out of him.

You bastard. I'm not done yet.

Oh yes you are, old man.

He was on his knees, not even knowing how he'd got there. His arms were wrapped about his chest as if he strove to hold himself together. He fought for control, to suck in one gasp of air, another, but the cough came again and now there were flecks of moisture on his lips and skin, scattering to the unseen floor.

He was going to die, here, alone, in the dark and the cold. Not a fighting death, not the death of a warrior, not facing some great creature or starved bweao, not saving the world or his friends – but alone, in a ditch, forgotten.

Then a voice in the darkness said, "Let me help you."

And with it came a choice.

No.

The man's arm was muscled and string-thin, writhing with faded tattoos and needle-scars. There were flesh-tunnels in his ears, and his face held a look of such absolute sincerity that it was hard to focus past it to the truth of what he offered.

Peace.

But at the cost of passion, of personality, of want and need and freedom.

He offered a drift of nothing, and he offered it like a prize.
No.
Ecko's refusal was like the first rise of the tsunami.
No.
You won't fucking do this to me.

He turned her against the wall, his hands over hers, his weight and strength behind her. He held her there, helpless, his breath warm on the back of her neck – held her just long enough for her to understand that he had complete control, just long enough that she was pushing back against him, craving despite herself, needing to feel the heat of his skin.

Little priestess.

She felt him laugh, his dark chuckle deep in his chest; she felt him hold her harder, hurting her hands against the stone wall.

You'll do anything I say.

And then something in her baulked.

The rejection was as abrupt as it was absolute, a conviction she felt to the core of her being. Under the hot touch of Maugrim's hands and breath and body, it was the strength of the stone under her hands, and it was the only thing that made sense.

She drew a breath, feeling herself solidify. She turned her head, tried to look round, to see him over and behind her. But as he pressed into her harder, mocking, her vision became a blur: his face was there but double and triple, his smirks layered one upon another and sliding away from her eyes.

He gripped her harder, hurting.

But she'd had enough. Like a prisoner taking hold of her fetters, she fought for her focus, to stand upright and pull away, to deny all of this.

Somewhere in her heart, she knew the truth: *This isn't happening.*

As she moved, he grabbed her hair, wrapped it round his hand and tried to force her back into the wall. He grabbed a wrist with the other hand, went to twist her arm up her back. He pressed himself into her more closely, still with that dark and tempting chuckle.

Little priestess.

Little girlie.

She was not going to take this. The hardness she felt made her angry, there was no lure of temptation – her resentment had crystallised into a savage knot of hate, as cold and strong as the stone.

I said no.

She wrenched her arm free, fought to stand straight. He grappled for her and missed, then punched the back of her neck making her see sparks and driving her almost to her knees, before yanking her back up again, hard enough to make her eyes water.

"You're *mine*, Amethea. You gave yourself to me."

"And I take myself *back*."

He pulled her hair harder, tugged her head back and up. She felt her entire understanding of the world spiral in on that one sensation, cling to it as if it were the only thing that made any sense.

This isn't happening.

Amethea was a healer. She'd seen people in the most terrible pain, helped them focus through broken bones, through infection and loss, through fear and horror. And now, that focus was coalescing in the corners of her heart and mind.

Maugrim let her go, stood hard on the back of her knee.

"I'm not here." Stumbling to the floor, she found it was stone – she remembered how it felt, its strength and solidity and calm. "I'm not here," she repeated. It was something she could trust and rely upon, something that had been there for her once before. "I'm not here."

She turned to look up at Maugrim, his lined face curled in scorn, and said it again, louder, "I'm not here." As she heard herself voice the thought, so it gained authority and confidence. Her hand caressed the stone as if it was a friend. "I'm not here." Her head still spun, but she could move, could find her feet and control the urge to throw up. "I'm not here."

She got her feet under her, crouched there.

Maugrim's face contorted and he came at her, fists and feet and hatred, but he was fading now, like smoke, dissipating in the pale light of a morning sky.

Her resolve strengthened. She lifted her head, stood up.

He fell back, face stretched into pure, naked hate.

She told him, "I'm not here."

She watched him shout at her, and she watched him fade, ashes on the wind, carried by the roar she could hear in her head. She watched him fight to coalesce, to bring a last attempt to bear her down, but it was a fake, a feint, and she was just too damned strong.

"You hear me?" She roared at him in a rush, a blood-rush like combat; she was almost laughing. "*I'm not here!*" The room swam, her stomach with it, but she had this now, she had her belt-blade in her hands and by Saint Ascha and the Goddess herself she was going to –

Everything was gone.

In an eyeblink, she went from a fury and sunrise to a still, cold darkness – even as she heard her own cry ringing, she staggered from the lack of resistance. Her hands were empty of fury, of stone, of blade, of hope and courage. Her ears shrieked at her, after-echoes of her own defiance.

Or could she still hear screaming?

She carefully felt the back of her neck and the pounding pain was gone, as if it had never been.

But there was another noise in the dimness, a female voice, crying out in pain or horror – she couldn't tell which.

What?

Amethea stumbled, uncomprehending, fell against a wall. She stood still, her heart thumping, her skin tense, wary, struggling to make out where the rhez she was, what she could see, what had just *happened*...

Was this more trickery? More figments? Or was this cold on her skin real?

She shuddered, tried to gather her thoughts. She remembered – she had fallen, surrounded by the ruin of stone and flesh, by the injured and the twisted. She could see them as if they were all around her still, here in the dark, reaching with their open hands, their open wounds...

She remembered – pieces of legends. Aeona. Midden city, oubliette. The fading town that'd lived and died on the very edge of the Varchinde. A place for the lost.

A place that was real.

She stood upright, breathed deeply. Steadied herself.

Then she checked her body carefully for injuries, stretched her back and neck. She could see little, there was a stripe of light falling from an arrow-slit, high in the wall, and there...

Midden city.

There, in the tiny rectangle of illumination, were the people that the CityWardens of the Varchinde had not wanted. The people they'd kicked under the rug, the abandoned, the undesired and the undesirable, the criminals and the smugglers.

The inconvenient and the forgotten.

Amethea stared, heart pounding hard in her mouth. She prodded the remnants with a toe. The floor was a scatter of human remains – bones, bared and brown and broken. Some were fleshed still, though the meat had wasted to a thin covering. Skulls watched her with wide grins and empty eyes, some still had hair even, or glitters of terhnwood jewellery. Here and there were tattered fragments of garments, rotted to grey wisps.

They were oddly desiccated. Her apothecary's eyes told her that something about them was wrong, the smell, the scatters of dust across the stone.

As a bone rolled over, and sighed into brown dust, she withdrew her boot with a shudder.

Something in her heart half-expected them to reassemble, to get up and come clattering at her with ancient blades and flopping, gaping, chattering jaws... But this was not a tavern tale, a saga spun in the bazaar for trinkets and food.

She had to move. She had to think. She had to find Redlock and Triqueta.

Ecko.

For a moment, something flickered moth-like at the edges of her understanding – something about the horrors, about the chearl refusing to fight, something obvious that she'd missed. But her concern for the others was too strong and she stood up, hands touching and exploring the odd, striated stonework of the walls.

The feminine cry came again, outrage and pain and fury, familiar this time.

"Triq?"

Carefully, she picked her way across the remains underfoot, across the rectangle of light. Her hands reached for her belt-blade, assuring herself it was still there. From somewhere, the cry came again, softer now.

"Triq? That you?"

The walls of the room were carved into peculiar friezes, patterns of spirals, of madness and empty eyes, creatures demented that watched her as she walked.

Then a cry of rage made her pause, straining to see into the darkness on the other side of the room.

"Triq?"

The cry came again.

"Triq? Where are you?"

Amethea's eyes were beginning to adjust to the darkness. She could just make out a stone lip about the wall that served as some sort of seat, the persistent creeper that grew into the spirals. Triqueta was somewhere beside the single, sealed door, almost as though she'd fallen there even as she'd entered the room...

There!

Amethea saw her, curled on the floor, hands over her head – as if to protect herself from unseen assault. She was screaming defiance, crying and shrieking.

"Triq!"

As she came closer, Amethea saw that her friend's half-hidden face was etched in lines of grief. Through her fingers, Triq said, "I did it all. The fire, the stone, the blight. It's my fault. I did it all."

"Dear Goddess." Her own figments yammering at her, taunting her with horrors, Amethea grabbed the Banned woman's arm and shook her. "Triq, it's me."

"No," Triq said again. She curled into herself, shuddered. "I abandoned my family, I deserve no better –"

"Triq!"

But she clawed her hands into her hair, knotting round great clumps of it, banging her head against the floor.

"I'm sorry, I'm sorry, I'm sorry..."

"Oh, by the rhez." Amethea dealt her friend a ringing slap that stopped her dead, eyes wide. "*Triq!*"

The woman stopped, letting go of her hair, burying her face in her hands. She shook for a moment, then uncurled, looking up at Amethea, blinking as if in shock.

"Thea? What the rhez –?"

"You okay?"

"I had a nightmare, I think, I –"

"Had one too. Don't even ask." Her lip shook, she controlled it. "Figments, playing games with us. Where are the others? Redlock?"

"Figments." Triqueta touched the stones in her cheeks, echoed the word with a short, humourless laugh. She looked around at the spiral walls, the creeper, the grinning and shrivelled death that was scattered over the floor. She said, "I don't know, but I think... I think they took him away."

17: MERCHANT MASTER FHAVEON

Going back to the market had been Mael's first mistake.

His second had been loitering there too long.

The market was gutted now, a hollow remnant of its former thriving self. Many of the stalls and placements stood empty and skeletal, fabric fluttering forgotten in the sea wind. Many of the kitchens and alehouses were deserted, others stood with doors open like requests, though there were few people around to respond.

The people who remained were closed-faced, sharp-eyed and wary. The soldiery were everywhere, hands on weapons and prowling watchful; every barter was observed, every offer weighed and measured. Above their heads, the worn stone face of the GreatHeart Rakanne still stared out towards Rammouthe as though she craved the return of the city's time of legend.

Legend, Mael had snorted to himself as he rolled up his charcoals and styli in their pocketed fabric case. Legends were stories to be told, and storytelling was for busier markets than this one. Stories were for happier times, when people had the leisure to listen, and they were not afraid.

He slipped his tools into his little pack, alongside the picture of Jayr.

The sea wind was cold, and it tasted of winter.

Mael let down the awning on the front of his stall, and turned to look out at the dying marketplace, a taint of his grey mood flickering at him just as his curtains flickered in the chill. The alehouse where he and Saravin had sat so many times, the stalls where they'd stopped to browse and talk, the overgrown garden where they'd seen the girl that was covered in moss... Every tile in the mosaic under his feet held an image, a memory, there was another in every rise of the buildings around him.

Sentimental old fool. Mael wasn't sure if the voice was Saravin's or his own, but he turned back to lace the last fastening shut.

Then a noise made him look up.

At the back of the marketplace there was a commotion, shouting and shoving. There was a cluster of stalls there, still trading in woven fabrics and pottery and bright, wrought-terhnwood art. As Mael watched, he saw flashes of military colours, heard the strident demands of the tan commander Ythalla.

His heart trembled in his chest.

Even as he squinted, trying to see what the old bitch was doing this time, he saw one of the stalls tilt sideways, creak alarmingly, and then go down with a crash and a shattering of pottery. There were shrieks of protest.

Horrified, Mael forgot to breathe.

Movement made him glance back over his shoulder, and see that the last denizens of the market had come to stare, gathering on the mosaic, faces etched in almost comical horror. Rain was starting to scatter from the grey clouds that lowered overhead.

It didn't take an artist's vision to know how this picture was going to end.

Dear Gods.

Mael shouldered his little pack, looked this way and that for a quiet route out of the market. He was no fighter, and had no wish to wind up in the hands of the soldiery answering unnecessary questions. Then he caught sight of the height and inked chests and odd, inhuman gait of the Merchant Master's newest recruits.

Over the mutterings of the small crowd, he heard Ythalla's voice.

"The market is closed until further notice. It is the word of the Lord Foundersdaughter Selana Valiembor, daughter of Demisarr, son of Nikhamos, that all traders and merchants will return to their homes and halls, and all their goods will be handed to the soldiery, for redistribution as befits the life and health of the city of Fhaveon. If you are not a resident of the city, you will be required to hand over your trade-goods and depart before the death of the sun. The market is closed. I say again, the market is closed."

"Is it, by the rhez."

The mutterings grew louder.

"I don't think so."

Caught like a rodent surrounded, Mael looked back to where Ythalla stood, to where her forces were even now loading the terhnwood from the broken stall onto following porters, and hustling the stallholders away. One of them protested, was trying to reach for a hand or a hold on something he had lost, but a gauntleted fist in his face dropped him like a stone. The tan stepped over him as if he was not even there.

"Any resistance will be treated as an offence against the Lord of the City herself. Return to your stalls, and hand over –"

"Bollocks!" The word grew into laughter, scattered support that rose in confidence and volume.

Ythalla – Mael could see her clearly now, spear-lean and metal-grey hair as cold as her expression – raised a hand, gestured.

The old scribe winced.

The man who had spoken, dropped to the mosaic. He fell on his face with an arrowshaft in the back of his neck, Fhaveon's white feathers dulled to grey in the rain.

The crowd silenced in shock, the people closest pulling back.

"Make no mistake," Ythalla said, striding out to face them, severe and absolutely fearless. She was probably close to Mael's age, but a lifelong fighter and still fit as a horse. "I do not negotiate, and I do not play games. The next man or woman to speak will take another shaft. And so on, as many as it takes until you heed what I say. Return to your stalls and hand over your goods, as you are told. If you do not fight, you will not be harmed."

These people were only traders, the last few who had hung on, hoping to turn success from the perishing life of the city's trade-cycle. They didn't have the courage or the numbers to stand up to her, and as she strode forwards, the rain making both her hair and real white-metal armour sparkle with threat, they backed away, muttering.

By herself, she had enough presence to terrify them. And she had monsters at her back.

Realising that he had stayed far too long at the fair, Mael attempted to slide carefully round the other side of his stall to where he would not be seen.

But her eyes were as sharp as her blades.

"You! Scribe Mael!"

He could hear the grin in her voice, pleasure like a predator coming across a fat and helpless esphen.

"The Foundersdaughter wants to see you."

The Foundersdaughter, predictably, did not want to see him at all. The person who wanted to see him was Phylos. The Merchant Master's massive Archipelagan physique was seated in a carved wooden chair by a huge open fireplace.

The fire within had burned down to ash. The cook and his helpers had gone from the communal kitchen and the huge, stone room was dark and clean and quiet. Phylos's red robes were as dark as drying blood and his face was hidden in shadow.

"Scribe Mael," he said softly as the grunts brought Mael to a halt, and let him go. Phylos's tone was amused, his fingers traced over his chin in a gesture that might have been thoughtful.

"Merchant Master." Mael was stooped and blinking. He looked at Phylos through eyes that watered with age and –

"Enough of that, Brother. You and I both know that your mind is sharp as a white-metal edge. And I'm sorry about your glasses – I will, of course, see they're replaced. Acquiring such a rarity is the least I can do after the – indignity – you've just suffered."

Mael had no interest in playing old friends, or in any false display of gratitude. He eyed the fire tools warily, and wondered whether the Merchant Master would torture him himself or if he had an expert on his household staff.

Phylos must have followed his gaze. "This is Garland House, Brother, the halls of the late Rhan – the fire-tools still bear his craftmark. I should probably have it removed."

As I removed its craftsman.

The words were unspoken, but loud as a shout in the vast, chill room. Mael still said nothing. Phylos tapped his fingertips together and then leaned forwards, his face just catching the glow from the ashes in the huge hearth.

"Scribe Mael," he said, his voice now pure, cold metal. "I understand that you entertained the Lord of the City in your private rooms? And that she was unattended?" He let the comment rest for a moment, and then said, "Do you not think that… inappropriate?"

Mael blinked – for real this time. In the far and darkest corner of the huge kitchen, there was a scuffle and a squeak – an errant rodent, seeking grain. He knew how it felt. In his mind though, something in the room, some image he'd seen from the corner of his eye had jogged a memory, something about the rodent and the fireplace and the mention of Garland House…?

Pinned by Phylos's gaze, he tried to see what had touched the tiny flame, tried to remember what it was trying to illuminate.

"A man of your age and station, Brother, does not welcome the Lord Foundersdaughter into his rooms without a reason. Her welfare is of primary concern to me, as I'm sure you're aware. Perhaps you'd like to set my mind at rest?"

Mael had to play for time – but he was no good at these games. These were things for tavern tales, for laughter over a warm nut ale and a bowl of –

"*Tell* me!"

Phylos's bark nearly made his heart stop. In the corner, the scuttlings froze.

Mael opened his mouth, almost squeaked with tension, and then somehow found his voice to speak normally.

"The matter is private," he said.

"Really?" Phylos raised an eyebrow. "And what can be private between a man of your returns and a lady young enough to be the daughter of your children?"

"I have no children." This was better – maybe he could keep this conversation to some banter of wits. "I –"

"You will address me as 'My Lord Seneschal'." Phylos smiled. "It's not quite accurate – yet – but you may as well get used to it."

Lord Seneschal.

Mael's heart was in his throat now. Trying to do so surreptitiously, he looked all around the fireplace, trying to locate the memory, the thing that he'd seen.

"My Lord." The words almost came out as a question, but he controlled it at the last minute.

Phylos's smile deepened and he sat back, his fingertips still steepled together.

"You failed to answer my question, Brother."

Mael silenced a pique that wanted to demand that Phylos address him by his name – and then he saw it.

On the mantel that stretched above the huge fireplace.

It was a feather-quill, white. No inkpot, and he had no idea why such a thing would be in a kitchen, unless Phylos was keeping records of his foodstuffs. But it didn't matter. It was enough.

He took a breath and wished that he could pray.

Then he said, "I demand the Right of Appeal. My Lord." The last two words came out rather more insulting than was wise.

"The what?" That one had caught even the Merchant Master on the hop, apparently.

"The Right of Appeal, my Lord. I illustrated the document for a patient, once, when I was still in the hospice. It required me to draw a feather." He looked into Phylos's face, though it was still in shadow and he could see no expression. "Seemed an odd choice, and I've never forgotten it." Indeed that much was now true, he could see the very wording there in his mind's eye. "Perhaps I could recite it for you, if you've forgotten?"

Even as the words were out, Mael realised that he'd made a bold gamble – there was no one else in the room, and if Phylos decided to smash in his skull with the poker, no one would be any the wiser.

He tried to remember how many people had seen them come down here – the guards, the porter, the young man who ran the household, had his name been Scythe?

But Phylos merely tapped his index fingers in a short annoyed tattoo. However close he may be to the chair of the Seneschal, he hadn't made that final move. Not yet. There was still hope.

"Very well then." The Merchant Master turned, raised his voice. "Bring the Lord... *ask* the Lord Foundersdaughter if she'd be kind enough to attend me. And make sure she's escorted, this time." He sat back, controlled a short, exasperated sigh. "And as for you, Brother, you have neither the aptitude nor the training for this choice of path – I think you're getting in over your head." His grin was audible. "Don't you?"

When Selana saw Mael, she paled.

She swept into the kitchen, all cloak and skirts and hair and beauty, exactly as an artist might have drawn her. She descended on Phylos with a certain amount of justifiable indignation, but it crumbled like a harvest garland when she saw Mael standing there.

Phylos had not offered him a seat, and his feet and back were starting to hurt.

But that didn't matter now.

"Brother Mael," Selana said.

Her tone of voice held barely concealed fear – Mael understood that he'd played right into Phylos's hands by asking to see her. If Phylos didn't get the answer he wanted out of the old scribe, he would get it out of the girl, Lord or not.

Maybe he was out of his depth, but it was swim or drown.

"Brother Mael has asked to see you, My Lord," Phylos said. "He has invoked the Right of Appeal."

Selana blinked. "What is he charged with?"

"Nothing." Phylos's red shrug said *yet*.

Mael watched the girl, his mind racing. Not sure what his plan was or even if he had one, he said, "The Merchant Master asked me why you came to see me."

Selana inhaled, tension rising from her body.

Mael said, "I merely wanted you to be here when I answered the question." He turned back to the chair. "I asked if the Lord of the City had been permitted to see her uncle, whom I understand is in the hospice?" One glance at Selana's pale face told him that she'd been permitted nowhere near her uncle Mostak, or anyone else for that matter. "Perhaps," he deliberately left off the "My Lord", "you can offer an answer?"

For a moment, Phylos was absolutely still – as though he'd not expected Mael's sheer daring to be that big. He understood completely what Mael had done – he had placed Selana squarely in a position where she had to choose, and in front of both of them.

Mael quelled a rise of panic and hoped to the name of every merciful God that this was not utter idiocy.

He could hear Saravin, *What are you doing, you daft old sod?* He could hear his own heart thumping in his ears. He could hear the scuttlings in the corner of the kitchen – the rodents that would be getting his personal leftovers when the cook turned him into stew.

Phylos learned forward, picked up a poker. With a flawlessly innocuous gesture, he prodded at the ashes, and a flare of heat washed against his face.

Selana backed up a step, but Mael did not move.

He was staring at the Merchant Master's face, the height of his forehead, the slightly aquiline set of his nose, his high cheekbones and square jaw. The Merchant Master was typically Archipelagan, a handsome and powerful man with a very distinctive face – a face no Grasslander could mistake...

A face he knew.

A face he had seen recently, on a young woman, a face etched in harsh Kartian scarring.

Mael would have gambled every last damned thing he owned, up to and including his own ageing skin, that Phylos had a daughter.

Jayr.

Dear Gods.

They had taken his pack from him, but he remembered the picture. His mind was racing now – a tumble of questions. As the flare from the ash faded again and the close-up of Phylos's face was gone, Mael could still see it as if it had been heat-brazed onto his thoughts. Phylos had a daughter, a daughter that had been gifted or traded to the Kartians – there was no other way she could carry scars like those.

He had a lever, but for a moment he had absolutely no idea how to use it, what to push against. There was no shame in Phylos having a daughter – but the slavery? That was another matter. And what of her mother?

Jayr's colouring was Grasslander, darker of eye and hair and skin-tone than Phylos's ice-blue gaze and pale skin. Why had the Merchant Master lost – given – his daughter to the Kartians?

He was hiding something. Mael had no idea what it was, but the knowledge alone was enough.

He straightened, let out a long and slightly unsteady breath.

Phylos had not answered his question, and was still sitting with the poker in his hand. If he actually decided to crash Mael round the face with it, then all of his insight and cleverness would come to nothing...

But the Merchant Master put the poker back in the rack and held his hands to the new glow in the fire's ashes.

The cavernous kitchen had suddenly become a great deal warmer.

He said, "Brother Mael, I had expected more gentleness from a man of your background. The family Valiembor has taken terrible damage, and Mostak is not possessed of his full wits. With his brother dead," he glanced at Selana, who stood like a carven statue, unspeaking, "and with what happened to Valicia, forgive me, he is exquisitely distressed and really cannot be disturbed. My Lord Foundersdaughter understands this."

Mael gazed at her, willing her to speak, to stand up to Phylos, to voice a thought, anything. But it seemed she did not dare.

The scribe picked up the feather pen from the mantel. Twisting it between his fingers, he said, "It's a funny thing, the importance of family. How close one can be to ties of *blood*."

There was just enough emphasis on the word, just enough of the flicker of the feather between his fingers, to make Phylos's eyes flash with an interior light. To make Mael's spine freeze as that gaze crossed his own.

The Merchant Master would have been through Mael's pack – he would know that the scribe had seen Jayr.

And *exactly* what Mael meant.

For a moment, they were at a dead draw, unspeaking and immobile. Mael's heart was screaming in his ears – he was an old man and more out of his depth than he had ever been in his life, but he swam on, determined not to go under.

Selana glanced from one to the other, understanding that something had passed between them, but not knowing what.

"I think, in the light of what's been *drawn*," Mael said, "that the Lord of the City should take more of a... personal interest in her uncle's welfare?"

Phylos glared, and Mael imagined him considering the play that had been made. He had no idea how much Mael knew about Jayr – or didn't. And he had to weigh very carefully what he would do next.

Mael nearly fell over when he said, "Very well then. If that is her wish."

Selana's mouth opened in shock. She shut it again almost immediately, stood up to her full height.

"Yes, I... yes, I would like to see my uncle. I would..."

Phylos leaned to pat her arm. "I will send the senior apothecary down to him, my Lord. To see... how he is."

Dear Gods.

He had no doubts as to what *that* meant.

Now, the old scribe found himself in an odd position. He had the upper hand – but he didn't know why, or how strong it was, or quite what to do with it. Like his opportunity with Selana, this was huge...

…and it scared him.

Heart in his mouth, he said, "Perhaps we should all go down together. Now."

The tension in the great stone room froze. Mael almost panicked, he had no idea if he had just overplayed his dice.

Phylos withdrew his outstretched hands from the odd, clammy warmth of the ashen fireplace and said softly, "Don't push your luck, Brother. I have a lot of – questions – I need to ask you. And I'm going to have answers."

Again, he raised his voice to call and the young man called Scythe came in, inclined his head politely.

Phylos said, "Prepare a room for Brother Mael, he'll be... staying... for a while. And please escort the Lord –"

"Wait." Selana's voice had a faint tremor, but her command was clear. She said, "I want to see my uncle now."

Phylos gave a gentle laugh. "My Lord, he's very unwell. I'm afraid –"

"I said 'now', Merchant Master."

Mael bit back his smile, but his heart sang. *Good girl, brave girl. Well done!*

Don't get cocky, Saravin grumbled at the back of his thoughts.

Scythe paused, one eyebrow raised.

Selana gave the young man a glare, then turned to look down at Phylos.

"Well?" she said.

"Well enough, then." With a billow of scarlet, the Merchant Master stood, opened his hands and bowed to her, the gesture sweeping and exaggerated. "I obey your wishes Lord, we will visit your uncle. Now. Please understand, though, that he is unwell, and may not be quite himself."

Selana nodded, turned to Mael. "You'll accompany us, Brother? I understand the hospice is known to you."

She made as if to say something else, but Phylos spoke over her. "Brother Mael may accompany us if he wishes, but he will be returning directly here." His smile was elegance itself, a gracefully concealed blade. "I feel he should be a guest of my household. Probably for a while."

18: BURNING IT DOWN AEONA

"What do you mean, they took him away?" Amethea's voice was all shock. "Took him where?"

Triqueta kicked a laughing skull straight in its bared teeth, sent it skittering.

"What're *you* looking at?" She glanced up, said, "Syke told me. Don't ask."

"Syke?" Amethea stared at her friend.

Triqueta bit back a sharp retort. At the corners of her vision, she could still see Syke and the others, still feel their rejection and the strike of their boots. Her anger died unspoken. Whatever Amethea had seen, she had been strong enough to break out of it – to throw back the figments that had come to drag the horrors from their souls.

"I'm sorry." Triq's apology was awkward. "I saw stuff – stuff I didn't need to see."

Family.

The loss of it roared loud in Triq's mind, it caught at her lingering fears, made them surge into anger at whatever game this was, at whatever creature was twisting their figments back in upon them.

Make us victims, would you? Oh, I've had about enough of this.

Amethea was looking at her lap, at the floor, at the scattered remains, as though she couldn't bear to look up. Triq reached a hand to her friend's shoulder but the girl was already moving. She was frowning at the spiral designs in the walls and the lightless creeper.

She said softly, "Where are we anyway? Is this the place the – creatures – were guarding?"

"I don't know, I guess so." Triq's blood was thumping a tattoo in her temples, her fury was twisting a knot in her throat. She needed someone to answer for this, someone to blame for the figments that had tormented them. For Maugrim, for Ress's madness, for Syke, for every damned thing they'd seen since they'd left Roviarath.

For Redlock, for *Ecko.*

Amethea had picked up a jawless skull, was turning it over in her hands.

"You know something?" As Triq spoke, her mind was clearing, her thoughts hardening, her voice gaining volume. "I'm going to find whoever's done this, whatever the rhez it is. And I'm going to carve out its insides. Nightmares and figments, pieces of our pasts – they're not funny. I'm going to take this *back.*"

She spun, and one of her long horsewoman's boots slammed out sideways, hard into the heavy wooden door. The door juddered, but held.

"Triq, what are you...?"

"I'm getting us out of here."

She welcomed the door's resistance – she needed it to defy her, needed something to pit herself against, something upon which to vent her helplessness and rage.

Triqueta had no weapons, no kit. The Banned were gone, her friends, her family, her little palomino mare. Her opal stones hurt as if Ress's blade really had tried to prise them from the bones of her face.

She had only her courage and determination, the old breeches and shirt she stood up in, her boots.

But that was enough.

Triqueta kicked the door, harder this time, enough to make the sound echo tightly in the small room. The wood shuddered, tumbles of dust fell from the frame.

The bones on the floor clattered in echo as if they applauded her.

Amethea said, "Do you really want to do this? We've got no idea what's out there."

"I don't care." With a snarl that could have been Redlock's, she kicked again.

"Wait!" Amethea's voice was stronger this time. She was holding the skull out to the slant of light from the arrowslit, turning it to see the flesh-shreds that still clung to the bone. "Honestly, Triq, think. This isn't right. Something about all of this –"

"What? People being walled up to die? You're not jesting." Triqueta kicked the door again. This time, it buckled under the blow and there was the distinct sound of splitting wood. She heard the drop-key rattling hard against its housing.

"Triq, stop." It wasn't a request. "Stop now. Before we mess up anything else."

The Banned woman halted. Arms crossed, she glared.

"That isn't funny."

"Like you said, I'm not jesting. Look." Amethea held out the skull.

"He's dead, Thea. Been dead a while."

"No, he hasn't." Amethea brandished the thing as evidence, though Triqueta had no idea what she was supposed to look for. "He's probably been dead for less than a return. Quite a lot less. Nothing's eaten the flesh off him, it's like it *shrivelled* –"

"So?"

"Will you listen? Something drained him, Triq, sucked the life right out of his skin –"

"How can you tell?" Triqueta was out of patience.

"His bones are a young man's," she said. "But his skin – it's desiccated. It's like he rotted."

Arms still folded, Triq eyed her friend, looking at her filth-streaked face and crazed, pale hair. Then she held out a hand, took the skull, dropped it and put her boot down on it, shattering it to pieces.

"Whatever it is" – she kicked the door again – "I hope it's out there *waiting* for us."

And she kicked again, and again, shouting defiance as she did so.

"You hear me, soul sucker? We're coming for you!"

Rolling her eyes, Amethea groaned.

And the door splintered, shook under the heavy blows. It took the shocks, but every one was breaking it further, every one telling as the wood split under the sheer force of Triqueta's boots.

She kicked it again. It juddered against the drop-key, but bounced back. She was sweating now, giving a hard, furious shout with every blow. This door was everything in her path and it was going to *break*.

Ha! Come on, you bastard! Ha! I'll get you! Ha!

It shuddered, twisted on a hinge, sprang back. She kicked it again, and it held as if it were taunting her.

Exhausted, infuriated, Triq paused to swear in frustration.

Amethea looked up. "Triq, stop. You're crazed. You can't break –"

"I can damned well do this!" Her back was hurting, but she bit down on the pain and turned to kick again at the door.

This time, she heard the splinter of the drop-key housing.

"By the Goddess." Amethea's words were awed.

"No. By my feet." Triq's teeth clenched, her face reddened, contorted. She kicked and kicked and *kicked* – not caring about the noise, not caring about anything other than getting out of here.

And then it gave, suddenly and completely: the drop-key housing came away from the frame and the whole thing slammed open like she'd ridden a horse into it. She staggered, almost fell. The door smacked back against the outside wall and then hung there, broken.

Amethea was on her feet, speechless.

Triq wanted to say something, but her knees went and she was on the floor among the bones, her back twinging with shocks of white agony. She couldn't move, couldn't...

"Calm," Amethea said. "You've gone into spasm, try and breathe..."

"I *am* breathing!" The words were barely a gasp as she hauled cold, damp air into her hurting lungs, uncramped her side and back. "No time. We need to get out of here before" – she smacked the brown and broken remnants away from her and looked up – "that soul-sucking monster of yours gets hungry."

"And go where?" Amethea eyed the doorway as if she didn't dare step through it.

Finding her breath, Triqueta said, "Thea, are you just going to sit in here and be tragic and wait to be rescued? You stood up to Maugrim in The Wanderer, right at the end, you spat in his face. You kicked that damned bandit. Well, find your balls 'cause we're getting the rhez out of here, and we're rescuing the boys on the way."

Mustering an effort she would never show, setting her expression against the hurt, Triqueta stood up.

I can still do this.

You damned well watch me!

Outside the door lay a sunken courtyard, silent and circular. It was brilliant with sunlight, open to the sky and all crafted from the same odd, striated stone. The creeper grew more thickly here, sliding over everything and upward towards the light. About the edge of the circle, there were more friezes, though these ones were carven. In the bright sun, they were picked out in shadows, more spirals, or dancing figures crafted into the wall.

In the courtyard's centre was a round pool, cracked and long dry.

There were other doors, four, five, six of them, spaced at odd intervals about the wall. Several of them were broken, or overgrown.

The heat was oppressive. There was no wind. Nothing moved.

Opposite them, however, on the far side of the circle, there was a set of long steps, wide and decorous, rising upwards towards some high and roofless plateau. A second circle stood above them, walled like a lookout platform – it rose against the sunlight and cast its shadow back across the empty pool, a long blur of grey.

Amethea said softly, a catch in her voice, "I don't like this. It's too hot, I can't breathe…"

She was right, it was close, as still as death, airless despite the open sky above. Triqueta's skin itched with tension. She felt the loss of her blades more with every moment. Yet there was nothing here, no flicker of life, no monster, no Redlock, no Ecko, no soul suckers, no creatures wounded and bleeding. There was only the ancient stone, a haven for the sunshine and flowers.

Flowers, for Gods' sakes.

The edge of the sunken yard was too high to climb easily, the tall steps were the only way out.

But there was no cover. If there was anything up there, it could spike the pair of them full of arrows before they'd passed the doorway.

"Hang on." Triqueta eyed the edges of the yard, crept out towards the lip of the pool. She remembered Redlock in water, laughing with her despite her increased returns, laughing even in celebration of them, and the memory gave her a sharp twist of real fear.

Red. Where are you?

If anything had happened to him. To Ecko...

By the rhez! How had they even come to be here? Following Ecko, following Nivrotar? Following some haphazard trail that seemed to have no sense, no meaning?

"Triq, look!" Amethea was pointing. "The mwenar! Look!"

She didn't see what her friend meant right away. Behind the creeper, one of the friezes in the wall was a creature like the human-faced predator, powerfully muscled, its snake-tail curved upwards over its back. The carving was old, blurred with time, but there was another beside it, another creature, a beast like the one they'd seen in the alchemist's house, the mwenar with its four arms –

By the rhez!

Understanding went through her like a shock – suddenly their haphazard trail seemed oddly, frighteningly deliberate. Triqueta didn't know if they'd been led or sent – she tried to think through a tumble of connections to work out how they'd come to be here. Nivrotar had wanted a weapon. And Ecko had found that yellow brimstone crystal...

...in the alchemist's house.

Dear Gods.

She shivered, her skin suddenly prickling despite the heat. "The alchemist – Sarkhyn." The words were no more than a breath, an exhalation of shock. "Thea..."

But Amethea was pointing at another frieze. She was trembling and pale, her navy eyes wide, sharing Triqueta's shock.

"Triq, look! Can you see what it is! Saint and Goddess!" Her hands went to her mouth as if to hold back a torrent of shock and words.

Triq almost didn't want to know.

The wall was overgrown, the creeper sliding across it as if

trying to hide its secrets. She reached out with a flaking, itching hand and pulled it away.

Then she stopped dead, her heart screaming in her ears. She felt sick.

I know what that is.

Centaur.

Rearing and powerful, its claws splayed as if to tear the stone asunder – the damned thing was huge, like the stallion, like the creatures that had fought them at the Monument, Maugrim's watch-beasts...

Amethea was talking, words falling over themselves. "How could we have been this stupid?" She was looking about around her, eyes wide, the sunlight glimmering from her pale hair. "Maugrim *told* us he didn't make them. He said –"

"We're damned fools, the lot of us. It all *fits*. Whoever – whatever – this CityWarden is –"

"Whoever's here, they made all of this. The centaurs, the mwenar, the chearl. Everything." Amethea brushed her fingers over the friezes, turned to look at her friend. "But then... we can't be here by chance, surely? How did we...?"

Her shock was visible, a reflection of Triq's own.

"I'm starting to wonder," Triqueta said grimly. "Pieces of a story, all suddenly fitting into place. We came here following Ecko, following Nivrotar's need for *weapons*."

Amethea stared. "You think she sent us –?"

"I don't know what to think, not yet," Triq told her. "But by the rhez, I'm going to get to the bottom of this, and I'm going to find the others before the Gods alone know what happens to them." She yanked up another bunch of creeper, pale flowers wide open, like bright eyes. "Before they get made into something, for Gods' sakes."

Amethea said, softly, "Or before we do."

The remainder of the rooms that surrounded the courtyard were empty, their occupants the same scattered and broken remains. Despite Triqueta's fears, they found no black eyes or teeth among the scattered bones of the Varchinde's lost, no red hair.

Amethea had picked up a loose fingerbone, was turning it in her grip as if she sought an answer, needed to follow a thought through to its ending. Something about the deaths of these people was bothering her, something that didn't yet fit the emerging pattern – but she didn't seem to know what it was.

Triqueta, keeping an eye on the tower above them, only knew that this was all damned crazed. She understood her share of city politics and gaming – and here she was, beginning to wonder how they'd really come here, whom she could trust, what dice were being rolled – and by whose hands. This place was crawling her flesh, taunting and worrying her. There were figments still in her mind; still lurking in the creeper-grown spirals that seemed to be everywhere she looked.

Creatures created.

Amethea said, "There's nothing still living down here. If I had to guess, I'd say this was the reject pile. Those that the CityWarden didn't want to... to make into anything." She was still frowning at the fingerbone.

"Meaning the ones on the clifftop were – what? The failures?" Triqueta shuddered.

Amethea shrugged, grimaced. "It makes sense."

In several places clumsy marks had been scraped into the wall – forgotten sigils made by the desperate and the dying, last messages that would never be read, or understood.

Amethea touched a fingertip to one of them, said, "This place is old, Tusienic probably." She glanced at Triqueta from the corner of her eye. "What did he show you? In your nightmare I mean? What did you see?"

Not meeting the look, Triq was scanning the high stairs, looking for the ambush, the creatures that guarded the exit – or the entrance.

"Whoever rules here, I think he likes to make people victims."
Amethea dropped her gaze back to her bone.

"And *no one* is doing that to me," Triq said. "Or to you. I want to find this CityWarden and have a little word in his ear. Assuming he has ears. Maybe I'll carve him some more, just to be on the safe side."

She thought that Amethea would say something more, comment on her lack of sharp objects, ask her how she, of all people, could have been made to feel like a victim, but the girl only nodded.

Then, at the bottom of the wide steps, there was movement.

Ecko was not home.

This was not the Bike Lodge, not a hospital bed, not some mass of 'trodes and scanning gear. It wasn't Grey's base – he wasn't plugged into the world of anywhere-but-here. There wasn't a fractal fucking algorithm in sight.

Instead, Ecko could see sky.

He expected a rush of dejection, a momentary flash of outrage that he hadn't managed to bust and bullshit his way outta here, that he hadn't broken the program.

But all he managed was a certain wry lack of surprise. *Nah. Too many layers for that shit.*

Ok, let's do this. Let's see whatcha got.

He was flat on his back, his wrists and ankles now held in metal, his skin against cold stone. Over him, the sky was bright and blue, incongruously summer; the air was stifling-still. Around this platform, whatever it was, there rose some sort of wall or parapet, and from it reared carved creatures – gargoyles clawed and fanged, but worn and ragged with age. They peered over at him, casting odd shadows.

Behind them, birds wheeled in the sky.

Chrissakes, if they didn't come to life and try and eat him

before all this was over, then Ecko was a monkey's fucking cross-dressing uncle.

But the stone creatures didn't articulate, manifest or puke; their blind eyes continued to stare at nothing, pointless and without end.

Then movement made him turn his head.

There was someone up here with him – but that someone, thank fuck, was not Eliza. Instead, he could see the calm, thoughtful face of an older man, one of his eyes covered by an embroidered patch. He was greying at the temples, his hair tied back, and a series of leather thongs hung about his throat. Tattoos covered his face, they moved lazily under his skin, shifting as he advanced through sunlight and shadow.

He looked like an old hippie – and Ecko had seen him before.

Yeah, I know you...

Younger but still with the eye-patch, he'd been on the silk hanging in the house where they'd found the burning dead McBeastie with the four arms – and the sulphur.

Coincidence, apparently, had packed its bags and gone on vacation.

Great, so I walked into a fucking trap.

Now what?

But the man showed no response to Ecko's curiosity, he only walked around where he lay. He was in no hurry, humming tuneless snatches of something between thoughtfully pursed lips.

Ecko spoke, a rasping mutter. "Know anything by BiFrost?"

"What?" The man paused, as if surprised at the interruption. He blinked for a moment at his specimen spread-eagled, hands and feet held fast in metal clasps that even Lugan couldn't've busted his way out of.

Ecko bared his gap. "If you're gonna try an' torture me some more, I reckon I get to pick the music. Y'know, last wish an' all that?"

The man stepped back. "Last wish?" The words seemed

to puzzle him. "Ah, Ecko." His voice was scholarly, objective and calm. "I've worked very hard to bring you here and you surpass everything I could have dreamed. The figments have shown you some interesting nightmares and they've taught me much – who you are, where you're from. And what you want." He flickered a smile. "Which is where I – we – can help."

"Jesus." Ecko groaned. "Spare me the cryptic willya? If you're gonna peel my skin off" – he lifted his head, grinned – "go ahead. Give it your best shot."

The man's single eyebrow came up in surprise.

"Ecko, you once made a threat." There was a yellow glitter, sunlight on stone, and the tiny sulphur crystal was in the man's hand. It shone like a promise, like gold, like the opal stones in Triqueta's cheeks. "And we've got the potential for you to fulfil that threat. You can own this world, or you can break it. You can do anything you wish." His smile deepened. "And yes, if you want to, you can burn it all down."

Burn it all down.

For a moment, his long outrage was there in the sunlight, real and immediate. He was thrumming with it, lost for a sharp comeback. The stone caught the light like a promise.

Burn it all down.

The man stepped forwards, laid a hand on his flank as if feeling his response. The gesture was paternal, possessive, oddly eager.

"We want to help you, Ecko. We want to help you make it burn."

His voice was soft as blackening paper, as ash falling like snow. He was way too close and way too eager and his enticement was like flame, like the Sical. He was freaking Ecko the fuck out.

"You wanna help me?" Ecko snarled. "Let me the fuck up."

The man laughed, a sound that had an odd, bass undertone – as though something else laughed with him and in him. *We.*

He said, "You want to make people fear you, respect you, make them know you're there, in the shadows, stalking the rooftops." The laugh rolled around the walls, rose into the bizarrely blue sky. "You want music? We can turn your name into the single greatest legend the Varchinde has ever voiced." The hand stroked him, predatory. "We can show you how to burn it all. If you'll trust us."

The thought was as bright as the little crystal, dancing with light, with tangible temptation. Ecko was caught by it, staring at it, his rage still clamouring in his head... Could he hear screaming?

But the sound was gone under the man's thrum of enticement and power.

"You can help us, Ecko, help us recraft the Varchinde entire. Help us with madness, with war. With weapons." His voice was oddly calm, though that throb of hunger was there, buried deep. "I talk of crafting the greatest creations of my long life, of watching them rise and fight with your help. I talk of taking control of all that your Eliza – our World Goddess – has made here. You can own it, Ecko, you can make it yours to do with as you wish. You can be free of your real tormentor."

Your real tormentor.

Eliza. World Goddess.

The crystal turned, glittered. The hand was hot on his skin. Ecko shifted on the cold stone of the table, turned as best he could to look the man in his single eye. The tattoos writhed like familiars, sliding up his throat and into his face, sliding under the eye-patch like worms after a feast. The hidden eye was a ball of heat, like steam. Warmth seethed under the man's skin. Whatever he was, he was no more fucking human than the chimera-thing from the woods.

Burn it, own it, anything.

In his head, it was already burning – the grass, the trade-roads, the markets and the cities. He could see it, he could smell the smoke as he had smelled Pareus's melting flesh.

Struggling against the image, though not even sure still why, Ecko managed, "Who the hell are you?"

The man laughed again, his hands still exploring Ecko's skin with a clinical interest that was somehow more chilling than any blades or threats.

"Me? I'm Amal, the Spectator, the Host, many other things. I was outcast from Amos in the days after Tusien fell, made exile and pariah for practices of forbidden alchemy." The patting became a stroke, a fine touch that ran down the centre of Ecko's chest. "I came here, to Aeona. And I struck a bargain so my learning would not be wasted."

"So – what?" The man was back to using "I" not "we" – and Ecko was trying to clear his thoughts and focus. He so wasn't thinking about the crystal, about the rise of the Sical, about the burning Monument, wasn't thinking about any of it. He strove to concentrate, to find his voice, remember who he was. "Why do you wanna let me burn stuff, anyway? You the bad guy?"

Amal smiled. "The 'bad guy'? I'm just a craftsman, Ecko, I need to learn. I create things – just to prove they can be made. The burning," he shrugged, academic and careless, "is inevitable."

Inevitable.

The flame in Ecko's head was higher now, the glitter of the sulphur crystal, the roar of the Fawkes' night fire, the rage and hunger and glory of the Sical. He had to blink to focus, to see the sun and the sky.

Fighting to keep his mind clear, he said, like a last hand clutching the windowsill of sanity, "Maugrim –"

"Maugrim was a visionary, a wielder of an ancient art not entirely unlike my alchemy, in its own way. He 'prenticed to me, when first he came here. He would have cleansed the Varchinde, Ecko, if you'd let him. He would have ushered in the new age it so desperately craves, the new age that Phylos now heralds from the high walls of Fhaveon." Amal shook his head, sorrowful. "And you killed him – you brought the blight upon us all. Kazyen is come, the nothing, the death of emptiness – and we will all die" – he leaned forward to whisper – "unless we burn first."

Crops, burning. Grass, burning. His own flesh, burning under the sun. The Varchinde, wildfires across the plains.

Inevitable.

Held there, skin to the stone, that stroking touch still travelling down the centre of his chest and his mind full of fire, Ecko said, "Tell me. Tell me how to burn it down."

19: THE STORM BREAKS FHAVEON

The hospice in Fhaveon embraced Mael like an old friend.

As the scent of the place filled his nostrils, herbal incense and astringent cleaners never quite masking the melted-together taint of blood and pain and hope, he remembered being a younger man, bucking his responsibilities and playing hookey over the back wall. Those had been days of too much ale and not enough study – as he looked around the calm quiet of the colonnades, they seemed suddenly very close.

He smiled, momentarily uncaring of the red robes of the Merchant Master, of Selana's pale hair that gleamed gently in the rocklight, uncaring of the heavily armed pair of goons that followed them. *Simpler times*, he thought to himself, *when the great city of Fhaveon seemed all sea air and sunshine.*

Now, the city simmered with outrage and fear, a rising fury that boiled just under her rattling lid, threatened to detonate and tear the very rock asunder, to rive the city down to her stone foundations.

With the closing of the market, the people had had enough. Their livelihoods had gone, they could not trade – and they could not secure what they needed to survive. Haphazard

kitchens had sprung up on street corners and were doing
their best to feed the city's roving and restless, but they, too,
struggled with the lack of trade-space and with the threatened
withdrawal of farm-tithes. Mael knew little about the
convolutes of the trade-cycle, but he knew that it was falling
to pieces.

In the city, there were voices on every corner, calling for
uprise and retribution. They were too many for Ythalla and
her forces to counter – as she rode after one, it would melt into
the stone around it and another would rise, somewhere else,
sounding the same rally. For the moment, they had no cohesion
– but Mael knew that the time was coming when they would
muster. All they needed was the right voice.

All around them, bloodshed lurked, circling the island
calm of the hospice. And it seemed that the apothecaries and
herbalists of the building knew this all too well.

Phylos's presence brought tension to the cool air of the
healing house.

"My Lord." The senior apothecary, younger than Mael and
his face unknown, ignored the Merchant Master completely
and responded instead to Selana's slightly hesitant authority.
"You've come to see your uncle?"

There was an edge in his voice that might have been hope.

"I trust he's well?" Phylos's voice was cold. The young
apothecary gave him a look of dislike.

"As well as can be expected."

Had Mael imagined it, or had that comment been laden
with implication? As Phylos took the lead, striding down the
corridor, the others almost tumbling in his flowing red wake,
Mael caught the eye of the young man and gave him a barely
perceptible wink. The man started, stared, then looked away.

As Phylos turned through an archway and down a short
flight of stone steps, the apothecary recollected himself and
addressed him accordingly. "It's well to see you back here,

Merchant Master. We have concerns –"

With a gesture, Phylos cut him short. He turned through another archway and Mael saw a plaque on the overhead wall inscribed with an old sigil, ten-sided like the High Cathedral itself.

Many times, as a young man, he had wondered at that correlation. He wished he had the leisure to wonder now.

Selana ventured, "My uncle…?"

"He's resting," the apothecary said. "Though I fear he's less than himself. His… heart is troubling him and he's very weak."

His heart, Mael wondered, as they passed under the archway and the sigil and kept walking. Mostak had been training from when he was old enough to hold a spear. There was still Archipelagan blood in Valiembor veins – they were strong, there was no history of a weakness to the heart in the family.

"Poor man." Phylos's comment was bleak. He turned through several corners, came to stop by a door. "Brother Mael, you will wait here." He caught the eyes of the goons and they nodded, unspeaking.

But as the door opened slowly into the small, quiet room, as Selana ran forward with a cry, Mael saw exactly what he'd needed to see.

Even sleeping, Mostak's face was white, sheened with sweat in the rocklight. His rest was erratic, his hands and jawline twitched, shadows moved under his eyelids and his limbs fidgeted as though he dreamed of running, of fleeing as far from this crazed city as he could. His covers were pushed down, and his limbs were sinew-thin.

Mael was no apothecary, but by the Gods he knew the symptoms well enough.

The man had been poisoned. And by a dosage heavy enough to drop a chearl. But how did the apothecary not know? If Mael could see it…?

Or did Phylos now control the church as well as the soldiery?

Mael glanced at the young apothecary, but the man refused to meet his gaze. He was looking at his feet as if his shame was bunched on his shoulders.

The old scribe felt a momentary sense of panic. This game had moved board, and while he understood the plays that had been made – that were still being made – he still wasn't sure what the rules would and would not let them do.

Behind him, the goons stood silent.

Selana was gently shaking her uncle's shoulder.

"Please. You have to wake up. It's me, Selana. I need to speak to you. Please…"

Mostak stirred and muttered. Mael shot the apothecary a sharp look.

"Get Phylos out of there," he said. "Let the Lord speak to her uncle alone."

The apothecary looked back at him as though he were crazed. "I can't –!"

"Phylos, you may go." Selana had spoken to the Merchant Master as if he were a minion, giving Mael a sudden, hot rush of hope. For the smallest moment, Phylos stiffened, the tension in his huge frame flickered through the room and reached Mael where he stood in the doorway. The goons shifted.

The apothecary was holding his breath – in anticipation or fear.

The moment tilted, shifted, and was gone.

"Very well, my Lord." His expression schooled to a thunderous calm as he turned, the Merchant Master came back through the small door, a snapping rage of scarlet. He shut the door behind him, eyed Mael, then beckoned to the apothecary. "I need to speak to you on a matter of some urgency."

The apothecary bowed and scuttled.

Mael could have guessed at the content of the conversation, would have given his eye-teeth to go after them, but he didn't dare. As talks happened around him that could decide the fate of the Varchinde entire, he twisted his hands in the hem of his shirt and wondered if he could stay ahead of this crazed and carnival gaming, just a little longer.

When the hospice offered them food and water, Mael refused. It was too simple, too obvious – he had no intention of ending up in the cell next to Mostak's with a matching facial sheen. Beside him on the stone bench, Selana sat studying her perfect nails, her face troubled.

One of Phylos's grunts stood over them like some damned guardian statue; the other had accompanied the Merchant Master out into the elaborate walkways and plantings of the formal hospice gardens. Around them the little quadrangle was open to the storm-grey sky and the central pond ruffled slightly with the wind.

This was an opportunity – and Mael knew that he had better take it.

"My Lord," he said, clearing his throat awkwardly. "How is your uncle?"

Selana said nothing. He glanced sideways at her and saw her swallow, blink.

After a moment, she managed, "You've killed us both, you know that, don't you?"

Mael wasn't sure if her "both" meant Selana and Mostak, or Selana and himself. He opened his mouth to ask, but her shoulders rounded and she collapsed in on herself with a deep sigh that should have brought the colonnades tumbling down in rows.

She said, "If Phylos doesn't kill me, the mob outside will blame me and tear me to pieces. If my father could see what we've become…" She raised her face to the grey sky, the roil and threat of the clouds. "I'm the smallest child of a diminishing name. It's all a jest now, Mael. It's all *over* –"

"I don't think drama will help, my Lord." His tone was light, but the reprimand was fully intended. If he had to fight this, then she had to damned well fight it with him. "We –"

"You're a fool. You and Saravin both." Her voice was gentle, but grief and anger were entwined under her words. "You have no idea what that man's really capable of, or where this will end!"

"He wants to be Seneschal –"

"He wants to be *Foundersson*!" Selana turned her gaze on him, bright with grief. "Haven't you got that yet? You and all your learning? He's Archipelagan – he's Saluvarith's *blood*, his great-grand-nephew or something. I might be the Founder's direct descendant, but Phylos has more pure Valiembor blood in his veins than I do. He's got more damned right to rule the Varchinde...!" Her tone worked itself to a peak, and then subsided. She spread her hands helplessly as if striving for the rest of the thought. She said, "He's been planning this for more returns than I've drawn breath."

He's been planning this...

What?

Mael stared, unseeing, at the statue in the centre of the flickering pond – a leaping beast, long and lean with a graceful tail, forever poised on the very edge of its potential. The thought hadn't distilled, not yet, and the beast's blank eyes seemed full of shadows. Amid the shock, he found himself asking, *But if you know that...?*

He voiced it aloud, not caring for caution. "But if you know that, my Lord, then why are you letting him rule you? Perform acts in your name?"

"I didn't know it," she said, "not at first." She offered no further explanation, but Mael's mind had jumped – had followed a sudden and terrifying tangent.

By the Gods.

Jayr.

That was why Phylos had bridled so strongly at the mention of his family, *that* was why Jayr was such a colossal lever. Jayr the one-time Kartian slave, she was blood Valiembor – and if Phylos did take the palace...

She would be his rightful heir.

Mael was beginning to wish he'd questioned Phylos more closely in the kitchen, poker or no poker. If Jayr was Phylos's daughter, then how had she become a Kartian slave?

And if Phylos had wanted to deny her, surely he could have just strangled her at birth? Was there some Archipelagan superstition, some tradition or fear, that had stopped him? Or had he not known when she was born?

And, if that was the case, when had he found out?

Mael tried to think. Archipelagan culture was one of elitism, of high art and high ambition. They were a scattered people, extremely long-lived, arrogant by Varchinde standards, and there were only a handful of them in the grasslands – he knew no more than that. Frustrated now, his thoughts yanked him up off the bench and had him pacing the edge of the pond, the beast's eyes seeming to watch him. He went back to the original question.

"If Phylos is blood Valiembor, my Lord, why doesn't he just take control of the city? Have you killed?"

The way he killed your father.

Selana was watching him as though the sun had just risen in his face, was even now blazing from his eyesockets as if he were some kind of damned prophet.

She said, "What? What're you thinking?" She was on her feet now. "He's promised to make me his wife!"

Wife?

Oh, of course he has. Mael could have kicked himself. If Phylos was her great-great-something uncle, their Valiembor blood was probably distant enough. And how better to buy her loyalty, to secure his own power and bloodline? The old scribe snorted, partially at her naïveté and partially at his own.

He said, "How do you know he won't have you killed anyway, in the end?"

Her face paled, but any answer was halted by a sudden commotion in the colonnades. The angered Phylos, tailed by scuttling staff, now billowed out into the quad.

He barked, "Seal the doors. We must take shelter. Now!"

Selana was upright, and now Mael could smell smoke, the faintest hint of ash on the wind.

He thought, *Oh, my Gods...*

Phylos answered his silent shock. "The riots have started."

He strode through the corridors and they tumbled in his wake as if they could not help themselves.

Selana called, "Where are we going? Where are we going?" But Mael knew all too well. The hospice had cellars, cool chambers of dried herbs and full kegs, places where the records had once been kept.

Where he'd once worked.

The corridors now were as familiar to the old scribe as his youth itself, places he'd loitered trying to get access to the more interesting ends of the herbery. There was the door to the gardens, carefully tended under a scatter of rain. There was the huge hanging banner that reminded all of them that the hospice both belonged and answered to the Fhaveon church. The fat old High Priest Gorinel never came here, but it was his nonetheless.

The banner shifted in the air from the doorway. The wind was picking up now and the smell of smoke was stronger. There were shouts coming from somewhere – doubtless the rioters had equipped themselves with torch-and-pitchfork and were on the doorstep at this very moment, demanding that their accusations be met, that various heads be served up on platters with suitable garnish.

"If they get in," Phylos said, "they will kill you."

Mael noted that he said "you" and not "us".

Selana said, "What about my uncle?"

"He's too sick to move." The Merchant Master shook his head, a show of sadness that made Mael glance sideways at the hurrying girl. "The main doors are sealed, we can only hope. I'm sorry."

Trust Phylos to turn the situation to his own advantage – he was leaving Mostak to die.

Selana's face twisted into a worried frown, and she looked back along the corridors as if she, too, had reached the same conclusion.

I can't do this for you, child, Mael thought. Though something in him wished that he could.

They came to the head of the stone steps, steep and rocklit and worn low in their centres.

Selana said, "Stop... stop." She put her hand on Phylos's arm, seemed to gather herself. "I'm not going down there."

"Yes, you are. My Lord." The pause was infinitesimal, but spoke more than a scholar's volume. "It's for your own safety."

"No," Selana said, lifting her chin. "I'm not."

Figures scurried past them, faces drawn with concern. There were flakes of ash drifting through the air and the shouts were growing nearer. Phylos's grunts were nowhere to be seen.

Phylos turned. "You must."

Mael watched her, willing her to security and strength.

She said, "No. I want to go and speak to" – she hesitated over the phrase but used it anyway – "to my people."

Good girl. Mael said, "She should do so, Merchant Master. If she can hold them..."

"Don't be ridiculous, she's a child." Phylos's face darkened for a moment like the roiling storm that blackened the sky above them, the city around them. Then it cleared and he found his cold smile. "I fear only for your –"

"That is my concern, not yours." Selana took a step back. "You'll open the doors to this building and you'll allow the injured to be tended and helped. You'll secure my uncle, and Brother Mael, and you'll let me *go*."

Phylos inhaled like he was striving for control. He glanced to and fro down the corridor, then leaned forwards.

"What did he say to you? Your uncle. What did he say?"

She lifted her chin. "My father's blood is on your hands, Phylos Valiembor. Isn't it?"

Startled, Mael could have cheered.

For the faintest moment, the Merchant Master's jaw dropped – his face was etched in absolute and genuine surprise. Then the darkness and thunder rose in his skin and he lunged and grabbed her, slammed her back against the wall.

She smiled. "I'm the Lord Founderssdaughter of Fhaveon. You as much as touch me –"

But she was cut short as he bundled her down the first two steps, shoved, and sent her stumbling. He turned back for Mael.

"And as for you, you wily little bastard. I don't know what rock you crawled out from, but you're going straight back under it. In pieces, in a *sack*." A second lunge grabbed him by the neck of his shirt and spun him through the door. "I'll deal with you when I get back." Mael stumbled at the top step and went down them sideways, hitting the bottom, shoulder-first, with a sickening crack.

He tried to get his hands under him and failed. The room spun. Selana was picking herself up, turning to help him. Phylos stood at the top of the steps, staring down at them like some accursed and avenging daemon come to rend them soul from flesh.

The herbery was small; there was only the one door.

Phylos slammed it on them, dropped the key.

The game, Mael figured, was over.

* * *

Outside, a tide of anger was rising against the tall walls of the city – passionate and riled and flowing, roaring, from building to building almost undiscriminating as to its targets. There were those who had felt the bite of hunger, of despair, the loss of their livelihoods and crafts and trade. There were those who had felt Ythalla's brutality and her hard, mailed fist, those who had felt the Merchant Master's cutbacks and harsh limitations of tithe. The farmers had refused to relinquish what crop they had remaining, the hay and the terhnwood that they needed for themselves – the manors stood helpless and the tithehalls' stored resources were all but empty.

Now, the voice of the city was demanding explanation and recompense. It was demanding a solution that Phylos did not know how to give. One thing remained true – whatever his scheming, and however many returns he had planned and built for this, laid the foundations and carefully chipped away at the walls, the blight had not been his doing.

He had only played it, turned it to work for him.

Now, it seemed, he could make that turn again.

The wide-eyed apothecary met him in the corridor.

"Merchant Master. My Lord Selana is secure?"

"Have the door to the herbery watched. What of her uncle?"

"Merchant Master. I –"

"Execute the contingency."

The apothecary stuttered again, "I –"

"The poor man's heart will finally fail him. A tragic loss."

"Please –"

"Are you *deficient*?" Phylos rounded on the man, snarling. "I'd not intended to do this now, but if the rioters want something to hang, why don't we give them exactly that? Rid us of Mostak and *hold* the door to the herbery until I tell you to bring the girl forth."

The apothecary nodded and fell silent. His hands twisted one about the other. Phylos reached the main door.

Outside, rage and chaos burned as bright as the light of the city itself.

"Now," he said, and deep in his heart the slow steam of the other, coiled presence heard him, "we finish this."

Yes. You have done better than I could have believed. The Varchinde is yours, Phylos Valiembor.

Utterly unafraid of the howling horrors beyond, Phylos, the last true-blooded son of the Founder, threw open the doors of the hospice to face the crowd.

20: CHOICES AEONA

It came running, head-down and snorting, on hooves inhuman and with a speed that stole the breath from Triqueta's lungs. It was agile, swift of movement – it was animal, and crazed.

Swearing, Triqueta instinctively went for weapons, but she had no arms, no armour – only her agility and wit. And her luck, if she still had some left.

The creature was big, its shoulders shone with muscle; it had a spear, shaft patterned and decorated with feathers at the tip. Somehow, it suited the spirals in its skin, the layers of decorous thongs about its throat.

Something about it reminded her of the centaurs.

"Triq…" Amethea's voice was tense with complex warning. The girl hung back, watching, wary.

Triqueta stepped in front of her, swallowed hard.

I can still do this.

The beast slowed and looked up, met her eyes, raised the spear. For a moment Triq hoped the creature would throw it, but it wasn't that damned stupid. As it closed, it slowed and took the weapon in a two-handed grip – gave it a deft spin more like that of a staff-user. Triq drew in a long breath like courage and came forwards to face it, hands outstretched, to pace round it in a careful circle.

You want to dance? Come on then.

"Watch the parapet!" She barked the instruction at Amethea, didn't take her eyes off the creature to see the girl nod her response.

The creature grinned. Its eye-teeth were pointed, its hair a mass of tangle and darkness. She could see a short, irate tail. Something about it felt savage, elated and wild.

Triq beckoned it. *Come on, then.*

And it came fast, the spear point feinting at her throat and then the opposite end cutting round and under and slamming upwards towards her hip. She was quick enough still – it missed, and they circled again.

It said something, a word of angles and threat. She had no idea what it meant, but she bared her own teeth in a snarl of response. She didn't care what this thing was, or where it had come from, or what it was *armed* with, by the rhez – her blood was warming to this now and her snarl spread into a grin, an outright warning.

This, she knew. She'd been raised fighting the trade-roads and, even unarmed, she would take this thing to bloodied pieces.

Watching its gaze, its shoulders, she moved quickly, aiming to get her hands on the spear shaft and twist it out of the creature's grip. But it saw the move and stepped back, bringing the point to level at her belly.

Again, they circled.

Amethea said, "There's something up there, I can't see –"

"Just watch it. If it has a weapon, throw rocks at it! Make it keep its head down!"

The response distracted her for a moment too long. The beast came forward, now with the spear-point low. It caught her kneecap, twisting and sickening and impossibly painful. She staggered but kept her feet.

"Triq!" Amethea was moving. "You okay?"

"Stay there!" The scrape was a nasty one, warmth oozed down her shin. She needed to finish this damned thing – and fast.

Her right hand moved, a lunge towards its groin, but the motion was a feint – she got her left hand on the shaft of the spear. Using it to brace herself, she slammed one long boot round, hard, into the side of the thing's skull. The impact jarred her knee, but the creature fell back, shaking its head.

But Triq still had hold of the spear. If its grip lessened, even for a moment –

Then her back went into spasm, dropping her like a rock.

In a moment of horrible clarity, she realised she'd pushed herself too far kicking down the door – her body simply couldn't take it any more. *I'm too old for this, for Gods' sakes!* A sharp stab of pain shot through her spine and flank. She was on her knees, frozen like some damned crippled elder and she absolutely could not move.

The creature stood over her, grinning, teeth gleaming.

It knew that she was helpless and it was drawing it out, enjoying it.

From somewhere behind her, Amethea was moving. With a loco disregard for anything resembling sense, the girl came past her as if she was going to tackle the beast herself...

...but she didn't get time.

The creature dropped the spear completely and threw itself at Triq, bearing her to the stone floor, wrenching her back and making her spit shards of pain.

She hit the ground twisted, one leg caught under her, couldn't move.

And it was over her like a lover, hard muscled and grinning, its breath fecund and steam-warm. The spirals on its skin writhed and it shifted its weight, fought to get her arms over her head.

Furious, she jack-knifed, not caring about the pain. She

tried to free her leg, twist, throw the beast from her, hoped that Amethea would have the courage to pick the spear up and impale the damned thing clean through...

Then Triqueta realised what it wanted.

Dear Gods!

She'd felt this once before, this exact sensation, this odd pull of sensuousness and helplessness and loss and elation. This peculiar, nauseous drawing of her soul from her flesh.

Like Tarvi, the damn thing was stealing her *time*.

Now, her fury edged on panic – she had no more damned time to spare. Tarvi had robbed her of returns, this thing would kill her, drain her to ash and bared bone, just like the damned skeletons in the cells. She thrashed, got one hand free, wrapped it around the beast's neckthongs and twisted, knotting them round her knuckles and driving them upwards into its throat.

Make me a damned victim, will you?

Its eyes bulged, its grip lessened. The pulling sensation stopped and it shifted its weight – it was all Triq needed.

Amethea had the spear in her hands but hesitated, not really knowing where to stick it. Triq twisted out from under the creature, threw it down and sideways and shouted, "Thea! Now! *Now!*"

With surprising strength, Amethea jabbed the spear at the creature's flank.

It shrieked, but the tip glanced from a rib, gave it a nasty triangular tear. It reached out a hand, grappled to get its spear back but Amethea was too fast. With a shudder, she kicked it in the face.

Triqueta cheered, giving it the ululating warcry of the Banned – then realised that whatever was on the tower would hear her and come running.

They were out of time.

Literally.

Triq was on her feet in a moment, ignoring the sickening

twinge in her back. She took the spear from Amethea and rammed it, point first, into the beast's mouth, straight back into its skull.

Its hooves kicked, just for a moment, then it collapsed.

It didn't move again.

Now, my estavah, my brother, now is the beginning of all things. With the creation we have before us, so do all things change.

We've done well.

The creature in Amal's mind was stronger now, stronger than it had ever been. It was there, always there, teasing at the forefront of his thoughts. It caressed the barrier between them with sharp fingers of heat and impatience. It was starving, a predator stalking for lust and sustenance. It was all he could do to remember where it ended and he began.

Yet he remained academic, emotionless – he knew what would happen if he lost control. It craved freedom, and its hunger, its naked *want*, was too close to the surface for it to conceal.

The creature had no interest in his learning, his crafting, in building armies. The creature wanted its freedom – it wanted to master the destruction itself.

Ecko was the key to its cell, and its expectation burned fervent and silent and white-hot.

But as the creature had played Amal to bring Ecko to Aeona, so Amal had played it in return – without its strength and insight, he would not have the manifest skills for his crafting. Flex and stretch, their pact had always worked this way. They craved time, both of them. Amal craved it to further his own, to learn and study and craft; his creature craved it to feed its strength, to one day shatter Amal's control and break free.

Their bargain had been a balance, and down through long returns, the delicate tilt and shift played on.

Now, that balance was to be tested. Ecko was its pivot, and

Amal would not have liked to guess its outcome.

Yet he must retain control.

Peace, he told the creature, *wait. There is knowledge to be gained, a new army to be crafted. New creatures and figments, new nightmares.*

The creature snarled at him, *We will bring war!*

I will give you your war, but in my own time. Wait!

It sneered at him but subsided, fading backwards, almost out of touch. Yet that sense of *want* remained, shimmering faint and hot and cruel. It teased him like the tip of a brand, like a noise in the background that he couldn't quite shut out.

You will do what I say, my creature. Lore must be gathered, and used to greatest effect.

Amal walked slowly round the strange, mottle-skinned, fibre-muscled little man, his back held hard against the stone, his wrists and ankles caught motionless. The shadows of the gargoyles made the colours of his skin shift, almost as if they tried to stay out of the sun.

Tell me how to burn it down.

The little man's eagerness felt uncannily like the creature's own.

Ecko bared his teeth, said, "So? Let's get this road on the show."

He thinks as I do. The creature was still there, coiling and rustling like laughter at the back of Amal's thoughts. *Yes, yes, yes...*

I said, you will wait!

Ecko clanked his wrists against the metal. "Gimme the sulphur or whatever. Let's *go.*"

Amal chuckled. "The brimstone has served its purpose – we make new weapons here." He smiled passionless, took Ecko's chin in his hand and said, "Weapons of flesh."

Ecko's sneer grew. "Chrissakes, what d'you want? My user manual?"

I like this one. The creature's lingering humour was like

greed. *He's funny.* And then that laughter was suddenly gone, torn down, closed away, and it was surging forwards once more, as if Amal's barriers and controls meant nothing.

Now open him.

The force of the command sent a sharp shock through the alchemist's flesh, brought a sudden, hot taste to his mouth. In his head, the creature was rising, sudden and terrible, surging to full power. Destruction came with it, surrounded it, images of flame and crumbling walls, of tiny people fleeing hopeless.

Why play petty games, pieces of what must come? You will gain your greatest learning with your greatest action! We must bring war to the Varchinde now – we must rise now!

Wait! Amal had long returns of control. He'd lived with the creature since the days of Tusien and now he strove to hold it back. He did not dare flinch, even for a moment. If he weakened, that pivot would turn, and it would tear him from the inside out.

The burning was inevitable, but it was also eventual. He would not relinquish the opportunity.

Amal was a master, creator of chearl, of nartuk, of bretir, of creatures half-human and of humans half-creature... understanding Ecko was imperative.

I must know it all!

Ecko was his life's opportunity. He was insight, an ultimate creation. To win understanding of that lore, Amal was prepared to risk playing the creature's game as far as it suited him to do so, to dare the creature's hunger and greed.

Here on the table – *this* was the thing they both craved, the thing they'd lured to the midden city.

This node. This critical point.

Yes! The creature was raging now, passion and power – anticipating its freedom and the devastation it would wreak. *Now! Now!*

No! I am in control here! Amal fought back, fought harder than he ever had –

There came a sudden cry from the courtyard below – unexpected, petrifying the striving as if it were suddenly set in stone. The voice was high and female, defiant and angry. For a moment, both Amal and the creature paused in disbelief – and then the alchemist cursed, with frustration and anger.

The creature fed on his emotions, revelled in them.

Birds on the parapet took flight, cawing in distress.

Amal spun, startled and furious and forcing the feelings away. He ran for the top of the long steps, his heart thundering, his blood playing tunes of fear. He had no staff here other than the crafted vialer; there was no one else in Aeona.

In his mind, his creature coiled and hissed. It liked his outrage and it made it stronger.

What is this? Its voice was hotter now, eager. *What is this new thing that comes? That makes you so... angry?*

Feet on the steps. Amal paused at their head, stared down at the small, bright figure that was racing upwards, at these crazed creatures that challenged the moment of his greatest breakthrough.

There was a woman, small and slight and strong and desert-blooded, eyes as bright as the yellow sun, the opal stones in her cheeks burning with indignation.

The creature was laughing at him now. *Her time is good, Amal. I remember this one, I remember her taste. Bring her, bring them both...*

Amal heard its lust in his own pulse-beat, in the tattoo of alarm drumming in his skin.

Behind the desert woman came a second figure, younger, pale-haired and quite beautiful. The creature's laughter rose, but Amal had paused as if the Count of Time himself had cupped his grey hands over the gargoyles on the tower...

Waiting.

Triqueta. Amethea.

Banished to the city's cellars because he had no desire to

craft with either of them. Their time may yet feed him – them – but these two had no further use.

They had seen him now, and they were running.

Bring them to me now. The Count of Time is upon us, Amal! Rhan rises; he comes to face me down and he comes with power. My old army rises, your creatures and creations from returns gone, locked into the Fhaveon stone. The city stands ready for my return!

The creature's usual mental caress, its coaxing tones of "my brother, my estavah", were gone, shredded in the gale of eagerness and elation.

My *return.*

Not "our".

No more games, Amal realised. No more tilt and shift.

In his chest, his heart seemed to freeze. The Count of Time held his hands still.

Waiting.

For that striving of soul against soul. For that tiny pivot that would turn either way, and affect the pattern of all things.

Then the two women reached the top of the steps.

Triqueta was upon Amal in an instant, her captured spear at his throat, words racing from her angered mouth.

"I know you. From the hanging, in the house in Amos – this some *game*, is it?" The word was an accusation. "What the rhez have you done with my friends?"

Amethea, behind her, stared at the table, at the crouching stone grotesques that watched it so carefully. Her hand was over her mouth, then she too, was spilling words. "What the rhez are you *doing?*"

Take them both! The creature raged, rising and fighting against his flesh, his fetters of will that held it in place. *I am out of time, Amal! Take them both, take them –!*

"Silence!" Amal barked the order, sending the creature reeling like a rolling weed, stopping both women in their tracks.

"This is Aeona and this is my *home*! I say what goes here!"

Triqueta aimed the spear at his chin. "I don't think so. Where are my friends, you…"

He stepped back, with a taunting gesture that was almost a bow.

"Shit!" Ecko was twisting his body awkwardly on the stone table, trying to look round. "What the hell're you doing?"

"Ecko!" Triqueta was running now, relieved, spear still in her hands. "I should slit your damned throat myself!"

"Fucking nick-of-time-rescue bullshit. Don't you fucking *dare.*"

She stopped as if he'd slapped her. "What?"

Struggling to sit up, failing, Ecko snarled at both of them, a wraith of darkness and fire and savagery.

"Don't you fucking *dare* come up here." He twisted further against metal and stone. "You're too fucking *late*. I'm done with this, all of it. I'm done doing what I'm told, being the good guy, saving the world. I'm gonna burn it all the fuck down, show Eliza just what she can do with her Virtual fucking *Rorschach*!"

The creature was alight now, blazing, its lust and wonder burning like a plainswide fire. *Yes! Now! You must do this now!*

But Amal was still fighting, still thinking. He had to have time – not stolen time, but the time to take back control of this crazed tableau, both internal and external.

He moved back, stood at Ecko's head, a blade across his throat, and said, "Either of you as much as breathe, he dies." *And you,* he said to the creature, *will gain no time or strength from his blood-letting. So be silent!*

The creature raged at him, furious. It understood, in that gesture, that it had not fooled or led him, that he had absolutely no intention of letting it loose, that he prized his lore above all things.

And so the last pitch and sway of their long bargain began.

Triqueta paused, the spear held steady in cracked hands.

Amethea said, "Horseshit. We'll take our chances. He's tougher than you realise – and you're going to kill him anyway. Or you'll try to."

Triqueta chuckled. "If you don't want to be impaled like an eager bride, step *away*."

But Ecko was shouting at them. "Chrissakes, are you two fucking deaf? I don't want a fucking *rescue*. You hear me?"

"By the rhez, Ecko, do you have to make everything as difficult as possible?" Without moving the spear-point, Triqueta fumed her exasperation. "We're your friends, we came here because we love you, because we won't abandon you" – her expression shadowed for a moment – "because we don't walk out on family. You're a part of us, Ecko, we've been through the rhez together, and come out the other side. This... *man*," she pointed with the spear though Ecko couldn't see, "this man made the centaurs, he made the mwenar you burned in the alchemist's hall. He's Maugrim's *master*, for the Gods' sakes! Which side are you even *on*?"

"Side?" Ecko snorted, twisted again against the table. "Good and Evil, whatever, yadda yadda – you people are so fucking naïve. We're not the good guys – we caused the blight. And I'm not jumping through any more 'good boy' hoops. I am what I am: misfit, casualty, creature created, creature of chaos. I don't know names any more and I don't care. What I do know is that I'm *done* sucking Eliza's cock. And if that means the world burns – then let it burn. I'm Ecko – and I'm gonna do whatever it takes to stay that way." He turned, shouted up and past the gargoyles above him. "This program? Has *failed*."

INTERLUDE: THE FATE OF THE WANDERER
THE BIKE LODGE, LONDON

Karine had been having nightmares.

White light, rage and flame, passion so powerful it had woken her, sweating and shaking, and she'd left her chamber to pace the silent and empty floors of The Wanderer.

To feel the warmth of the building fading even as she needed it.

The Wanderer was hurting. Cracks ran through its walls, spreading with each day, each rumble of vehicle. Its captivity was impossible – she could feel its hurt grow steadily worse. Roderick and Lugan were gone, the Bard was with Ecko's "Mom", the commander gone after Ecko himself. She'd lost little Silfe, Kale had died on the streets of the city, and Sera was fading fast.

Karine wanted wine, a means to lessen her haunting horrors. She knew it wasn't a solution, but she was drinking it anyway – and with the taste in her mouth and the carafe in her hand, she paced, her fingers brushing the scars of the silent tabletops.

The bar itself was broken, her neat rows of stock shattered and left where they'd fallen. The windows were askew, they no longer fitted. Looking at it all, she found it hard to breathe.

The harsh white lights flickered as the huge, overhead rumble came again. The tavern shook with the racket. Trails of dust fell from the rafters, more pottery smashed.

The sound cut like shards – like everything she loved and knew was coming to pieces. With another slug of red, she took herself away from the damage, fled down into the cellars, anything to get away from the emptiness and fear and harm that lurked above.

She felt like her nightmare was real, like Kas Vahl Zaxaar himself was rising in her heart.

Walking, like wine, helped to clear her agitation.

The cellars were warm, their familiarity settling. It felt safe down here, shielding her from the layers of impossibility over her head. Slowly, a sense of ease began to creep through her muscles, unknotting her chest and throat. Her heart began to slow.

Everything would be all right – the Bard had never let her down, he'd always been there. He was her friend, her protector, her eccentric uncle and she *knew* he would find a way to fix this.

If he would only come home.

She should find something to do, maybe, take her mind from her own uselessness. A stocktake could take days – she had no idea how long it had been since she'd done the job properly...

Days.

The thought caught her, cut under her guard like a blade. Her heart started to hammer again, her pulse to rise, her breath to ball hard in her throat. Her hand tightened on the carafe.

Did they have... *days?*

What would happen if The Wanderer fell? Would she ever go home?

Time and hopelessness stretched ahead of her like an empty road, redoubled her blood to a thumping panic, beating in her temples like a war-drum. She rested a hand on the stack closest to her, needing its support.

Days.

Somehow, she'd been expecting him any moment – every sound had made her glance up, waiting for the light to change, for the door to open. Fuller had come in and out, but his face had furrowed into a heavy frown. He'd taken her to see Sera, but her friend's faltering life had only upset her more.

Days.

Something moved by her feet, startling her. She stumbled – then realised the cat had followed her down and was curling about her ankles, seeking friendship or food.

She put the carafe on a shelf and picked the little beast up, buried her nose in its fur.

"It'll be all right, little one," she told it. "It'll be all right. I promise."

But the creature stiffened suddenly, struggling to escape her grip. She tried to calm it, but was holding a writhing, spitting monstrosity. It scrabbled and clawed, flipped onto the ground and spat at the darkness, at something ahead of her in the stacks.

Then it stood, tight to the ground and growling, spiked tail lashing behind it in a way that reminded her forcibly of Kale.

Karine checked her belt, kicked herself for leaving her cosh behind the bar. She glanced quickly at the stack beside her for anything she could use as a weapon…

But it was not monsters that the creature had seen.

It was movement.

The little cat's senses were blade-sharp. It took a moment for Karine to realise that the stack beside her was quivering, shuddering like a tree being hit with an axe. Her carafe teetered, rocked and fell, tumbling with impossible slowness to the floor. Then the whole thing was shaking and pottery was falling and breaking and the cat was scattering in a scrabble of hissing and claws. But it was not the stack that was moving, it was the floor under her feet, a queasy, shuddering motion that made the shelving and her belly both lurch together.

The cracks in the walls…

Somewhere ahead of her, the stacks – *oh dear Gods* – the stacks were *falling*.

With rising horror, she understood the noise now – the shuddering *whump* as each one fell, struck hard into the stack next to it. The scattering and shattering that was everything sliding and hitting the floor. Then it came again, the next *whump* as the following stack, in turn, toppled and hit its neighbour. The floor juddered as the noises grew faster and louder.

And closer.

The air shook. Ahead of her, the entire cellar was collapsing.

Karine wanted to howl in protest, at the mess, the loss, the chaos, deny that such a thing could happen – here of all places, after so long being cared for and loved – but she was standing solid on the spot as though moving would somehow make it all real.

No! This is my home, *damn you! No!*

Then her mind yowled at her, *Idiot girl! Run!*

Her scream tore her throat, though she could not hear herself over the noise. There were tears on her cheeks, she blinked them back as they stung her eyes. And then she was moving, turning on her heels and fleeing as the cat had done, the *whump-whump-whump!* getting even faster now as the stacks fell one into one another and the shattering of everything she loved grew closer. She stumbled, the horrific destruction seeming to follow her, to echo through the cellars as though the entire building was going to come down around her ears. The falling shelves were hounding her, the noises right there, up and behind her like some figment monster prowling through her waking dreams. She skidded around a corner, another, running like a Banned horse as the destruction was almost right over her, laughing at her, thundering at her heels...

She skidded momentarily, came out into a more open space, a dipped half-circle of stone floor and a flat, decorous wall with a single barrel set to one side. Reaching the wall, she turned, placed her back flat to the stonework.

Maybe, maybe, there was enough of a space…

And, as if the Count of Time itself had slowed, she watched the outermost of the stacks shudder as it was struck and then slowly, slowly tumble – boxes and carafes sliding free, falling to the floor and then smashing into shards as the whole thing came down.

She covered her ears and cringed.

It missed her, slammed to a thundering, billowing boom on the floor. She felt the air as it hit.

And then it was quiet.

For a moment, Karine didn't dare move. Her heart was thundering, her ears screamed, a high-pitched whine she couldn't shut away. Then, as she uncurled, she heard the aftermath of the devastation – the occasional shatter of something hitting the floor, the uneasy creaking of the piled shelving.

Standing upright, she stared, stunned by how close the tavern had come to killing her.

And by the chaotic jumble of its own loss of life.

From somewhere, she heard the cat, its little voice raised in a quavering cry.

She had no idea how to reach it.

Karine found she was biting the inside of her cheek, fighting tears. The poor little beast, she didn't even know where it was. The Bard was gone, everyone was gone, her *world* was gone – and now this. The Wanderer had been her life, the one thing she understood and clung to. She'd fallen in love with this building from the very first time…

In the devastation, the vision was strong – fleeing that harsh man who'd wanted to break her down, own her on every level. Funny how one decision – to flee when and where she had – had brought her to The Wanderer, to Roderick, and to everything that had happened since.

The cat cried again. She wanted to call to it but she didn't dare make a noise in case anything else came down.

She thought about Ecko and patterns. Just like the stacks falling, one into another, she thought about how one decision could change everything that happened from that point on. How would her life have been different if she hadn't run round that corner on that day?

Then a flicker of movement caught the corner of her eye.

Yanked out of her thoughts, Karine put her back to the wall and stood still, heart trembling. The light was dim down here, old rocklights that had not seen the sun in returns. She scrabbled for one of them and held it high.

There was no clear way out – not unless she wanted to try clambering over the mess in front of her. Maybe, if she stayed close to the wall…?

Oh dear Gods…

She told herself it was the cat, though the little creature's crying had stopped.

No, there *was* something out there.

Some*one.*

What?

Alarmed now, prickle-fleshed and wary, Karine pressed her back harder into the wall. She picked up a heavy piece of broken, sharp-ended pottery. Closed her hand round it like hope.

Who in the world would be down here in all of this?

Almost choked by fear, she stuck to the wall, breathless and trembling.

And then she saw it, a single figure in the devastation, a faint silhouette, shadowed in rocklight and dust. It was half-crouched, moving carefully, lithe and agile and dark, clothing indecipherable. As the figure moved closer, she could see that it was probably tall, taller than Fuller and too slender to be Lugan.

She knew who that was!

Heart and hope leapt, but she stayed motionless, still somehow unsure…

By the Gods. It had to be – didn't it?
Oh please, please, let the Bard have come home!

But if this was the Bard, then his face was concealed and something about his movement was twisted, wrong – he moved like a man in pain, like a man who had been to the very edges of the Rhez and then climbed back to the light, daemons clawing at his back.

He moved like a man *angry*.

Karine slid along the wall, carefully easing away from the incoming figure. The Bard was a welcoming man – open, expansive of voice and gesture. This man was closed, his body defensive.

Yet, she stared, transfixed.

He was closer now – she could see that he was tanned, bare feet picking carefully over the wreckage, steadying himself on the ceiling with one long hand. Occasionally, he stopped, picked something up and looked at it with an air of – almost confusion – before putting it back down and continuing to move.

He leaned down and picked up a rocklight, glimmering its last.

It *was* the Bard!

But...

Karine gaped.

His habitual shirt had gone. In its place was a garment more like one of Lugan's, long-sleeved and black. It had a hood that covered his hair, left his face in a hostility of shadow. Beneath it, some sort of scarf covered his nose and throat.

As Karine stared, hands resting on the wall of the tavern as if to draw comfort from the bricks, he stopped again, looking at something at his feet. When he crouched, his stance changed, his shoulders dropped, and he reached his hand out to touch something.

The gesture was absurdly gentle.

For a moment, he lowered his head, and something across his black-clad figure flickered like sorrow.

Without even knowing how she knew, Karine realised that he had found the cat.

A lump rose in her throat and she blinked.

Then he stood up, raised his gaze to the light.

And her heart froze solid in her chest.

He was no longer Roderick.

Not the Bard, not the Final Guardian, not the idealistic and slightly feckless witness of the world's jumbled thoughts.

The name was ludicrous, comedic, inadequate. Everything he had ever been had been hooked out of him on barbs of pain, on the razor-sharp edges of an understanding that he had – willingly – traded his soul for. Down there in the darkness, in the deepest darkness of heart and mind, in a horror that he had no words to articulate, even now, he had found the very depths of his own insanity. He had found his beliefs, his ego, his memory and his understanding, and he had dragged the whole lot out into the bloody and painful open.

Dragged them screaming.

During the time he had been there, under Mom's fingers and blades, she had been there for him and with him. She spoke words of comfort even as she carved out his skin, his throat, his vocal cords and his windpipe, even as she cut him right down to his spine.

And he had opened himself to it, let the pain and fear come, let her kiss him and tell him exactly what he would become, let her open his throat like a lover and coax from him silent screams of utter terror that no one would ever hear or care about.

This was what Ecko had lived through. Not only Ecko, but Thera, and who knew how many more? And he had submitted to it willingly, in order to understand, and to have the capacity to do one thing.

To *remember*.

He knew now – he needed to *be* the world's memory. He needed to live those memories, to be able to see and feel and touch them, he needed to hold them and be a part of them, and never let them go.

Down there, in the belly of the dark, as the layers of his skin had peeled back, he finally recognised what it was that he had seen in the water, so many returns ago, finally knew what the world truly feared – and how he could fight it.

The waterfall of the Ryll, where he had studied under the Guardians, had a sister, the Ilfe, the well of her memory. The Ilfe had been lost, and so the world's memory had rotted with it, had mouldered and been forgotten. The soul of light had sunk beneath the waters of the eastern sea, and the Elementalists had faded. The Council in Fhaveon had laughed at the Powerflux, at Kas Vahl Zaxaar, at Rhan – they had taken notice only of themselves and terhnwood.

With his pain, he had bought the capacity to hold the world's memory. To take it upon himself and to wield it.

But he had also bought something else.

A new power, a power that could shatter the Powerflux and bring down the very sky.

Once he had that memory, he could give it voice.

That was what Mom had given him, down there in the bowels of the dark.

She'd called it *Khamsin*.

He held out a hand and said to her, "Come."

Karine could find neither answer nor motion. She was flat against the old wall as though his very presence pushed her backward, as though the simple word he had spoken had enough force to flatten her into the bricks themselves.

She tried to say his name, but the question reached her lips and stopped, as if it were afraid.

He said to her, "Come."

The word was a command, like nothing he had ever said before. His voice had changed, was firmer and stronger, almost metallic – it had complex layers of power, a thrum of presence that could bring down the very Kartiah. She shook her head, still unable to comprehend what he was even doing there. His eyes, the only part of him she could see between the hood and the scarf, were as cold as chipped stone.

She knew him – but she had no idea who he was.

He said to her, "Come."

And this time, she couldn't help herself. She went towards him as though called to her own ending, stood before him like some sort of crazed sacrifice. The devastation around them seemed somehow appropriate.

She found her voice, said, "What happened to the cat?"

It sounded ludicrous, when the building was dying.

He said, "She will stay and guard The Wanderer." His voice was resolution, inevitability and courage, and a grief that went beyond anything she had ever heard or felt. "Take a moment and say your farewells. But be swift, the Count of Time is come for us."

Karine caught a sob, couldn't catch the second one and buried her face in her hands, her shoulders shaking. Her mind repeated, stupidly, *poor cat*, but there was so much more – this was the end, the final moments of The Wanderer, the tavern would fall and there was no way she could help or save it. This was wrong, all wrong. This man was not the tavern's owner, not the sparkling-crazed passion of Roderick the prophet...

This was not happening.

But there was a closeness to the air like the sky in a storm, like a rise of thunderclouds, a swelling and heat that presaged a detonation.

"Why?" She wiped her face. The question could have been anything, everything, but he understood.

"She should not have come here." His sorrow was vast. "In a moment, this will all be over."

"But... Sera..."

"He stays. The balance is necessary."

"What balance?"

Nothing was making sense. The building was shaking now, not just the stacks, but the floor, the ceiling, the wall behind her. As she turned and looked, the plaster ran with cracks from top to bottom and fragments began to fall like snow.

He said, "We go."

He did not change his tone, place any emphasis on the words, but her feet moved as though he had pulled them. She found the strength to pause, say, "What happened to you?"

He looked at her with that same, silent flicker of sorrow. His faced was lined now, haggard, she could see, even under the hood. He looked like he'd been through a war.

He thought for a moment and then said, "I made a choice."

"What choice?" The response was reflex, a whisper.

Carefully one of his long hands came up to the edge of the hood, the other to the scarf at his mouth. As he showed his face, Karine let out a wail.

She had no idea who he was.

Gone was his long blue-black hair, gone his sense of mischief, his humour. His eyes were cold, his head was shaven, there were cruel scars in his flesh. But his *throat*...

Karine stepped back, tripped, fell. Without even realising it, she was pushing away from him on her hands and backside, sobbing still, scrabbling backwards to get away, to get *away*...

His throat was alive. From the neck of his garment, to his chin, to his lower lip, was a thick mass of metal serpents, things that wove in and out of his flesh – as though his very vocal cords had attained a life of their own and been put on display. As he drew breath, they slid about one another, up to his ears, into his mouth; as he turned or moved or spoke, they shifted and writhed with him. They were his new voice made manifest, the coldness of his gaze, and they made her feel sick.

"Dear Gods…" she breathed.

He replaced the scarf and hood, said, "This is how it must be. We have a war to fight."

As if in answer to the statement, the barrel beside her suddenly shattered, broken ribs and gushing liquid and a sharp shock of scent. It soaked her hands and clothing.

Pieces of the ceiling were starting to fall.

Momentarily, his eyes shattered – she could see a heave of pain and loss, a vast anguish she dared not even try to understand. Then it was gone, and the stone returned. He held his hand to her again, and this time she took it, stood up.

She was dripping with the Varchinde's best malted spirits, the contents of the most precious barrel they had ever owned.

But it didn't matter, not any more.

The tavern was dying around them, and they needed to go.

PART 4: DESTRUCTION

21: NO TIME TEALE; AVESYR

They came into the small harbour town as the clouds rose to swallow the sun and the sky thickened with evening.

The streets were silent, grey and empty, whirlwinds of debris scudded across the cobbled stone like figments. The rocklights in the doorways were streaked with old dirt, illumination blurred out into the road.

There was no sign that anyone still lived here.

Jayr suppressed the urge to shiver, turned to make sure Ress had properly fastened the front of his cloak. He was hunching along behind her, fixed only on his own horrors. He was tired and his mutters ghosted like shadows across the air.

Poor Ress. Since leaving Fhaveon, he'd been a man demented, determined and focused on the journey that lay ahead of them. Even on the edge of exhaustion, he became agitated if they stopped, twitched and muttered constantly. Now, his eyes flickered from doorway to doorway as if he expected the gloom to rise up and claw at them.

Frankly, Jayr reckoned, looking round them, *it might just cursed-well do that.*

Unease breathed cold across her skin, prickling chillflesh.

She rubbed at her scarred arms, bit into a nail, spat out the shred. She was looking for a sheltered place to stop, somewhere to get Ress out of the scattering threat of the rain while she went to look for signs of life...

...or of anything else.

But this place was deader than an overworked slave. The paint on the closed shutters was peeling, faded with salt and light.

Ress said, quite clearly, "Kazyen. No time, no time, no time, no *time*..."

Jayr ignored him.

Facing the weary buildings, the harbour was cradled in two long, curving stone arms, one ending in a lighthouse, the other in some crumbling grey statue, now a rain-misted blur against the grey. The fishercraft sat high in the water, patiently waiting; a row of houseboats offered faded, painted signs and sprawlingly untended plants.

In Fhaveon, the old scribe had said they'd find passage here, a boatmaster or fishercraft prepared to take them where they needed to go.

But it looked pretty cursed unlikely from here.

Unable to help herself, Jayr looked out across the water, eastwards at the faintly dark stripe along the horizon. It had been there, shadowing them, all the way over the wooded hills that separated Teale from Fhaveon.

Ress followed her gaze and his agitation increased. He shook her shoulder, his mouth working round words of urgency and fear. "No time, no time, no time..."

"We'll get there somehow, I promise," Jayr told him. "If I have to row you all the damned way."

"Kazyen," Ress said, now sounding on the verge of tears. He looked round at the harbour, shook his head. Then he brightened, pointing. "Look! The crustaceans are safe!"

"What?"

He pointed again, his face lit with wonder, a child's gentle smile. There, at the edge of the harbour's wall, the hanging wicker-woven cages were door-loose and empty. Whatever beasties had been caught in there had long gone.

"Gods' sakes." Jayr was scanning the harbour, wondering if any of the boats would take them across the strait, if she could handle one without help. She knew less than nothing about water – currents and double-tides, something stupidly complicated about the moons. For a moment, fears clamoured at her, reaching with cold hands and trying to bring her down, but she stood, fists clenched and solid, until they subsided to resentful muttering and left her alone.

She was Jayr the –

Oh for Gods' sakes, Syke and his nicknames. The Banned were long gone. They would never go home, she understood that now. She was Jayr the Damned, or Jayr the Damned Fool.

"One of us is howling loco, you know that?" She grabbed Ress's elbow and pulled them both under the front of a building, out of the wet. "Didn't the scribe say there was another fishing town, further north?"

"Must go. Now." Ress yearned out over the harbour, out towards that ever-present shadow. "*Please!*"

His mouth contorted as if he was trying not to cry.

Then, in the corner of her vision, movement caught Jayr's eye. *What the rhez?*

Up there, high above them on the wooded slopes overlooking the small town – there was something moving, shifting oddly in the half-light. There was some kind of empty stone theatre up there, rocklit against the darkening sky – but the motion was an uneasy seethe, and lower down.

Was there something in the *woods*?

Several times as they'd followed the roadway, Jayr had felt that they were being trailed, or watched – but she'd seen nothing. Even the pirates had packed their little pirate bags and gone home.

No, she wasn't jumping at figments, there *was* something up there, something that roiled through the trees like...

Her heart lurched in her chest – a sudden spike of nervousness that sent her body thrumming, ready. She was tensed, staring.

"Ress," she said carefully. "Can you see –?"

He ignored her, still staring out at the water. "Must. Go!"

"Ress..." Jayr pulled back into the shelter of the building's doorway as the rain came in harder, slicing sideways across the harbourfront. Ress looked up at it, blinked, opened his mouth to catch it and then gave a sudden, odd laugh as his hair soaked through and darkened, plastering back from his face.

Jayr pulled him back out of the deluge, swearing. She was struggling to make out the hillside through the shining grey blur.

The figure that came round the front of the doorway to speak to her almost made her jump out of her skin.

It was a woman, a woollen shawl over her head and clutched under her chin, though she was soaked through. Long lines of age and grief cut down the sides of her nose and mouth. She glanced back, beckoned to them.

"Come with me." Her tone was low and urgent.

"Why?" Jayr asked her.

"The town..." She shook her head, drops flying, pushed a wet strand of greying hair out of her eyes. "Whole place has gone to the rhez. You need to come with me. And quickly before they get down here. You can't stay outside any more – you're lucky Tawkarn spotted you."

As Jayr watched her, trying to understand the threat, the woman clicked her tongue in exasperation. "Quickly!"

Ress blinked. "No. We have to go. Have to..." He started to walk out of the doorway, towards the harbour. Jayr lunged and caught him.

She said, "We're not going anywhere..."

He turned on her, furious, his face suddenly contorting, his voice lifting into a thin, frustrated shriek.

"No *time*! We have to *go*!" He lifted a hand, went to grab at the front of her tunic. "We *must*!"

Startled, Jayr stepped back, blocked the reach, but the movement was awkward in the tiny space and it unbalanced her footing. She twisted an ankle, swore, and stumbled hard against the cracked wood of the door.

The door was too battered to take her weight. It creaked, pivoted on a shattered hinge and twisted sideways into the room behind.

And Jayr went over it, crashing clumsy into the dirt and the dust and darkness. Ress, still screaming, still grappling for her throat, threw himself straight in after her, his hands grappling for her face. She caught his wrists, but his knee came down in her belly and the air coughed out of her lungs.

"What the rhez are you doing? Get off me!"

Ress was still shrieking.

In the doorway, the shawled woman peered after them, a startled shape against the rain.

"Is he okay? Are you? We need to shift – and now."

"Shut up!" Jayr's Kartian-trained ears could hear movement. Close movement.

Movement in the room with them.

Ress was still shrieking, but Jayr was focusing now – tight and sharp, more alert than she'd been in days. She was out from under him, flicking him to the floor with a deft twist of hip and shoulder, then flipping herself to her feet and moving into the room, ensuring he was behind her.

"I said shut *up*!" she hissed.

Ress's shrieking stopped as though she'd torn it out of the air. Its echoes rang in her ears and she shook her head to clear them.

The woman, no fool, was reaching for the nearest light.

And then the movement came again, soft. A rustling, a breathing, a wakening.

The woman said, "Oh my Gods. Get out of there, get out of

there!" Her voice was soft with crushed horror.

But the air was shattered into ringing fragments by the sound of wooden poles tumbling, rolling, clattering across a stone floor. Jayr crouched still in the dimness, heart thumping, her fingers splayed and her eyes and ears and skin all searching.

Under the clangour of the falling poles, the movement came again.

Closer.

Then there was a thin, almost plaintive wail from somewhere in the back of the gloom. The air smelled faintly of terhnwood, of husk and dirt and fibre. Jayr turned slowly, her skin alive, waiting for the assault.

Come on then!

By the Gods, she was looking forward to this, wanting it...

From somewhere in front of her, there came a faint slightly uneven footstep. Another echoed it, further back. The woman in the doorway was lifting the rocklight, still telling them to get out, to get out *now*.

And then, in the dusty tumble of the light, Jayr could see them.

There was a huddle of people down by where the poles had fallen, a ragged bundle of faces and eyes and hands. They were gazing at her, stretching their hands out, opening their mouth and their breath was wrong, wet and somehow –

Again, Ress began shrieking, splitting the air with inarticulate rage and frustration, with a howl that sounded like a man helpless as his friend or lover died. He strove to get past her, but she held him back.

The huddle of people uncoiled to meet him. In the dirty light, they were somehow eager.

And then Jayr saw the real horror.

Jayr the Infamous had been a Kartian slave. Had spent a childhood in darkness and violence. Few things in the Varchinde scared her – but this, though, this was Gods-damned *wrong*.

The poles on the floor were cut lengths of old terhnwood,

and somehow they were still growing. Green shoots came from their ends and from the rings in the bark; even in the darkness, they strove for new life.

In among them, the coil of people were reaching hands towards Ress as though they sought to welcome him, as though they wanted to embrace him and close over him and bring him down among them.

And they, too, were alive with growth.

Shoots of terhnwood came from eye sockets and mouths, came from fingernails and coiled under and through skin, bursting forth and burrowing back. The nested horde had a sense of hunger to them, an overpowering sensation of need that was suffocating in the dusty air of the small warehouse.

The woman in the doorway was shouting still, but Jayr couldn't hear her over Ress's fury, over the drumbeat of her own blood in her ears. As Ress reached the huddle of people, they stood up to welcome him, to hold him to them until he too, became woven with the growth of the terhnwood...

Jayr shuddered to the very core of her soul.

Then she picked up one of the wood-lengths, lunged past Ress to ram the first figure hard in its overgrown mouth, send it slumping back into the heap. She spun the staff, back end upwards, slamming the second one over and back, came back with the off-swing to take Ress's feet out from under him and send him skidding across the floor in a rattle of poles.

Ress was shouting something, outraged, indignant. She didn't understand – and she didn't care. An upper-cut fourth blow caught a third figure in the jaw and cracked its head back, sending it sprawling back into the morass of its friends.

For the moment, the horrible, crawling, keening, prowling eagerness paused in confusion.

And Jayr could feel something prickling against her palms. *What?*

It felt like tiny, soft teeth, like some sort of rash. Like

something nosing at her skin as if trying to gain entry. Not letting go of the makeshift staff, she opened one hand, turned it over, peering at it in the dirty light. Her palm was itching, there were marks in her skin where –

Where the growth of the terhnwood was trying to penetrate her *flesh*?

She looked back at the huddle, at the suffocating knots of plant that wove through them from the inside. Had these people...?

Jayr swallowed, suppressed the urge to throw the staff as far from her as possible.

"Ress," she said, backing up, "don't touch the..."

"No." He was staring up at her, still crumpled where he'd fallen, staring at the terhnwood in her hands. "She's only trying to heal," he told her. "Kazyen empties her – she's only trying to heal." He blinked, his eyes glinting oddly in the rocklight. "Jayr." His voice caught, cracked, sobbed. "If she doesn't, everything... will die. We have to *go*!"

The people had closed in a cluster about their injured. They were probably eating them or something ghastly, Jayr reckoned, but at least they were no longer a threat. They curled about themselves and occasionally looked up into the rocklight, their green-woven flesh pale and sweating.

Jayr glanced back at the woman in the doorway. "We need a boat."

"A what? To go where?" The woman's voice was startled. "Ikira's even worse than here, the blight tore through the crops like black fire. Everyone" – her voice caught as she waved a hand at the huddle – "everyone who tried to help..."

"She's trying to *heal*!" Ress was scrabbling to his feet, one of the lengths of terhnwood in his hands, he was shaking it like some prophet's staff. "The blight, the nothing, the Kazyen!" He pointed the staff at the coiling knot of people. Jayr half-expected him to blast them with the same awful force he'd used to kill Jemara, but he only shouted, "Look! She's trying to *heal*!"

"What is he *on*?" The woman stared at him.

"The *world*. The *world* is trying to –" Ress broke off, exasperated, shaking with the effort of control. "It's here, can't you see it? The nightmare is *come*!"

The knot of people was still, watching him now, a glimmer of many eyes. They seemed oddly intent.

Jayr took her hands from her staff, one at a time, rubbed them down her trews.

The blight, the nothing, the Kazyen.

She's trying to heal. The nightmare is come.

It was the same thing he'd seen in the library. The thing that had cost him his mind. It had something to do with the blight, something...

...something he's trying to remember.

"He's fine," Jayr said shortly. She was watching the huddle watching Ress. "He had a problem with some poetry. I *said*, we need a boat."

"Poetry," Ress said. He was ducking in some strange dance, trying to dodge or weave through the gazes that had fixed upon him. "The Final Guardian; the Master of Light. Ecko. They're not enough, the pattern's incomplete. We must *remember*. Or everything will die."

"The Master of Light," the woman said. She glanced at them, eyes sharp as blades. "Did you say, The Master of Light?" Something in her voice had an edge, a flicker of pain, of understanding.

"Yes," Ress held out a hand to her. "He touched you, didn't he? Loved you once. I can see his light in your face."

But this was all damned loco and Jayr wasn't really listening.

Slowly, the people were beginning to unknot themselves once more, to creep forwards, hands open as if begging for scraps or mercy. The keening had stopped, now they were completely silent, but they were fixed upon Ress as if he was their saviour – or their cursed dinner.

"Come on then, you sonsofmares." Jayr turned to face them, staff still in her hands. "You just bring it over here."

The woman said, "Where are you going?" The peculiar, indistinct tension was still in her tone.

"Why? Coming with us?" As the huddle came on, Jayr wasn't in the mood to guess.

"Yes, I am." She gave a short, humourless laugh. "I can pilot the boat, if you need it. You might say I've... seen the light."

Jayr spared a glance, saw the woman's expression was sombre, absolutely serious. She looked older, suddenly, like she'd seen some sort of figment, some tragedy, some risen shade of her past. Ress, too, had stopped and his head was cocked to one side as he watched her.

"We're going to Rammouthe," Jayr said. "We're not expecting to come back."

"Memory," Ress told her. "We need the Ilfe. We have to remember."

"Maybe we do." The woman's acceptance was calm, the tension in her voice had gone – their destination seemed to have offered her some sort of personal resolution. "I'm Penya. If you want me to, I'll do my damned best to take you."

Rhan stood at the edge of the water.

Flecks of ice-cold teased the skin on his face, rainbows danced crystal and shimmer, but he stood motionless, watching the froth that seethed below him, the tumble and surge of the current at the foot of the huge falls. This was the Ryll, the thoughts of the world, the waterfall at the northernmost tip of the Varchinde.

This was his absolution, and his answer.

He'd wanted Roderick with him – but the Bard was gone, long gone, even more lost than Rhan himself. They had made such an almighty mess of this, both of them... so much for being champions. Faced by the world's woes, they'd had trouble finding their backsides with a map.

The water thundered, filling his head and chest with noise. He shook with it. It was in the bones behind his ears, in his skin. And it shouted fury, elation, power, just for him.

The cry with which Phylos had sealed his execution, had branded him a traitor to four hundred returns of service: *He is a lodestone and a drain upon us, a figure of indolence and luxury. Who can know what takes place under the roofs of his home? I say, that if there is a daemon, it is the daemon* sloth, *it is the daemon* idleness, *it is the daemon that keeps us from our crafthalls and tithehalls and farmlands and markets! This – creature – has believed that he is above the laws of this city! He has traded in substances we abhor, he has corrupted our youth, he has murdered the loved Lord of this city and taken his wife by force...*

Over him, the water thundered with power, filled his ears, his chest. *You are an* infection! *You have sat in this very room and pulled our strings like puppets!* Moisture stained his face like tears.

He watched the roar of the falls, the constant shattering of the water's surface before him, the carving of whirls and surges that could pull life from flesh and flesh from bone.

No man, no woman, no mortal, had ever touched these waters. Only Roderick, daring with the very tip of his finger – and he had seen the world's nightmare made manifest and been crazed ever since, convinced of a truth that no one else could understand.

Rhan knew it now: he did not have the Bard's courage.

He was afraid.

Above him, mountains towered, holding the sky upon their whitened shoulders. Below them, he was nothing, a tiny fragment of life, squeaking in protest at a fate he could have avoided. Away beyond him, the mountains tumbled into the

Forest of Skaide and the Han-Shen Moors to the west, to the ragged line of the Belazian Range to the east. Northwards, a breathless climb might have taken him over the end of the Varchinde plains and into the tundra proper; south, the way he had come, Avesyr stood a silent and grey-walled guard at the mouth of the mountains – and she was a grim city indeed.

A city dying.

The blight had ravaged her crops and farmlands; the lack of trade had gutted her like a caught fish. Many of her people had simply fled. As Rhan had come northwards, both road and river had been laden with the lives of the beaten.

The last surviving Guardians, those who had taught the Bard as a boy, who had outcast him for his heresy, even they were gone now – Rhan did not know where.

He was alone, alone at the very top of the world.

Carefully, he took a pace towards the edge of the stone, and looked down past his own feet.

How does that old saying go? Third time lucky.

And then he stepped off the edge.

The water hit him like a fist. The cold was terrible, it robbed him of breath and tore the heat from his body. The fall battered him down, forcing him deeper and deeper under the Ryll itself, tumbling him helplessly, bruising his flesh, tearing his skin. There was anger in these waters, outrage and fury and helplessness and power. The hand of the Goddess his mother spun him headlong, thrashing him like an errant child.

Take my life, Mother, if you will; I beg you, spare my soul.

To confront the might of the Goddess directly was death; no man dared.

Rhan was not a man.

From somewhere there came the first spark of passion, borne from the anger of the Goddess and leaping through the water like a surge of rainbow lightning. What gave him the right to lie down and die, just because he could not bear to fail? He had moaned and slouched and blamed everything but himself, tried every way to avoid facing his responsibility. There was a battle to be fought, and he had to damned-well fight it, with whatever weapons he could garner.

Get up, the Goddess told him, *and get on with it.*

The force of the water tumbled Rhan's helpless body like a toy, like the winds of chaos had once torn his wings. Yet now that force was a powerful, physical reminder of cleansing, of pleasure, of the strength that came from surviving pain.

Flashes of the world's thoughts came past him: the pulsing veins of the Powerflux, critically damaged when the OrSil, the soul of light, had sunk beneath the eastern sea; Kas Vahl Zaxaar, his brother awakening in power; Phylos ascending in blood and glory; Roderick – *dear Gods* – screaming in silent and impossible pain, his thin body stark with horror, his throat laid open, a scarlet wound; the hole in the world's heart, the blight that crept ever-inwards; a slight man, eyes of pure darkness, skin that shifted with all the world's colours; the shores of Rammouthe, as if seen across the bows of a tiny, wind-torn boat...

Penya?

She turned to face him as if she were the Goddess herself. *Fight, you fool!*

Death was not an option.

Knifing through the freezing water, Rhan swam out from under the pressure of the falls and headed for the surface, the water's chill strength singing through every muscle of his body. His head broke free into the sharp air, the cold wind stung his face into a crackling of ice; his heart was burning with the chill, burning with the passion of it. It was impossible that he could contain this much strength without his skin ripping like silk.

Rhan Elensiel raised his voice and cried aloud to the surrounding mountains, to the grey walls of Avesyr, to the Varchinde stretched out to the south.

And that cry was a pulse of power, through the Flux itself, through the air, through the very rock. The mountains rang with it. His own skin flamed lambent with power.

He could feel the soul of light, feel the Flux's warp and weft – he could feel –

Rhan raised his arm, though he already knew it – the binding that Phylos had put upon him was gone.

The Powerflux was in him, woven through him, it was his to wield, as it always had been. Its strength was in his heart and soul.

Now, my brother, he said to the bright cold sky. *Now, I am coming.*

22: MANIFEST AEONA

The creature's laughter was ringing in Amal's head, surging into his mind, his skull, his ears, his blood. It was not the soft, hot laugh of a threat or a tease, but a rich laugh of pure power, as if it knew that it had won.

Amal began to tremble, feeling its strength within him, feeling his own heart quailing. For the first time, he wondered if he was really strong enough.

And if, in that very doubt, his own death was assured.

"Get out. Both of you." His blade caught the light of the sun and his voice was flat, pure threat.

Triqueta said, "Fat chance. Where's Redlock? You've got 'til I count to... dear Gods..."

Her voice tailed into open-mouthed horror, her jaw dropped lax. Amal didn't know immediately what had stopped her, then he realised that he could feel his own skin changing, the heat rising in his face. The creature was massing its strength, coalescing like steam. It was wrapping its hands about the long returns of their bargain and it was straining at those bindings.

And this time, it was breaking free.

Triqueta stared, horrified. Amethea had fallen back, her

hands at her mouth. Amal could feel the heat in his skin, the heat in his heart. He could feel the time-spirals twisting as they unravelled. He raised a hand and saw that his flesh was heating, he smelled like cooking meat. He should be screaming from the pain, but all he could feel was the sheer rush of ecstasy, of pure glory, that came from the creature as it rose.

"Ecko." The word came out of his mouth, though he did not say it. "You can free me fully, if you wish. The greatest destruction of all can belong to you. Maugrim, Amal, the nartuk, the Sical, your brimstone – all of these things are nothing compared to the weapons I can give you. Free me, Ecko, let me –"

"No!" Amethea threw herself forwards. "For the love of the Goddess, Ecko, don't. If you free it – it'll kill everything. Us. You too."

Laughter came from Amal's throat.

But he was not laughing, he was fighting to take his own voice back, fighting to throw this thing, this possessor, back down into the place it had always lived, right to the back of his thoughts.

Beside Ecko, Triqueta spat savagely onto striated stone. "You absolute little shit. I really should slit your throat myself. You've led us here on some damned chase, just to tell us that you don't care? That you think it's okay to just let this – whoever the rhez he really is – burn our world down? To help him? He's going to wind your guts onto a drop-spindle and I'm going live long enough to *watch*."

Amal was helpless. The creature was moving him, shifting his arms and legs, the motions becoming more fluid as it grew used to holding control. A prisoner in his own thoughts, Amal threw himself against it, shouting. He may as well have thrown himself against a hot metal wall.

He felt his hand tighten on the blade it held, felt himself look down at where Ecko lay.

Felt the rush of saliva in his mouth, like a starving man faced with a feast.

His mouth said, "You may fight me if you wish, or you may choose to flee. Either way, it will not matter. In just a moment, your time –"

"Your *time*." Amethea stared at his tattoos, at the crouching gargoyles, at the labyrinthine patterns of spirals that wove about the walls. Somewhere under the onslaught of the creature's presence, Amal realised that she knew – somehow, this girl had worked her way through the maze, had followed the trail and found the answer none of them had come seeking.

"Time – all of this," Amethea said. "The spirals are all about the Count of *Time*."

The creature grinned with Amal's mouth. "Come to me, little priestess. Come and tell me what you've learned. What Maugrim taught you."

"Stop yanking my rope." Amethea was white-faced with horror, backing up, pushing Triqueta behind her. "Ecko, haven't you even realised who... what... this is? Haven't you understood what you've – we've – been brought here to do? Saint and Goddess."

Even the sky seemed to freeze, poised to hear the words as they fell from her mouth, crashed to the stone below.

She said, "This isn't just some craftsmaster, some crazed old Tusienic alchemist. How could we have been this stupid?"

"Then who am I?" The creature smiled like a predator, waiting for the truth. Amal had no doubt that the words would be death for all of them.

"You're the daemon," Amethea said. "You're Kas Vahl Zaxaar."

And Amal's mouth smiled at her understanding.

* * *

Kas Vahl Zaxaar.

The words hit the stone like the crash of a wave and Ecko saw it all, like a laser-flash, burned into his retinae. He looked at the one-eyed man, at the creature that was now living within him like live steam, eating him from the inside out.

And something in him knew he was in the right place still, that nothing needed to change.

He said, almost like a dare, "I don't care if he's fucking Merlin. This place is still gonna burn."

The alchemist, daemon, whatever the fuck it was, began to laugh. The man's body heat was off the scale, Ecko could see the temperature even without his oculars – the shimmer of the superheated air above the man's shoulders rising to the jaws of the gargoyles above. He should be slumping to melted flesh and charred sticks, but he was grinning like insanity and the blade was resting at the hollow of Ecko's throat ready to carve him straight in two.

Ecko's adrenaline sparked, but he was so fucking beyond afraid. Beyond hope, beyond dismay – he didn't *care*. He'd fucking *won* – he'd gone through the woods, he'd left the path – and this was the ultimate fuck you to Eliza's control program.

The alchemist, Kas Vole Zack's Ass, whatever the hell it was, raised his eye-patch, showed the searing, burning orb beneath.

Dimly Ecko could hear Triqueta, Amethea, but he couldn't move. He didn't want to. That eye had caught him like a hook buried hot in his face.

Kas Vahl Zaxaar.

The daemon, the daemon was really *in* there. He was a smoulder, a blaze, a burning lust of need, a fire of energy and purpose and strength. He was Maugrim and he was the Sical and he was more; he was everything that the Varchinde was not. Passion, rage, fallen starlight, steam and flame incarnate.

And there was a hunger in him, something that he *needed*.

The first cut of the blade went unfelt, Ecko could do

nothing but stare at that eye, that window into the soul of the daemon. There was no pain, the blade moved and he did not feel it – instead, there was a sensation of pulling, an odd and momentary sensuousness that seemed to tug, tug again, and then stop, confused.

The eye blinked. The blade stopped. Blood streaked, the pain cut in.

The adrenaline cut straight over it a moment later.

Ecko was tense, confused, wrists tearing at the metal that held him, uncaring as to what it did to his skin. He found himself shuddering, freaked the fuck out.

"Let me up, let me *up*. What the hell was that?"

Something was all the fuck wrong, that wasn't how this was supposed to go.

Ecko's oculars were fizzling: he could see a figure, bright red robe, arms raised like he was fucking Christ Almighty. The man was on a balcony, scenes of destruction at his feet...

Come to me, he was saying. *Fhaveon is ready and I am waiting for you. Come.*

But the daemon, the alchemist, whatever, was stumbling, falling back. He was laughing, but that laugh was hollow now, it lacked the bass undertone – it was mortal, human once more. The man was slumping, grey-faced and sick, suddenly weak as a fucking kitten. He raised a hand to the eye-patch, Ecko heard him cry out, "No! No!" speaking to something that none of them could see. Then he'd fallen completely and the eye-patch was back in place, and the daemon had fucking *gone*, vanished up its own ass, vanished clean in the bright sun of the tower top...

The gargoyles grinned.

Ecko struggled to sit up. "What the hell just happened? What *was* that?"

The alchemist was white-faced, wheezing weak laughter as though trying not to cry.

"I played a game," he said. His temperature was falling, his skin losing its outrage and seethe. "I played a game within a game within a game." He was hunched, shivering, laughing, on the edge of hysteria. Ecko had to strain to keep him in sight. "All this time, since the moment we knew you were here, I've known what Vahl really wanted. I've known he would betray me. All this time, Ecko, and I've known the truth. Why, ultimately, his need would fail." His laughter faltered, he coughed. "I've known... all along... that you didn't have... the one thing, the key, Vahl really needed."

Amethea moved to the side of the table and winced at the deep cut in Ecko's throat. But Triqueta stood over the alchemist.

"What the rhez are you talking about?" she said. "What game? What did Vahl really need?"

"You..." He was panting now, his breath short and his skin grey. "You know... Banned lady... because Tarvi... couldn't touch him either. Daemons need it... like we need... air." He coughed, cleared his throat, said, "He has no time... no *time*..."

No time.

Ecko's skin crawled.

The flickering digital readout in his oculars when he'd first arrived.

No time.

Tarvi's passion, Triqueta in Amos.

No time.

The madman Ress, in the corridors.

No time.

The enlightenment was terrifying. He felt suddenly like he was in freefall, like nothing now made sense. How the hell did that happen, how the hell was it even possible?

No time.

It meant – did it? – that this world was somehow real.

"You, Ecko." The alchemist was still speaking, his voice and face fading to grey. He was shuddering now, his hands palsied.

"You're a stranger… come from another world. Our Count of Time… can't touch you. But I had to hide it… from Vahl… right to the end. I had to distract… the daemon… play his game… or he might have remembered… that Tarvi could not hurt you…"

Ecko snorted, bitter and painful. "Couldn't hurt me, huh?"

The alchemist laughed again, coughed flecks of blood. Then he said, as though his heart were broken. "But I lost… as well. Vahl never told me… he had another host…" He tried to haul himself upright, said, "I fear Fhaveon will fall. Now, come here to me, lady of the Banned. Help me to the parapet. I want to see the sea… before I die…"

Triqueta was shaking her head, trying to understand. She blinked at the man, and then came forwards to extend her hand.

Ecko tried to move, but Amethea was in the way, her hands all over him. He tried to call, to shout, to stop her…

No, Triq, don't… for chrissakes, don't!

Daemon or no daemon, Ecko didn't trust that old fucker an–

There was a disturbance in the air.

Not like his vision of the man in the red robe – exultant and gloriating – the air on the tower was twisting in on itself, sickening. The sensation was familiar, somehow, something he'd seen or felt before – something that he knew deep in the darkest corners of his heart.

He struggled, useless, against his bonds. "Fuck's *sake*." He swore as Amethea blocked his view, still trying to look at his throat. His stomach was churning, he was chafing his wrists, hurting himself, but he had to see, to see…

He knew what this was.

But it couldn't be.

No fucking way…

Amethea turned, her own startlement taking her hands from his throat. Ecko stared, barely daring to believe. He heard Triqueta cry out and stumble back, away from where the alchemist had fallen; heard the alchemist wheeze disappointment like it was the last breath of his life.

Then there was a soundless snap. There was a flicker of a reality that he knew, something he recognised like the smell of the River Thames on a Sunday morning.

Lugan?

Beyond hope, beyond time, beyond worlds, could it be...?

But it was not Lugan.

It was the Bard.

The gargoyles that leaned over them were frozen with impossibility. Ecko stared, the pain in his wrists and his throat forgotten. Amethea had fallen back against the table. Only the alchemist breathed, his wheezing laughter somehow framing the enormity of the moment.

The Bard had come *back*.

Back from the dead; back from another world.

Ecko's memories clamoured at him – this man was his conscience, his guide, his Jiminy Cricket. He could hear Triqueta saying, *He died believing in you*, hear Nivrotar's need for the lore and learning of this man, for his guidance.

But this man was not Roderick of Avesyr, the Bard that Ecko remembered.

He was tall, grim. He was wearing a hoodie, for chrissakes, something so urban that it screamed out of place. His hair and face were covered. He looked like some stylised street-thug, angular and harsh, with eyes of stone. Something in Ecko's head expected him to heft a crowbar with one hand and skin up with the other.

But that something was a whim, buried. The rest of his mind was fixated on the fucking *hoodie*, the label, the zipper. His own thoughts screamed at him, looping insane...

Where the fuck?

Amal was trying move, to push himself backwards out of the hooded man's path, but the man paid him no attention.

He seemed unimpressed by the scene before him, took it in with a glance of cold eyes, showed no flicker of emotion or surprise.

Ecko's head shrieked questions. Where was the tavern, Karine, Kale, the others? Had The Wanderer been in London, for chrissakes, how the fuck was that even possible?

The man strode across the tower like he owned it, boots slamming hard on the stone.

He said to Amethea, "Get out of the way." His voice was –

Holy fucking shit on a stick.

His voice was *mechanical.*

Amethea paled, but didn't move.

Ecko gaped, utterly fucking dumbfounded by the masked figure that now stood over him, his shadow harsher than the fang-toothed gargoyles that blocked out the sun.

Roderick.

The name was ludicrous.

What the fuck did you do?

He scrabbled to sit up, failed. His heatseeker was in overdrive – looking for flaws, excuses, anything to allow him denial. The man had a throat that seethed with warmth and colour and harm; a skull that offered twin cold plates, one down either side. And the work didn't stop there – the heat fluctuations followed across his collarbones and shoulders, down into his chest. They retreated too far under his skin for Ecko to work out what they were, but...

Holy fucking shit.

There was only one person who'd do work like that.

"You went to Mom." It was a whisper, laden with implication. "You went to *Mom.* Jesus fucking Harry Christ – *why?*"

His mind staggered sideways like a backstreet drunk.

"And – *how?*"

But the Bard didn't answer. Instead, one gloved hand gripped the bloodied mess that was Ecko's throat, thumb and fingers, ready for throttling. The other took the scarf from his face.

Pressure squeezing, threat and promise, he said, "This is

over. No more drama, no more games. You tell me again, Ecko, how my world isn't real. How it doesn't matter. How you can play as you choose and damn everything to perish. Tell me again how you're the only thing of importance."

Tell me again, Ecko, how my world isn't real.

He couldn't process it, couldn't begin to wrap his brain round what all this meant. The Wanderer had been in London – in *London*, for chrissakes! – a figment of Ecko's program, a piece of his fucking imagination, had existed *outside*. He wanted to reverse away like Amal had done, wanted to escape the thought, what it meant. Wanted to shriek denial of the man's presence, of what Mom had done to him. He clanked against the restraints, struggled against the man's grip, panicked – he was looking for the exit, the hole in reality, the shimmering-gate-through-time, the whatever-the-fuck-it-was, but there was nothing there.

What the fuck?

He spluttered, still twisting against the metal clasps and unable to gather his shattered wits. "You... but... *shit*! You *died*! What the fuck happened to you? How...?"

The man's face was thin, now, pale and hard. His amethyst eyes were like chips of gemstone, cold. There was no mercy in his expression, none of the humour and empathy that Roderick had offered to those around him – there was only the hand across Ecko's throat.

Whatever Mom had done to him, it had reft him of his sanity, his humanity. It had fractured his soul – just as it had fractured Ecko's before him.

What was the word they used? *Estavah*, closer than brother.

But brother or not, this time, Ecko feared that he really did face his own death.

That not only had the program failed, but that it would take him with it.

23: RAGE FHAVEON

The shouting began.

Trapped in the darkness and the rich, sweet scents of the herbery, the young Lord Foundersdaughter and the old scribe listened to the rise of fury in Fhaveon.

Selana was sobbing, Mael could hear her gulp and sniffle. He didn't blame her for a minute, poor child had been through the rhez, but he restrained the urge to pat her awkwardly on her shoulder.

She was afraid, and out of her depth, and the release was good. Frankly, he could have sniffled a bit himself.

Get up, you fool. But there was no time for fear – he could hear Saravin as clearly as if the big warrior was beside him, hulking and hairy, there in the dark. *Get up and get on with it!*

Sometimes, Mael figured, *you have to do these things – simply because there's no one else left.*

He got up.

Selana shifted, responding to his movement, but he said nothing. Instead, he stood still in the darkness, fighting down his rising panic to listen, turning his head and feeling the air, trying to orient himself. They'd done this as 'prentices – more returns ago than he cared to count – drawn lots and then arranged to get locked in so they could access certain protected substances. And if Mael hadn't lost his damned mind completely...

He remembered. That tiny filter of light coming from a chink in the stone – it was barely more than a figment, but it gave him direction.

That way.

He picked his way across the floor, counting steps, his hands stretched in front of him like a sleepwalker's. Eight paces, kicking with his toes as he went, and he found the wall. Two sideways, and there was the old scar in the stonework. Three handspans down...

...and *that* was the axis point.

He couldn't remember who had found this – a stone idiosyncrasy that lurked here unremembered and unseen. The loose piece of wall weighed more than Mael could shift – more than Saravin could have shifted for that matter – but had been crafted with such skill that a touch in the right place and it swung outwards like a door into the very back of the hospice garden.

When it swung closed the fit would be almost flawless.

The spreading arc of light touched Selana as she turned, eyes wide and face streaked and sparkling.

"You moved the *wall?*" she said.

Mael allowed himself a chuckle. "Tekissari built the hospice, my Lord. Thank your forefathers, and my misspent youth, and let's get out of here. And quietly!"

Scrubbing at her face, Selana scrabbled to her feet. As she did so, the rush of angry noise came again, startling both of them – it was a rising crescendo of outrage, a tide of wrath on its way to crash against the walls of the higher city.

They could hear hooves, shouted orders, the clatter of weapons. From somewhere, a single voice – Phylos possibly – fought for control. The tone was strident, demanding discipline and obedience.

Dear Gods.

A blossom of very real fear grew in Mael's heart. For all their bravery, they were an old man and a young girl, facing streets now probably streaked with the angry, the righteous and the violent. How they were supposed to win through this...

Stop moaning, you old fool, and move!

The scents of the herbery brought flickers of his youth, memories of 'prentice antics and personal rebellion.

Just who are you calling old, you galumphing great oaf? Call yourself a warrior?

Mael felt a sudden rush of pure nostalgic wickedness, allowed himself a grin. Feeling younger than he'd done in returns, he said, "Come on!" His heart thumping, he caught the girl's sleeve and they ran together through the tiny and overgrown end of the garden, stingers biting at them as they went. Then they rounded into the gardens proper, neat rows of planted flowers, dancing statues that spat water in perfect arcs.

Mael ducked them into a side-arch, said, "We have to stop this, my Lord..." He drew a breath. "We've got to go out there."

"Out there?" Selana gawked at him. "You're crazed!"

From somewhere there was a taint of smoke, cries, flecks of ash.

Mael swallowed, aware that he must be pale as a corpse.

"You gave a brave speech earlier, Selana." He used her name deliberately, a confrontation. "I'm hoping you meant it. We're going to get your uncle and we're going to open the doors to the hospice. And then, we're going to get you into the palace."

She drew a deep breath, said, "Okay. Okay. I suppose... we can go round to the back door. Into the kitchen."

Mael nodded. *Good girl.* "Then we're going up to that balcony to stop Phylos."

Somehow.

He didn't need to add it to the end of the statement.

* * *

It had started in the tithehalls and the marketplaces with the seizures and demands, with the casual brutality of the soldiery. With the overturning of stalls, and the breaking and burning of stock. With small knots of outrage, and a gradual rising of voices that would take no more.

It had started in the lower streets of the city, with those who'd heard the words of Fletcher Wyll, with those whose companions had been dragged away to face the wrath of the Justicar. With the Lord city's roadways being patrolled by things inhuman, beasts of hoof and horn with the bodies of men, and skin woven with spirals of seething ink. With the kicking down of doors and the accusations that followed; with neighbours dragged, bleeding, from their hearths and families. It had started as the people of the city realised their homes were not safe and that their anger was greater than their fear.

It had started the moment a victim had hit back.

It might have been a stone, a thrown pottery carafe, an explosion of shards; it might have been a knife between the ribs, a flash of flame, or a rocklight raised in anger and brought down shattering-hard. Whatever that first spark, it caught to sudden light and the blaze that spread from it was pure rage.

Under her perfect skin, Fhaveon had been simmering with it.

Rage at the blight, at the people's helplessness, at the soldiers' brutality. Rage from traders and craftsmen denied their livelihoods, from warriors who could express themselves no other way. Rage from brewers and bookkeepers who had seen their tallies tumble and had taken a rope across the back for it.

Now, that rage had an outlet. Fhaveon's people swarmed the streets, the squares, resentment and righteousness giving them strength and determination. They gripped tight whatever weapons they had – staves, belt-blades and woodsman's axes – and as they moved onwards so they became more, so their shout was heard further, and so their might and number increased.

They raided the hoarded stockpiles, tearing down the guards from their duty and wresting away their weapons. They took everything they could and then torched what remained. They burned out of indignation, teaching the city a lesson, firing stores rather than letting Fhaveon's rulers keep them – and then they watched defiant as the sparks and smoke rose into the autumn sky.

Their roar became a scream – revolt and outrage.

But then, the city answered them.

And her walls came to life.

The grey stone of the main hospice was sealed. Its apothecaries and herbalists rushed from corridor to corridor as though the building was listing this way and that, and they had to hold it upright lest it fall. Scurrying in, secure under its shelter, Mael stopped at a line of pegs and threw a cloak at the Foundersdaughter, then they ran down the colonnade, just another pair of figures racing in the panic.

One corner, two, and they found themselves back at Mostak's door.

In the room was a figure, leaning over him.

Mael paused, but Selana shoved past, grabbing the figure's arm.

"Wait!" she cried.

Startled, the apothecary – the same man they'd spoken to earlier – turned to say something, and then his expression and his shoulders sagged with relief.

"My Lord, you're all right, thank the Gods! The city's going crazed. Phylos told me… but I couldn't, I…"

"You're a brave man," she told him.

As she spoke, Mael heard the crack in her voice – he realised that Mostak's hand, callused and thin, was reached out to her.

Choking, the Lord of the City fell to her knees in a billow of stolen fabric.

The commander struggled to sit up. He was pale, but the sheen to his skin had gone and his eyes were clear. Whatever orders Phylos had given the apothecary, the man had apparently found his own courage.

Mostak laid his thin hand on Selana's shining hair, looked up at Mael.

"It's all right," he said. His voice was weak but steady, a soldier's determination. "It's all right. I know all of it. Now, help me stand. It's starting, out there – and we need to get to the palace."

The first one came from the city's lowest streets, tearing itself bodily from the stone. It had been a creature of lost Swathe, perhaps, or a crafting of the Founder's forgotten masons – now it was a blunt thing, misshapen and clumsy, its mouth stretched in dismay and its strength shattering buildings. The crush of people in the roadway paused before it, those at the front pulling back as their anger was suddenly leaking down the insides of their thighs.

Further back, the rage continued and the press tried to surge forwards – there were cries and seethings and fallings, there was a mass of trampling and feet. As the stone thing rose, stinking of age and rank air, stinking like rotted breath, like the inside of a dead cavern, so the front of the crowd broke and tried to flee through alleyways and over gardens – but those behind had no warning and could not move for the press that was pushing them forwards.

The creature hit the mob head-on like a fist, hammering, shattering bodies, crushing flesh into the roadway, broken and screaming. It picked bodies up and slammed them down into the stone, it roared at them in bafflement and pain.

People screamed, horror crystallising and anger forgotten. All they wanted was to get away.

But from the alleyways came the vialer, the creatures of hoof and horn, with weapons raised and eyes of chaos. They hit broadside and slashed and tore their way through the people. They laughed like a rising storm, exalting in blood and pain. They pulled people to the ground and disembowelled them or kicked them to death. They tore clothes from skin and skin from bone and they wrapped themselves in all of it, laughing in gore and glory.

At the back of the crowd, the press was still pushing, shouting, making demands – though there were the lucky ones, the wary ones, who'd peeled away from the sides. These fled outward into the streets – some crying in terror, others looking for friends and retribution.

At the centre, though, there was a core that stood unbroken. A core that had seen enough of Fhaveon's brutality and that feared neither creature of dust and history, nor the madness of the vialer. There were hands that gripped weapons and eyes that hardened.

And there was a resolution that would not be broken.

In the upper tiers of the city, in the central market, another resistance was gathering.

This was not a haphazard mob, rampaging loose through the streets, this stood solid, answering to the cry of a single voice. She was Mistress Cirel Alaxien, a senior member of the Harvester's Cartel and hers was a strident shout across the thunder of the people's anger – she was rallying point and focus, and she was crafting that anger into a weapon that would hit back. The city, she said, had betrayed them, and the city, she said, would be made to pay.

When the cavalry came in a thunder, a shaking of ground

and a rising of dust against the pale blue of the autumn sky, it was Cirel's voice that held the people steady. She turned them, she commanded them, and she hurled them back at the incoming horses.

And then the madness really began.

In the market, the people had torn down the last of the stalls, had armed themselves with wooden stakes as long as spears and hacked to crude points at one end. As the horses came closer, sweat and dust and hooves and muscle, the very city seeming to shake beneath their weight, so the stakes were braced hard against the ground. They were not dug in, the flags would not allow it, but they were enough.

As the last command was given and the horses went from canter to full gallop, so the first rank of the mob peeled away to the sides – revealing the death-spikes aimed at the charge. Unable to stop on the smoothness of the stone, the horses hit the spikes chest-first. Many of the spikes were not braced hard enough and simply skidded – many, but not all.

The air was suddenly filled with screaming, terrible and high-pitched and rending the sky from top to bottom. Some of the horses fell, rolling; others went up on their hind legs, cracked forehooves kicking. A horse who still had the stake embedded in his chest turned, the whites of his eyes blazing, his teeth bared, pulling his rein out of the hands of his rider. Blood frothed in his mouth, on his chest, scattered across the faces of those before him. Another horse had taken a long scratch – a tear in her hide. With her rider bent hard over her neck she came through the barricade and hammered straight into the heart of the waiting people, kicking and plunging and biting, her rider striking out with blade and fury.

Smoke billowed from the torched remnants of the stalls. Some riders fell, went for weapons, were cut down as they tried to stand. Others stayed in their saddles, fighting for control or rallying their mounts to rage into the heart of the mob. The tan commander called for them to muster, to fall back in on his location, but around him horses were rolling, tack and armour clattering. Some among the mob were close enough to attack the fallen animals, and as the horses tried to stand they were injured and hacked down, slipping in their own flooding gore, skidding and panicking until they finally fell. Others in the mob, those with more wit or courage, mounted the beasts themselves and rode them back at the attacking cavalry, mount to mount, kicking and fighting.

Chaos screamed like the fallen horses. Ash and smoke were blinding. Terhnwood weapons clattered, shattered, shards spiralling, shining in sudden breaks of sun.

On foot, the people were bewildered, surrounded. The smells of rich blood and horseshit and fear all meshed one with another, heady and confusing. In some, adrenaline raged and they fought their way through to the attacking soldiers, needing to vent their anger and helplessness. Others, overwhelmed, tried to cower or flee and were cut down where they stood by those riders who had penetrated deep into the mass of the mob.

The last of the stalls were burning, the flames hot on skin and rising into the clear air. And now, in among the attacking forces, came new things, creatures with the forms of horses and the upper bodies of men and women, creatures heavier than the cavalry mounts with huge claws that rent any flesh they found. The people screamed and thrashed, ran this way and that, but the monsters were everywhere and they were pure destruction, tearing the world asunder.

In the midst of it all, Cirel slipped quietly away. Her task was done and she was less than a shadow, sliding back the way she had come – sliding back to the side of the Cartel itself and back to where Phylos was laughing.

She had done enough.

* * *

It had all happened exactly as he had designed it.

Rage carefully crafted and built, now ignited and channelled into the ash-and-blood streets of the city, where it broke against the walls and tore down the crystal trees. It had been stoked to the point of detonation, and now it had its outlet.

Above it all, celebrating in its eruption, Phylos stood upon the palace balcony, his red robe blazing and his arms outstretched. Behind him rose the white wall of the Valiembor building, rose the sky, rose the blazing sun; before him, the zig-zag streets of the city roared with fury as though their people had climbed from the very rhez itself.

Yes. Witness what I have crafted. What I have done!

In his mind, Phylos could feel Vahl's presence stronger than it had ever been, massive and exultant. The Count of Time was upon them both, and Phylos had brought the city to exactly where they needed her to be.

So many returns, scheming. Waiting.

Fhaveon was in the grip of her own death.

To his left, Phylos could see the remnant of the central market blazing, filling the air with ash and shrieks and smoke, could see the destruction wrought by the cavalry and the struggling, failing people. The great mosaic was covered with blood and vomit and garbage. Above it, Rakanne's imperious face stared outwards, insensible, as if she couldn't find it in her stone heart to care.

And somewhere, still out of his reach but getting stronger, Vahl was laughing.

Phylos knew that down there, somewhere loose in the morass, was Ythalla, armed and brutal, her soldiery given leave to do anything they pleased. They had been force-fed with their own might and righteousness, and now they were off their rein, given their freedom. They were savage and gleeful, exalting in their brutality – the death toll was rising, and the injured were left to rot where they lay. Even as Phylos stood, so the mob was shattering under their force – anywhere the people of the city rallied, the soldiers broke them like wooden uprights, burned them and cast them down. Until there was no protest any more, just scattered groups and odd individuals, stumbling and coughing, hoping only to flee with their lives.

The city was a mass of destruction and any sense of unity or defiance among her people was hunted down and cut out, an infection to be exterminated.

Vahl's laughter was as rich as the spilled blood of the people.

Yes! See what we have brought to pass!

Phylos *wanted* his forces to be feared. He wanted the riots to be put down. The contest at the harvest, the arrest of Fletcher Wyll – all of this had brought the city to this moment.

What we have brought to pass!

On the edge of the mosaic, where the last of the market burned, there was a gathering growing – the final massing of the city's people, the rioters that had found themselves so utterly outmatched. They knew they were dead, but they didn't care, they were fighting fierce, taking on all comers and savagely defending the burning market as if it were a symbol, some icon of their lost livelihoods.

Phylos shouted his scorn at the pure blue sky.

And they came to him, Amal's inhuman fighters – twisting themselves from the very walls, falling free and rising up, monstrosities, creatures of power and beauty, bare-chested and wild-haired, centaurs and mwenar and vialer. They came to smash the last of the resistance and run rampage, deal death through the streets. They bore burning brands and chased and tortured the survivors as if in sport. They assailed the soldiers indiscriminately, trampled any human in their way, dismembered screaming victims. And Phylos let them, watched them, revelled in their strength. He let the chaos reign, let Vahl enjoy the last blaze of the city that had been built solely to defy him.

The single point of regret – Maugrim had failed and Roviarath still stood firm. But Vahl's joy was high and Phylos knew that the death of Fhaveon would be enough.

So many returns of planning.

And this was perfect.

Perfect.

It was enough to bring tears to his eyes.

The final moments were almost upon them. As the chaos became too much for the city to bear, as she teetered on the brink of death, so he would step forth and control the violence. He would free the people, establish his absolute leadership, be hailed as hero and deliverer. He would buy the city's soul, and wed its legitimacy.

The Varchinde would belong to the true son of House Valiembor.

And to the lingering eagerness of Kas Vahl Zaxaar.

This moment had been so long in the crafting, that he almost did not want it to come to pass, did not know what would fill his life when it had. He stood upon its edge, waiting.

And below, the city burned.

24: KAS VAHL ZAXAAR FHAVEON

The palace seemed immune to the madness, a rock in a blood-sea tossed by storm.

Upon the balcony, Phylos still stood like a god, his laughter thrown skyward. In his heart, he could feel Vahl's awareness and glory meshing with his own, feel the creature's seethe of pleasure.

He could also feel it rising – it was coming closer.

Vahl had only ever spared a shred of his awareness for Phylos – the Merchant Master did not know where Vahl was hidden, but had been promised, long ago, that Vahl would come when the Count of Time was ready. When Fhaveon was prepared, when the way was clear, when his place of hiding had outlived its usefulness, then Vahl would manifest in the city and finally win his war.

He would rule through Phylos's arm and might.

Blood Valiembor would be all.

His heart trembling now with fierce anticipation, Phylos could see Ythalla, riding a man down, the hooves of her heavy chearl hammering him, screaming, into the gore-slick mosaic. She turned the creature, raised her metal blade in circular gesture, commanding her tan of elite cavalry to follow her lead.

Behind her, a grinning, wild-haired vialer pulled a shrieking lad down to the floor and gutted him, swift as a butcher. Then it stood, arms crossed, and watched its victim thrash in his own intestines until he died.

But the Merchant Master's attention was not fully on the fighting below. The images were there, but he barely saw them. Instead, his attention was increasingly turned inwards, towards the tremble in his chest, to the rise of adrenaline in his muscles, to the fulfilment of the bargain he had made so long ago...

Come to me, he said. *Fhaveon is ready and I am waiting for you. Come.*

And he knew that Vahl could hear him.

On the other side of the mosaic, a new knot of resistance had gathered – someone had enough of a voice to rally the loose and panicked people. But somehow, through the scream and the smoke and the clangour, Phylos could see another place, the top of a faraway tower, gargoyles perched with fangs bared at the scene below. There were figures – a small, strange man clasped to a stone table, a woman of the Banned lined with long returns, a man with one eye...

The vision eddied like smoke on the air. Ythalla's cavalry exploded through it, shattering the resistance, fragmenting Phylos's image and blowing it away. He struggled to keep track of where it had gone. One thing he sought, one thing – the man with the eye-patch...

There! I know you, I can see you!

Screams of outrage rang somewhere in his head. He heard a chearl bellow as it fell, heard the deep thunderous rumble of the cavalry. And in an odd moment of billowing quiet, he heard the snapping of a single, overstrained terhnwood weapon, a loud retort in the air. The Count of Time slowed round him, and he met the man's single eye.

And he could see where the daemon had been hiding.

In the city's lower streets, the creatures of stone ranged free. Hurt, confused, bewildered, they raged in pain and tore at anything that came close.

They roared. They slammed through buildings, bringing them down in avalanches of stone. They destroyed the city's parks and tore down her crystal trees. They ripped the people one from another and limb from limb. When they came across pockets of resistance, they simply raised their heads and called like the rolling of great rocks down a hillside and more of their kind came, ripping themselves out from the walls.

Upon one roadway, down in the lowest tiers of the city, a great stone creature faced a block of resistance, a massing of the people who would not fear, would not retreat from the monster that confronted them. Goaded by the viciousness and chaos of the vialer at their flanks, they hurled themselves at the lumbering stone thing with death-wish ferocity – hammering at it with terhnwood weapons that shattered, but each one taking a chip, a chunk, and then finally an arm from the shoulder, causing the thing to stagger, confused, to cry aloud in pain.

The sound of it shook the very sky.

It grabbed at them with blunt hands, human and vialer alike, uncaring or unseeing, then it collapsed like a crumbling wall, its almighty roar replaced with a keening like the splitting of stone.

They swarmed over it, putting out its crystal eyes, and then they surged outwards and upwards towards the heart of the city, leaving the thing behind them, lopsided and blind and broken.

The incoming vialer, celebratory and indiscriminate, tore it to pieces and laughed as they did so.

* * *

"Follow me. Stay close and stay quiet."

Tan Commander Mostak was shaky on his feet and clad in only an undershirt, but his courage was severe, cold as stone. He had acquired a short belt-blade from the hospice staff, and he held it hard in his hand like it was a rock for his sanity – the only thing that made sense in a world gone crazed.

Mael and Selana followed him like errant children. They waited as he opened the side-gate and peered out into a high-walled stone alley, a strip of bright sky above.

"Clear," he said softly. "Now, stay with me, and do everything you're told, without question. You hear me?"

"Yes, Commander." The old man and the girl spoke together, both of them too overwhelmed by what spun around them, by what the city had become.

Somehow!

Mael desperately wanted to ask him questions, to plug the holes in his own understanding – how had Mostak known that Phylos had killed Demisarr, assaulted Valicia? – but now was not the time. Carefully, his old heart trembling in his chest, he followed the commander out into the alleyway.

The air was hot, too hot, and it left him breathless.

Silly old fool. Saravin was shaking his head, grinning through his beard. *How do you get yourself into these things?*

Shut up! Mael told the figment firmly. *It's the getting out of it again that's the problem.*

The smoke was heavier out here; the thick sense of storm that hung tense in the air. Fragments of madness went past them at the alley's end – tiny frames of life struggling to survive before being swept out of view. Here was a man with a child clutched to his chest, hunched and panicking; here a woman with a woodcutter's axe, red faced and screaming with fury. Here was a rearing monster, four arms and a bow, laughing at the madness raging round it. Here was an old soldier – Mael flinched at the sight – with a bloodied blade rammed to the hilt in his shoulder.

Mostak said, "We'll stick close to the wall, I know how to get from here to the palace kitchens. If you're a praying man, Brother –"

"Actually, I'm not –"

"Fair enough, then. We depend upon ourselves. Let's go."

They came to the alley's end and paused, afraid of what they might find ahead. Then they slid out along the wall, into the smoke, into the noise, into the blood. Above them, the city's fabulous carvings snarled, threatened them with ash-stained and helpless teeth. The confusion was incredible; the onslaught of smells terrifying. They passed the dead and the dying, people trampled and abandoned, people looting the fallen, or helping them, or ending their lives with a blade that might mean either mercy or greed. Briefly, Mael thought he saw a face he knew, but it was hooded and gone in a moment.

He was sweating. He felt sick.

But they crept on, cautious, and as swift as they dared to be.

Selana was shaking. He heard her say, "My people..." for the second time, as if she struggled to understand the words.

"Not now," Mostak said, with a harshness that could have been compassion. "Do this when you're safe."

She nodded, white-faced. They came to a corner and halted.

And then they saw the horror.

It wasn't very big.

It was belly-low on four clawed feet, a long tail lashing whip-like behind it. Its fur was matted and patchy, carved with old scars, its face was animal and savage, twisted round yellow teeth as long as Mael's fingers. A bubbling snarl came from deep in its stomach and pink froth fizzed on its jaws.

Selana drew back, pulling Mael with her.

Mostak's hand tightened on his blade.

As the commander closed, watching the thing, circling slowly, Mael had the oddest impression that the beast was familiar – that he'd drawn it or seen something like it somewhere before. But his old memory was flickering faint and he stared at it, trying to sketch its features in his mind, trying to remember...

Where had he seen something like this before?

It crouched, its hind end quivering. As it sprang, Selana squealed though it was nowhere near them, but the commander, even straight from his sick-bed, was far too fast for it.

It moved like a bweao, low and swift. Mostak moved sideways, turning with a lightning swiftness, cutting round his own back to bite his blade into the thing. Its snarling redoubled and it spun with him, ignoring both Mael and Selana completely. There was something oddly human about its face, its burning eyes – something that fascinated the old scribe. He watched the creature as though he were rifling through every sketch he'd ever done, every patient he'd ever studied, every moment of his past, 'prentice and master and retired market artist.

Selana clung to his arm. "What is that thing? What is it?"

"I don't know."

Look at it, you old fool! He didn't need Saravin to tell him that one.

Around them, chaos raged. Eddies of smoke curled through the air. Mael could hear screaming, the clatter of hooves. From somewhere else, a tirade of anger in a high female voice.

In front of him, the beast was on its hind legs, as easy on two feet as it had been on four. It lashed at Mostak with its foreclaws, almost manlike. The commander evaded each slash, drawing the thing forwards as he retreated. Mael wasn't much of a warrior, but he could see the commander was a calculated fighter – watching and carefully weighing his options. The beast missed its footing, just for a moment, and Mostak took the opening, cutting a slash down the thing's odd, almost-human face.

Feet raced behind them. Selana turned, turned back with a shudder, but Mael was intent on the creature with a fascination that bordered on –

Did it have a mark on it? Some sort of…?

Dear Gods.

Just for a moment, he had seen the scarred fur in its shoulder, the matting seeming almost to make a sigil, some sort of craftmark. He wasn't sure, but –

The beast had seen him looking.

Its head suddenly swung, low and lethal and its eyes fixed their smoulder on him, upon Selana. Mostak paused, watching it, waiting to see which way it would go. As it crouched to pounce on the old scribe and the girl, he was after it, blade biting its flank, and again, and again.

But as it came, Mael could see that the wound in its face was shallower than it had been, that the cuts in its flank were not so much as slowing it down. He backed up, shoved Selana behind him – though what good that was going to do he frankly had no idea.

The beast watched him, teeth bared.

Where had he seen something like this before?

And then, as it sprang, he had a moment of absolute clarity, a flash like it had come from the very Gods themselves. He had seen a beast like this – in the most unlikely of places. He and Saravin had been drinking in The Wanderer, perhaps only a cycle or two before, and it had been in the kitchen…

He didn't get time to ponder the significance of this. The beast was moving, faster than a thought, than a whip. Mostak was moving after it. Discarding the blade, the commander had his arms outstretched and his knees forwards. As the beast came at Mael so the commander landed on its back, his fibre-strong arms wrapped about its neck.

There was a ghastly snapping noise.

For a moment, the Count of Time seemed to stop. The beast's eyes were on Mael, Mael was watching it in return, Selana's hand was to her mouth and the commander was knees first, dragging the creature's head right back, snapping its back, its neck...

Then creature and commander hit the stone together, skidded in old blood.

The light went from the beast's smouldering eyes, the tension in its body faded.

And then it began to shimmer, its form twisting in the air.

As Mostak struggled back to his feet, Mael stared, trying not to be sick, and Selana swore under her breath with more creativity than the old scribe would have given her credit for...

The creature shimmered and became a normal human man, naked and dirty and wild-haired, lying with his neck broken in the middle of the road.

And the symbol was still there, its ink tattooed in his shoulder.

"What...?" Selana began helplessly. "Why...?"

"Whatever it is, it doesn't matter," Mostak said. "Run!"

Mael ran, but something in his memory made the sketch of that craftmark – it was something he didn't want to forget.

They ran through the destruction of the city's wealth and power, through the collapse of her masonry and the crumbling of everything she had ever been. They saw the vandals gaud the front of Garland House; saw the soldiery slam into the great doors of the High Cathedral, apparently seeking those who had found sanctuary inside.

They saw Phylos upon his balcony like a blood-fleck, burning in the sunlight. He stood like a daemon manifest, his glory blazing eager.

As they came at last towards the palace, thanking every God and their own strength that they had made it unscathed, the noise of hooves made them look up.

At the tan commander Ythalla, her heavy mount with hooves bloodied and her grin as wide as the smoke-filled sky.

"Commander." The woman's voice was as sharp as a spear-point. The chearl beneath her scraped a hoof impatiently on the stone.

Mael paused by the wall, unsure. Selana gazed at her uncle, at the pallor of his skin, at the line of sweat that ran down his temple. Master Warrior he may be – but he was still sick. There was no way he could win this one.

"Go." Mostak gave the word as an order, expecting it to be obeyed without question. "Left, and then make for the toolcrafter's alleyway. Sel, love, be brave. You know where the gate is. Go now."

"I can't leave you." Selana went to go to him, but Mael held her arm.

"He's right," Mael said. "We need to do this."

Ythalla sneered, "Oh how touching. The commander gives his life that the Lord might survive. I'll gut you like a fish, you bastard, and I'll ride her down and crush her into the stone, the old man too. You're done, Valiembor, you and her both. Phylos will bring the city under his law, martial law, and then it's *mine*."

"You're a bully, and a poor fighter," Mostak said flatly. "Skill is more than sitting on chearlback and terrorising traders."

"Are you trying to make me dismount and fight you fair?" Ythalla laughed. "Your health is poor and you're carrying a knife. I can do *this* and you'll – hoi!"

"*This*" had been a playful, one-handed jab with the spear she carried. The "hoi" was her shock as Mostak pulled it neatly from her grasp, reversed it in a single fluid move, and pointed it up at her.

"You were saying?"

Mael suppressed an urge to chuckle.

"That's not fair!" Her protest was high-pitched and petulant.

Mostak shrugged. "Whether you stay on the beast or not, Thalla, I trained you. I know your styles and weaknesses and the chearl won't make the slightest damned difference. I know I can kill you."

Her sneer was almost audible.

But Mael didn't wait to see them fight, to find out if Ythalla would dismount to duel her commander fairly, or if she was enough of a mean old mare to ride him – and then them – down. He understood what Mostak was doing, and he intended to take advantage of every moment he could give them.

They must reach the palace.

No matter what.

Somehow.

Hugging the wall, his heart thumping, *thumping*, he began to scurry. Selana was with him still, her feet sure, but her face streaked with filth and tears, her expression torn with grief. Poor child – to have regained a member of her family only to lose him just as swiftly – Mael could not begin to imagine her heartbreak and confusion. He slowed and took her elbow.

"We must be quick. Please, my Lord. We must get to the palace and get you up to that balcony. And you must call the city's wrath upon Phylos; you must make your accusations, and lead your people." *Somehow.* "You need to find your courage, child, your Valiembor heart, and you must do this. For your uncle, and for your father. For Rhan."

"Yes." The girl stumbled. A bretir had fallen in the road and was flapping helplessly, one wing burned or broken beneath it. It cheeped at them. There was a message ring about its clawed foot but Mael dared not stop, not for the message and not to put the thing out of its pain. He turned away from it, hurting, and they went on again. Hooves came past them, and were gone in the smoke.

They fought on.

The palace was just ahead of them – there was a surge of

people about the huge front gate. They were looking up at the tiny red figure, the bloodstain that was Phylos, there on the balcony, his arms still open like a welcome, a benediction.

And then, like an arrowshaft shot clean out of the northern sky, they saw the light.

25: HERO AEONA, GLEAM WOOD

Leaning over Ecko, the man that had been the Bard said, "This ends here. Now."

Ecko had no words. He was transfixed by the man's presence, by the mess his throat had become, by the multiple layers of sound, by the seethe and ripple of power that made up his voice.

From somewhere behind him, he heard Karine's more human tones. "What are you doing?" she said.

Her voice brought a slew of memories, the warm wooden glow of The Wanderer, the feeling of family, wrapped in belonging. He found himself staring at Roderick's frozen gaze and suddenly – oh God – really *wanting* this to be over, wanting that hand to close his windpipe, wanting only to go the fuck home – and then catching up with that realisation.

Home.

Something in him was looking for *The Wanderer*, for chrissakes. Something in him missed it, needed it – its warmth and safety. Something wanted his little room under the eaves, the overstuffed cellars, his cache of kit...

No, I don't care. I don't care!

Shit!

The Bard was right in his face. He smelled of metal and venom, savagery and cold determination.

"You little shit. You think you can sacrifice my whole world on your stubbornness and ego? How fucking dare you?" The word was deliberate, a jab of understanding. "I've been where you've been, lived through the same tortures, the same darkness, the same terrifying love. And you know what? I'm not impressed. Get the fuck over it. Quit whining. You're going to help me, Ecko, or I'm going to stand here and throttle you myself."

He let go, stood back, arms folded. Gone was the gentle, confused insight of the Loremaster, his eloquently tangled pleas. The gesture was an outright challenge – *Help me or die.*

Ecko had nothing, no words, no sharp comeback. No fucking understanding. Was this just Eliza calling him out, once and for all, her last shot at making him knuckle under?

Get the fuck over it.

Or had The Wanderer really gone to London? And if it had, then was it *real*, was the life of the Varchinde really his to save? After everything?

Quit whining.

Above him, the sun shone in a clear and surreal blue sky. The gargoyles stared unseeing, bared their broken teeth.

But – *shit!* – he had so many questions! His thoughts tumbled one over another in a mass of incomprehension – he couldn't find an end to untangle the knot. He'd gotten no clue how the man was here, where he'd been, what dark epiphany had struck him. And if Roderick had seen Mom, then where was The Wanderer, where was Lugan, where was the Bike Lodge, where was every fucking thing he understood?

What was real, for chrissakes, the inside or the outside?

If he died here, would he go home?

Turn back to page one.

Did he… did he even want to?

It was a tiny spark, buried deep. It glimmered somewhere alongside the sound of Pareus's death, the feel of Triqueta's friendship, the knowledge of the Bard's absolute faith in him.

The warmth of The Wanderer.

Shit!

The bloodflow from his throat was beginning to slow – somehow ironic that a gift of Mom's should now be saving his ass. He jerked his shoulders against the cuffs.

"Get these fucking clasps off of me, willya?" His rasp was low, halfway between lethal and absolutely bewildered.

"No." The Bard held a hand to stop Amethea responding. "Not until you tell me."

"Tell you what?"

"Were you actually willing to do this, turn your back on us, Ecko? Let us die? *Help* us die? Because if you were, then you won't get off this table."

Somewhere, screaming taunted him, and it carried understanding – the Bard's absolute faith had not changed. Roderick had been to Mom – yet he still believed utterly that Ecko was the hero that would save his world. And now he stood, cold and brutal, finally with the courage to make the single greatest gamble of his existence.

It wasn't Ecko's life he was betting.

It was the life of the Varchinde entire.

Were you actually willing to do this, turn your back on us, Ecko? To let us die? Help us die?

It was an epiphany, stark and shocking, and Ecko foundered. He felt like he'd walked in on himself – that there was no lead-in, no context any more, like all he could see was his own whinging and anger and self-pity.

If Roderick was really prepared to go this fucking far, then maybe the Varchinde was damned – monsters and daemons and blight. Maybe he *was* the only person that could save it.

But I don't...

His protests ran down, out of batteries. The shadows of the gargoyles were shortening as though they were pulling back from him, denying any attachment or responsibility.

He struggled to find his cynicism, managed, "I can't, I... I don't even know my score."

His response made Amal wheeze with laughter.

The alchemist had fallen against the inside of the parapet. He was fading: his age was manifest in his face now, cracking visibly through his lined skin. He cackled as they turned to him.

"Help you... do what... Master Bard?" The title was mocking, bitter. "You're too late... for heroism. My friend... has gone... four hundred returns... waiting... and he's left me..." His voice broke, he sounded like he was almost in tears. "Left me to die."

Roderick took a pace, slammed a long black boot into the heavy wall by the man's head. But the old alchemist didn't flinch, he just wheezed another laugh.

"If you're... trying to make Ecko... face the daemon... save the world" – the last words were a creaking sneer – "you've failed."

But he only made the Bard snort, a sound that rippled with new power, echoed merciless into the sky.

Roderick said, "The daemon is not Ecko's enemy, never has been. Vahl will go to Fhaveon. To Rhan. Ecko must face another foe, far more deadly than Vahl has ever been. If he has the balls."

"The blight..." Amal wheezed again, nodding, then he lifted a trembling, palsied hand. "Help me, Roderick of Avesyr... as one Loremaster... to another. My learning... can serve..."

But the Bard stepped back, clearly seeing straight through Amal's thirst for time – through his tricks.

"I remember you, Amal. Now, I remember many things. Not everything – not yet – there's still a final drop-key to fall before I can see the world's memory clearly. But even so, I remember *enough*." His voice was rich with pain and hope and scorn and fulfilment. "I know enough not to need you."

Amal coughed, withdrew, hunched further over himself as his skin shrunk into his skull, cracked open to reveal bone and yellow teeth beneath.

He said, like a lost child, "Vahl promised me... I would live..."

"He lied." With a gesture of utter disgust, the Bard rammed his boot heel, sudden and brutal, straight into the old man's face.

And the alchemist crumpled, broken and almost bloodless, to the stone.

Roderick turned to Ecko.

"Right," he said. "Do I let you up, Ecko, or do we all die?"

In the end, Ecko capitulated.

What else could he do?

The stone shuddered beneath them, and they ran.

As the walls splintered and cracked, so they gathered Ecko and their wits and they raced, scattered and panicked, for the long stairs down to the courtyard. Shadows shifted, the stone table cracked, and the grimacing gargoyles tilted and then slid free from their bases, falling at last.

Fleeing the shattering missiles, the flying shards, they chased madly down the tiny steps. They could feel the tower behind them shuddering, see dust trickling from the walls. The steps cracked as they ran, the rocks beneath them shook. Stones came loose and turned ankles. Behind them, parts of the parapet cracked completely and came free, and scree and rock fell down to the water far below.

Hit with a splash that sounded like horror.

Triqueta shouted, "To me!" and they paused by the empty pool, panting and wild-eyed, looking about them for an exit.

Ecko tried to ask about the tavern, but Roderick cut him short.

"She was never meant to go that far," he said. "She didn't

come back." His voice was layered with severity and an appalling, complex grief.

Ecko had no idea who he was, who he'd become – but he didn't have time for that now. "Where are the others?"

Karine said, final and fatal, "There's only me."

Triqueta had not let go of her spear and her cracked and flaking hands were white upon its shaft.

Scanning the walls, the carvings and creeper, Ecko skidded as the stone cracked and then tilted, right under his feet. He was verging on panicked, now, his adrenals in a ball in his wounded throat. His cloak and webbing were gone, he'd no fucking clue where. He was thin and pale and exposed, bared to the sunlight, clad only in hastily borrowed breeches. His knees shook, his wrists hurt, the cut down his chest stung like a motherfucker. There was a pink, straight scar slicing down through his skin like he'd been marked for butchery practice.

Behind them, more of the parapet cracked and crumbled. Another gargoyle fell clear, slammed into the tower with a shattering impact that sent cracks of shadow through the long stairs.

Fear flickered from face to face.

"We're not leaving without Redlock." Triqueta's tone was half-threat, half-statement.

"Chrissakes." The crack under Ecko's feet was growing wider. "You're fucking kidding me."

It was like the Bard's choice in miniature, *help me or die*, like the tiny repeated pattern that made up the big one. It was all piling up against him now, pushing aside his fury and denial as if his whole fucking wall was just so much sand, as if he was finally coming to pieces like the keep around him. He'd done his fucking best, but the fight was fading – he'd tried to burn it all, and he'd *failed*...

What was left?

The Bard said, "Ecko. Get us out of here."

Help me or die.

Shit.

"There!" The crack under his feet widened yet further – he jumped sideways and pointed. One of the cell doorways was showing warmth and light. "Let's go!"

Beside him, the dry pool suddenly splintered to a spider-web of cracks – as if something underneath it had given way. Fragments and corners began to fall into some huge hollow below.

Karine was bellowing, "Come on, come *on*! If Ecko can see, he'd better go at the front…"

But Ecko wasn't waiting. He darted for the doorway, warily eyeing the lintel. He could see where the back corner of the cell had cracked down one wall. It was tight, but he pulled at the creeper, kicked at the bones, turned sideways and managed to cram himself into the gap. Getting through it just as if it was the stinking side-tunnels of the old London Underground.

Hell, if Rodders had seen Mom too, then he should feel right at fucking home.

Now, Ecko was beginning to grin – feel almost like himself again – then the crack suddenly opened out into clean air and light, and he found he was teetering on a high ledge over a carefully organised garden. Rows of flowers and plants, walls and pathways – the ornamental garden of some stately fucking home.

What the hell?

He was in shadow, the long grey shape of the keep was cast ahead of him. He clung to the edge of the vantage, scanning. Behind him, the others were a mass of shouts and chaos, he could hear them scrabbling and swearing.

"Watch your butts," he shot back at them. "We gotta way out but there's a drop. Who's got sixty foot of rope?"

"What?" Karine, next in the gap, was having trouble fitting and didn't get the joke.

Ecko turned back to the garden.

It was walled, open to the sky. At its far end he could see the walkway that joined the bailey to the edge of the cliff and the haunted forest. There were other routes, archways and more grounds, all of them beginning to crack like water-parched earth...

Earth, for chrissakes.

The word made him snort.

Then the ledge underneath him lurched and he jumped, pressing his back against the stone. He clung harder, feeling a sudden sense of déjà-vu.

Earth. Hell, maybe if I let fucking go I'll hit the sidewalk at Blackfriars Bridge, after all...

Yeah, right.

There was an almighty shatter of falling masonry. A sudden crack ran through the wall and out into the garden. He heard Karine shouting.

In a flurry, Ecko scrambled down the side of the keep. He leapt for a bush, ducked, let his skin shift to the colour of leaf and shadow.

And then he realised that the garden had a watcher, a last guardian.

A centaur.

At first, he couldn't see it clearly – it was in the sun on the far side of the keep's shadow, pacing the length of a bright-flowered garden. It was different to the other creatures he'd seen: it seemed somehow unbalanced, almost crude by comparison to the elegance and power of the beasties he'd seen previously. Its gait was uneven, peculiar, and it seemed oddly unfinished, scarred somehow, as though...

As it came closer, crossing into the shadow with its huge claws raking at the stones, Ecko's telescopics got a clear fix. He realised what he was looking at.

And his mind said, *Holy fucking shit.*

The others were dropping down the wall now. There were

curses as the stone shook under them; the crack was getting worse. The entire sodding keep was going to crumble to rubble and they needed to move. Like now. They needed to get the fuck out of these gardens and off this peninsula before they all took swimming classes.

Triqueta came to join him, skidding into a crouch behind the bush, her spear clutched in her hand.

She said, "Just one?" She was grinning. "C'mon, Ecko, we've fought bigger beasties than that..." Then she tailed into silence, as she, too, realised what she was looking at.

Her mouth opened as if she would say something, but no sound emerged.

Ecko watched her, the congealing horror in her expression. He felt his heart shrink in his chest, his throat close. He put a hand on her arm.

"Triq..." He had no fucking clue what to say to her.

"No. Take this." She stood up, shoved the spear into his hand. "I'm going out there."

"Chrissakes, don't. You –"

"Shut up!" She rounded on him, voice breaking. "Roderick was right – this is all your fault! We should have stayed with Syke, stayed in Roviarath. This has been loco – all for nothing. Nothing! What have we gained from coming here?"

Her yellow gaze was too much, and he looked at his hands, colours shifting.

Something behind them rumbled and the ground shook.

The others were behind him now, scattered and unsure. As Ecko looked back up, the shadow of the keep shifted and changed. The rumble became a roar and stonework fell, harsh and splitting. From somewhere came a long, rumbling crash as masonry hit the ground. There was a splash, another, the heavy slosh of water.

Chrissakes. We gotta move.

But Triqueta was walking out to meet the monster.

Amethea came to a halt by Ecko. She stared, shocked, horrified. Then swallowed, muttered, "You can't let her go out there…"

But Ecko shook his head. He was shaking, sickness or reaction or adrenaline, he didn't even know.

Triqueta walked to the creature.

And the creature came to meet her, like something out of a particularly twisted soap opera.

It was chearl-bodied, bulky in comparison to the monsters he'd seen before. Its torso was of normal, human size, powerfully muscled and heavily scarred, but the two had been joined poorly – the thing looked like it had been jammed together by an impatient child with plastic cement.

But even that was not what made Ecko stare, what made Amethea catch her voice in a sob and bury her face in his shoulder. He patted her, stupidly, his brain reeling.

He knew who this was.

The creature's bitter, confused expression was so human. His hair and hands were the same ones that they'd known through their long journeys together. He still had his axes. But the look in his eyes…

The keep shuddered again and the ledge behind them crashed, making Ecko start and his adrenals jackhammer an insane, impossible tattoo.

Karine was on her feet, shouting, "We have to go, we have to *go*!" but the Bard, too, had come to stand by Ecko and Amethea.

He said, his voice as dark as the falling shadow ahead of them, "We should know how he feels."

Triqueta reached the monster. It towered over her – she extended her hand to it.

Ecko heard her speak to it, even through the sounds of destruction that surrounded them.

She said, "Redlock?"

* * *

Her mind wouldn't take it in. He was there, he was warm and flesh and his face was the same, his heavy shoulders, the scattering of grey-threaded red hair down the centre of his chest, the heavy scar given to him by Maugrim's chain.

She said, "Redlock?"

She extended a hand, but couldn't bring herself to actually touch him. It would make him real, and he couldn't be, he *couldn't* be. This was another figment, like her sire, like the boots of the Banned.

But the keep behind her was falling in upon itself; the gardens beneath her were cracking to the core. The beast raked a claw in the stones and shook itself as though trying to speak. Its – his – face contorted as if he had forgotten what the words were, or how to make them.

She said, her voice a whisper, "Redlock, please. It's me."

But if he understood her, he didn't show it. He exhaled, shook his hair in a gesture that was so frighteningly chearl she backed away, her heart trembling. She had no idea how much of the man was still there, how much of the creature was not only a part of his flesh, but a part of his mind.

Then he focused on her. He blinked and stepped sideways, head thrown and knees high as if he were spooked.

He stopped, made a sound, frowned, made another. With an effort, he managed something that might almost have been her name.

She said again, as if she voiced some kind of terrible truth, "Redlock..."

Then there came a heavy, terrifying rumble from behind her, a massive male cry that seemed to echo clear into the sky. The voice was the Bard's and it said, "*Run!*"

The ground shook at the sound.

Triqueta turned and saw the entire front wall of the keep coming down. Heart hammering now, she turned back, just for a moment thinking that the creature would rescue her like this was some kind of saga, that he would pick her up and race away across the gardens and there would be some kind of...

Some kind of *what*?

But the creature looked at the falling wall. He blinked, puzzled, edged backwards, scraping the stones under his claws. As Triqueta held her hand out again, she realised that she'd missed the chance to touch him, to reach him, to tell him that it would be okay.

He was backing away, eyes wild, hands resting on axes as they always had. His claws left long scars in the stones.

Then Ecko hit her in the back like a trade-road bandit. "Shift your ass, willya?"

On the ground before her, the shadow of the wall was moving. Even as she watched it, the whole of the front of the tower slid free, crashed with a roar into the courtyard. Stones came over the wall like missiles, like a wave of thrown rock and Ecko ran, holding her wrist and dragging her with him.

They raced for the cross walk, for the haunted forest.

As they reached the courtyard, the wall cracked asunder, splitting from top to bottom, so she turned one last time to look into the crumbling garden.

The centaur was standing there like a carven statue, watching them go.

When they were clear, they stopped on the clifftop, wind and sky and flowers. The sun was sinking towards the distant Kartiah and the sea shone like polished metal. The keep, whatever it was, had fallen and a cloud of smoke hung like a pall in the clear air.

Triqueta tore a handful of bright summer colour up by the roots, threw it at Ecko sobbing, caught somewhere between fury and grief. But Ecko couldn't face her and he turned away, looking out over the gleaming water.

Roderick was right – this is all your fault! This has been loco – all for nothing. Nothing! What have we gained from coming here?

The Bard stood beside him like an accusation, silent and cold.

"All right." Ecko said. "I'm on side. So what the hell do we do now?"

26: HALF-DAMNED FHAVEON

It came to him, as he had always known it would.

And Phylos was on his knees, his hands at his throat. He was gagging for bare life, struggling to understand, to handle this huge thing, this presence, this colossal whack of pure might that had just ravaged him body and soul. It screamed in his mind, brought blood to his heart and eyes and mouth, rang a clangour of hot laughter in his ears.

It said, mocking, a seething voice like ash and steam, *You wanted me, Phylos?*

In that moment, Phylos understood a single truth – that any bargain he had made with this creature was a fallacy, that it had no time for him, it wanted only its own victory – and that if it ruled Fhaveon, it might be in his flesh, but he would not be sharing it.

Kas Vahl Zaxaar had come.

Phylos came to his feet, wrenching at the neck of his robe, tearing it open across his chest. He could see the darkness writhing beneath his skin; see an eruption of inks that seared like branding, burning designs into his very flesh. He could smell himself crisping, burning from the inside out.

But he was Valiembor-blooded. He was Phylokaris, son of Salukaris, of the line of Saluvarith; he was nephew to the Founder himself. And pure-blooded, not some cursed half-breed – his elite Archipelagan race was untainted. He was born better than these foolish Grasslanders, better than the weak and wasted remnant that Valiembor had become.

That Rhan had made them.

Rhan.

Vahl heard the thought, and his teeming wrath paused. The daemon eased its raging and its striving for control. *Rhan.* For that moment, they meshed perfectly – they had a mutual enemy and they were of one mind, and one purpose.

Rhan.

Vahl knew he was coming...

...and he knew that Phylos had already beaten him once.

It was a pinpoint, bright and white and rainbow, too many colours to see, impossibly brilliant and getting bigger by the moment. Across the city, people pointed, turned, their anger forgotten. It was approaching with incredible swiftness.

And it was aimed straight at the heart of Fhaveon herself.

It grew larger, became brighter than the sky, searing out of the north. Everything stopped.

The air, the wind, the water. The city, her seething streets and bloodied riots, her chaos and creatures, her soldiers and dissenters. Mael and Selana. The tan commander Ythalla, still mounted; the cornered Mostak, fighting to hold his life and his ground.

On the balcony, Phylos could see it clearly – he knew exactly what it was and he welcomed it. He stood with his arms still outstretched as though he were pulling that streaking light straight into his heart, some long-lost brother, some sibling blazing back from the dead.

And within him, Vahl was laughing with a blood-eagerness that tainted them both.

Rhan.

Brother, estavah, soul of my soul. Welcome!

The Merchant Master stood trembling, his body all but alight. Mortal and immortal, they waited together, a supra-human pulsebeat of anticipation. Vahl had waited in hiding for four hundred returns, and his victory was upon him. Phylos had schemed and manipulated, destroyed the Council and the city, left the last child of the Founder alone and afraid.

His, whenever he chose to take her.

The light was blinding, almost upon them. It was screaming for the city like some avenging comet, like the last star of the night sky come to reclaim the day.

On the ground, the people shrieked and scattered.

"There is no need to fear!" With a roar that shook the very walls, Phylos rent his robe from neck to hem, showing the ink and spirals and darkness that writhed within his flesh. "The city stands strong!" Without even realising how or why, he – they – threw themselves upwards and into the incoming blaze.

Rhan.

As he hit, dazzled and tumbling, robbed of breath and sight, Phylos thought he was screaming, but had no idea if the noise was even his own. The air burned around him, in him. The impact was more than his mortal mind could tolerate – but Phylos was long-lived, noble-blooded, Archipelagan, and Kas Vahl Zaxaar was with him, riding the detonation and holding him against it. The two creatures met – light and fire, too similar, and for a single crazed instant, they were almost one, united as brothers down through all the long returns of the world's existence. Blasted by the detonation, Phylos could barely tell which one was alight in his soul and which one blazed about him, wrath incarnate.

But the pain was glorious, like the adrenaline that wins you a race despite bones broken, that brings through exhaustion to the elation of the mountaintop. For a moment, they spun, through and over and under, in and around each other like a tornado. Then Phylos was falling, suddenly cut loose and ragged. There was a flash of an awful loss, a bereavement – the loss of the bright halls of the heavens, vanishing above him – and then with a jar like coming suddenly out of a dream, he was crashed down and reeling, breathless, stumbling, across the broken remnant of the city's mosaic.

The fall should have killed him, but he had landed on his feet.

The sensations were fading, even as he wondered what had happened. But Vahl was there, had held him to life, had brought him through the impossibility – the daemon was still with him.

You are Phylos. Hold to your faith and trust me.

Phylos looked at the tiny, shattered tiles. Blinked for a moment. Looked up.

Rhan was standing over them. He wore the smoke of the city behind him like a cloak of wrath. He bore the sky like a personal light, the sunshine like anger. He did not need to say it aloud. *Vahl. I've been waiting for you.*

Still with the theatre? Vahl laughed with Phylos's mouth, laughed as if the city, the smoke and the ruin were his to own, as if the Varchinde itself belonged to him in ash and rubble and loss. *Save it, I can see through you.*

Aloud, he said, "Brother."

Pressed flat against the wall, Mael and Selana stood, stunned, at the outmost edge of the mosaic. They had seen the streak of illumination, seen it strike the balcony, seen Phylos rend his robe and hurl himself from the balcony's edge.

There had been a detonation, a massive whack of air and light that had knocked everyone – everything – back from the point of impact. People sprawled, screaming; dust and rubbish tumbled. For a moment, the city seemed to contain a whirlwind, coiling heat and light in an inseparable, crazed spiral, then Phylos hit the mosaic with an impact that sent cracks through the pattern, cracks through the city itself – and over him stood the blazing-white figure of the Seneschal.

"Rhan. Oh my Gods…" Selana's hands went to her mouth. She had tears in her eyes that glittered with rainbows of refracted light. Mael had no idea if the gesture was fear or relief, whether she still blamed Rhan for the hurt that had been done to her family, or whether she was overwhelmed to have him back with her, and for her.

Mael *somehow* had just found an answer.

He said, "Now, my Lord, now while we can. We must reach the balcony!"

But he couldn't tear her away.

Slowly, some manifest monster, Phylos stood up.

The mosaic had dented at his impact, as if he carried new weight, an authority never before seen. He wore only his clout, his massive physique writhed with patterns of ink and darkness – he looked as though he could explode, seethe into a tentacled growth of something else entirely, grow roots, wings. He looked as if his soul were suddenly larger than his flesh and could barely be contained.

And he was laughing.

The sound shuddered through the mosaic at his feet, through the city itself, it echoed from the palace wall. Every creature in Fhaveon heard him as he spoke.

"Brother."

The word was a death knell.

And then he turned, raising his arms like a priest from some ancient and forgotten saga. He threw them wide, encompassing all of the madness and the destruction and the inhuman and impossible creatures that now stood, stunned, about the edge of the mosaic.

"Now," he said, "let us show my brother his homecoming."

And around them, the stunned creatures began to shift into motion.

Selana shuddered at the sound of his voice. Mael could hear it – as clear as the sky itself. He was no longer Phylos, he was something darker and softer, something more elegant and smothering – something far more dangerous. As the ranged forces at the edges of the mosaic came slowly to life, began to move forwards towards the single figure in their midst, the young Lord shook herself and lunged, crying aloud, "Rhan! I'm here! *Rhaaaaaan!*"

Mael made a grab for her arm.

Surrounded by violence, the Seneschal almost turned, almost heard her, but the tide of darkness was seething forwards now, creeping over the broken mosaic, soldiers armed and angry, creatures twisted with righteous rage, burning with steam that shimmered in the air. That tide was all around him, incoming and threatening to take him down – and at its centre Phylos pulled it to him and wrapped himself in it, used it as cloak and glory and weapon.

For a moment, Mael stared at it all blindly and wondered where all of the people had gone. If the riots had just been...

...a distraction.

Dear Gods.

He pulled Selana's arm. "My Lord. My Lord. We must go!"

For an instant longer she stood there, straining, as if she willed Rhan to fight, willed him to hear her, as if by sheer force of wishing she could undo all of this madness and go back to just being Selana, the only child of a gentle father –

Move! Saravin's voice in Mael's ears made the old scribe shake the girl, Lord or no, and *run*.

Rhan was home.

Home to a nightmare, home to a city destroyed by four hundred returns of his brother's scheming and building and patience.

And now they came for him – weapons raised and mouths stretched in hate – soldiers, monsters, creatures. They came from every direction, faster now, burning with eagerness and clawing at each other in the effort to reach him first. They came with eyes of darkness, of fire, eyes that reflected his own light. As they closed in upon him, they tussled to gain ground, they turned on each other, snarling and fighting. Among them, lost and crushed, or carried forward by the flow, came the ordinary people of Fhaveon, those few survivors who had taken to the streets in protest and now found themselves caught in this crazed war not of their making.

They were cut and crushed and trampled, forgotten, into the mosaic below.

And Phylos – Vahl – just stood back and watched them die.

But this was what Rhan had been made for. Defending the city, not against manipulations and politics, but against the manifest physical flesh of her foes – against his risen brother.

At last.

This was what mattered.

Phylos's fetter had gone, and even though the soul of light was sunken, Rhan could still attune himself to the vibrations of the elemental Powerflux with a skill that made Maugrim look like a 'prentice.

And he was *angry*.

The first creature dropped with a fist to its temple – brutal and satisfying – he didn't even see what it was. And then there were two of them, three, four, five, and they were on him like a deluge. For a few moments, it looked like he would be overwhelmed, there were too many; they were coming from every direction. The sheer weight of them was too much, and they were bearing him down to the mosaic to be crushed along with the people of the Lord city. He was faltering, falling...

No. It's not that damned easy.

With a roar that was as much force as volume, he regained his feet, threw them back. They tumbled from him, bloodied and dying, like he was the heart of his own explosion, like he was the Powerflux itself. Here was a vialer, broken and discarded; here a soldier, picked up and thrown back, his head shattered on the tiles. Here was a trader, carried forward by the tide and crushed between the force before him and the incoming creatures behind. Rhan did not even see him.

In the midst, a lone centaur, head and body higher than the rest and claws raking the tiles as it came. He was young, bore blades that he wielded with impressive skill, hacked his way through friend and foe alike to reach where Rhan was standing.

The tiles were *melting* under the Seneschal's feet.

The centaur bellowed, and Rhan turned to face it. He did not even pause – he was laughing like his brother now and he simply raised a hand and gestured, throwing the creature away. It faltered, screaming like an injured horse; it dropped one weapon to cover its eyes. Blind, it careered, clawing and crushing. A moment later, a soldier behind it ripped a hole in its gut in an effort to save her own life.

The creature tumbled sideways, kicking, took several members of the woman's tan down with it. Its remaining weapon slashed at anything that came close and the awful scream went on.

The tan turned on it, hacked it to pieces.

Phylos was still laughing.

Raging now, elated and hard and pure, Rhan picked up a sneering nartuk bodily and threw it, its body combusting even as it left his hands, and turning into crisping flesh and charcoal. The stink was sickening. It crashed into a huddling group of rioters, taking them down and sending the survivors screaming for the shelter of the roadways.

Smoke rose from the corpse.

At the edges of the mosaic, people were fleeing now – the

soldiers among them. Rhan was berserk, purging himself of long returns of inactivity and laziness and guilt, oblivious to anything but his own savage release.

And Phylos was still laughing.

The door to the back of the palace kitchens was closed.

Selana shrugged, knocked on the door three times and then twice.

There was a long silence, a space that seemed to last until the end of the Count of Time. Mael checked behind them, watching the scattered savagery. He could hear his heart beating despite the roar that was rising from the city's streets... and then the door eased open and half a face peered around the edge.

"Yes?"

"It's me." Selana was through it like a bolt from a slingshot, Mael following.

The young man who had opened the door wore a cook's greasy overshirt and a frown. "My Lord! You shouldn't be here. They're trying to breach the gates!"

"We must get to the balcony." On her home ground now, the Lord pushed the young man gently out of the way and eyed the long arch of the corridor before her, rocklit doorways to either side. She said to Mael, "Can you still run?"

His heart was thundering.

"I'm not done yet, my Lord."

From somewhere, they could hear rising sounds of panic, then a solid boom as something hit the front gates. The floor under them shook. Selana paled, gathered her skirts and her breath, and they ran.

Behind them, the young man called, "But what are you going to do when you get there? My Lord? My Lord!"

Mael had got this far by wit and luck and the seat of his breeches – if they got to the balcony and Rhan had fallen, they had better make this convincing because it was the last thing either of them would ever do.

Cries came down the passageway. Selana skidded round a corner, another, raced past the long foodhall, stumbled up a flight of steps and came out in the main entranceway of the Fhaveon Palace.

"By the Gods." In the midst of the madness, Mael paused.

He'd never been in here, never had reason. The huge door, the tiled floor, the sweep of steps, the colossal painting that covered the ceiling – Saluvarith himself, blessed by the Gods, laying the first stones of the city on the site of the legendary Swathe. The room was huge, it echoed with emptiness and it robbed Mael of words and breath. He –

Behind him, the door juddered under a massive impact. The walls quivered. Raised voices outside chanted mockery, echoed the sound of Phylos's steam-filled laughter.

Selana cried, "Come on!"

She was gone up the huge stairway, faster than Mael could follow. His heart was labouring in his chest now, the rhythm oddly strong and too fast, but he didn't have time to worry. For just a moment, he wished that Saravin was with him, that the old warrior could have done this instead of him – perhaps he would have done it differently, or better.

The door juddered again. The drop-bar shook and dust fell. There were whoops and cries from outside – another impact like that one and the damned thing would give.

In the hallway below, a strident voice was assembling a tan of the palace guard, a small and decorative force that, by Mael's reckoning, would last about as long as a sneeze. They stood like a gaggle of nervous dancers, fidgeting with weapons they had no idea how to use.

When the doors went, they would scream and scatter and die.

He didn't have time to even feel pity for them.

Selana was bounding upwards. She rounded the corner of the stairs and paused to check the landing. The judder and boom echoed again from below, and Mael could hear the voice calling the straggled force to rally and hold firm. He glanced, but could not see the commander. As he reached the top of the stairs, he stopped, hauling breath into wheezing lungs, his heart thundering, swift and relentless, counterpoint to the rhythm of the battering below.

Then there was a terrible weight in his chest, a sudden hot thumping in his ears. His vision was going dark, tunnelling in about him. He tried to go after Selana, but he really couldn't breathe and his legs were like water and he needed to sit down.

Just to catch his breath.

Just for a moment...

You silly old fool, said Saravin. *You've done it, you've really done it. You can stop now. Everything will be fine.*

Brother Mael slid to the floor, one hand on his chest. He really wanted an ale, but he decided, all in all, as his vision blackened and his heart seemed to labour even harder, that his old friend was probably right.

He'd done what he had to. He could stop now.

Rhan stood alone amid the cries of the dying.

He was breathing hard, stained with blood and filth and ash. His light dimmed with weariness, but he was still standing, and the mosaic was his.

Only Phylos still stood, watching him with the eyes of his brother.

In the streets, the fighting continued, knots and ripples of violence. The steady boom of the assault on the palace – the war for the city was not yet done. Here, though, there was silence.

Then Vahl said, soft as ruin, "Your skill does you proud, my brother. Your returns of idleness have not made you soft."

"Get out of my city." Rhan spat contempt and anger. He was in no mood for word games.

"Your city?" Vahl laughed at him. Ink writhed across Phylos's flesh, as if it strove to break free and coil through the stone beneath. "Your city? The city that you've lost, brother, the city that you've failed, despite Samiel's charge?"

"I've failed nothing. *Brother.*"

"You've failed everything." Phylos spoke with his own voice, with Vahl's tones sliding through and round and under them. "Don't you remember? Samiel cast you down for loving his daughter, for laying your hands upon the body of the Goddess. Don't you remember how she felt, Kas Rhan Elensiel? How she tasted? Calarinde – she rises in glory above you every night of your immortal life, and you can never touch her again." Phylos came forwards as he spoke, insidious and mocking. "Ah, but you never knew the truth of it, my poor estavah, my half-damned brother. You didn't seduce the Goddess – how could you? Look at you. She came to you, took you, loved you – just so you'd be cast down. Samiel set you up, you fool, and then he damned you for it." Phylos's smile was as wide as the sky, too wide for his face. "And still, you've failed."

Rhan said nothing. His light paled against the sky. But Vahl was not done.

"Look at you. Indolent, selfish, bored. The world rotted because of you, stagnated because of you. I bring change, brother, new life. Progress." He was close now, all smirking and warmth. "Am I the daemon, Rhan?" His smile was pure venom. "Or are you?"

Am I the daemon?

Rhan stood, surrounded by ruin, awash with memories he had not dared touch, not down through all the long returns of his exile. *How she felt? How she tasted?* In the streets there were echoes of noises, tails of fighting, the steady boom still came from the palace gate, but here, there was silence.

Samiel set you up, you fool, and then he damned you for it.

Rhan let go of the light, the pulse and power of the Flux. He paled until he was his normal self, recognisably the Seneschal, though weary and faltering under the weight of his brother's truth.

He said, "When did you give up your soul, Phylos? I hope the trade was a good one."

Vahl laughed, the noise ringing in the morning light. "Is that all you have left?"

"No. It's not." Rhan looked up, shook his head. "I've missed you, my brother, my estavah, soul of my soul. But whatever truths you reveal, you've forgotten something." His voice became stronger, regaining its usual sardonic boom. "Calarinde is the Goddess of Love, or so they say. I may have served four hundred returns for her touch, but you know what?" One hand lashed out, closed on Phylos's throat. "It was *worth* it."

And he squeezed.

"Now, Dæl Vahl Sashar. You're out of options. You can't own me, and there's nothing else here strong enough to hold you." His hand tightened. "I call you damned, brother. Once, and for all time. Go home, go back to the Rhez, and leave my city, and my people, and my family, *alone.*"

Phylos gagged, hands clawing at the arm that held him, but it might as well have been carven stone.

"And as for you, Phylos, killing you gives me more pleasure than I can describe. And if that makes me the daemon, then so be it." His grin broadened, his hand crushed harder and the man's eyes bulged, his jaw worked as he strove for air. "Ah, the times I could have done this across the Council's table! You and your smugness and your damned games." His hand crushed harder. "No trickery, no Elementalism. You'll die by my bare hands."

Phylos shook, scrabbled with hopeless grip. He fought for one last moment, his face blackening almost as if the tattoos were spreading through his skin. Then he gagged, pissed himself, and slumped.

Rhan threw him down, discarded like garbage.

But over him, an odd haze, like shadow in the morning sun, was something else entirely.

Selana Valiembor, Lord of Fhaveon, came out onto the palace balcony to see her city in devastation. Death and pain filled the streets, smoke drifted across the sky. Buildings were in ruin, walls torn down, trees ripped up by their roots. The sunken half-circle of the theatre had formed a rallying point for the remains of the soldiery. The GreatHeart Rakanne still stared out over the water, still oblivious to the threat that had crept in under her guard.

Selana stood silent, looking out at her city. She could see that the market was no more, a scattered ruin of ash and char, fragments of livelihoods discarded and forgotten. There were figures wandering the remains, confused – as if looking for some shred of their crafting, some reason, some hope.

Below her, there was fighting at the palace gate – the rattle and boom of the great doors had stopped, it seemed the guard commander had mounted a sortie. She could see them now, a woman armed and armoured, and the sight gave her a fierce rush of joy. She wanted to run down there and embrace her, crying at her courage.

It was Valicia, her mother.

To her other side, the great mosaic was shattered, its fantastical design now torn up and scattered, melted and blasted. Rhan still stood at its centre, though his light was faded. Phylos lay dead, his body twisted and stained.

Selana felt a moment of relief, a sudden need to cry.

Then she saw the thing that faced him, the shadow, standing over Phylos like a predator. It was oddly nebulous, as if crafted of smoke or somehow had no flesh of its own.

Something about it made her skin crawl.

It was like nothing she'd ever seen: it was old, stooped, shrivelled somehow, with a vast sense of power and eagerness that she could feel, even from here. It was emaciated, its smoky body wasted. There were long scars at its back as if it had once had wings, but they had been cut or torn away. Its skin was thin and cracked in places and it could not stand fully upright. It flinched and flickered at the light of the sun.

As yet, as she looked at it, something in her heart was moved to a vast pity.

And it looked back at her, eyes burning blue like the heart of the fire.

She shivered, pinned and staring, held to the spot.

And slowly, she felt its smoke filter gently into her thoughts.

Vahl was a broken thing.

No longer the beauty and strength of the Gods' most favoured form of life, no longer hale with might and presence – no longer even flesh. He was shattered, crouched and cracked and sneering. He wavered in the sea air.

Rhan had waited four hundred returns for this – and now he found he couldn't lift his hand. Phylos was dead, the city was safe... his brother was broken.

Vahl. Kas or Dæl, he was estavah, closer than any creature had ever been, would ever be.

Up on the balcony, Selana was standing like the carven statues of her family, staring down at them.

He watched his brother for a moment, beyond victory and beyond heartbreak.

And then he took a breath, and blew the creature away.

27: PATTERNS AMOS

In her high tower, wrapped in chill and shadow, Nivrotar of Amos stood silent as death.

The wide stone bowl before her was layered over with fine ice, smooth and absolutely clear. Reflected in it was a young girl, blonde and pretty, her head bowed. Beside her stood a man injured, his arm folded in cloth and a long scar torn down his cheek. At her other side was an older woman, her face similar in features but tired.

They did not speak.

They did not need to.

Upon a pallet before them lay an elderly man, grey-faced and motionless. His eyes were closed, but his chest still fluttered – barely. His lips were parted as if hoping to draw some life from the still air.

Nivrotar knew the inside of the Fhaveon hospice well enough; knew Selana and Mostak and Valicia, the last faces of House Valiembor. She had watched Phylos's final moments, the return of Rhan and the fall of Vahl Zaxaar – and she watched now, observed the ongoing life of the Varchinde as she always had, always would.

Selana said, "Funny isn't it – he's not a warrior, not a champion, he's not anything really" – there was a weight of sadness in her tone – "he's just an old man."

"We owe our lives to Brother Mael," Mostak said quietly, "all of us."

Selana nodded. "We owe him the city." She turned as the door behind her opened, said like a flare of hope, "Can you save him?"

Rhan was drawn and ashen, as grey as the man on the pallet. He looked weary, as though his returns had loaded his shoulders with cares he had no way to lessen or voice.

"Honestly, my Lord?" he said, "I don't know. But if there's attunement and light left in me, Gods willing, then I'll give it everything I've got."

Selana nodded and stood back, letting him approach the pallet.

Nivrotar was old. Perhaps as old as Amos herself, she honestly couldn't remember. She could feel the Powerflux in her aged bones, in her Tundran blood. She could feel the spreading seethe and webwork of elemental strength that wrapped the world, flowed in the seasons and the growth and death of the grass. As Rhan opened his focus, accessed that web for himself, she could feel him like a node, a bright flare of immortal awareness.

She could feel just how terrifyingly powerful he really was – and how close he had come to losing.

Yet he knelt beside the old man like a supplicant, one hand on his thin chest, his weak, limping heart. He lowered his head, inhaled. Then he blew, a single long breath that was almost visibly warm, a gift of life.

Heal and Harm, the oldest elemental rule – none could learn one without learning the other.

Slowly, the old man's chest ceased its desperate fluttering, the colour returned to his face. A second breath, and he was relaxing, his heart rate steadying. A third, and he was asleep.

Rhan sat back on his heels, his hands shaking and his skin

like aged parchment. His face was sunken and his expression exhausted.

"Sometimes," he said, his voice a low rumble, "the greatest heroes are not visible – they're not immortal guardians, not lords or warriors. Sometimes the greatest hero is an old man who lost his best friend and wanted to do the right thing."

The last word caught in his throat, and he swallowed. "I'm shamed by his courage."

"We all are." Mostak's tone was gruff.

"You know," Rhan said, looking back round at them, "I did not harm your brother, nor you, Lady."

Valicia lifted her chin. "I know that now," she said. "Or you'd be having a very close encounter with a very sharp knife. Mostak – in the hospice –"

"Phylos tried to kill me." The commander gave a brief, eloquent shrug. "Warrior I may be, but I'm not that damned stupid."

Rhan made no attempt to stand. "Then my service is yours, as it has always been." His voice broke, with exhaustion and grief. "If you still want it."

There was a moment of silence, more compassion than consideration.

Then Selana said, "Yes, my Lord Seneschal, I do. On the presumption that Brother Mael is appointed Merchant Master and the Council of Nine reformed. After all," she gave an impish grin, "you wouldn't want me to be a tyrant, would you?"

"And," Mostak said bleakly, "no more narcotics."

"You have not only my service, Commander, but my word and my focus." A faint, wary smile flickered over Rhan's face. "Somehow, I feel my brother may lurk closer than we realise."

In the gathering gloom of the tower, Nivrotar pulled her attention away from Rhan and his family. She touched the edge of the wide stone dish, moved the focus of the ice within until she could see the shattered streets of the Lord city, the death and debris, the drifting smoke. The hospice doors were open, but there were too many injured for the building to hold and the gardens were filled with the hurt and dying, some of them tended by friends, others crying out and alone.

Yet they were the lucky ones.

All through the streets, in buildings broken and charred, there were others who had not been able to move. Some had simply lain down and died, others called out for help. Opportunists roamed the emptiness: a slit throat or broken skull was an easy end to the pain.

In some places huddles of people had gathered, bristling-wary and waiting with sharp eyes until the streets were clear. In others, there were lone icons of bafflement, staring at a dead monster, an old building, the end of their livelihoods. Soldiers, too, were loose in the mess, but making no more sense of what had happened than anyone else.

Nivrotar felt an odd tug at the edge of her awareness.

For a moment, she didn't know what it was – thought perhaps she'd heard something in the palace itself. But no, the tug had come from the ice before her and she moved the bowl again, shifting its focus, looking for the origin.

South – from Fhaveon to Amos herself, following the coast. South again, past her own city down into the pathless figments of the Gleam Wood and Aeona, the midden city that lurked like a shadow, the outermost edge of the grasslands.

On the clifftop, damaged but alive, were Triqueta and Amethea, leaning on each other for support. Ecko, his colour-shifting cloak missing and his head bowed. He was clad in trews and a shirt, both too big for him. At wrist and neckline, his skintones flickered with the fabric's colours

And there – beyond worlds, beyond hope – Roderick was with them. He walked silent, stark and brutal, hard-edged, his Tundran blood seeming frozen in his veins. Carrying no concern for the weariness of the others, he blazed with an odd, new strength, something quintessentially elemental yet unfamiliar – something almost forced, somehow tainted.

His attunement felt... artificial.

As she looked at him, he turned as if he could feel her gaze.

She withdrew, nudging the focus of the stone so that he was only the tiniest glimmer of power.

What had happened to him?

Walking behind him, almost as if she was being pulled in his wake, was Karine of The Wanderer, warily exhausted, slump-shouldered and drooping. There was no sign of Redlock, nor of the remainder of the tavern's staff.

Nivrotar felt a flicker stir her heart – somewhere, deep in the ice, a spark still glowed. What had happened to the Bard was critical – and she lacked the lore to comprehend his transformation.

Roderick turned back and kept walking.

The clifftop itself was empty, the buildings fallen, the castle keep at the water's edge a ruin. Nivrotar had known about Aeona, about Amal, of course she had – many of her own failures had found their way through the trackless nacre of the Gleam Wood. She had known about Sarkhyn, about the peculiar alchemical substances her old friend had hoarded.

A faint smile touched her lips as she wondered if Ecko had found the weapon he sought.

It was all patterns, Nivrotar had always known this. Everything was a pattern: each tiny event, each meeting, each decision, changed everything about a person's future, about the futures of the people and places they touched. And each new series of events spread out, linking one to another and unfolding into vast illustrations, huge pictures whose eventual complexity even she could not see.

Nivrotar had taken a wager on the unfolding of this particular picture that, if sent into the Gleam Wood, Ecko would find

Aeona, and would be strong enough to withstand Amal's coercions. A wager that he would survive, and come back.

On the clifftop, the small bright blaze that was Triqueta had faltered, fallen in the soft grass as though she couldn't go on. Amethea turned to her friend. Nivrotar nudged the stone to focus closer, saw her extend a hand, her face torn with pity.

Ecko was saying, "C'mon, he musta gotten out."

"'He'?" Triqueta spat it at him. "You mean 'it'."

"We should keep moving." Roderick's voice made the ice in the bowl crackle. "If there's anything still living here, it'll be looking for us. You can do personal trauma when we're out of the woods."

Ecko muttered, "We're not outta the woods yet."

Triqueta eyed the pair of them, but seemed to think better of it. Amethea pulled her to her feet.

Nivrotar watched them.

Slowly, they stole through the woods and the air about them faded to a thick, haunted dusk. The trees began to gleam: that white nacre that lit faces to a pallor of ghostliness and fear. They pulled closer together; even Ecko stared about him as if he expected corpses to rise rotting from the ground.

Only the Bard walked apart, his face bleak. As the others drew tighter together, he seemed almost to disdain that contact, to flicker with an edge of contempt. He walked as though he dared the very woods to defy him...

They were being followed.

The Lord of Amos nudged the bowl again, and the image shifted across the ice, coming back into close focus.

The follower was not human – it was huge, a powerful horse-shape that loomed in the darkness, a mass of body and pain. It had a human toso, hair that shone red in the pale light – then the ice clouded and the beast was gone, a figment in the gleaming, a dream upon awakening, a nightmare begging to be denied.

Touching the bowl's edges, looking for lost focus, Nivrotar heard Triqueta: "Redlock! Redlock!" The Banned woman caught her breath on a sob.

The Bard's voice said, "Enough. This place is laden with nightmare. We walk until we're clear – the trade-road is a long way."

And Nivrotar leaned back from the stone, a cold smile flickering on the side of her face.

She had been staring out of the window, her mind filled with her own dark thoughts, when a scatter of light made her blink and turn back to the room.

A flicker like firelight but pale and distant was coming from the frozen surface. As she watched, the wide bowl filled with it and grew brighter, closer. The light danced from the stone walls and the forgotten apparatus of the tower.

She studied it for a moment, reached a hand for the stone bowl. But it was hot to the touch and the ice was sublimating straight into steam and she pulled back, startled, knocking the bowl's focus. Carefully, hand wrapped in an end of her robe, she went to find it again, her heart suddenly trembling.

She'd no idea what the bowl – the steam – was showing her.

Images writhed. Not Fhaveon, though flickers and smoke remained. Not Roviarath, Larred held his city with strength. Not the Bard, nor Ecko. The images were much closer than all of that; they were...

It was the faint taste of ash on the air that made her realise that the fires were closer than she thought.

The images were Amos.

For a moment, Nivrotar was torn – part of her needed to chase down the long and spiral stairs and demand explanations of her useless court of philosophers... but they were sleeping, or thinking, or whatever such creatures did.

This was immediate, and she needed to understand it now.

Hand still wrapped, she moved the focus of the bowl to her own city, its outskirts, the terhnwood-covered cliffs that flanked the mouth of the river valley. She blew the steam from the air, eddying, taunting, strained to focus through it.

There!

The fires were on the clifftops that flanked the city. They were in the terhnwood crop.

They were in *her* terhnwood crop.

Briefly, the Lord of Amos was floored – her heart seemed to freeze in her chest. Everything she had gambled upon was burning to ash in one realisation...

I am too late.

Had her wager failed at the last?

Fhaveon was in ruins, Roviarath still under threat. The Lord city's soldiers were still scattered throughout the Varchinde, now leaderless and brutal. The blight crept inwards faster than any could have dreamed and the harvest had failed – destroying the delicate balance of the grasslands' trade.

And Ecko...

In the smoke, Nivrotar could see the madman Ress as if he stood in the very room with her. From the moment she had found him and Jayr in the Library, this was what she had been piecing together, had been hoping for...

Kazyen. The impossible foe. What Roderick had seen and forgotten, what Ress had seen and what had driven him loco. The void, the nothing, the death of the terhnwood and the grass.

Patterns. Games and ploys. The steam wafted and thinned, fading into the moonlight from the window. Turning back to the bowl, she nudged it again, looking back down at the Gleam Wood, at the haunted edge of the world.

But the bowl was still hot and her hand slipped, she jerked back too fast. The ice had melted and water slopped on the floor, wetting the hem of her black skirts. She snatched her fingers back, shaking them, biting her lip with the sudden pain. Even though it was only a touch, it seemed to sting like the touch of Vahl himself.

With the ice melted, her focus was not as good – but she could see the rising coastline of an island, jagged against twin moons. It took her a moment to realise where the island was – it took her a moment longer to see the tiny dark shape of a boat, resting almost motionless on the swell of the glittering water.

A boat? At Rammouthe?

Urgency gathered in her chest. She knew who was in that boat before she even looked. Bringing the focus closer, she could see Jayr, her scalplock all but lost in a new growth of hair; she could see another woman, older, curled and asleep. And she could see...

Ress!

All her attempts at finding him had failed – her spies and soldiers had reported, wide-eyed, that he had simply vanished. Even those who had been on duty at the palace itself had seen nothing.

But she could see him now.

He was huddled beneath a blanket, rocking, looking up at the vast shadow of Rammouthe over him. There was a resignation about him, a swelling of courage and inevitability – as if he knew he was going to die, but it was as it had to be, and he had made his peace with himself.

Rammouthe!

The Island of the Accursed. The one place no mortal might set foot. Roderick had tried, some forty returns previously, and barely escaped with his life – he had been laughed out of the Fhaveon Council when he tried to speak of great enemies.

But Vahl had not been on Rammouthe, had never been on Rammouthe. The legend had been a part of the creature's vast deception.

So why...?

Nivrotar had a strong image of Ress and Jayr in the Library – it seemed so long ago. The books they had been reading, the great work of foretelling they had found.

The Ilfe. The Well of the World's Memory. Sister to the Ryll now guarded only by the deserted Avesyr. Truly, Roderick really was her Final Guardian.

Her heart trembling in her chest, Nivrotar turned to look out of the window, back up at the flames, a tiny shred of hope burning even as the fires torched her crops and her future.

Memory.

If Ress's madness was insight, if Jayr's strength was enough, then the world could really remember.

Her gamble had paid off – all of it – and in a way she could never have anticipated.

Nivrotar shivered – a feeling crawling over her skin that all of this had somehow been orchestrated. Not by Phylos's games, not by Vahl's, not even by her own, but by something far, far larger – almost as if the pattern had no limit, no end. She was not a woman of faith – certainly she knew the Gods existed, but she also knew that they had long since grown bored of their plaything and had simply abandoned it to fend for itself. Now, she wondered if that belief was simply a convenience, a shield.

Something that had let her believe in her own power.

Patterns. All patterns.

Nodes of strength that wove together to make the full picture – Rhan, the Bard, Ecko. Herself. Vahl Zaxaar, in his own way.

The little boat that bobbed on the water.

And as the moons rose high over the island, let their rays fall on the huddle of hope that was gathered under the gunwales, Nivrotar of Amos wondered what could come next.

EPILOGUE MALALAU, THE KUANNE

The man in leathers walked alone through a sunless world of decay.

The air was chill and dry, it caught in his lungs like cobwebs. Emptiness surrounded him, mocking his footsteps, telling an echoing tale of desolation. Carved stone walls, their pictures worn down by touching hands, now seemed forsaken in the silence – abandoned but for the crawling fingers of long-dead creeper.

The few tiny windows were splintered into fragments by the ivy's clinging corpse, putting out the panes as though they were eyes. Amid the breath and smell of crumbling stonework no light could reach him, no hope would dawn.

The man did not know who he was, or what he was doing in this deserted place. Existing only to go forwards, to pursue this dream path, he came through a carved stone archway into a cathedral-vast hollow. A tower, rearing over him as if he were a trapped rat.

Its height alone was giddying. If he looked up, he could see light – a lifetime above him. It struck a poignant chord, he had to reach it, but to do so he must unravel and climb the dizzying network of stairways, ledges and platforms that lined the walls above him.

Some seemed to defy his senses, standing out from the wall too far to be stable, or seemingly unattached; silently existing outside everything the man understood.

He looked back down as the room's whirling grew too much, but his boots were still upon the broken-tiled floor – the air was unmoving. It was his mind that was spinning upwards to join the distant sun.

Struggling for something to focus upon, he was mildly surprised to find that he was carrying an electronic device in his hand. He recognised it as a "phantom", a radio-beacon tuned in to track a particular signal, but he did not know why he carried it, or what signal it was tracking. He examined the display, the light emitting diode lighting his face to a wash of green.

It pulled him east, a call he could not ignore. He understood that it was important, although he could not explain why, or how he knew. This filled him with a faint sense of unease, and he went through the pockets of leather and cut-off, trying to find an answer.

A spanner, a screwdriver, a handful of steel washers. A policeman-style pen and pad. A pocket full of dog-ends and a pouch of tobacco. A hip flask and a leather wallet. A small box of ammunition for the weapon he carried under his right arm.

In the wallet, a card with a face on it, his face perhaps, which identified him as "Alexander David Eastermann", Personal Ident Code 0998-127-4806-9R, Status Rating G12.

Alex, he thought, *Alexander David.* Reason told him that it should be his name, but it sparked no memories. It bothered him faintly, but reaching the light was far more important. He was trapped in a lifeless stone cell, amid the dead weed and the forgotten remains of a decaying city. He started up the first of the flights of stairs, striving to find the air.

The man had no way to measure the time but by the strain

in his hands as he swung from an upper ledge above a slavering fall, and by the dead ends and frustrated attempts that forced him to retrace his steps. Here, the creeper was his friend, providing him with handholds and secure footing, almost as if it wanted him to find the light at last.

As he climbed painstakingly higher, the carved façades of the rising walls seemed to mock his impossible attempt, coaxing him to look down to the floor, now far below, or to despair that he would ever climb away from their silent oppression.

His breathing was harsh in the stillness. Shaking now with sweat and fear, the man stopped upon a ledge and sat still. He did not lean against the wall – he did not trust the carving. Instead, he sat cross-legged in the ledge's centre, looking out across the mad, plunging view of the tower's inside.

How high had he climbed? He did not know, but his shoulders throbbed with the effort it had taken, the muscles in his legs shivered with strain. He looked at his hands, flexed his fingers.

Gloved hands, cold hands. Hands numb from gripping handlebars...

The image was gone as fast as a thought, but the man stayed still, not daring to breathe, as if trying to grasp it back. A fragment of a life washed up, like garbage on the riverbank...

Who...?

His unease struggled to find a focus, to ask the questions that needed answers, and the towering, rotting maze about him pulled his concentration away from such idle thoughts. He was over two-thirds of the way up the inside of the tower. Above him the light was closer, and the stairways and archways seemed to challenge him to reach the top.

Below him was a drop into darkness. One slip, one misjudged leap...

He stood up, a tiny, upright figure in the maze that spiralled outwards from him. In two steps, he reached the limit of his ledge and tensed his body for the leap that would take him to the next platform, above him and a chasm away. The lip of the stonework was crumbling under the toes of his boots.

He tensed like a spring, and threw himself forwards.

His hands caught the lip of the ledge, and his feet swung over the drop for an instant, then he pulled himself, trembling, onto the tiles.

From here, he could climb the creeper to a ledge high over his head.

A little closer to the only thing that mattered – the light.

The man had no past, and no future. He accepted this present time as all he had. For all his existence, all he had done was climb the tower to seek the sunlight.

Secure in the inside pocket of his now dusty leather jacket, the phantom device struggled to track its signal across wide miles of forest and mountains, and empty grassland.

ABOUT THE AUTHOR

DANIE WARE is the publicist and event organiser for cult entertainment retailer Forbidden Planet. She has worked closely with a wide range of genre authors and has been immersed in the science-fiction and fantasy community for the past decade. An early adopter of blogging, social media and a familiar face at conventions, she appears on panels as an expert on genre marketing and retailing.

WWW.DANIEWARE.COM

For more fantastic fiction from Titan Books in the areas of sci-fi, fantasy, steampunk, alternate history, mystery and crime, as well as tie-ins to hit movies, TV shows and video games:

VISIT OUR WEBSITE **TITANBOOKS.COM**

FOLLOW US ON TWITTER **@TITANBOOKS**